Gabrielle Kimm is the author of *His Last Duchess* and *The Courtesan's Lover*, also published by Sphere. She lives in rural West Sussex, and teaches English part-time at a small performing arts school.

The Girl
with the
Painted Face

GABRIELLE KIMM

SPHERE

First published in Great Britain in 2013 by Sphere

Copyright © Gabrielle Kimm 2013

The moral right of the author has been asserted.

A CIP catalogue record for this book
is available from the British Library.

ISBN 978-0-7515-5034-4

Typeset in Fournier by M Rules
Printed and bound in Great Britain by
Clays Ltd, St Ives plc

Papers used by Sphere are from well-managed forests
and other responsible sources.

MIX
Paper from
responsible sources
FSC
www.fsc.org   FSC® C104740

Sphere
An imprint of
Little, Brown Book Group
100 Victoria Embankment
London EC4Y 0DY

An Hachette UK Company
www.hachette.co.uk

www.littlebrown.co.uk

For Katy and Beattie

Acknowledgements

I owe a huge debt to Pete Talbot and his wonderful modern Commedia troupe – the Rude Mechanical Theatre Company. Pete truly brought the traditions of Commedia dell'Arte alive for me in a way no book could possibly have done and I'm not sure I could have written the book without him. Thank you to Rebecca Saunders and Louise Davies for their tender care of my story and to the rest of the Little, Brown team. Thank you as ever to Judith Murray. Thanks to Annie, Chloe and Loree – your feedback is always spot on and apposite. I don't know what I'd do without you three!

Several books were very useful:

The Italian Comedy, Pierre Louis Duchartre (George G. Harrap and Co. Ltd, 1929)

Commedia dell'Arte – an Actor's Handbook, John Rudlin (Routledge, 1994)

Scenarios of the Commedia dell'Arte, Flaminio Scala (translated Henry F. Salerno, Limelight Editions, 1967)

At Home in Renaissance Italy, ed. Marta Ajmar-Wollheim and Flora Dennis (V&A Publications, 2006)

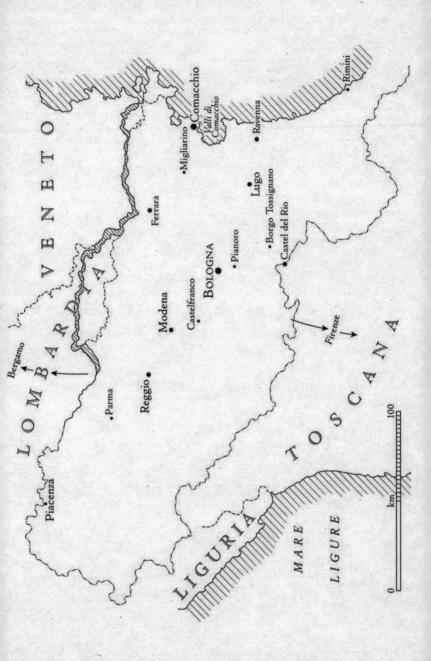

'Good my lord, will you see the players well bestowed?
Do you hear, let them be well used; for they are the
abstracts and brief chronicles of the time.'

Hamlet, Act II, scene ii

William Shakespeare

The Castello della Franceschina, a few miles outside Bologna, October 1582

Sebastiano da Correggio does not anticipate the blow to the back of the head which will end his life. Steadying himself against the bedpost, giddy from too much wine and with a bright bruise flowering along the edge of his jaw, he is laughing as he bends to pick up his dropped doublet.

The blow, when it comes, is hard and fast and heavy. The base of the iron candlestick hits him and he crumples onto the floor of the study without a sound, though the fingers of his right hand twitch for a moment before they are still.

1

Modena, two months earlier

Sofia ducks into a narrow alleyway, banging her shoulder hard against one wall as she skids around the corner.

'Come back here, you thieving *bitch*!' The voice is hard, and gritty with anger.

The blow to her shoulder is painful – Sofia gasps and swears – but she does not slow her pace. Kicking over a basket of apples as she swerves past an old woman seated on a doorsill, she shouts a breathless apology. She jumps over a sleeping dog and runs down a narrow flight of steps, taking them two at a time, her skirts bunched in her fists. At the bottom of the flight she stumbles, falls forwards and lands heavily on her hands. A sharp pain shoots through one of her fingers. Scrambling back onto her feet and bundling her skirts up in her arms again, she checks over her shoulder, then, taking a sharp left turn, runs flat out now, across a wide and crowded piazza, her breath heaving painfully; she zigzags between stalls and carts and the grasping hands of market-goers eager to become involved. Her hair is falling about her face and between her teeth and she spits out a mouthful, flicking her head to one side and the other, but she dares not release her hold on the fistfuls of skirt in case she trips. Dodging the outstretched arm of a smirking poultry-seller, Sofia races away from the piazza, pausing for a fraction of a second to check her options.

Another narrow side street or the long Via Bologna?

She takes the side street.

Two paces up, though, she sucks in a shocked breath as the thick-necked man with the heavy belly appears at the far end – less than a hundred paces from her.

Red-faced, mouth a rectangular hole, he points at her. 'There she is, the little whore!' He begins to run towards her, heavy-footed, hands now fisted. Several other men follow him.

Sofia doubles back out of the street, half crying now, dragging in a dry, breathless sob at every pace. A few yards up the Via Bologna, a narrow, pointed-arched vault leads into another dirty-looking alley; she scrabbles around the corner and into the shadows.

A door stands ajar. She flings herself at it, opening it wide; then, slipping in behind it, she pushes it shut, leaning up with her back pressed hard against it, mouth open, chest heaving. Her breath is ragged and rasping, her throat close to tearing at each gasp. Her heart is pounding so wildly she can feel it in her neck, her ears, her face; her damaged finger is hot and pulsing. She holds the sore hand up against her bodice, and rakes the other through her curls, scraping her hair back from her face. The sweat that has gathered inside her tight bodice feels suddenly chill now against her skin; a cold trickle runs down between her breasts.

'Now what?' she mutters in between breaths. 'What . . . in the name of heaven . . . do I do now?'

A head-high pile of baskets stands just inside the door in a dark, stone-flagged passage. Taking a step forward in the gloom, she bumps up against the pile, and it falls, teetering for a second and then tumbling slowly to land with a muffled crash. The top two baskets break open and half a dozen cabbages roll away down the passage.

'Oh, *merda*!' she hisses.

Heavy footsteps outside: several people running.

A shout thuds out in time with the speaker's heavy footsteps. 'This way! I'm sure she came this way!'

Sofia holds her breath. Eyes wide, still breathing through an open mouth, she presses herself flat against the wall behind the door. She'll fight, if they come in.

But nobody comes and within seconds the cries and the footfalls fade.

She waits for several more pulse-loud minutes. Then, easing the door open, she peers out into the alleyway.

It is deserted.

Glancing to left and right, she takes a tentative step outside.

'Hey! You! What do you think you're doing?'

Sofia smothers a cry.

A big woman with a round, flat face like a plate glares at her from the next doorway. 'Who are you? What are you doing, sneaking like that out of Signora Martello's house? I know she's not at home.'

Sofia thinks fast. 'She's my aunt,' she says, smiling brightly. 'I saw her in the piazza just now, and she asked me to tidy up the baskets in the passageway there – all those damned cabbages! She's too busy this morning to do it herself. Bless her! So sorry if I worried you. Thank you, signora – *addio*!' Ignoring the woman's blustered response, she turns on her heel and walks as fast as she can without actually breaking into a run, until she reaches the corner. Looking back, she waves farewell, then turns the corner and speeds up.

*

Some twenty minutes later and well over a mile further east, Sofia finally slows her pace. The Piazza Vecchio is crowded and noisy, and she moves gratefully into the anonymity of the bustle of market-goers, resisting the urge to glance over her shoulder as she weaves her way between stalls and shop fronts. Reaching a flat cart, untidily laden with misshapen loaves and sweetmeats, she edges her way through the throng of market-goers to stand next to two large, well-dressed women who are busy haggling with the baker.

'Oh, no, no, no, Domenico Rossi, you must be having a joke at my expense!' The larger of the two wags an accusatory finger at the flour-dusted and weary-looking man behind the stall.

He raises both hands, palms up like a priest at the offertory. 'Signora Bellini, I would never, *never* even *dream* of doing such a thing – to you or to anyone.'

Shaking her head, the woman says, 'To charge a king's ransom for such a paltry specimen of a loaf – just look at it! You might as well charge for bags of dust swept off the floor of your bakery.' She picks up the offending article and shakes it at the baker.

As the baker reacts angrily to this, leaning out and snatching his bread back from his angry customer, Sofia edges back behind the two women and walks away towards where several dozen people have clustered together, facing something or someone she cannot see. Whatever they are watching is clearly entertaining them: several men are jeering loudly, and most people are laughing. Curious, Sofia sidles through to the front.

A slight, grey-haired man, dressed in a shabby black doublet and breeches, is standing on an upturned half-barrel, a tall black hat perched on the back of his head. In his outstretched hand is a red bottle, tightly corked and neatly labelled, and on the floor by the barrel, a wooden box stands filled with similar bottles.

'. . . and here,' he is saying, 'just as I have described to you all in so much *glorious* detail, is the very stuff itself. Right here. Never again need any of you gentlemen go through the inconvenience — nay, that word simply will not suffice to describe the shame of it: let us say rather *the ordeal*, of facing your wife with . . . how shall I put it? . . . *the contents of your codpiece* failing to *leap into action* as you have been hoping it will . . .' The man waggles his eyebrows, gesturing as he speaks with the bottle and a jerk of his hips.

Whoops and catcalls from the crowd.

'Never again will you have to experience the *shame* of watching it *wilt* like a tired fig-leaf . . .' He allows the bottle to droop dramatically to the horizontal.

Several people whistle.

Someone shouts, 'You've probably just pissed in that bottle, you old fraud. That's all there'll be in it!'

More laughter from the crowd. Sofia glances from one face to another, enjoying the spectacle.

The mouth of the man in the black doublet has dropped open in theatrical outrage. 'How dare you! I've just told you what's in here!' He shakes the little bottle in the direction of the man who shouted. '*Arugula* seeds, basil, *cilantro*, liquor from the finest oysters . . .'

Someone else takes up the cry, interrupting the litany. 'He's right, all those things might well be in there . . . but you probably just ate the stuff yourself and then pissed into the bottles!'

The man on the barrel draws in a theatrical gasp. 'You insult the very history of medicine!'

'Not half so much as you insult our intelligence!'

'You don't *know* the half of it! I've told you about the *cilantro*, the *arugula*, the cudweed and the oysters — but the full recipe for this extraordinary Lifter of Amatory Spirits is known only to those of us who have declared allegiance to the Brotherhood of Apothecaries. Think of this, signori and signore – a bottle of this very elixir was bought last week by none other than Signor Francesco de' Medici, the Grand Duke of Toscana, for thirty *scudi*—'

'Signor de' Medici? Are you serious? The man has seven children! Are you telling me that a man with seven children can't get it up?'

The man in the black doublet throws back his head, smirking. He points towards the heckler with the little red bottle. 'Hah! Of course he can! Night after night! Several times a night, most probably. No doubt about it! And why? Because he's been buying supplies of my elixir for *years*.'

More cheers from the crowd.

Sofia goes to push her hair from her face, but winces and pulls her hand back, looking down at her fingers, one of which is now decidedly blue and swollen. Grimacing, she tries to bend it.

'As I say, the Grand Duke of Toscana paid thirty *scudi* for his most recent bottle of the Lifter of Amatory Spirits.'

The crowd '*oohs*' softly.

The little man continues, 'But for you, my fine friends, because I know how badly *some* of you are in need of it ...' Here, he makes an extravagant, sweeping bow towards the two hecklers, and the crowd cheer again. '... because of this, I'll let it go for not thirty *scudi*, not twenty, no, not even ten. Not even *one*! No – any of you fine people may purchase this ... this *invigorating* draught ...' Another upward jerk of the hips on the salient word. '... for the mere trifle of thirty-five *giulii*.' He pauses and then adds rather more quickly and prosaically, 'Or should you want to lay in supplies, I can let you have three bottles for a *scudo*.'

'I'll take a bottle. Might liven up my boring nights a bit,' one woman says, pulling out a few jingling coins and jiggling them in her palm. There is a murmur of laughter.

The woman next to her nods. 'If you're taking one, Caterina, then so will I. Been so long since Gianfranco's been able to do anything other than piss with *his* pride and joy, I've nigh on forgotten what I've been missing.'

The man in the black doublet beams at them. '*Bellissime signore*, I shall be honoured to think that I shall be playing a part in restoring your nights to the wild and wonderful adventures in lovemaking they once were.'

Several women shriek. 'Wild adventures, with Gianfranco Bello?' one of them says, cackling. 'Ha ha!'

'How dare you!' Gianfranco's wife's colour deepens. Elbowing past the half-dozen people who separate her from the laughing woman, she stands facing her with her hands on her hips. 'You're a fine one to criticize, Loretta Fiori – your Enrico is hardly anything to crow about.'

'And how exactly would *you* know?'

Gianfranco's wife makes no answer, but raises an eyebrow and smirks at Loretta. Then she turns away, shaking her head and saying clearly enough for most people to hear, 'Cock that small – if he hadn't been so noisy, I'd hardly have known he was there.'

Sofia grins. The crowd whoops, and then laughs louder still as Loretta Fiori kicks out at Gianfranco's wife, catching her hard on the backside with the flat of her foot. Gianfranco's wife stumbles forwards onto hands and knees.

'That how Gianfranco likes you?' somebody calls out. 'On all fours?'

Gianfranco's wife, now red in the face, clambers to her feet and stalks away from the gathering, to a farmyard cacophony of hoots and jeers.

A number of people now jostle forward, pushing past Sofia, to buy bottles – some cheerfully, some proclaiming their future plans with vulgar enthusiasm, others shamefaced and furtive – and the man in the black doublet takes the proffered coins, drops them into a leather pouch at his waist and doles out his wares, smiling and exchanging pleasantries with everyone. The crowd finally begin to disperse into the piazza, talking and laughing. Eventually, Sofia is left alone with the little man in the black doublet.

'Are you after my elixir, by any chance, signorina?' he says. He glances down into the box at his feet. 'I have a couple of bottles left, and will be happy to furnish you with one, though I have to say, you don't strike me as someone who needs to—'

Sofia shakes her head. 'No. No, I'm not after the elixir. But, signore, would you be able to look at my hand? I've hurt my finger. Might you have some form of salve I could put on it?'

The man reaches out, and Sofia places her hand upon his palm. With surprising tenderness, he gently turns it this way and that, examining it with a furrow of concern between his brows. 'How did you do this?' he says after a moment or two.

'Tripped and fell.'

'Ooh, that does look sore.' He presses very gently along the length of the finger, eyes closed, the tip of his tongue just visible between his teeth. 'Well, it's just possible that it's broken, but I think you might be lucky – it may just be a nasty sprain.'

Sofia clicks her tongue against her teeth. 'Oh no, please, signore, tell me you're joking.'

The man shakes his head. 'It's at least a sprain, and I cannot guarantee that you have not broken something in there.'

'But I'm a seamstress. I can't work if it's broken. Specially this one – it's my needle finger. Please . . . say you're wrong.'

Another shake of the head.

'What should I do?'

'Come here, and I'll strap it for you.' The man jerks with his head towards a small tilt-cart. 'I'll give you some comfrey, and I'll strap the hurt finger to the one next to it. That's the best I can do for you, my dear.'

'How long will it take to mend?'

The little man sucks his teeth, considering. 'If it's a sprain, then a week or two at the most. If it's broken, then three, maybe four weeks till you can take the strapping off.' Turning away from her, he climbs up into his cart and begins rummaging in a painted box.

'Four weeks!' Sofia puffs out a breath, trying not to panic. 'She won't wait that long.'

The man in the black doublet looks up from the painted box, holding a strip of linen, a tuft of wool and a tiny pottery jar. 'Who won't wait for what?'

'Nothing. It doesn't matter.'

The man pats the upturned barrel, inviting Sofia to sit upon it. She complies. He gives her the little jar, which she opens and sniffs. Then, stoppering it tightly once more, she tucks it down inside the top edge of her bodice. Taking her hand in his, the man places the tuft of wool carefully between Sofia's middle and fourth fingers. Then he winds the strip of linen around them, binding them snugly together. Tearing the last few inches of the strip into two he ties a neat knot, fastening it securely near Sofia's knuckles. 'There,' he says. 'Better?'

Sofia nods. 'Thank you, signore,' she says.

'How did you come to fall so heavily?'

Sofia looks at her companion. There is something innately trust-worthy in his eyes, she thinks, despite the nonsense she knew he was talking moments ago. His expression is kind. 'I was running,' she says. 'They're trying to make out I'm a thief.'

'Who are?'

'This man and his servant.'

'And are you?' The man smiles. 'A thief?'

'No. I'm not.'

'And what do they say?'

She hesitates. 'Well, I was asked to deliver an undershirt to this man in the Via Magdalena – a shirt I'd mended for him.'

The little man tips his head to one side, listening.

'His servant asked me to wait in an upstairs *sala*. He said his master wanted to inspect the repair – make sure it was done to his satisfaction.'

Shuddering at the thought of what had happened then, Sofia explains what followed. She recounts the shameful suggestions the man had made to her . . . and explains how she responded.

'And then I fled, while he shouted to a servant that I had stolen his purse – which of course I hadn't – and now I might not be able to sew for weeks . . . ' Sofia lifts her bandaged hand. ' . . . and Signora Romano won't pay me a single *baioccho* if I can't work.' She draws in a long breath. 'She pays me little enough as it is.'

The man in the black doublet shakes his head. 'You poor, poor girl. What a tale. You have indeed been unfortunate, signorina.'

'Yes. But lucky to meet you. I'm very grateful to you, signore, for helping with my hand.'

'Ah well – as one who has . . . has been run out of town by the authorities myself . . . ' The man paused. ' . . . I am never averse to helping out a fellow creature found at the mercy of the rich and powerful.'

'You're very kind,' Sofia says.

'Bless you, child, not at all, not at all. Now listen, I have some bread, and ale. Far too much of it for myself alone – in fact, I would welcome some company in the eating and drinking of it.'

Sofia smiles at him. 'Then thank you. I should be honoured. May I ask your name, signore?'

The little man stands back and bows low, sweeping the tall black hat from his head with a flamboyant flourish. 'Niccolò Zanetti. One-time apothecary and now purveyor of the highest quality medicaments and curatives.' He pauses, then adds in a conspiratorial whisper, 'And of a fair number of medicaments of a somewhat lower quality, too, I'm afraid.'

Sofia jumps down from her barrel and curtsies. 'Sofia Genotti. Seamstress-in-training.'

'Well, well, Sofia Genotti, seamstress-in-training, let's find somewhere more comfortable – like the back step of my cart – to take some of that ale and bread and rest awhile.'

They sit pressed together side by side in companionable silence on the wooden step of the tiny covered cart, eating hunks of torn bread and watching people coming and going across the piazza. As Sofia brushes crumbs from her mouth, Niccolò Zanetti pours ale into a pretty silver cup and passes it across. The ale is sweet and fresh; Sofia wraps both hands around the cup and rests it on bent knees, her feet drawn up under her on the tilt-cart step. 'My mother was a healer,' she says. 'She never called herself an apothecary, but she knew everything about plants and herbs and . . . ' She tails off, wishing she had not mentioned her mother. The memories are still too painful – even after all these years.

'Was?'

Sofia nods. 'Yes. She's . . . she's dead.' She cannot be more specific. Not to a stranger.

'Oh, I'm sorry, my dear.'

'It was several years ago, when I was a little girl.' Please, Sofia thinks now. Please don't ask me how she died.

But Signor Zanetti does not ask. He looks at her for several

13

seconds, then pats her on the back of her hand and says, 'In my experience, women often make by far the best healers.'

'How long do you plan to stay in Modena, signore?' she says, deliberately changing the subject.

'Me? Oh, I shall be on the road again this evening. Me and Violetta here.' He jerks his head towards a large and ugly donkey picking at a pile of hay some feet away.

Sofia is surprised to feel a pang of loss at the thought of Signor Zanetti's departure. 'It must be a difficult way of life,' she says, 'never knowing where you are going to sleep, not having a proper home.' Not that I really have one myself, she adds silently.

Several long seconds pass. Niccolò Zanetti seems lost in thought. 'There's a little house up in the mountains about twenty miles from here,' he says softly, staring with unfocused eyes at something Sofia cannot see. 'A pretty little place called Faenza. It overlooks an ancient landscape, thick with old oaks and sweet chestnuts, with beech trees and conifers. It's a pretty place, and my daughter and her husband have lived there for . . . oh, nearly ten years. When the weather is too bad for travelling and living out of the cart, I like to go and stay with her – and I think she likes to see me, too.' He smiles at Sofia. 'You put me in mind of my daughter.'

Sofia opens her mouth to reply, when a voice rings out above the buzzing hum of the remnants of the crowd.

'*Why?* You want to know why I've been traipsing halfway across Modena and back? *Why?* Because that thieving little whore abused me and my hospitality; she stole my property and I'm determined to have her for it!'

'*Merda!* Oh God, signore, that's him!' Sofia is on her feet, her heart racing again, her skin instantly clammy with chill sweat. 'That's the man who has been hounding me across the city . . .'

*

She is hand in hand with her mamma as they approach the centre of the little town of Comacchio, and Sofia is skipping happily, when a shout stops them both in their tracks. Three men are standing shoulder to shoulder across the pathway some few yards ahead.

One of them points at them.

'That's her!'

Mamma drops the bag she is carrying and turns to run, dragging Sofia with her, but Sofia is too small, she cannot keep up and she stumbles. Mamma turns to face the three men, pushing Sofia to stand behind her. Holding her there, she backs with her towards a wall, shaking her head, and the panicked pleas that begin to tumble out of her mouth as the men approach make no sense to Sofia.

Niccolò Zanetti takes her arm. 'Get in the cart,' he says, quietly.

Clambering up and over the tailgate of the cart, she crouches under the curve of the canvas cover as Zanetti flips a string and unrolls the back flap. Edging past a couple of boxes, she squats down in a cramped space behind a rack of stoneware jars, aware that she is now well and truly trapped: there is no other way out. She swallows, feeling light-headed.

'And you!' comes the booming voice, now clearly just inches from where she was sitting: the man's shadow, dark and distorted, slides up and over the other side of the creased canvas. 'What about you, signore? Have *you* seen a girl – about sixteen? Yellow dress. About this high.' The shadow-arm lifts as the heavy man indicates her height. 'Dark hair. *Tette* like a couple of peaches. Probably breathless with running.'

'That I have not, signore.' Zanetti's voice is calm and steady. 'I'm sure I should remember someone of that description most particularly.'

'Bastard whore stole a purse full of coins from me.'

Sofia hears Zanetti tutting his tongue against his teeth. 'Despicable indeed!'

There is a long pause.

Then the heavy-bellied man says, '*Cazzo!* We're a pair of bloody idiots! We've been wasting our time. Luigi!'

'Signore?' The servant's voice.

'We've been running around this damned city for nothing. God, I'm a fool! We don't need to find her – we need the mistress. Luigi, go now, straight away, and find Signora ... what was her name? The seamstress. Romano. That's it: Romano.'

Sofia puts her hands over her mouth.

'And tell her what a treacherous, thieving bitch her little needle-woman really is.' There is a moment's pause, then Sofia hears the man mutter, 'I'll show that filthy little *puttana* what happens to anybody who dares to treat me like ...'

The big shadow moves away from the cart, fading and blurring as it goes, and Sofia misses the end of the sentence. A minute passes. Then a corner of the back flap is lifted and Sofia sees Niccolò Zanetti's face peering in. 'He's gone,' he says. 'Quite gone. I saw him leave the piazza.'

Sofia climbs awkwardly out of the cart. Feeling sick, she stares around her for a moment, then looks at Niccolò Zanetti. 'Thank you, signore. I'm very grateful to you for ... I'm ... but I'm sorry – I have to go.'

'But—'

'I'm finished in Modena, signore. This is it. You heard him – he's going to tell Signora Romano that I'm a thief.'

'But he's mistaken. You are innocent. Will she not understand that when you tell her?'

'No,' Sofia says, shaking her head. 'She won't. She won't understand. She'll want to have me put away, or run out of town. I can't stay. I have to get out of the city – straight away. At least for the moment. Till the fuss dies down. But thank you. Thank you so much.' She reaches out and takes Niccolò Zanetti's hand for a second, and then turns from him and begins to run once more, across the piazza towards the Porta Nuovo.

'Signorina!' she hears Zanetti's voice calling behind her. 'Stop! Listen! I have an idea. Why don't you . . . ?'

But her footsteps are clattering on cobbles now and his last few words go unheard.

2

A couple of miles outside Modena

A black-masked figure, barefoot, in untucked shirt and patched breeches, sidles out from a patch of shadow, carrying a ladder under his arm: half of it projecting out before him, and half behind. It is clear he is anxious about being overheard – each step is being carefully taken. He looks around him continually, eyes wide behind the mask, as though expecting disaster.

Another figure – noticeably older, shorter, stockier – creeps in step some paces behind him; this newcomer is clearly taking even more elaborate care than the first to remain undetected. This second man then drops something metallic, which clatters as it hits the floor. Startled, the masked man spins around, whirling the ladder, as the second crouches down to pick up the fallen object. The ladder skims above the head of the crouching figure, who then stands up. Coming around full circle, the ladder hits the second man hard in the backside. He falls forward onto all fours.

'Yes, yes, that works rather well,' he says, getting to his feet and dusting off the knees of his breeches. 'But I dropped the key too soon, I think. Let's just try it again before we stop for this evening. Once more, please, Beppe? And then, if it works, let's run through that little piece of dialogue, too.'

Beppe puts the ladder down on the ground and pulls off the black mask. Rubbing his face, he pushes his fingers through already untidy, cropped black hair; then, yawning and stretching long limbs, he nods. 'If you'd like to.'

'Take it from where you come on. I need to give you a little more time with the creeping before I drop the key – build up the tension that little bit more.'

'Mmm. If I stop and start a couple more times, then you can stop and start with me – exactly as I do – and then on the . . . ' He frowns, considering. ' . . . on the fourth stop, that's when you can do the drop. And I'll spin.'

A woman's voice calls from some way off to the left. 'Agostino!' The second man turns round sharply. 'Agostino!' comes the voice again. 'How long are you going to be, you and Beppe?'

'Not long, *cara*!' he calls back. 'No more than a few moments!'

'Your soup's ready.'

'Thank you, *cara*. I won't be long!'

'Beppe, there's enough for you too, if you want some.'

Beppe grins at Agostino. 'Thank you, Cosima,' he calls back. 'I'd love some.'

'You do know it will be unspeakable, don't you?' Agostino says, shaking his head. 'She gets worse by the week.'

'Better than no soup.'

Agostino raises an eyebrow. Beppe laughs. 'Well, maybe not,' he says. 'It'll fill your belly, though.'

'Hmmm.' Agostino shakes his head. 'Let's run through the *lazzo* again before we face the . . . ' Closing his eyes, he claps the back of his hand to his forehead in a gesture of exhausted despair. ' . . . the

Ordeal of the Soup. I want us to have this little piece absolutely right before our first performance in Modena.'

Beppe picks up his ladder. Holding it upright, as though it is leaning against a wall, he climbs up some half-dozen rungs, and stands there balancing. Then, as the ladder begins to wobble, he jumps nimbly backwards and lands back on the ground, pulling the ladder neatly with him.

Agostino laughs. 'Oh, I like that, Beppe – use it somewhere. How high can you get?'

Beppe shrugs. 'About six, seven rungs.'

'See if you can make it to the top.'

Beppe shakes his head. 'Too risky.' He thinks for a moment. 'With a shorter ladder I might get up and over the top, though. And down the other side. It'd seem as though the ladder were stuck to the ground.'

'I'll get Vico to make one for you. Say six, seven rungs high?'

Beppe bends and picks up his ladder again. He carries it off to the edge of the little makeshift stage, then once again creeps out from the shadows, staring around him fitfully, eyes wide, mouth slightly open. Agostino follows him. Beppe takes one big step and pauses, foot high. Agostino takes a much smaller step, but pauses in time with Beppe. Beppe gingerly puts his raised foot to the floor. Agostino copies him. Beppe shuffles a step. So does Agostino. Beppe takes three long strides. Agostino follows suit, with shorter strides – and then he drops the key. As he crouches, the ladder whirls over his head. He stands up, and is knocked to the floor once more. 'Oh yes, much better,' he says. 'Dialogue now.' He draws in a breath, leans dramatically forward from the hips and, peering myopically towards Beppe, says in a very different, higher-pitched squawk of a voice, '*Arlecchino! Is that you?*'

Beppe, hopping from foot to foot now, says, '*Yes, sir. Oh yes –*

*it most certainly is. I told you I'd be here ... and here I quite defin-
itely ... am.'*

'I want you to go and fetch my daughter.'

*'In a moment, sir, in a moment. I'll have to hurry — she's about to
explode!'*

Agostino, who has been turning away from Beppe, whirls back
round again, mouth dropping open into an O of surprise.
'Explode? My daughter?'

'No, no, no! My pot of stew! She's been on the fire too long.'

'On the fire?' Agostino seems to wobble with bemusement and
his voice becomes even more shrill.

'I don't want her bottom to burn ... '

'Her bottom? My daughter's—?'

Beppe puts his hands on his hips and doubles over for a second.
Straightening up, he shakes his head violently. *'No, no, no, no! My
pot of stew!'*

*'Oh, you really are the most aggravating creature — get on with you!
Quick!'*

'The quickest way is up the ladder, sir ... '

Beppe breaks off. 'Hey — tell you what, Ago, if I had the shorter
ladder here, I could make quite a nonsense of trying to get up it,
and keeping on finding myself back on the ground again because
I've gone up and over without realizing.'

'Yes — that could be marvellous. I'm sure Vico will be able to
knock up the new ladder in time for Bologna.'

'Good. Sorry — let's get back to it. From *quickest up the
ladder ... '*

Beppe repeats the line. Agostino's stance changes again. Bending slightly, one hand now on his crotch, he leans forwards once
more, screwing up his eyes and glaring at Beppe. *'Get on with you,
you pestilential little ... er ... little ... '*

'*Little what, sir?*'

Agostino glares at him. '*I have little patience with you, that's what!*'

Beppe lays his ladder at an angle against a big wooden chest. Scrambling up and along it on all fours like a monkey, he squeals loudly when the ladder up-ends and seesaws him down towards the ground again on the other side of the chest. Rolling, head over heels, still holding the ladder, he somehow manages to stand upright with it again, and hurries off, away from Agostino.

Agostino claps his hands together a few times. 'Thank you, Beppe, that was perfect. Now let's gird our loins and stiffen our sinews. It's ... time ...' He shudders. '... for ... soup.'

Laughing, Beppe leans the ladder up against the edge of the makeshift staging. He picks up his discarded mask, and, swinging it by its leather straps, jumps down from the stage and begins to make his way over rough ground towards where four covered wagons stand grouped together beneath a large oak tree. A fire is burning in a brazier some yards from the wagons, and an iron pot hangs above the flames.

Seated near the fire, staring into the flickering light, is a handsome woman, dressed in vivid red, with a bright parti-coloured wrap around her shoulders; her hair hangs down her back. She looks up and smiles as the two men approach; reaching out behind her, she picks up two wooden bowls, then ladles soup from the iron pot into each.

'There you are,' she says in a voice husky from tiredness, handing them their bowls and then big torn hunks of bread. 'Eat up. Everyone else ate earlier. I didn't like to interrupt.'

Beppe sinks neatly to sit cross-legged on the grass near the fire next to Agostino, and places his mask down by his side. He takes the proffered bowl, spoon and bread, thanks Cosima and, avoiding

Agostino's eye, begins to eat, trying not to grimace. As expected, the soup is thin and insufficiently seasoned; the vegetables and beans in it are badly overcooked. It does, however, as he had promised Agostino, fill his empty belly. A moment later, wiping out his bowl with his bread, he places it down on the grass beside him and lies back; fingers interlocked behind his head, knees crooked up, he stares at the stars. Someone – probably Vico – is playing a guitar nearby and Lidia is singing. Beppe listens for a moment, soothed by her lilting voice.

A dog comes near, sniffing Beppe's face, its nose cold and wet against his cheek. Beppe reaches out and begins lazily to fondle its ears. The dog sits, pressing itself up against him.

Someone sits down on his other side.

'Rain tomorrow.' Cosima's voice.

Beppe turns his head towards her. 'Why do you say that? That's a wonderful sky.'

'It is, isn't it? But see over there, Beppe – see what's on its way towards us.' She points westwards, where a thick bulwark of ugly, stuffed-looking cloud hangs menacingly low over the horizon.

Beppe rolls onto his side and peers in the direction Cosima is pointing. He swears softly. '*Merda*. Probably going to pour just as we start performing on Saturday.'

The dog thumps its tail on the ground and licks Beppe's ear.

'Might well do, but we're in the Piazza di Porta Ravegnana in Bologna on Saturday, aren't we? We can work under cover there.'

Puffing out his relief, Beppe sits up. 'Oh yes. I'd forgotten. Thank God for that.'

'Not often we get such a sheltered spot for the stage.'

'Not often enough, that's for certain.'

'And then it's the big Correggio house outside the city in October, don't forget ... what's it called? Franceschina. That's it –

the Castello della Franceschina.' Agostino leans forwards and claps a hand on Beppe's bent knee. 'Our venues are becoming ever more prestigious, are they not? The Coraggiosi will be performing in palaces every week within the year – you mark my words, Beppe, my boy.'

Beppe smiles and shrugs. 'Maybe so. But you know me – I'm just as happy in a piazza.'

'What? You have no ambition, *amico*, that's your problem!' Agostino shakes his head. 'Look at the Gelosi – they're being fêted and talked about wherever they go now!'

'Oh, the Gelosi, the Gelosi. The bloody Gelosi – they are no better than we are!' says Vico, sitting down on the far side of Beppe.

Agostino glances across at him. Dark and wiry, Vico is scowling. 'Vico,' he says, 'your loyalty to the Coraggiosi is indubitably touching, but the vile and vitriolic vituperation you aim at our nearest rival troupe at every possible opportunity seems to me to be entirely uncalled-for.'

'And the number of unnecessary syllables you stuff into every one of your endless sentences is as astonishing as ever, Agostino,' Vico says with a quick grin. 'I mean it, anyway. They're good, yes, the Gelosi. They're wonderful, in fact. But so are we.'

Cosima smiles at him. 'Bless you, Vico. We are. We're as good as the sum of our parts, are we not?'

Vico pecks a nod in agreement.

'Mmm – and if it's of any interest to anyone, I'd like to say that I'm in agreement with the general consensus . . . ' A tall, bearded man of about forty walks up from the wagons and sits down next to Agostino.

'Thank you, Federico, and I'm sure you know that we are equally delighted that you chose to come and swell our ranks.'

Smirking smugly, Agostino pats the newcomer on the knee. 'What is it – two months since you joined us?'

'Yes, about that long.'

Agostino looks from Federico to Beppe, Vico, Cosima and Lidia, who has settled herself just behind Vico, saying, 'But I feel I should remind you that the only way we will sustain this burgeoning success is if *all* the various parts of the whole bother to rehearse sufficiently.' His smirk fades and an expression of soldierly determination takes its place. 'So,' he says, 'listen to what I want from you all tomorrow.'

Beppe leans back on his arms. Agostino's instructions are clear, concise, demanding . . . and humorous, and by the time he has finished, everyone is smiling, but nobody is in any doubt as to how exhausting the following day is likely to be.

Agostino jabs a finger towards each of his company, saying, 'Go on then, off to bed, the lot of you. Poor old Giovanni Battista is already dead to the world, bless him, and I've seen neither hide nor hair of Angelo for at least a couple of hours, so I bloody well hope he's asleep too. Someone will have to fill him in first thing tomorrow.'

Beppe sees Vico and Lidia exchange glances.

Agostino says, 'I want you all up and ready to start by first light. Do you hear that – all of you? We make our entrance into Bologna at midday, we perform in the afternoon, and I want us to have run through the whole play at least twice here before we set off.'

Vico stretches and groans. 'First light? Twice? God, Agostino, you're a bloody slave driver!'

Lidia puts her arms around Vico and kisses his cheek. 'Stop complaining and come to bed.'

Getting to his feet, Beppe laughs softly. He raises a foot and nudges Vico in the shoulder with his heel. 'You won't get a better offer than that, *amico*. I'd make the most of it, if I were you.' He turns to Cosima. 'Shall I douse the fire?'

'No, leave it, *caro*. It'll burn itself out within the hour. Be off with you, and get some sleep.' She reaches out to Agostino, who takes her hands and pulls her to her feet. Kissing her, he drapes an arm around her shoulders and she leans in against him affectionately.

Beppe yawns. Patting Vico on the shoulder, pecking a nod to Lidia, he collects his and Agostino's soup bowls and spoons. Throwing them up one by one, he juggles with them for a moment, then catches them deftly and walks away towards the wagons, the dog at his heels, his footsteps soundless on the thick grass.

In the darkness over on the far side of the wagons, a young man with a perfect profile is leaning against a tree, a flask of grappa in one hand. Angelo da Bagnacavallo has been listening to Agostino's exhortations and rolling his eyes in irritation, shaking his head scornfully. On hearing his own name mentioned, he checks, holding his breath, listening to see if anyone is aware of where he has been. Quickly satisfied that his whereabouts still seem to be a mystery to all, however, he drains his flask, blinking a couple of times against the strength of the spirit, and prepares to wait another few minutes until the rest of the troupe have settled for the night.

He has no wish to enter into conversation with anyone.

3

Just inside the walls of the city of Bologna, as the afternoon edges its way into evening, a steady mizzling rain is blurring the edges of the buildings, catching in starry droplets in the hair and lashes of anyone unfortunate enough to be out of doors. Sofia's yellow skirts are clinging to her legs – a dark tidemark meanders around the fabric at knee-height – and cold trickles are running down from her hair into the neckline of her bodice. Gazing up at the heavy-bellied clouds as thunder growls softly, she hunches her shoulders and pulls up and over her head a length of sacking she found fallen from a passing cart. After two days and three nights out in the open, walking the twenty-five or so miles from Modena, sleeping in doorways and church porches, her now-broken shoes are oozing water at every step and her feet feel painfully chilled. The linen strip that Signor Zanetti so gently bound around her broken finger the other day is filthy now, and, within the sodden cloth, her fingertips have bleached and wrinkled.

Seeing a deep doorway, Sofia hurries to shelter under its low arch. A scrawny cat mews, stretches, and stalks across to rub itself against her legs. Sitting down on a dry step, and pulling her skirts in out of the wet, she strokes the top of the cat's head with the tips of her fingers. It closes its eyes, pushing up against her touch. 'Do you know,' she says to the cat, 'I'm so hungry now, I could almost eat *you*.' The cat mews again. 'Might you be able to catch me a mouse, little puss?' Sofia says. The cat begins to purr. 'We could share it, if you could.'

The cat snakes itself around her. Its fur is wet and it smells musty. 'What am I to do, puss?' she says, fingering its tattered ears. 'You tell me.' She picks a wet ringlet of hair from where it has stuck to her cheek and tucks it behind her ear. 'Do you know, I used to have a little cat a bit like you. Once. A long time ago.'

The cat gives another plaintive little mewing cry.

Footsteps sound out some yards away. Sofia looks up. The cat stiffens, and then slips silently away. A man approaches. Thick-set, broad-shouldered, grey-haired, he is wearing a heavy cloak and boots. Sofia gets to her feet and, as the man nears her doorway, she steps forward.

'Might you have a few coins to spare, signore?' she says, her heart thudding with shame. 'I have nothing to eat.'

He checks, his gaze raking her from head to foot, taking in her tangled hair, her soaked clothes and the mud-stained shoes. He runs his tongue over his lip. Sofia's heart beats faster at the look in his eye, and she starts to feel sick.

The man's gaze lingers on her face and then dips to her breasts. Sofia folds her arms across her front. The man shakes his head a fraction. Pushing a hand into a pocket in his breeches, he fumbles through its jingling contents; with one quick glance at the coins in his hand, he flings them at Sofia's feet without a word. He pulls his cloak more tightly around himself and strides on, away around a corner and out of sight. Sofia does not move until he has gone, but as soon as he has disappeared, she squats down and picks up the coins, rubbing the mud from them with her thumb.

Standing, she sees that dust from the dry step on which she has been sitting has now stuck to the wet cloth of her skirts, crusting around the sodden hem; she tries to brush it off, but it clings tenaciously, so, giving up the attempt and pulling the sacking over her head, she sets off back out into the rain, heading up the Via Piella towards the city centre, clutching the coins in her good hand.

It is some minutes before she finds a likely tavern.

A yellowish light is spilling out through its part-open door to lie in glittering puddles on the cobbles. As Sofia pushes it further open and peers in, she sees some two dozen people within. Most are seated at tables, but one small group is huddled in a conspiratorial cluster by the wide fireplace, and, in an empty corner of the room, two young men are standing nose to nose, fists up, faces distorted with fury.

Sofia slips inside and stands up against the wall near the door as the huge tavern-owner pushes a massive arm like a leg of pork in between the two fighters. 'Come on now, signori, that's enough. Settle down now,' he says, his voice surprisingly soft for a man of his size.

One of the young men glares at him. 'Oh, *vaffanculo*! Piss off, Alberto – don't get in my way!'

'Hey, hey, hey . . . now that's enough,' Alberto says again. 'Not in here, if you please, Pietro Goldoni. If you can't settle down, then you can both take yourselves off outside and deal with your problems in the street.'

Scowling, Goldoni shoves at the other young man's chest and then turns away. His companion staggers backwards, swearing in his turn; then, righting himself, he lurches back towards Goldoni, grabbing his upper arm and swinging him around. Drawing back a fist, he lets fly, catching Goldoni hard on the jaw. Goldoni grunts in pain. He reaches out and pulls the other boy in towards him by his shirt.

Several of the people seated at the tables gasp. Someone pushes a chair back, scraping its legs across the stone flags.

Alberto shakes his head and puffs out a sigh. Taking a handful of Pietro Goldoni's doublet in one hand, and a fistful of the other boy's shirt in the other, he parts them with ease. Turning them both towards the door, and lifting them so each is almost up on his toes, he half-walks, half-drags them through the jumble of tables to the entrance without a word. Kicking the door wide open, he swings both young men out into the street; both fall forwards onto the wet ground.

Alberto pulls the door closed and brushes his hands together. 'There – now stay out until you can sit and drink together in peace, the pair of you,' he says loudly to the closed door, wagging a massive forefinger.

He crosses the room, shaking his head.

'Good man, Alberto!' somebody calls.

The big tavern-owner nods in the man's direction but makes no comment.

Sofia follows him. 'Excuse me, signore,' she says as he stops and lowers his bulk onto a stool which looks far too flimsy to support him.

He raises an eyebrow and inclines his head.

'Er . . . might you have a room spare? Somewhere I could stay for the night? And something to eat?'

Alberto's gaze takes in Sofia's filthy clothes and sodden hair. 'You need to go and sit yourself down near that fire, signorina,' he says, pointing towards the hearth. 'Get yourself dry.'

'Thank you. And the room, signore?'

'What money do you have? I've just the one bed upstairs for travellers. A place in it and a blanket can be yours for half a *scudo*. And a bite to eat for fifty *baiocchi*. I've a stew on the fire.'

Sofia holds out her coins.

Alberto moves them about on her palm with one thick finger. 'Not quite enough,' he says. 'Do you have any more?'

Sofia swallows awkwardly and shakes her head.

'Well, perhaps . . . ' The big man pauses. He raises an eyebrow. ' . . . you can pay the extra . . . some other way?'

Sofia's mouth opens a little, but she says nothing.

Her heart races.

Alberto sucks his teeth for a moment, then he frowns and says, 'Perhaps you might see your way to washing a few pots for me?' He nods towards her fistful of coins. 'You have enough there for a meal. Then you could wash a few of my dirty pots to earn a bed for the night. How does that sound? Could you do that?'

Sofia almost laughs. 'Oh yes – with pleasure, signore.'

Alberto smiles. 'Eat first, I think. Don't you? Then do the pots.'

The makeshift bed in the tavern's upstairs room is low and very wide – wide enough for at least three sleepers. Straw-mattressed, its foot-end is strewn with a jumble of shabby blankets. The one small window in the room is unshuttered, and the steep-sloped ceiling is merely the underneath of the roof-tiles; smears of lime mortar show between the tiles, and chinks of the night sky are winking through at various places above Sofia's head. Every now and again, she feels the cold prickle of a raindrop which has found its way through into the room.

Sofia drops the big folded sheet Alberto has just handed her. It lands on the floor with a whump and the candle on the shelf gutters in the draught, then settles again.

She picks up all the blankets and the three limp pillows and heaps them on the floor. Standing at one side of the bed, she flaps out the sheet and watches as it settles across the uneven mattress. The far edge flips back on itself, and Sofia shakes it out again a couple of times until it lies flat. She works her way around the bed, tucking the sheet in under the mattress, wincing a couple of times as her damaged finger takes more weight than is comfortable.

She replaces the pillows side by side across the generous width of the bed, and turns to the blankets. There are six of them; Sofia folds four and places them neatly on the sheet at the foot of the bed, ready for any other sleepers who might come into the room. Picking up the other two, she blows out the candle, then wraps the blankets around her and lies down on the far side of the mattress, fully dressed, cocooned in the shabby wool, which smells of sweat and dust, of unwashed skin and faintly, faintly of sheep. She curls on her side, drawing her knees up. Her skirts are almost dry now, warmed through in front of the tavern fire, and her belly feels full at last – full of the mutton stew and bread Alberto has given her in return for her begged-for coins.

Her eyes seem not to want to close, so she turns her head and stares up at the needle-points of light between the tiles. Her thoughts fragment and disconnect as she moves her eyes from point to point.

She has no home.

No money.

Nowhere to go. She has become a stray . . . like that cat.

She has nothing. Nothing at all. Where should she look for work? For lodgings? How is she to pay for anything for the next few weeks, while she cannot sew? She begins to fiddle with the strapping on her broken finger. The finger feels hot now it is no longer wet – hot and swollen, and itchy within the binding. Sofia picks at a tiny strand from the tuft of wool, pulling at it, teasing it out; but it feels suddenly as though the whole thing might come loose, and she lets go quickly, pushing it back down inside the strapping with the tip of her other forefinger.

The door to the upstairs room creaks open.

A man comes in, carrying a candle, shielding the flame with cupped fingers. He is short and stocky, with sparse hair and a doughy face. Someone whom Sofia saw earlier downstairs, she realizes, but of whom she had taken no notice.

She holds her breath, draws her blankets in more tightly around herself.

The man sets the candle down on the shelf, next to the stub of the one Sofia has just blown out. He turns to look at her. She catches his gaze, then closes her eyes tightly.

'I know you're not asleep,' he says, quietly.

She does not move.

'I was watching you in the tavern room. I saw you leave to go upstairs.'

Sofia remains silent. She opens her eyes a fraction, wanting to see what the man might be doing, hoping he will not notice. He is taking off his doublet, his gaze on her face. She does not move. The man sits down on the end of the bed and pulls off his boots; the straw stuffing in the mattress scrunches beneath him as he moves. He picks up and shakes out one of the blankets; then, crawling across the bed, he lies down next to Sofia, pulling the covering up and over himself.

His breath smells of grappa. He lays a hand on her shoulder, pressing gently with his palm, lifting his fingers as though he were going to stroke up towards her face. But Sofia turns right over without a word, away from him, clutching her blankets around her.

'I'll pay,' he murmurs, pressing himself up close to her back and replacing his hand on her upper arm, gripping it tightly this time. 'I'm not asking you to do it for nothing. I wouldn't do that.'

Feeling the man now stroking down towards her elbow, she jerks her arm backwards, pushing him off.

He hesitates for a moment. With a lurch of her stomach, she feels him pick up a curling strand of her hair; he tucks it behind her ear, then runs his hand down to cup her shoulder again. 'It wouldn't take long,' he whispers. 'And I'll make it worth your while. I have a whole *scudo* . . . p'raps two I can give you. But we'll need to be quick – someone else might come.'

Two *scudi*. Four nights' bed and board here at this tavern.

Pulling the blankets more tightly around her, she draws her knees up towards her chest, curling herself into a ball – and then the door creaks open once more.

A stripe of yellowish light from the staircase falls across the bed; then it narrows and vanishes as the door is pushed shut again. The man edges away from her, swearing softly under his breath.

Sofia holds her breath. Another one? She feels sick. She cannot fight two of them. Her back is to the door; she dares not turn to look at the newcomer, but strains her ears, trying to hear anything that might give her an indication of what sort of a person the new arrival might be.

His movements are slow; the footsteps she hears are shuffling and a little unsteady. Oh God, Sofia thinks, her heart beating so fast now she feels light-headed, if he's drunk . . . Please, I can't fight off two men. Then the newcomer coughs, clears his throat, and coughs again, and Sofia almost cries with relief. This is an old man's cough: a sound of frailty and ill health. A noise of no threat.

The man next to her has turned his back to her and is lying still. After a moment's immobility, though, she feels his body start to jerk. It is a muffled, furtive movement, rhythmic and intense, and every few seconds he lets out a barely audible gasp, stifling the sound in his pillow, clearly trying to remain unheard. Sofia screws her eyes shut and holds her breath. The man's back trembles against hers and the straw mattress rustles under him. Pulling her blanket up, Sofia presses it in against her ears. After a moment or two, the man shudders and is still.

In the silence that follows, Sofia becomes aware of the old man, who is still on his feet. Turning slightly, she looks over her shoulder and starts to watch him in the flickering candlelight. Chin tucked down to his chest, he is taking his time in unfastening his doublet with stiff, unbending fingers – Sofia can hear the soft scrape and tick of the laces being pulled through their eyelet holes – and then he places the doublet down on the chair near the door. It slips off and falls to the floor; the old man grunts softly as he bends to pick it up again.

'Blow the candle out, Nonno,' the man in the bed mutters.

Shuffling footfalls cross the room, the old man puffs out the flame with a wheezing gasp and darkness fills the room.

Sofia lies still, tensed and hardly breathing, for several minutes, dreading the thought that, despite what he has just done, the man next to her might resume his attentions in the dark, but the seconds pass and nothing happens. Still she does not move. The old man begins to snore softly on the far side of the bed – a quiet bubbling in the back of his throat – and Sofia finds herself listening intently, counting the seconds in between the snores. From the man next to her, there is only ragged breathing. Sofia tries to shift position without drawing attention to herself: her shoulder and hip are stiff now, from lying on the same side without moving, but she dares not turn towards her companion, fearful that he might interpret the move as an invitation.

Finally, she can bear it no longer, and, turning as smoothly as she can, she shifts position to face in towards her companion. The man's back is bulky, his shirt creased and warmly damp. Heat is coming from him and Sofia smells the prickling bitterness of stale sweat. Staring up at the light-speckled ceiling for a moment, her eyes begin to feel leaden; she closes them.

She will, she thinks, ask the tavern-owner for more work in the morning. That will be a place to start from. And if Alberto has nothing for her, well, she will at least have had a meal and a sleep. A sleep . . . she has to sleep: each breath is fluttering in her chest. But how can she sleep, lying here next to a man who wanted to . . . wanted to . . . What if he tries again? While she sleeps? What if he decides that the old man will not wake, if he tries his luck again? The thought makes her feel sick.

Here, in this bed, next to this heavy, sweat-smelling, unattractive stranger, Sofia imagines having agreed to the man's earlier suggestion; she pictures herself naming a price, the man laying his hands on her, unfastening her dress, pushing his way up under her skirts. She sees the greedy look in his eyes as he edges himself into position. Her face distorting with disgust, she imagines herself touching him. She hears the chink of coins thrown down onto the pillow and imagines his muttered thanks as he pulls away and adjusts his clothes.

Yes. She will ask Alberto for work in the morning. That will be a start, she thinks. Running through how she might frame her request, she feels herself sliding away into sleep.

4

The Castello della Franceschina, a few miles outside Bologna

'Sebastiano, please, listen to me!'

Sebastiano da Correggio picks up a silver goblet from the heavily laden table in front of him and flings it at the woman seated on the opposite side. She ducks, gasping in shock as the goblet smacks against the wall behind her and bounces down to the floor, splattering wall, floorboards and the sleeve of her dress with red wine.

'Don't fucking tell me what to do!' he shouts, his mouth twisted with anger. Flecks of spit land on the table in front of him, darkening the damasked linen cloth. 'You pathetic, inebriate bitch – why the hell should I listen to you?'

The woman bites her lip. Tilting her chin up, she is clearly struggling not to cry; fat tears gleam along her lashes. The fingers of her left hand tighten around the stem of her cup, her knuckles standing out white. 'Please, Sebastiano,' she says again, in little more than a whisper this time.

'Did I not say to you that you were not to tell *anyone*?' da Correggio says through gritted teeth.

The woman says nothing.

'But such an instruction was clearly too complex for someone of your limited intelligence to grasp.'

The woman flinches. She stands up.

'Where are you going?'

Saying nothing, the woman walks around the end of the table towards where da Correggio is sitting. Crouching down next to his chair, clutching its arm with both hands, she gazes up into his face. 'I can explain, Sebastiano.'

'Don't trouble yourself!' Shoving his chair back from her, Sebastiano da Correggio lifts his right arm and swipes at her back-handed. The blow catches her across the cheek with a crack like a horsewhip; she cries out and stumbles backwards, banging her shoulder hard on the edge of the table as she falls.

'Get up!' da Correggio says. 'It's pathetic! What do you think you're doing grovelling down there like a dog?'

Grabbing the edge of the table, the woman pulls herself to her feet, pressing her hand to the side of her head. 'I'm sorry,' she mutters.

Da Correggio reaches out and grasps her wrist. 'Listen, Maddalena,' he says, 'you know as well as I do that I want to keep my sources a secret. You promised me you wouldn't tell anyone. You've let me down.'

'I'm so sorry,' Maddalena whispers. 'I only told Lisabeta—'

'Your fucking maidservant?' Da Correggio lets go of her arm and shakes his head in disbelief. 'One of the loosest mouths in Emilia-Romagna, so I've heard.'

'It was only because I'm so impressed with your plans.' Maddalena is now almost inaudible.

'You know I want to be very careful with how the information spreads. If other possible dealers start to realize what potential this liquid has beyond the curative, then my position will become precarious in the extreme.' Da Correggio turns away from her, adding in a much softer voice, more to himself than to Maddalena, 'She will need to be made to remain silent.'

Maddalena stiffens, but says nothing.

Several long minutes pass. Then Sebastiano da Correggio reaches across the table, snatches up Maddalena's cup and drains its contents. Maddalena stands unmoving, her hip pressed against the edge of the table, her gaze fixed upon da Correggio's face as he stares into the now-empty cup.

'I'm sorry I made you angry,' she whispers.

Da Correggio grunts.

'I never meant to—'

'Do you know,' da Correggio says loudly, as though Maddalena has not spoken, 'I think this might all have gone on long enough. I think it might just be time to let your cuckold of a husband know exactly what sort of a needy little whore his wife really is.'

Maddalena wails and drops to her knees, clutching the arm of da Correggio's chair. 'God, no – please, Sebastiano! I want to be with you. You can't!'

'Oh, I think I can. If I choose to. Don't you agree?'

'Please! I beg you, Sebastiano—'

Da Correggio lifts a hand, palm towards her, to silence her. 'Be quiet. That's enough. You want me to keep your secrets? Well, you'd better fucking well learn to keep mine. You know what you need to do to persuade me not to talk to him, don't you?'

Maddalena hangs her head.

5

Bologna

Not long after midday, the four painted wagons of the Coraggiosi troupe rumble through the great gate of San Sotero, making their exuberant and noisy way along the Via Emilia towards the centre of Bologna.

Much to everyone's surprise, the rain is holding off. The sky, as Agostino pointed out that morning, resembles nothing so much as the sagging underside of a heavy grey mattress, but, as yet, to the delight of the Coraggiosi, the streets are still dry.

Beppe is out in front with Vico. Masked once more, but no longer in his tattered shirt and breeches, he is wearing a long jacket and leggings of multi-coloured diamond-shaped patches, and has a soft black woollen hat on the back of his head. He is arguing vehemently with Vico. Vico – shorter, stockier than Beppe – is also masked, and is dressed in what appears to be a couple of grubby old flour sacks cinched in at the waist with a length of rope; he is clearly coming off second-best in the altercation. Hopping from foot to foot in a counterfeit rage, Beppe shakes his fist at Vico, chattering at him in what seem at first to be recognizable words, but in fact make no sense at all. He grabs one of his friend's hands. Vico tries to snatch it back – but to the two men's apparent astonishment, their hands seem to have instantly fused together. The two men pull and push and struggle to free themselves, dodging in and out of the path of the wagons, to cheers from the watching people. Beppe lifts first one leg over his and Vico's clasped arms and then the other, tangling himself in knots, ending by flipping head over heels and landing lightly on his feet, waggling both newly freed hands as though they have been burned.

The people now lining the streets laugh and catcall and shout encouragement. One small boy runs out into the street and, with a look of great daring, pokes his tongue out at Beppe. Beppe backflips again in shock, then pokes his tongue out in return. The little boy doubles up with laughter and runs back into the crowd to a spattering of applause.

Lidia, driving the furthest wagon, calls out to them, 'We perform this afternoon in the Piazza di Porta Ravegnana. Don't miss it! *The Foolish Notary* – we start in two hours! Come and join us!'

The crowd cheer and wave. Several children begin to run alongside the wagons.

Two people are riding, one on either side of the wagons, on a pair of pretty dark brown ponies: Cosima, and a young man with features of such symmetrical perfection, he might have been modelled in marble. This is Angelo. Both Cosima's dress and Angelo's glittering, jewelled doublet and breeches are a vivid, joyous red. Both are beaming and waving at the crowds with regal dignity and Cosima is throwing flowers from a basket on her arm.

His face split in a wide smile, Agostino is standing up in the foremost wagon, reins in one hand, and with his other arm around an old man with sparse grey hair and reddened cheeks. He calls out to the crowd, 'Signori and signore, it's here at last! The moment you have all been waiting for for months! The wait is at an end! The Coraggiosi will perform this afternoon, in the piazza, in little more than a couple of hours' time. Here in the shadows of that august and hallowed establishment, the *university* .. :' Agostino gives a deep bow and the crowd cheers. He continues in a voice now mournful and slow. 'Here we shall enact for you a terrible, sad tale: the catastrophic demise of an eminent professor of philosophy, a man so steeped in learning that, like a cabbage left long in a butt of brine, his brains have ... *pickled*.'

Someone in the crowd whoops and shouts and people around him laugh.

'And here he is!' Agostino claps his companion on the shoulder. The old man – Giovanni Battista – shakes his head, his expression one of pompous disbelief.

'Is this man not every inch the great scholar?' Agostino shouts, turning first to one side of the street, and then the other. 'But you must come and see for yourselves this afternoon just how quickly it becomes clear that sometimes knowing *too much* can be as dangerous as knowing *too little*. Look, for example, at that pair of idiots ...' He points forwards towards Beppe and Vico, who break off their continuing altercation to bow extravagantly to right and left, grinning widely to loud applause. 'Could it be that a couple of empty-heads like these come off best in a battle with the academic establishment? Come to the Piazza di Porta Ravegnana this afternoon, and, in the shadow of the Two Towers, you will find out for yourselves!'

He stops. Seeing a familiar face in the crowd, he points and waves. 'Niccolò! Niccolò Zanetti! My good friend! Purveyor of the most extraordinary medicaments to the people of Emilia-Romagna since goodness knows when! How excellent to see you! Will you be coming to see us in the piazza this afternoon?'

A slight figure in a dark grey doublet takes off a tall black hat and waves it energetically. 'Wouldn't miss it for the world.'

'Make sure you come and find us – it's been too long since we last saw you.'

Niccolò Zanetti waves again. 'I'll be there, *amico*.'

'I'm sorry, signorina, I can't help you,' the big tavern-owner says, shaking his head. 'I've neither the money nor the need for anyone. I only offered you the pot-wash last night because I couldn't bear to turn you out of the tavern in weather like that.'

Sofia looks up at Alberto's great round face. She forces a smile. 'Thank you anyway, signore. You've been very kind,' she says. 'I'll not take up any more of your time.'

'Listen,' Alberto says quietly, jerking his head a fraction in an invitation for Sofia to come near enough to share a confidence. 'Come here.'

She takes a step towards him.

'Listen,' he says again. 'I'm sorry I can't offer you what you need. But ... ' Hesitating, he says, 'Here – have this. Go on, take it.' Pushing a hand down into a pocket in his breeches, he pulls out a small leather pouch. 'It's not much ... ' He gives the bag a quick shake and the contents chink. 'Please. I'd like you to have it, signorina. It's not much, but ... ' He tails off.

Holding out a hand, her face flaming, Sofia takes the little purse from him. She tries to smile again, but her face feels stiff and heavy and her mouth seems unwilling to move. She pecks a quick nod, now unable to meet Alberto's eye. 'Thank you again,' she mumbles. 'I think I should go now.'

And, stumbling over a stool in her haste to leave, she lifts the latch on the tavern door and hurries out into the street and away towards the centre of the city. With the bag of coins tucked into her belt, she walks along for several minutes, her thoughts in turmoil.

Where now? And what to do? Fingering through the contents of Alberto's money-bag, she decides there should be enough for a couple of meals and another night somewhere. But where? And what then? What will happen to her when the money runs out? Alberto has been so very kind, she thinks, but even if she ekes it out carefully, she cannot see his money lasting her more than a couple of days. Panic begins to swell in her throat at the thought of the only option that seems to be left to her if she is not to starve. She holds her breath, fighting back tears. She cannot do it – especially after last night. Even contemplating the prospect of unknown hands fumbling with her clothing, pushing their way up into her skirts, the feel of unknown lips on hers – it makes her feel sick. She thinks of the man in the bed in the tavern room, and then pictures the glistening mouth of her accuser in Modena, ringed around with hair and smelling of ale and rotten teeth. Of what will *they* smell and taste, these men who might want to pay to touch her – and to have her touch them? And what might they ask her to do? Would she even understand their requests? Will they laugh at her if she does not? She has never so much as kissed anyone. Once, in a tavern, Sofia overheard a whore laughing drunkenly to a friend about some of the things she had done with her 'tricks' . . . Sofia presses a fisted hand to her mouth and swallows uncomfortably.

The narrow, winding street she is in suddenly opens out into the vast Piazza Maggiore: a wide space dominated by a series of castellated colonnades and already bustling with life. Sofia slows her pace, staring around her, her anxieties momentarily pushed aside in the face of such a vivid and enticing sight. She begins to make her way around the northern edge of the square, gazing about as she walks.

Fish merchants and poultry-vendors are busy setting up their stalls and laying out their wares: mournful-eyed sardines lie in depressed-looking rows on piles of glittering salt; boxes of angry crayfish with tightly strapped, waving claws jostle for room beside baskets of squawking chickens; and on hooks hang clusters of rabbits and several limp ducks. On one stall a wet tangle of octopus tentacles gleams in the fitful light like a melting Medusa.

A little way down the colonnade, a long table is stacked with books: some big, fat, heavy, bound in brightly coloured leather; others smaller, with scuffed wooden covers. One or two are lying open, showing dark woodcut illustrations, but most stand upright, spine out, ranked neatly along their table. Their owner, a tall man in a black doublet and breeches, sits on a high-legged stool behind the books, one large tome lying open in the palm of one of his long-fingered hands. Engrossed in what he is reading, he seems entirely uninterested in his surroundings and equally unaware of any potential customers.

A scrawny young man hurries past Sofia with a bulging basket on his back. He stops just near her, swings the basket down onto the ground and opens it. She watches as he pulls from it a dark green cloth, which he spreads across the cobbles; then, reaching back down into the basket, he brings out bright handfuls of ribbons, buttons, laces, glittering beads and several pairs of embroidered sleeves, which he starts to lay out across his cloth. Whistling softly, he sits cross-legged on the ground behind his display, reaching from time to time to tweak and fiddle. Lastly, he takes from the basket a small iron bowl, which he places at his side.

Pulling a few coins from a pocket in his breeches, he drops them into the bowl.

Sofia gazes longingly at the ribbons and laces. They are beautiful, vividly coloured and enticing, and she longs to run her fingers through them. The sleeves are exquisite too, she thinks, itching to pick them up and examine them.

'Want to come and have a look, signorina?' the young man calls, grinning at her.

Embarrassed to have been noticed, Sofia shrugs. 'I haven't any money.'

'Don't stop you lookin' . . . '

Sofia cannot resist. Crouching in front of the young man's display, she reaches out and picks up a bunch of bright crimson ribbons. They slip between her fingers like water, smooth and cool against her skin. She holds her hand up with the ribbons draped across it, and strokes it along her cheek. They are of a high quality – smooth and fine grained.

The young man watches her. 'Like them, do you?'

'How could anyone not like them? They're beautiful.'

'Only ten *baiocchi* for the bunch.'

Sofia shakes her head sadly. 'I'd love to have them. But I can't. No money.'

The boy, dressed in dirty breeches and a doublet several sizes too large for him, stares hard at Sofia for several seconds, his gaze travelling over her bedraggled dress, her uncombed hair and the bandaged hand. He reaches across his display and takes the ribbons from her. Embarrassed, she begins to stand, but the boy says, 'No, wait. You don't understand – don't go!' He slides a couple from the bunch and holds them out to Sofia. 'Here, have them. Stitch them onto your sleeve – they'll look pretty. Or put them in your hair.'

'But . . . ' Sofia begins.

'Come here. I'll do it for you.' He holds out an arm, flicking his fingers, beckoning her.

Sofia hesitates, but the boy is now on his feet. Bending over his basket, he pushes both hands down into it and rummages for a moment, then straightens, brandishing a small square of leather. Sofia sees that it is glittering with pins. The boy flaps it towards her. 'Here – come here, and I'll . . .'

She does not move, so he hops nimbly over his display and stands in front of her. Taking back one of the ribbons he has given her, he flips it back and forth a couple of times, creating a four-looped bow. Freeing the loose ends, he holds it by one of the loops between his teeth and pulls a pin from the leather square, which he then pushes back down into his breeches pocket. With the knot of ribbon in one hand, and Sofia's elbow in the other, he neatly in-and-outs the pin through the ribbon and fastens it to the sleeve near Sofia's shoulder.

'There!' he says, nodding in approval at what he has done. 'Now the other one.'

He pins the second ribbon.

'There, now. Fit for a duchess!' he says, grinning.

'Thank you. You're very kind. But you shouldn't be giving your things away . . .'

The boy looks suddenly serious. 'Nah, don't suppose I should. But, well . . .' He shrugs.

Sofia says, 'I'll come and find you when I have some money. I'll pay for the ribbons then. I promise.'

The boy grins again. 'I'm here quite often,' he says. 'Keep looking. And mind them pins when you take your dress off tonight.'

Sofia feels her cheeks burn. The boy's grin widens and he winks.

Not sure whether to smile or cry, Sofia moves off across the piazza.

*

Over in the Piazza di Porta Ravegnana, a stage is being erected in the shadow of the Two Towers. Some two dozen trestle supports have already been put in place, and Beppe, Vico, Agostino and the perfect-profiled Angelo are standing one at each corner of a large wooden board. The brightly coloured costumes have gone, and all four men are back in shirts and breeches.

'On the count of four, then,' Agostino says. On 'Four!' they all lift the board to just above chest height and slide it out across the trestles. Beppe ducks down beneath the board and flips a number of little pivoting pegs into their corresponding holes, to hold the board in place.

'Ready for the next one?' Agostino says.

Scrambling out from between the trestles, Beppe nods. The four men repeat the process. Half a dozen times they lift and shift; half a dozen times Beppe crawls under the staging and fixes the boards in place.

'Go and get the poles, will you?' Agostino says.

Vico and Beppe run across to the wagons. Three long wooden poles, each about three or four inches in diameter and some ten feet long, have been slung under the biggest of the wagons along with two long coils of rope.

Beppe tugs at the end of one of the poles. It sticks for a moment, and then comes suddenly free so that Beppe stumbles backwards. He eases the whole length of the pole out, lays it on the ground, then pulls the second and third ones free. 'Can you bring the curtains, Lidia?' he says as he slings the rope coils around one arm and, together with Vico, picks up the poles. 'Get Cosima to help you.'

'Won't be a moment,' Lidia says, peering out from inside the largest wagon.

Towards the back edge of the staging three holes have been cut in the boards, one at each corner and one in the middle. Each of the poles has a deep groove a few inches from its top and bottom ends. Laying them down on the ground in parallel, Beppe takes one of the lengths of rope and knots it around each of these grooves. Then, with Vico's help, he lifts, positions and drops each of the three poles into the holes so that, feet on the ground, they project upwards from the staging some seven feet, like oversized bed-posts, with the rope stretched tautly between them. Beppe takes another length of rope and fastens it around the bottom end of each pole.

Lidia and Cosima appear, carrying between them a big pile of dark cloth. Grunting slightly, they throw their burden down onto the ground, where it lands with a dusty-sounding 'flump'. Right around the front edge of the staging, at hand-span intervals, is a row of small iron hooks. Lidia and Cosima now begin lifting the cloth up onto the hooks so that it drapes down from the stage to the floor, effectively creating a large hidden storage area below where the actors will perform. As they do this, Beppe, Vico and Angelo are up on the stage, unrolling two huge lengths of canvas, on which are painted two halves of a scene. These they flap up and over the rope, weighting each down on either side with stones placed in little pockets at ground level, so that they hang – fairly evenly – right across the back of the stage, displaying a street scene: recognizably Bologna. A different picture (for a different show) faces out backwards.

Angelo now puts both hands in the small of his back and stretches. 'I'm going back to the wagons. I need to start getting dressed,' he says, to no one in particular. Without waiting for a response, he sits on the edge of the stage, then jumps down, landing neatly like a cat.

Nobody comments on his departure, though Vico raises an eyebrow and shakes his head, pushing his lips out and shrugging.

Agostino, standing back on the ground some few yards from the stage, shades his eyes with his hand and stares critically at the effect of the newly placed scenery. After a few seconds' careful scrutiny, he nods and, muttering to himself, begins to walk back to the wagons.

He takes no notice of Beppe, Vico and Lidia, who are now hurrying from wagon to stage and back, putting into the storage space behind the curtains an odd assortment of items: two buckets, a long string of onions, three chairs, a pile of books, a cloak, a stuffed dog with a string around its neck and Beppe's ladder, among many other things. Agostino clambers into the smallest of the wagons, to reappear a moment later with a slim leather-bound book in one hand, and a wooden board in a gilt frame tucked under the other arm.

He climbs to the hidden space behind the backdrop and props the board where it will be seen as the actors stand waiting for their entrances. Opening the book, he takes from it a handful of small squares of paper. Perusing these scraps, he places each carefully onto the board in a particular order, pinning each one with a tack. Once all twenty or so scraps are in place, Agostino stares at the board for several minutes. 'Good,' he mutters. 'That will work very well indeed.'

'All sorted, Ago?' Vico says cheerfully as he crouches, knees high like a frog, to push a large plaster cake into the under-stage space.

'Absolutely, absolutely.' Agostino glances once more at his board, then climbs back down the little ladder from the stage to the ground. 'Is everything where it should be?'

Lidia crawls out from under the stage, her skirts bundled in her arms. Getting awkwardly to her feet, she puts her arms around Agostino's neck and kisses his cheek. 'Stop fussing. Everything is *exactly* where it ought to be, *caro* – where you've *told* us it must be – where we *need* it to be.'

Beppe has balanced a walking stick on its tip on his index finger; his eyes are fixed upon its wobbling end. 'Everything will be wonderful, as always,' he says. 'And, as always, it'll be thanks to you.'

Agostino draws in a long, long, shuddering breath, closing his eyes and pushing his fingers up into his hair. Beppe flips the walking stick up vertically into the air and catches it one-handed as it falls back down.

Pointing at his actors with an accusatory finger, but smiling as he does so, Agostino says, 'Go on, get yourselves dressed then! We start when the church clock chimes two.'

There seems to be a new purpose to the jostling of the crowd, Sofia thinks. Having spent the morning wandering through the great piazza, gazing at the riotous and colourful stalls, listening to the vendors and purchasers arguing and haggling, she has been pushing to the back of her mind, over and over again, the fears that have lurked like hooded intruders in the shadows of her consciousness since her flight from Modena. She has just spent two of Alberto's precious coins on a slice of cooked pork, an apricot and a small flagon of ale, and has been sitting for several minutes on a stone ledge at the bottom of one of the piazza's long colonnades to eat her purchases. She is cold again, and her finger aches; she wants to unwrap Signor Zanetti's binding and see how it is healing, but has so far resisted temptation, afraid of not being able to refasten it once she has inspected the damage. Pulling the binding outwards at the top end and peering in at her fingertips, all she has been able to establish is that the finger is darkly bruised, and still considerably swollen. The tuft of wool smells quite strongly now – Sofia sniffs at it and pulls a face.

She watches the bustle of people moving through the piazza, everyone now seemingly heading out towards the north-eastern corner. Men and women are talking and laughing together, sounding excited, happy. Getting to her feet and brushing crumbs from her skirt, she begins to walk with them, listening to the jumble of conversations around her.

'I saw them last summer – yes, right at the end of the summer, I think it was. Early September. I know it wasn't as warm as it might have been.'

'A little like today, then. What did you think?'

'Marvellous. *Cara*, you were with me, were you not?'

'I most certainly was. Wouldn't have missed it for the world.'

'To be quite honest, I'd say they're as good as the Gelosi . . .'

'You've seen the Gelosi? Lord, you are lucky indeed! When?'

'Oh, God knows . . . two, three years ago? They were superb.'

Sofia walks in step some two or three paces behind these conversationalists: four fashionably dressed women, animated and eager, each clearly relishing the prospect of whatever it is they are preparing to do.

Who or what, she wonders, are the Gelosi?

One of the women laughs then at a remark Sofia has missed. 'Oh yes, I'm sure *she* was delighted. The Coraggiosi's *inamorato* has to be *quite* the most beautiful man I think I've ever *seen*!'

'He's *adorable*, isn't he? I can't wait to see him again today.'

Much taken with the idea of seeing this paragon for herself, Sofia quickens her pace.

The Piazza di Porta Ravegnana is already teeming with people when she arrives there. She stares around her. Dominating the square are the Two Towers: close together, impossibly tall and narrow and decidedly mismatched. One of them leans drunkenly out to one side and they loom over the burgeoning crowd like a pair of giant, inebriated stilt-walkers.

And, out in front of the towers, is a stage. The size of a large room, with a busy street scene painted on a cloth at the back, it stands at chest-height above the cobbles, and curtains hang down from it right to the ground; several dozen people have already grouped themselves in front of it, and, even as Sofia watches, another twenty or so join them. Up on the stage itself, three chairs have been grouped to one side as though a small house party has recently broken up and the guests have just departed, and a broom stands propped against a painted archway.

More and more people are arriving now, and the piazza is becoming almost uncomfortably crowded. Sofia edges her way through towards the front, determined now to find herself a place where she will be able to see the action of the play when it begins. Finding a spot some ten feet from the front edge of the stage, she gazes about her, happily infected by the general air of enthusiastic anticipation.

'Hey! Signorina! Signorina Genotti!'

Shocked at hearing her own name, Sofia spins around. The voice came from the crowd to her left. She stares towards where she thought she heard it and it comes again. 'Over here! Signorina!'

6

Turning further around, she sees him. In his tall black hat, smiling broadly, Niccolò Zanetti, the little apothecary, edges his way through the crowd towards her, saying, 'Oh, my dear, how pleased I am to see you.'

Sofia tries to speak, but finds she cannot – her words just stretch out into a smile.

'You disappeared so quickly back in Modena, I didn't have an opportunity either to bid you a proper farewell, or to offer you my ... well, perhaps "hospitality" is too grand a word for it, but I *had* intended to ask you if you would care to ride out of town with me in my little cart, and there was to be a blanket for you to wrap yourself in for the night. I had had an idea, you see, and ...'

Sofia puts her hand in front of her mouth.

Niccolò Zanetti says, 'You ran off so fast. But what have you been doing since that day?' He hesitates. 'Forgive me if I am speaking out of turn, my dear, but I think it's safe to say that, looking at you now, these past few days cannot have been easy ...'

Sofia feels herself reddening. She stares fixedly at the ground, seeing, as though through Signor Zanetti's eyes, her filthy dress and ruined shoes, and her tangled, dirty hair.

Niccolò Zanetti takes her hand and lifts it, touching the stained binding around her fingers. 'Listen, child, I—'

He breaks off. Sofia looks up. The crowd's loud murmuring dies to a hum, and then to silence.

Zanetti whispers, 'We'll talk later. They're about to begin.'

Sofia stares up at the stage.

Two women slip out from behind the painted backdrop, followed by a stocky man in a baggy white suit and hat. The man's face is painted white; his head bobs back and forth like a chicken's as he walks and his elbows splay out sideways. One of the two women is strikingly beautiful; she is, Sofia sees now, dressed in a richly embroidered red gown, her hair is piled high in a mass of complicated curls and braids, and jewels glitter at her throat and on her fingers. The other woman – smaller, plumper, quicker in her movements – is dressed more simply. A servant, perhaps.

Although not as starkly white as the chicken-walk man, both the women's faces are clearly much paler than nature intended – paler certainly than their hands – with enormous eyes and reddened lips.

The beautiful woman pulls her companion aside and, jerking her head back towards the man, she hiss-whispers, '*He'll be asleep soon.*'

'*Let's hope so!*' the little servant girl says, peering over her shoulder. '*With the amount of potion I've just given him, I'm amazed the fat fool's still on his feet.*'

Even as she speaks, though, the man begins to sway and stagger, yawning widely and stretching his arms out sideways. A laugh slithers through the crowd.

'*As soon as he drops, go and find Oratio! Be as quick as you can!*'
'*Oh, I will – I'll run like the wind, signora!*'

Sofia stares up at the stage, entranced.

Behind the backcloth, a few moments later, Beppe is listening to the lines being spoken on the stage, where Vico and Angelo are deep in conversation: just a minute or two until his entrance. Staring up at the cloud-heavy sky, he breathes slowly and deliberately. He stretches and flexes his fingers, his arms, rolls his shoulders, crouches and stands again several times, bends each leg up in turn and hugs it against his belly. Bouncing gently on the balls of his feet, he touches the fastenings of his mask and adjusts the position of his black hat, pushing it to sit a little further back on his head.

He checks the gilt-framed board, running his finger down the various scraps of paper – the *canovaccii* – on which are written the instructions for every scene in the play. Finding the one he needs, he reads it, although he already knows by heart what it contains, then he taps it with a finger as though dismissing its services.

Agostino, in his baggy white suit, climbs up to stand behind Beppe; he smiles, and Beppe gives him a swift grin in return. Reaching out for his ladder, Beppe picks it up and tucks it under his arm. As Vico and Angelo come back out, Beppe pauses for a second, then, crouching slightly, edges the end of the ladder out through the gap in the cloth and steps onto the stage, each foot raised high at each step, eyes wide behind the mask, peering around him fearfully.

The crowd murmurs.

Sofia watches as the stocky man in the white suit, now apparently happily recovered from his earlier enforced sleep, creeps along behind the strange masked figure in the long patched jacket. Along with the crowd, she laughs as the masked man swings his ladder around too fast and whacks his companion in the backside, sending him sprawling.

'That's Arlecchino,' Niccolò Zanetti says into her ear, pointing at the stage. 'Played by my friend Beppe Bianchi – such a clever boy.'

'Do you *know* the players, then, signore?' Sofia whispers back, surprised.

'Oh yes, I most certainly do. I've known them for years. You must come with me and meet them at the end of the show. I've a mind to—'

'What's the name of the man in the red doublet?'

Niccolò Zanetti raises an eyebrow. 'Who? The one playing Oratio?'

Sofia's face flames.

'His name's Angelo. Angelo da Bagnacavallo.'

The Arlecchino character scrambles up his ladder, which is now leaning up against a big wooden box. It up-ends and flips him downwards. Rolling head over heels along it, he pulls it with him and stands up again, looking bemused, with the ladder held upright in both hands in front of him.

The crowd cheers.

Sofia laughs, entranced by the acrobatics. 'How on earth did he *do* that?' she whispers to Zanetti as Arlecchino scurries off out of sight.

Niccolò Zanetti chuckles. 'Oh, that boy can do just about anything,' he says.

The red-doubleted Angelo strides back onto the stage holding a lantern, and at the sight of him, Sofia holds her breath. His name suits him. He is truly angelic-looking. And 'Bagnacavallo' – that just rolls off the tongue. He moves gracefully, too, she thinks, watching him holding the lantern high, leaning in towards where the beautiful woman in the red dress is huddled in conversation with another, taller, bearded man in a bizarre, long-nosed, strangely indecent-looking mask.

But suddenly, Angelo shakes the lantern and shouts at the bearded man, interrupting what seems to Sofia to be something of a love-tryst. The bearded man and the woman leap apart.

'*Traitorous villain!*' Angelo yells. '*Isabella is mine!*'

The bearded man spins round and draws his sword. Glancing out at the crowd, and lifting his chin in a gesture of defiant elegance, Angelo spits extravagantly onto the stage and draws his own weapon. The two men stand facing each other for a few long seconds, swords pointed towards each other's chests.

And then the fight begins.

Several people in the audience gasp. The swords clash as the two men back-and-forth across the stage to whoops and catcalls from the crowd. Sofia holds her breath, her clasped hands in front of her mouth, hardly daring to look.

'Remind me, in a second or two, when we're on stage, not to give the self-opinionated little shit a good kick in the bollocks,' Vico mutters in Beppe's ear. 'Otherwise I might just forget . . . and do it.'

Beppe raises an eyebrow and shakes his head. 'Come on. Off we go.' He, Vico and Lidia push through onto the stage, each holding high a small lantern. As Lidia, seeing the fight, stops dead, gasps, and holds up her hands in horror, Vico runs full tilt into the back of her. Lidia falls forwards onto hands and knees, dropping her lantern, and Vico somersaults over the top of her, rolling to land in between the two swordsmen, his lamp miraculously still held tightly in one hand.

Both swordsmen stop mid-thrust, mouths open, weapons in the air, both staring at Vico.

Vico sits up and grins at them, head swivelling from one to the other.

The crowd laughs.

Beppe, some two steps behind, pulls from his belt what looks like a narrow, two-bladed bat. Still clutching his lantern, he waves it above his head, gibbering nonsensically at Angelo and at Federico – Angelo's bearded, long-nosed opponent. He charges forwards, leaping nimbly over Lidia, slapping the bat against his thigh. It rings out like a whip-crack and the crowd murmurs. The chattering tirade continues as Beppe dances around Angelo and Federico, waving his lamp at them, whacking his bat against his leg.

Lidia scrambles to her feet and pulls at Angelo's sleeve. He shakes her off, pointing furiously towards a painted door in the backcloth. Lidia, hand over her mouth, scuttles away and slips off the stage through the gap in the hanging.

Beppe whacks his stick against his leg again.

Federico shouts at him, '*Oh, go to the devil, you ignoramus! Can't you see that a woman's honour is at stake here?*'

Glaring at him, Beppe points his bat at Federico and says stoutly, '*A woman's honour at stake? Well . . . all I can see is a couple of* dis*honourable "steaks" here, who are "on a" hiding to nothing . . .*'

'Oh, Signor Zanetti, that was wonderful!' Sofia says as the crowd begins to disperse. 'I've never seen anything like it.'

'Have you not seen players performing before?'

Niccolò Zanetti sounds astonished, but Sofia shakes her head. 'No,' she says. 'I saw troupes passing through Modena on different occasions, but I never stopped to watch.'

'Well, I'm glad you've seen them today. Come with me now, and we'll meet them all.' He hesitates. 'You see, I have a suggestion for Agostino, my dear, something which occurred to me the day we met. Something which might . . . ' He tails off, frowning. 'No, I won't say now. I'll wait and see what he . . . '

'Who is Agostino?' Sofia asks.

'Agostino Martinelli. He runs the troupe. He plays Pedrolino – the silly one with the white face, in the baggy white suit. Agostino's married to Cosima – the *inamorata*, that is, the beautiful woman in the lovely red dress.'

'Married? The players are married to each other?'

Niccolò Zanetti laughs. 'Of course – some of them are. Why should they not be?'

Feeling suddenly foolish, Sofia looks down at her dress, starting to fiddle with the cloth of the skirt. 'I don't know. I just didn't think that . . . '

'And no more should you have. Come on, come with me.' He reaches out and takes Sofia's good hand, adding as he does so, 'And then we can have a peek at that finger of yours, and see how it's progressing. You'll be needing a new binding on it, if nothing else.'

Behind the stage, a confusion of bustling activity is under way. The performers are now hurrying back and forth between the stage and a number of large covered wagons. She stands and watches as they take it in turns to crouch and reach into a great space beneath the stage itself, bringing out lanterns and plates, chairs, bunches of flowers, the stuffed dog and the great plaster cake, carrying them off piece by piece towards the wagons.

The glitter and magic has vanished in the few minutes since the play ended, she thinks, watching the bustle. Most of the players have already changed out of their costumes and it seems to Sofia that, despite the daylight, it's as though a candle has been snuffed out and the vivid colours of the performance have faded to grey. The men who were wearing masks have now removed them; their hair is damp and spiked, and to Sofia, their faces now seem small and squashed after the oversized features of the masks.

The servant girl, leaning backwards now against the weight of the big wooden box she is carrying, sees her staring and smiles. Sofia smiles shyly back, realizing that, close to, she is much older than Sofia first thought. This is more a woman than a girl – she has to be at least twice Sofia's own age, if not even a little more. Close to, the woman's pale face and heavily painted eyes, which are now smudged and sweat-loosened, look exaggerated, even grotesque.

Sofia scans from face to face, looking covertly for the red-doubleted Angelo, but he is nowhere to be seen. She catches the eye of the young man who, though now dressed in a tattered, untucked shirt, is still wearing his diamond-patched leggings – what was it Signor Zanetti said his name was? His short hair is standing on end – he has clearly run his fingers through it a number of times – and he looks tired, she thinks, but, on meeting her gaze, his eyebrows lift and he flicks her a brief smile. His eyes, she sees with a little jolt of her insides, now that the mask has gone, are wide and dark brown, and his smile is warm and broad and uneven, tilting up a little more on one side than the other.

'Sofia, come here and meet Signor Martinelli,' Niccolò Zanetti says then. Sofia, who is still watching the boy with the tilted smile, starts and turns towards where Signor Zanetti is standing next to a stocky man with grey hair and a now smeared and blurred white-painted face. His hair too is on end. The young man in the diamond-patterned leggings picks up a wooden box and moves away.

'Here she is, Agostino, here she is! Signorina Genotti,' Niccolò

Zanetti says, putting an arm around her shoulders. 'Sofia Genotti. The seamstress-in-training I was telling you about.'

Agostino cuts across Zanetti. 'This is the girl?' He beams. 'Oh, how entirely marvellous!'

Sofia blushes as Agostino continues, 'Signorina, you might just be the answer to a particularly heartfelt prayer. We are sorely in need of a seamstress – see here . . .' He turns away from her, lifting an elbow, and Sofia sees a long rent in the side-seam of his ballooning white smock. Poking his fingers into it, he spreads them out, making the rent gape. Sofia sees skin beneath the cloth and is momentarily embarrassed at the unsought intimacy.

'Look at that!' Agostino says, shaking his head. 'Just happened tonight. And poor Cosima's dress is almost in *pieces* – being held together with the barest *web* of threads.' He lowers his voice to a conspiratorial whisper. 'I have to admit that we are struggling to keep our costumes together. To my shame, we're becoming more threadbare and shabby with every performance.' Pausing, he adds, 'None of us is gifted with a needle. Something simply has to be done.'

'Agostino has complained about this often, and so, the moment I met you in Modena and learned your story, I thought—' Niccolò Zanetti begins, turning to Sofia.

'You did – and it was an excellent thought indeed!' Agostino interrupts. He leans forwards. 'My dear, Signor Zanetti has just told me all about you. He's made me a suggestion, and so now I have a proposition for you. A preposterous but perfect proposition. Tell me what you think of it. We are here in Bologna for three or four days, so . . . so might you see your way to spending a little time with us here in the city and working on these damned costumes for us, getting them fit to be used? In return for a small remuneration, of course. We haven't a great deal to offer, but will pay you what we can.'

Sofia's mouth opens. She looks from Signor Martinelli to Niccolò Zanetti and from him to her bandaged hand. Poking at her broken finger, it is still hot and tight and sore. 'Oh, signori – oh God, I'd like nothing better. I truly, truly cannot think of anything I'd rather do, but . . .' She pauses, and despairing tears begin to prickle in her nose. 'I'm not sure that I can. It's my hand . . . I hurt my hand last week. My finger might be broken. And I don't think I can . . .'

Agostino frowns. 'Broken?'

Sofia nods.

Niccolò Zanetti clears his throat. 'Let me take another look at it for you. If it's a sprain, it'll certainly be on the mend.'

Sofia swallows. 'Now?'

'Why not? Let's see what state it's in, shall we?' He begins to unwrap the binding around Sofia's fingers. The tuft of dirty wool falls to the ground from between the two fingers as the linen strip unwinds and dangles, limp and stained; the final few inches come away and the strip too drops to the ground to lie sadly on the cobbles.

Zanetti takes Sofia's hand in his and examines it.

The sore finger is a greyish purple. Sofia turns her hand over; the bruising is darker on the underside, and the swelling more obvious. Slowly, holding her breath and grimacing against possible pain, she attempts to bend it.

'Oh, this looks much better than I had feared it might, my dear,' Zanetti says.

'But it still won't move properly and I . . . oh God . . . I don't think I can sew with it yet.' As the thought of the opportunity which is about to pass her by settles on Sofia like a sodden blanket, she bites the inside of her cheek, fighting tears, pressing the back of her good hand against her mouth.

7

Angelo da Bagnacavallo climbs out of the largest of the Coraggiosi's wagons. They all seem preoccupied, he thinks, watching them clustering around the little apothecary and whoever that girl is. She's pretty. Bedraggled and grubby perhaps, but very pretty, nonetheless. That mouth of hers is ripe and ready. Perhaps he should stay for a while longer, and find out more about her. Blowing out his cheeks, he puffs a soft breath, tapping his lips with a finger, staring back at the troupe, trying to decide.

Maybe it would be better to introduce himself to the girl before he goes? He ought to make sure that bastard Beppe doesn't move in and attract her attention, apart from anything else.

But then – he has arranged to see Sebastiano before dusk.

He has to see him: after today, Sebastiano will be back at Franceschina, and the troupe will have moved on, and he, Angelo, will be literally tearing his hair from his scalp. He cannot wait. The Coraggiosi won't be performing at Franceschina for several weeks. Even thinking about having to wait that long makes him itch. He cannot do it.

A few moments here should not make too much difference, though. He will introduce himself, see how long the girl is likely to be around; then if it seems likely she will be there later on, he can head over to Sebastiano's city rooms and buy what he needs. Edging past a teetering pile of boxes, he walks up to where the apothecary is holding one of the girl's hands in both of his own. Everyone is staring at him and the girl, their gazes flicking from the girl's face to her clearly damaged hand, to the apothecary's frowning expression. Angelo says nothing, but stares at the girl, quickly registering her taut prettiness, the swell of her breasts against the edge of her undeniably filthy bodice, the wildness of her curly hair. He runs his tongue over his lips. She is small and slight and almost edible.

She looks up and sees him, and a deep flush rises in her cheeks.

Pleased with this reaction, he smiles at her, allowing his gaze to dip to her mouth and back up. Then, lifting his eyebrows and inclining his head in the smallest of bows, he says, 'Who have we here?'

Agostino and the others turn his way. Angelo sees with some satisfaction a scowl rise on Beppe's face at the sight of him.

Agostino says, 'Angelo, you remember Niccolò Zanetti?'

Angelo, who has vaguely recognized the apothecary, has no recollection of the man's name, but he lies smoothly. 'Of course. Signore, how are you?'

'Well, thank you,' the man called Zanetti says with a swift smile.

'And this', Agostino says, patting the girl's shoulder, 'is a young lady named Sofia Genotti. Sofia, this is Angelo, our *inamorato*. Sofia has just seen the show, Angelo. Niccolò has brought her to us because . . . because, thank the heavens, she is gifted with a needle.' He beams. 'We are hoping she might have a stab at mending some of the costumes. Just what we need, do you not agree?'

'Oh yes. Indeed. We're a sadly scruffy bunch at present.' Angelo flicks a dismissive glance over towards Beppe in his torn shirt, then looks back at Sofia. The colour deepens in her cheeks as she meets his eye and she drops her gaze to the ground in confusion.

Happy that he has had the initial effect upon the girl that he would have hoped for, Angelo stares for another second or two at Sofia's mouth, then determines to make his way over to Sebastiano's to effect the all-too-necessary purchases. He will not be able to concentrate on this girl later on unless he does.

'I hope', he says, 'to make your acquaintance further later this evening. Will you be eating with us? I have an errand to run, but shall return shortly.'

'Yes, Sofia and Niccolò will be eating with us, but where are you go——?' Agostino begins, but Angelo has already turned away. Scratching at the back of his head, he walks off, through a confusion of narrow streets towards a wide piazza, behind which sit Sebastiano da Correggio's city rooms.

By the time he bangs on Sebastiano's door, Angelo has begun to feel an uncomfortable tightness in his chest: a puckering, like a drawing in of purse-strings. Sweat beads along his upper lip and when a salt drop slides into the corner of his mouth, he wipes it away irritably with the side of his thumb. The ground beneath his feet slopes suddenly away from him, dropping downwards and then pitching back up to rock him as though he were on the open sea. His stomach churns. Closing his eyes, he swallows, tasting a sharp sourness. He leans forward, putting his hands on his knees, and stands bowed, trying to will the earth beneath him to stand still.

The door opens.

'Signore? Are you ill?'

Angelo turns his head sideways and looks up, hands still on his knees. Frowning, he tries to focus. A young man is regarding him with obvious concern. For a moment there are two of him, and then the paired images slide together into one. Straightening, Angelo blinks several times, and rubs his eyes. 'Da Correggio,' he says. 'I need to see Signor da Correggio. Tell him I'm here. Angelo da Bagnacavallo. He's expecting me.'

'Please, come inside.' The young man holds the door open for him. 'I will tell Signor da Correggio that you're here.'

Angelo sits down on a carved stool. His pulse is racing. The giddiness which engulfed him just now is still swirling around him, and the wooden boards beneath his feet are bucking and heaving. A terrible sense of urgency is threatening to overwhelm him now – that increasingly familiar sensation which always seems to hover somewhere between exhilaration and panic; he can never seem to determine which, nor whether or not he enjoys the feeling.

Footsteps on the staircase overhead. One flight, then another, then another, growing louder. Heavy and quick.

'God, how much bloody grappa have you had?' Sebastiano da Correggio's voice is scornful.

Angelo shakes his head. 'Not much. Not enough.'

Sebastiano clicks his tongue against his teeth and rolls his eyes. 'Come with me,' he mutters. Taking Angelo by the elbow, he steers him towards the stairs.

The *sala* is long and low-ceilinged. The heavy rafters are thickly painted in detailed patterns, and yet, despite the cheerful colours, the place has an unsettling air. Despite the elegance of the furniture, the walls are bare and no ornaments or embellishments can be seen. Several large wooden crates stand piled at one side of the room. A general lack of love is obvious. Even though a fire is burning, none of the many lamps or candles have been lit, so the light is dim and flickering, and on the table is a row of bottles, each corked and sealed; the firelight catches on the facets of the glass and glitters there, giving the bottles a strangely animated air, as though the substance they contain is moving. Each bottle is full of what appears to be a viscous, darkish brown syrup.

Angelo stares at the bottles, fighting nausea. He pushes his fingers up into his sleeve and scratches the skin of his forearm, then scratches too down inside the neck of the doublet, elbow winged high, face distorted as he pushes his fingers down inside the wool, unable fully to reach the source of his discomfort. 'Do you have a glass?' he says, turning to Sebastiano.

'What? You want some now? Do you have to?'

Angelo struggles to keep his face impassive. 'I'd prefer to. Will you join me?' he says, trembling slightly. 'I have to be back with the troupe for the evening meal, but I should like . . . ' He tails off.

'I'll take a grappa with you, to keep you company, if you wish,' Sebastiano says. 'But I'd rather keep a clear head as I'm expecting a visitor.'

He leaves the room, returning a moment later with a bottle of grappa, two tiny glasses and a spoon, all of which he places on the little table. He pours a couple of fingers' depth of grappa into each glass. Then, drawing the cork from one of the bottles with a faint 'pop' and holding the spoon over one of the glasses, he tips a small amount of the sticky brown liquid into it. Tilting the spoon – slowly, slowly – he allows the liquid to fall into the glass. It swirls for a moment in the grappa, then fans out and dissolves, staining the clear liquid a pale honey colour. He puts the cork back into the bottle, pushing it in firmly with his thumb.

Angelo pulls one of the chairs over and sits down. Making a dome of his two cupped hands, he holds them around the glass like a protective cave, not touching it; then, staring down into it, he leans down and breathes in the sharp sweet scent of the syrup. The anticipation is almost as good as the dose. Almost. He closes his eyes. After a moment, he picks up the glass with the tips of his fingers, tilts his head back and swallows the contents.

8

Niccolò Zanetti holds Sofia's hand in his and rubs the broken finger gently with the ball of his thumb. 'Mmm. Looking at it now, I doubt this finger is broken, after all, but it's clearly still painful.' He looks up at Agostino. 'There is little possibility she could do more than cobble basic stitches together right now.'

Wiping her eyes and nose with her knuckles, Sofia sees Signor Zanetti hesitate. Then he says slowly, 'But here's another thought for you.'

She glances from Zanetti to Agostino and back.

'How about this? Might she not travel with you on to – where do you go next? Ferrara? That hand will be healed and back to normal in possibly as little as a week. If you keep her with you, she can start work as soon as she's fit. You'd have yourself a resident costume mistress.'

Agostino frowns, tapping his teeth with a fingernail, apparently considering.

'What's the matter, *caro*?' comes a soft voice, and Sofia turns to see the beautiful woman from the play coming over from the wagons, no longer wearing the sumptuous red dress, but clothed now in an unfussy brown woollen bodice and skirt, which still, Sofia thinks, seem to accentuate her lovely features. 'What is all this?'

'Oh, good – Cosima. You can decide.' Agostino takes Cosima's hand and holds it against his cheek.

'Decide what?'

'On whether or not we take this child with us when we move on.'

'Take her with us? Why? Why should we want to do that?'

Sofia swallows uncomfortably at this, but when she risks a glance at the woman's face, she sees that her expression is mild.

In a jumble of unfinished sentences and interruptions, Agostino and Niccolò Zanetti explain. Cosima listens carefully. 'What did this man in Modena say you had stolen?' she says to Sofia.

Sofia hesitates. She decides on the truth. 'Money, Signora. A purse of money.' She shakes her head. 'But I didn't do it. I wouldn't.'

'Who was he? Why would he have—'

Agostino interrupts. 'Oh, Cosima, does it really matter?'

'It might.'

Sofia says, 'I don't know his name. He was just someone who . . . who . . . ' She pauses while she tries to put what happened into words, staring at her own hands, which she is twisting together in front of her. 'Well, he wanted more from me than the mended seam he had paid for, and . . . then he became angry when I refused.'

The rent in the linen was long and ragged: Sofia suspects that it might have been torn in a fight. Slit with the blade of a dagger, perhaps. But her stitching is almost invisible. She hopes the gentleman will approve of her handiwork. Perhaps he will recommend her to others of his acquaintance.

The door opens.

'Ah. So it's you. I saw you in the workroom at the signora's, the day I delivered the shirt for mending. I asked if she might send you. Did you do the repair yourself?'

'I did.'

'Let's have a look then.' The man who is blocking the doorway to the sala is tall and bulky, with dough-coloured skin and hands like hams. His head is almost hairless, but a thin line of dark beard outlines a glistening mouth. Sofia is surprised at the width of his neck — it is, she thinks, nearly as big around as her waist. His doublet hangs unfastened, and the shirt beneath strains over a belly like a sack of grain.

She passes him the mended shirt.

He casts it a perfunctory glance, then throws it to one side, his gaze fixed upon Sofia. The shirt catches for a moment over the arm of one of the chairs, then slips and falls to the floor. The man does not pick it up.

'Neat work. I thought as much. You're clearly ... good with your hands,' he says, running his tongue over already wet lips. He steps towards Sofia, who backs away. *'Let's see what else you can do with them, shall we?'*

Sofia's eyes widen. She shakes her head. *'No, signore. If you please, I—'*

'Oh, I do please, you're quite right. You please me. In fact, I think you'll please me very much.'

Sofia backs right up to the wall and presses herself against the tapestry. The man pushes up against her, fumbling for her breast, one thick knee pressing in between her own. He smells of sweat and ale, and his breath is foul.

'Bloody get off me!' she says, indistinctly. *'Piss off, you bastard! Vaffanculo!'*

72

The man tilts his head sideways, trying to kiss her; Sofia shoves upwards under his chin with the heel of her hand. The man's teeth click together; his head jerks back; he grunts in pain. Sofia lifts a knee. The man doubles over and a high-pitched, wheezing groan spews out of his open mouth.

Sofia scrambles past him and makes for the door. The servant is standing just outside, but Sofia knocks him off balance as she runs out of the room.

'What the—?'

'Stop her!' comes a hoarse voice from the sala. *'Little bitch! She has my purse!'*

'Stop!' The servant starts down the stairs after Sofia, but she is too quick. She reaches the front door and is out on the street before the servant has even made the foot of the stairs.

'Come back here, you thieving bitch!'

Cosima watches Sofia for a moment. 'And you can sew, can you?' she says.

'When my hand is working properly, yes. Yes, I can. I was working for one of Modena's best seamstresses. I made this dress, signora.'

She shrugs apologetically, holding her skirts out sideways, and sees Cosima's gaze taking in the mud-stains, the creased and water-marked skirts, the rip just below the bodice. 'It didn't always look like this. It's the only dress I have now, signora,' she says. 'I didn't have time to bring any of my belongings away from Modena with me. I'm afraid it's been badly spoiled in the rain.'

'Yes, perhaps it has.' Cosima bends forwards, and takes a fold of the skirt between finger and thumb. Rubbing the cloth, she nods her approval. 'It's well made – I can see that. Your stitching is very fine.'

There is a long pause. Sofia lets her skirts fall back down. She holds Cosima's gaze. From the corner of her eye she can see that both Agostino and Niccolò Zanetti are watching her too. Then Agostino leans across and whispers into Cosima's ear. Cosima's eyes widen; then she frowns. Finally, lifting her chin a fraction, her gaze rakes Sofia from head to toe. She says, 'I could lend you a dress whilst you wash that one – it might be a little big on you.'

Sofia holds her breath.

Cosima said, 'I trust you will not be expecting luxury. We sleep in taverns only when we have the money; it's in the wagons, in barns or just on the ground when we don't.'

'Ha!' Agostino says loudly. 'It most certainly is. But as it so happens, we've even more of a treat tonight than a tavern, child! We've just been offered hospitality in the house of a well-wisher – real, genuine hospitality. Food and drink and somewhere to sleep – for all of us. You must be bringing us luck already! And, then, on top of that, it occurs to me that—' He glances over at Lidia, then checks. 'No, that should wait,' he says, more to himself than to anyone else. 'Now is not the time.'

Niccolò Zanetti puts his arm around Sofia's shoulders. 'Good,' he says quietly. 'That's good. Now shall we strap up that poor hand of yours again?'

'You'll stay with us tonight too, won't you, Niccolò?' Cosima says. 'You've said you'll share the meal, so stay with us afterwards.'

'What? Oh, I don't know . . .'

'Nonsense. Of course you shall,' Agostino says firmly. 'It's far too long since we've had the luxury of sitting down and sharing news.'

'Then yes, thank you, I should love to.'

Sofia starts as someone else speaks from just behind her, in the heavy Bergamo accent she heard on stage earlier.

'Hey, Niccolò. We haven't seen you in an age. How long have you been in Bologna?'

It is the young man in the diamond-patterned leggings. He shakes Zanetti's hand, clapping the little apothecary on the shoulder. Then Niccolò Zanetti reaches out and takes Sofia's elbow, drawing her in towards him. 'Beppe,' he says, 'Beppe, this is Sofia. Sofia Genotti.'

Beppe smiles at her. 'I saw you earlier, didn't I?'

Sofia nods.

'Did you enjoy the show?'

'I thought it was wonderful,' Sofia says honestly, feeling her colour rise under Beppe's scrutiny; he is watching her carefully. His face might not be perfectly proportioned, like the handsome Angelo da Bagnacavallo's, she thinks now, and his clothes are worn and threadbare, but Beppe's eyes are huge and dark and his smile warm and wide and infectious, and for a moment she does not know where to look. Her face feels hot.

'Beppe, Sofia is a seamstress! She's agreed to come along with us when we leave Bologna to restore our costumes to their former glory,' Agostino says loudly, putting a hand on Sofia's shoulder. 'What a gift from the heavens, eh? No longer will the Coraggiosi be forced to resemble a tawdry pack of brightly coloured raga-muffins! No!' He begins to wave his other arm in a grand, sweeping gesture of proclamation. 'We shall once more be fit to bestride the stage like the bejewelled colossi we—'

'God, Agostino, you do talk crap!' Another young man has come up from the wagons to stand near Beppe; his hands are on his hips and his eyes glitter with mischief.

'And, you, Vico Savarini, *you* are impolite, indecorous and ill mannered.' Agostino points an accusatory finger in Vico's direc-tion. A thread of anxiety tightens in Sofia's chest at his words, until she sees that Agostino's eyes too are dancing.

'No he's not,' Beppe says. 'He's just bloody rude.'

'Ah, but I'm an accurate observer, Beppe, my friend, you can't deny that. An accurate observer.'

Beppe laughs.

Vico snorts.

Agostino pulls an open-mouthed face of mock outrage.

Sofia stares from one man to another, astonished. She has never before met people who bicker and banter and laugh with such ease and obvious affection. She has no idea what to think.

Niccolò Zanetti says quietly, 'Don't look so worried – you'll become accustomed to their ways, Sofia. And, whatever they say, however rude and offensive they may sound on occasions, just remember that you will never have a more loyal friend than one of the Coraggiosi here. Never. If they have taken you as one of them, then they'll not let you down.'

Beppe says, 'You're right there, Niccolò.' He eyes Sofia for a moment, then, turning to Agostino, says, 'We should do things properly, don't you think? This evening? After the meal. After our hosts have retired for the night. A real *scelta* ceremony.'

'A *scelta*? Oh, Beppe, what a tremendous idea!' Agostino says, sounding delighted. 'Sofia, my dear, Beppe is quite right. We'll do it tonight!'

Sofia swallows uncomfortably.

'Sofia, this is a real privilege,' Niccolò Zanetti says quietly. 'It's not many are offered a proper *scelta*. It used to happen often, whenever a newcomer joined a troupe, but people don't seem to trouble with such things any more.'

'What will I have to do?'

'Oh, they'll do it all. You'll enjoy it. But you'll have to wait and see.'

*

The great *sala* runs the full width of the house, some thirty feet from side to side. The many windows are small and set high in the walls; below them, several huge tapestries run right around the room, depicting a series of tableaux set in an idyllic landscape filled with animals, birds, fruit and flowers. The high ceiling is painted in big chequerboard squares of red and black. On a *credenza* in one corner, a little yellow bird sits on a perch in a large cage. As Sofia watches it, it chirrups, fluffs its feathers and hops down on to the floor of the cage to peck at a few fallen seeds.

A fire is still burning in the huge fireplace at the western end, but the dozen or so big beeswax candles in brackets, which earlier filled the room with dancing light, have all but burned out and are now little more than a collection of soft stalactites, dribbling down from their sconces. The long table has been cleared of the remains of the substantial meal they have eaten: eels, oysters, lamb, *melan-zane*, beans, tiny parcels of pasta filled with pumpkin and sage, plums and peaches and enormous bunches of the biggest and sweetest grapes Sofia can remember eating. All that remains to remind her of the meal is a comforting feeling of drowsiness and the soft pressure of her full belly beneath the constricting waist of her skirts.

Sofia takes stock of the room. Rarely has she set foot in such a place – a room so large and well appointed – and certainly never as an invited guest. Only a handful of times in her seventeen years, when delivering finished garments to wealthy customers, has she even *seen* a place so sumptuous, let alone eaten and drunk within it. Niccolò has truly brought her luck.

A large pile of blankets has been collected from the bedcham-bers of the great house by a handful of servants; they have been heaped untidily in a corner of the room, ready for the troupe to wrap themselves in for the night. Eyeing the pile and imagining the night to come, Sofia wonders at the thought of how comfortable and safe she already feels in the company of these strangers – and how different it all is from last night in Alberto's cramped tavern room lying next to the ugly, sweat-smelling traveller who had thought her a whore.

Agostino, seated in a wooden cross-framed chair up near the fire, raises a glass. 'Let's drink another toast to the wonderful Signor da Campo and his lovely wife,' he says. 'Here's to their hospitality and generosity; here's to mountains of good food and spiced wine, and to a warm fire and to a good night's sleep ahead.'

'Here's to all that, indeed,' Cosima says softly, and the other members of the troupe murmur their agreement.

'Don't forget what we said earlier, Agostino,' Beppe says from his place on the floor on the other side of the hearth. 'About the *scelta*. The signore and his wife have gone to bed. Now's the perfect time.'

'It is.'

'And this room's the perfect place.'

Agostino smiles. 'It is, Beppe, it most certainly is.' He speaks to the room at large and his voice is lilting and musical. 'Signori and signore of the Coraggiosi, we are privileged indeed. Not only do we have the memory of a successful performance today to comfort us as we prepare to sleep; not only are our bellies reminding us of how well we have eaten this evening, and our spinning heads of the wine we have consumed – no, we are more fortunate even than this. For we have *increased*. We are greater than we were before. We have taken on a new member.'

Sofia's face burns so fiercely at this that her eyes began to sting. She closes them tightly for a second, then blinks several times.

'Sofia, here' – Agostino holds out a hand towards her – 'joins us tonight, as you all know. But Beppe suggests a proper welcome: a *scelta*. What say you?'

Sofia hears a general murmur of assent. She looks around at them all. Clustered together on chairs, on the rush-strewn floor, on the stone hearth up near the dying flames, warm and drowsy and well fed, they are all watching her now. Vico has his arm around Lidia; Federico is absentmindedly scratching his beard. Old Giovanni Battista, head on his hand, looks on the point of sleep and Cosima is curled against Agostino's legs.

Then Lidia says, 'Agostino, wait. Angelo's not here, is he? Shouldn't we have the whole troupe for a *scelta*?'

Frowning, Agostino glances about the room, as though Angelo might be hiding unobserved in the shadows. 'I hadn't noticed. Where is he?'

Lidia shrugs, and Vico says, 'He went off somewhere after the performance, didn't he? God knows where. He said he had an errand to run. Perhaps he's met someone – it's happened before.'

Lidia says, 'He's been very strange for weeks.'

Standing up and brushing dust off his breeches, Beppe says, 'That's all as may be. He's usually strange, isn't he? But I don't think Sofia should have to miss out just because our . . . our much-fêted *inamorato* has chosen to spend the night somewhere else.'

'No, Beppe, you're right,' Agostino says. 'The *scelta* will have to take place without him.' Crossing to where all the troupe's bags and packs have been piled at the far side of the *sala* and squatting in front of the pile, he pulls open one large canvas sack and rummages inside it for a moment, arms almost up to the armpits, muttering to himself, then he stands back upright. In his hand is a small, tightly corked earthenware pot. He goes back to his place, then pauses. 'So, let us begin. Who speaks for the newcomer?'

'I do. As the one who suggested the *scelta*, I speak for her.'

'Thank you, Beppe. And who else?' Agostino looks around him. 'Two must speak for a newcomer, after all, must they not?'

Niccolo Zanetti gets to his feet and clears his throat. 'Me, of course. I will.'

'Good,' Agostino says, nodding his approval. 'Nicco, Beppe, let's have you up here.'

Niccolò and Beppe move to stand side by side close to Agostino.

'Now you, Sofia. Come here, child.'

Her heart thudding, Sofia gets to her feet.

'Stand between Signor Zanetti and Beppe, here.'

Sofia steps over Vico's legs, holding her skirts up and watching her feet as she goes, edging out towards where Agostino, Niccolò and Beppe are waiting for her. Pulse now racing, she places herself in the gap between Niccolò and Beppe.

'Take one each of their hands.'

Signor Zanetti, on her left, gives her a quick reassuring smile. On her right, Beppe fingers the edge of her clean new linen bandage. He says quietly, leaning down towards her, 'I don't want to do anything to hurt your fingers. Are you happy for me to hold your hand?'

Sofia looks up at him and nods. Glancing back down, she watches his thumb, rubbing softly back and forth over the binding, and something shifts and turns over itself in her belly at his touch. Yes, she thinks – more than happy.

'Very well,' Agostino says. 'Are you ready?'

Beppe and Niccolò both answer in the affirmative, but, nipping the end of her tongue, Sofia says nothing. Much to her surprise, at their words, a stinging has begun behind her eyes and she can feel a thickening in her throat. Not since the death of her mother has anyone – *anyone* – shown an interest in her like this; Sofia is suddenly afraid that if she moves, or speaks, long-dammed tears might spill for the first time in years over their well-constructed barricades.

'Vico,' Agostino says then. 'Fetch your guitar. Give us some music.'

Vico scrambles across Lidia's legs and crosses to the far side of the room, where, pulling open the drawstrings of another capacious leather bag, he draws from it a small and elaborately decorated guitar. Coming back over and seating himself cross-legged at one end of the long table, he begins to play.

Federico reaches into the big wood basket and puts three more large logs onto the fire. Flames crackle and spark around the new wood, and the light in the room brightens and begins to flicker cheerfully.

'*Fratelli.*' Agostino speaks more slowly now, more deliberately, a little louder; his expression is solemn and serious, though his eyes, she sees, are alight with obvious happiness. 'You stand here with the newcomer. Speak for her now – the moment is right.'

Vico picks at the strings of his instrument.

Squaring his shoulders, Niccolò says, 'This child asks that she may be permitted to join the august company of the Coraggiosi.'

Sofia swallows. Her throat now feels full and tight and a little too small. She nips again at the end of her tongue.

'Two members must affirm her intentions,' Agostino says. 'Are you those two?'

Beppe and Niccolò speak in unison. 'We are.'

Niccolò adds in a hissed whisper, 'I speak, of course, Agostino, as a long-time *friend* of the Coraggiosi.' He pauses. 'Not as a member.'

'Ah, but you've been an *honorary* member for years, Nicco.' Agostino smiles at his friend; then, turning to Sofia, he says, 'Listen, child, I have several questions for you, which I need you

81

to answer truthfully.'

Vico's tune is now plaintive and tender.

'Are you ready for a life on the road in the company of vagabonds and mountebanks and ne'er-do-wells?'

Sofia nods.

'Say "I am",' Beppe whispers in her ear.

'I am.' Her voice sounds like somebody else's, blurting out into the stillness of the room as though it is coming from inside a box.

'Do you vow to be loyal to the Coraggiosi while you travel with us, and to refrain from divulging secrets of impending performances to other troupes such as you may come into contact with, or to anyone else who might disperse such information?'

'I do.'

'Do you agree to a fee of . . . how many are we, now you are here?' Agostino looks from person to person, counting. 'Nine, including Angelo . . . one-ninth. Do you agree to a fee of one-ninth part of whatever moneys we are fortunate enough to collect at a performance after costs?'

Astonished at the generosity of the offer, Sofia says, 'I do.'

'Good. We'll sign an agreement to that effect later,' Agostino says by way of an aside. He pauses; then, drawing in another breath, and resuming the previous tone, he says, 'Have you spent time as a road-dweller before?'

'Well, I hadn't – until last week. But . . . I have now, and I—'

'Just say "I have",' Beppe says softly.

'Oh. Yes. I have.'

'And with whom have you travelled in your time upon the road?'

Sofia swallows again. Unsure what to say, she opens her mouth, intending to try to explain to Agostino about meeting Niccolò in Modena, about the boy with the ribbons at the market in Bologna and her unpleasant experience in the tavern, but Beppe speaks up before she can utter a word. He says gravely, 'She's travelled with Genesius and Vitus, and they have pointed her in our direction.'

Sofia has no idea what he means, but Agostino beams. 'Well, then it is clear you have indeed been chosen for us, and are most welcome. And now you must sign the Tenure of the Road.'

'Sign . . . ?'

Agostino nods. 'It should by rights be dust from the edge of the highway, but we are most comfortably ensconced in here, and I'm sure Genesius and Vitus will accommodate the substitution.' Turning to Beppe, he says, 'Beppe, if you please?' and Beppe steps back and crosses to the hearth. Scraping up a small handful of ash from the very edge of the hearth, he brings it back and stands once again next to Sofia.

Agostino says, 'Sofia, take a pinch of the ash, please.'

Sofia picks a small pinch between finger and thumb from Beppe's palm. It is warm – almost hot.

Agostino uncorks the little pot. 'Drop your dust into the pot, where it can mingle with the dust of every member of the Coraggiosi, present and past.'

Sofia lets the ash fall into the neck of the pot and watches as Agostino recorks it and holds it high.

A loudly strummed set of three chords signals completion, and everybody claps.

Leaning forwards, Agostino kisses Sofia on both cheeks. Niccolò Zanetti hugs her, and Beppe lifts her hand to his lips and kisses her knuckles, his eyes fixed upon her face. Cosima stands and hugs Sofia too. Lidia claps and Vico pats the rounded end of his guitar with the flat of his hand.

'And now, all of you, the improvisation! A full *scelta* must conclude with an improvisation, must it not? To seal the welcome,' Agostino says, his smile now wider than ever as he tucks the pot safely back into the bag. 'A ball. We must have a ball, if we're to do it properly, must we not? Beppe, have you a juggling ball?'

Beppe grins and pushes a hand into a pocket in his breeches. He brings out a leather ball about the size of a peach; highly polished, it gleams like an oversized chestnut in the firelight. Holding it up for a moment like an ancient deity's trophy, he then throws it to Cosima, who catches it neatly, one-handed.

'Cosima, start us off, please!' Agostino says.

Sofia's eyes widen, her threatened tears vanishing in the face of sudden anxiety. She turns to Beppe. 'An improvisation? What is this? What does it mean? What am I going to have to do?'

Sitting himself down on a table, he pats the wood next to him, inviting her to sit. 'Nothing. Don't worry. You don't have to do anything. Just watch and listen. Join in if you can.'

Sofia sits; Beppe's leg feels warm, pressed up against hers.

'What shall it be?' Cosima says. '*Terza rima*, Agostino?'

'*Terza rima?* God, no – are you mad?' Vico says, his voice distorting through a yawn. 'Far too difficult for this time of night, and after this much wine. Choose something easier, why don't you? Start us off, and we'll follow what you do.'

Pausing, Cosima looks up at the ceiling, frowning slightly, the tip of her tongue caught between her teeth, the ball held loosely in her lap. Then she stares into the fire. 'Very well,' she says. 'Erm . . .'

'A young man was dreaming of love and of pleasure
As he sat by the roadside one day long ago.
He sighed as he pictured his fondest heart's treasure –

84

A beautiful maiden named Lina di Po.

'But his mem'ries were flawed and he didn't remember
That Lina had spurned him and left him for aye.
'Twas as well that he didn't recall what had happened,
For the truth would have left him a-wishing to die.'

Her voice is soft and slow and honeyed.

Beppe sits forward. His expression very solemn, he clicks his fingers, and Cosima throws him the ball. Spinning it on his forefinger, he says,

'Now young Lina's virtues were sadly much lacking:
She was known as a strumpet by most of her kin.
Her fame had spread widely before and around her;
'Twas well known just how quick . . . she'd be tempted
  to sin.'

Hand over her mouth, Sofia begins to laugh. Beppe flashes her a smile. He flips the ball in the air, catches it again, then throws it over-arm to Vico, who raises an eyebrow as he says:

'But one man knew nothing about Lina's virtue –
Or lack of it – one man believed her to be
Nothing less than an angel descended from heaven,
A goddess, a delicate Aphrodite.'

A snort of muffled laughter. Agostino draws in a long breath. Vico passes him the ball. In a deep voice of great moment, Agostino says:

'One fine night this young man went to visit his sweetheart.
In his arms was a bunch of the rarest of flowers.
He waited outside in a fever of longing . . .
Yes, he waited for hours . . . and hours . . . and hours.'

Everyone laughs. Cosima takes Agostino's face in both her hands and kisses his mouth. Beppe straightens his expression again. He clears his throat and holds out his hand. Agostino throws him the ball. Beppe says:

'He could picture her braiding her hair in her chamber,
Eager and desp'rate to see him again.
But if truth must be told – she was kissing another.
Who was this? Only one of a dozen young men.'

Lidia coughs. Beppe grins and flips the ball towards her. She says:

'Our lover he waited below Lina's chamber
Until he no longer could bear to stand still.
He climbed up a ladder right up to her window
And stood there a moment upon the stone sill.'

Clicking his fingers, Beppe summons the ball back from her.

'Hands cupped, he peered clear through the glass trying to
*   see her,*
But what he espied made his blood run quite chilled.
She was naked – and wrapped in the arms of a soldier
And the smile on her face made it clear . . . she was
*   thrilled.'*

He raises his hands, clearly now relishing the development of the story. Sofia looks up at him and sees that his eyes are alight with the pleasure of telling the tale. He continues, gesticulating theatrically.

> *'With a cry of despair he fell back down his ladder.*
> *Then he ran to a tavern and ordered an ale,*
> *Which he downed in a moment – then ordered another.*
> *The amount he consumed would have filled up a pail.'*

Sofia's thoughts race, as she struggles to put a verse together. Twice she opens her mouth to offer a suggestion, but twice she closes it again. Then a second later, the lines are there in her head, she is ready to speak; sitting up straighter, she looks at Beppe, breath held, running her tongue over her lips. Seeing her readiness, Beppe grins and passes her the ball.

'Go on, then, chick,' he says quietly. 'See what you can do.'

Sofia takes a deep breath and says:

> *'With belly a-churning and head spinning freely,*
> *The young man returned to fair Lina's abode,*
> *Determined to tell her how much he adored her,*
> *But . . . he tripped and he fell . . . and lay flat in the road.'*

Beppe and the others laugh and clap, Vico whoops, and Sofia bites her lip, chewing down a pleased smile. Reaching out, Beppe takes the ball from her, spins it again on his finger and says in a low, throaty voice:

> *'Like a pile of discarded detritus he lay there,*
> *And his tears turned the dust of the road into mud.*

But Lina (the whore) – in flagrante – heard nothing
But the grunts of her lusty and tireless young stud.'

Everyone laughs. Exhilarated to find that she is able to contribute with more ease than she would have thought possible, Sofia finds another verse blossoming in her head, but before she can speak, Vico snaps his fingers. 'Let's have the ball, Beppe,' he says, and Beppe obliges. Licking his lips, eyes glittering, Vico says:

'Yes – splay-leggéd and gasping, our Lina heard nothing,
As she bounced up and down on her new lover's bed.
Her small breasts were a-quiver and her buttocks a-tremble
And her sweet little cheeks flamed a bright cherry red.'

A bark of vulgar laughter breaks from several of the troupe. Lidia's mouth drops open. 'Vico!' she says, sounding slightly breathless. 'God, Vico – in front of a newcomer! Sofia, I'm so sorry – he's a disgrace!'

Vico is grinning broadly.

Sofia looks from him to Beppe, who smiles and shrugs, shaking his head.

Agostino, however, is clearly trying to look stern, and equally clearly failing to achieve his aim. He wags an accusatory finger at everyone. 'Well, Coraggiosi, on that appalling note I declare the *scelta* to be at an end. It's time we went to sleep, I fear, before our improvisation, delightful though it has been, descends into irrecoverable puerility!' He strides across to the stack of bedding. 'Sofia,' he says, turning back towards her as he goes, 'you are truly welcomed as a member of the troupe! And your unexpected skill at improvising is remarkable. Well done!' There is a soft patter of applause from the others, almost indistinguishable from the dying crackle of the fire. Agostino says, beckoning, 'Cosima, Lidia, Sofia: as the ladies of the troupe, you take what you want first. Put yourselves down there near the fire. Keep yourselves warm.'

'Erm . . . ' Sofia looks at Beppe as she slides down off the table. She says hesitantly, 'May I just ask you . . . ?'

Beppe inclines his head.

'Who were those people you said I'd been travelling with? And Agostino talked about them too.'

'Who? Oh, do you mean Genesius and Vitus?'

Sofia nods. 'I don't know who they are – I've never met anyone of that name.'

Beppe smiles. 'They're saints. St Genesius and St Vitus: the patron saints of actors and clowns.'

'Oh.'

'They keep an eye on us all, most of the time. And – well, they've looked after *you* pretty well, don't you think?'

Sofia stares at him. 'Yes,' she said. 'Yes, I think they have.'

With a tired, tilted smile, Beppe takes himself off to the far side of the room.

Holding the blanket she has been handed by Lidia, Sofia sits down on the rush-strewn hearth near the dying fire and in the almost-darkness looks around wide-eyed at the various troupe members settling themselves for the night. They seem to have a routine, she thinks, seeing Federico hold a blanket out for Giovanni Battista, who winds it carefully around himself without looking at his companion, before being helped to lie down. Agostino, having crossed to where Cosima has settled herself, casts a last, contented look around the darkening room at his troupe before lying down next to her and draping an arm across her shoulders.

And Beppe ... Sofia watches Beppe settle himself with unself-conscious ease; taking off his doublet, he folds it into a rough pillow; then, wrapping his own blanket around himself, he rubs his face with both palms and stretches. Curling like a cat, he closes his eyes.

A last red-glowing branch fizzles and flares before it sinks into the ashes; at its sudden hissing light, Beppe opens his eyes again. He catches sight of Sofia still looking at him and smiles again. Feeling the colour rise in her face, she pulls the blanket up around her neck. The corners of Beppe's mouth remain upturned after he closes his eyes once more, head pillowed on one hand; Sofia watches him until the last ember cools and the light dies completely and she can see him no longer.

9

Sebastiano da Correggio looks down with distaste at where Angelo has sprawled across the table, his head on his arms. He is deeply asleep, his perfectly proportioned face oddly childlike in its utter relaxation, though the sight of it evokes no tender feelings in da Correggio.

'For God's sake, wake up, you bastard,' he mutters. 'Maddalena will be here any minute, and I want you gone.'

He shakes Angelo's shoulder, but Angelo just murmurs, and tucks his head more comfortably into the crook of his elbow, showing no sign of waking. Rolling his eyes, and feeling his jaw tense with the effort of not hitting his companion, Sebastiano da Correggio glances at the far end of the table. The three empty glasses stand next to the bottles of the dark syrup. One glass has tipped over and lies on its side in a pooled puddle of grappa.

'I hope to God you haven't had too much,' he says through gritted teeth. 'I don't want to have to deal with a damned corpse.' He stares down at Angelo for several seconds. 'And it's bloody cold in here now that damned fire's gone out.'

He opens a wooden chest and pulls from it an intricately slashed and embroidered woollen doublet. Shrugging it on, he buckles a belt around his waist and tucks into this a short-bladed knife with a prettily jewelled handle; then, closing the lid of the chest, he sits down upon it. A pair of boots lies untidily next to the chest; these he pulls on, swearing under his breath as one catches around his heel. Standing, he stamps that foot hard down into the boot.

At the sound of the stamp, Angelo groans and shifts position, but he does not wake. Sebastiano da Correggio swears. He shakes Angelo again, with no effect. Grabbing a handful of Angelo's hair, he turns the sleeping face up towards him. Angelo's eyes open slightly, showing only a thin line of white, and his lips part, revealing even, white teeth and the gleam of his tongue. A thin line of spittle slides from the corner of his mouth.

'*Merda!*' Sebastiano says, dropping Angelo's head so that it slumps back onto his arms. 'You bastard, Bagnacavallo – she'll be here any moment now and you're cluttering the bloody place up like a fucking pile of laudanum-soaked laundry. Being one of the very first to realize the delightfully intoxicating potential of one of the newest and most effective relievers of pain in Italy looks set to make me a great deal of money, Bagnacavallo, once word starts to spread. If you swallow too much of it – greedy bastard that you are – and go and die on me, my reputation will be badly tarnished, so don't bloody do it.'

He pauses a moment, and a muscle in his jaw twitches. He shakes his head. 'Do you know what? This is the last time,' he says. 'You can get it for yourself if you want more – I have better things to do than play broker with you. You self-indulgent little pretty boy.' He kicks the leg of Angelo's chair irritably. 'That's the last time I believe your declarations of solvency. And you can fucking well pay me what you owe before your bloody troupe leaves the city or I'm having the bottles back. In fact . . . '

He grabs the grappa and all the unopened brown bottles, leaving just the single three-quarters-empty one, and strides out of the *sala*, climbing the stairs two at a time to the bedchamber. He will just have to bring Maddalena straight up here – the fire is dead and the *sala* is cold, after all, so she is unlikely to object. Putting the grappa and the laudanum down on a table near the bed, he takes another couple of small glasses from a shelf and places them next to the two bottles.

A knock at the front door echo-cracks into the silence of the house.

Crossing the room to the window, da Correggio cups his hands around his eyes and, face pressed to the glass, peers down to the street below: he can just make out the top of Maddalena's silk-swathed head. He runs downstairs. Even as he opens the door, she slips inside, sliding her arms up around his neck and starting to kiss him before he can say a word. Her mouth is warm and inviting, and she presses herself against him, pulling him in close, murmuring incoherently through her kisses. The heavy gold stitchery on her sleeves scratches against his neck.

'I thought . . . ' she says, between kisses, ' . . . I thought . . . you might not want to see me.'

'Come upstairs.'

'I've missed you . . . so much. Paolo has been so . . . mmm . . . boring and miserable . . . and I've longed to see you and . . . '

'Come upstairs,' Sebastiano da Correggio says again.

Maddalena pulls back from him. 'How long do we have?'

A flash of irritation. 'That's rather up to you, is it not? How likely is it that the eminent Signor di Maccio will notice his wife's absence *this* time?'

93

Maddalena shakes her head. 'He won't know I've gone. He was fast asleep when I left the house.' She pauses. 'He always sleeps soundly after—' She sucks in a sharp breath and breaks off, catching her lip between her teeth.

Sebastiano sees colour rise in her cheeks and feels the familiar anger swell in his chest. 'Have you just come from his bed?' he says in a voice like a gob of spit. 'I hate the thought of you doing that.'

Maddalena's eyes widen and she takes a further step away from him. '*Caro*, he *is* my husband, after all.'

Da Correggio hears a catch in her voice.

'It was a chair, not the bed, anyway. You know he can't . . . can't . . . get it up any more, but he does seem to like . . . ' Running the tip of her tongue over her lips, she hesitates. 'Well, apart from making me feel slightly sick, a quick *pompino* doesn't take too much effort. And if it pleases him, and gives us a few hours to spend together, then can you not allow me to . . . ?'

The vulgarity is shocking in her mouth, but even the thought of her performing that whore's act makes him greedy for her. He looks at where her breasts are pushing up against the top edge of her bodice, imagining with an unpleasant twist of his guts Paolo di Maccio's bony old hands fingering them, and says coldly, 'I don't like to feel I'm trespassing on damp ground that still bears the proprietor's footprints.'

'I only do it for you – you know that. To give us time. God, having that limp and flaccid old slug twitching away in my mouth makes me feel quite ill! I wouldn't do it by choice, would I? Do you want me to wash first? I will if you want.'

'Don't bother – don't waste the time we have. Come with me. We'll go straight to bed.'

'Has it been delivered?' Her voice is trembling.

'Yes. You can have some as soon as we've finished. Not before — I don't want you falling asleep.'

Sebastiano da Correggio only just hears Maddalena's soft sigh of relief. He takes her wrist – small as a child's within his grasp – and leads her back up past the *sala*, straight up to the front bedchamber. It's dark: no fire or candle lights the room; but the shutters are unfastened, and there is just enough light to see.

Sebastiano begins to unfasten Maddalena's laces, all but pulling her off balance in his haste. He jerks the sleeves from her shoulders, pushing the dress down so that it puddles around her knees in great creased swags. She steps out of the skirts and Sebastiano crouches to grasp the hem of her shift. She puts her arms up as he tugs the chemise over her head. She wears no other undergarments. The grey light from the window picks out the curves of her body, highlighting the rounded outlines of shoulders and breasts, the swell of her buttocks; she looks, Sebastiano thinks, like a voluptuous ghost. His fingers go to the laces of his doublet, but then he stops.

He likes it when he is dressed and Maddalena is not.

'Go and stand in the light,' he says, and, without a word, Maddalena crosses to the far side of the room, where the light lies in a distorted, pewter-coloured square on the wooden boards. She stands in the centre of the square, holds her arms high above her head and turns slowly as he watches.

Maddalena knows Sebastiano likes to watch her caress her own body. Head back, mouth slightly open, she moves her hands over and around her shoulders, arms and breasts, then, as her fingers stroke across the skin of her belly, she feels again that small domed swelling beneath the skin – hardly more than a vague denseness of flesh – which has risen and rounded there over the past week or two. Turning away from Sebastiano's fixed gaze, she arches her back and slides her hands over her buttocks.

She must at all costs keep him from noticing the inevitable, for as long as possible. A sick feeling of dread rises in her throat as she imagines how he will react when he finally discovers the truth – and she pictures her impotent husband hearing the same news. There is no doubt, after all, that it is Sebastiano's child. Facing him once more, she sees that he has seated himself on the carved chest at the end of the bed.

'Here!' he says. 'Come here. Since you began the evening with a cock in your mouth, you little whore, why don't we call that a rehearsal? And now you can perform. Show me what you've learned.'

She moves away from the square of light to stand in front of him, and he takes her hands. Tugging downwards, he pulls her into a crouch in front of him, between his splayed knees. She reaches for the fastening of his breeches; her mind is on the little bottle on the table and she is grateful for the darkness.

Several hours later, Angelo da Bagnacavallo stands in the street looking up at the dark bulk of da Correggio's house. A wave of nauseous anger swirls down through him. Straightening the neck of his doublet, he runs a hooked forefinger around inside the collar, pulling it loose; the single part-empty bottle he has been allowed – *allowed!* – to take with him shifts against his thigh inside the pocket of his breeches, and he puts a hand into the pocket to steady it. His fingers toy with the protruding edges of the cork.

Oh, so you've decided to grace us with your presence after – what – seven hours, have you? Da Correggio's sneering voice is as clear in his head as it was in the *sala* a moment ago. *I've been thinking,* he says. *I've been thinking — seeing that you tell me you are unable to pay for them just now, that perhaps I should hold back a couple of the bottles. We can discuss what to do with them at Franceschina in a few weeks. Hopefully, you'll have the* scudi *by then.*

Angelo hawks and spits; the gob of spittle lands in the dust and is trodden under his next step as he turns to leave the house. 'You bastard, Correggio,' he mutters. 'You bloody bastard. Who the hell do you think you are? One bottle! And it's not even full! I'd have paid — you know I'd have paid. I've never let you down before.'

He almost believes his own untruth.

The dawn is still more than an hour off and the streets of Bologna are softly dark. Not having thought to bring a lantern, Angelo's progress towards the piazza where they performed yesterday — where he left the troupe — is tentative, running a hand along the front walls of houses, eyes stretched wide, placing his feet carefully. As so often happens after a dose, his thoughts are jagged, fractured, fragmented; they whirl unchecked around his head like scraps of rubbish in a sudden breeze: da Correggio's sneering face; a glimpse of a woman on the stairs as he left just now; the pretty girl in the ragged dress after the show; the proprietorial expression on Beppe's face as he looked at her. God — that girl! He all but promised her that he would be joining her for the meal this evening. Judging by the colour in her cheeks as she looked at him, he has a chance with her — if bloody Beppe doesn't get in there first. As he contemplates this possibility, he finds that he is unsure whether or not the resultant swirl of anger he feels is at the thought of losing the girl, or of Beppe gaining her.

Heading back towards the Piazza di Porta Ravegnana, he walks for half an hour or more, and by the time he reaches the piazza, there is a glimmer of silver between the buildings; although it is still no more than half light, Angelo can see quite clearly that the stage has gone – the piazza is empty. The horses and wagons are nowhere to be seen.

The troupe has left.

A scrawny dog lopes out from between two pilasters and sniffs the air; after pissing up against a pillar it disappears.

Other than this, the square is quite deserted.

Angelo stands in the middle of the piazza, staring stupidly around him. Where the hell are they? The whirling-rubbish thoughts spiral more tightly and a general sense of ill usage begins to overwhelm him – da Correggio's condescending presumption; the Coraggiosi's continual dismissal of his abilities; his father's refusal to give him any more money – the injustice of his situation is intolerable.

Then he remembers.

Just before he left after the show – an invitation. An invitation from some well-to-do audience member. The troupe was to spend the night . . . God, where the hell was it to be? He scours his mind, trying to recall what Agostino told him after the show; he had been so focused on getting to Sebastiano's in time, he had barely taken it in. Sinking to sit on a stone step, he puts his face in his hands and tries to remember.

Bloody Sebastiano, why had he let him take a dose straight away? He, Angelo, would have been back with the troupe . . . with that girl . . . with a dose ready to hand, if Sebastiano had refused him. If he'd told him to wait. Bloody man.

The heels of his hands press against his eyeballs, and bright giddying patterns erupt. Into the swirling colour comes a name. He remembers. The name of a road – the name of the house where the troupe will even now be sleeping. Angelo looks up, blinking away the black blotches which quickly replace the vivid colours. It is nearly dawn: too late (too early?) to knock on the door of a private house. No, he'll go to a tavern, and join the troupe in a couple of hours.

Angelo strides away across the piazza. As he reaches the colonnade on the north side of the square, however, the toe of his boot catches on a cobble and he sprawls headlong, banging his hip and knee on the pedestal of a pillar as he skews sideways and falls.

A crack of glass.

Swearing profusely, Angelo gets to his feet and, as he straightens up, he treads on something brittle, which snaps beneath the sole of his boot. He scuffs it away. Brushing the dust from his doublet and breeches, though, he is dimly aware that something feels infinitesimally different about him. He runs his hands down the sides of his breeches: his pockets are empty.

A cold space opens up behind his face. 'Oh God, please, no . . .' he mutters and, squinting in the poor light, he crouches down to examine whatever it was he had kicked from under his boot. The last of the syrupy brown liquid is soaking away into the ground and only shards remain of the bottle – though the cork is still intact in the broken-off neck. Gasping out his helplessness, and fighting a frantic desire to dip his fingers into the rapidly diminishing puddle and suck them, Angelo gazes in dismay as twenty *scudi*'s worth of relief disappears into the dust of the piazza.

10

Sofia stares wide-eyed as Beppe clasps Lidia's hands in both his own. Pulling her in towards him, he makes as though to kiss her; she resists for a token second, but then, sighing loudly, tilting her face up towards his and closing her eyes, she puckers her lips into a pink-painted rosebud. Beppe's kiss is noisy, theatrical, and planted in mid-air an inch from Lidia's mouth.

For a brief second they stand thus, hands clasped, eyes tightly shut, lips almost touching, while Sofia, who is sitting on the bottom step of the smallest wagon, half-hidden beneath a ballooning pile of crimson silk, swallows uncomfortably, hardly able to breathe. She cannot take her eyes from Beppe's face. Her insides flip over. Her mouth has opened slightly and she has frozen with needle in hand.

'Putting you off your work, are they, those two lovebirds?'

Angelo has appeared from the other side of the wagon. Leaning against the wooden boarding, he picks up a handful of the crimson silk. 'I see you've made a start on this rag of Cosima's,' he says, fiddling the fabric between finger and thumb. 'That hand of yours better at last?'

Startled, Sofia pricks herself with the needle and smothers a gasp. Squeezing the tip of her finger, she stares as a bright bead of blood swells, round and perfect as a crimson jewel. Lifting her finger to her mouth and sucking it, she tastes warm iron. Face flaming, she nods. 'I've been working on this for a couple of days.'

'Let's have a look.' Angelo reaches down and takes Sofia's hand. She drops the needle, which falls to the ground. Angelo seems not to notice this, but makes as though to examine the damaged finger, which is still darkly bruised. He strokes her palm with his thumb, but Sofia pulls her hand away.

'The swelling has gone down now, and it hardly hurts. It's still a little stiff, but at least I can sew again.'

'And you're making a good job of it too, it seems.'

Sofia starts and looks around as she hears Lidia squeal and Beppe laugh. Angelo turns too. Beppe is shaking his head, grinning, while Lidia has her hands on her hips, glaring in open-mouthed mock-outrage at Vico, whose face is a studied picture of wide-eyed innocence.

'Piss off, Vico, you lecherous toad!'

'Ooh, such delicate language, *cara* . . .'

'Shut up! Beppe and I *have* to get this right before Friday, and I can do without *you* creeping up and grabbing handfuls of my bloody backside every five minutes.'

'But it *is* such a delectable backside . . .'

Angelo snorts softly and turns back to Sofia. 'Vico is unde-manding. I'm not sure a woman of Lidia's age can ever be said to have a . . . *delectable* backside, are you?'

Sofia does not reply.

'Just give us a few moments more, will you, Vico, then her back-side is all yours.' Beppe pats his friend's cheek with the flat of his hand; then he and Lidia resume their positions.

Angelo runs the tip of his tongue along his upper lip. Sofia finds herself watching him, despite herself intrigued by the perfection of his symmetrical features; then, catching his eye, irritated with herself, she looks away quickly, leaning down to search for the dropped needle. Fiddling in the dust at her feet, she frowns in concentration as she scours the ground.

A glitter of silver – the metal catches the light. She picks it up.

'Yes,' Angelo is saying. 'She must be – what? – well into her thirties by now.'

'What? Who?'

'Lidia. More a matron than a maid now, I think anyone would agree, and Beppe, her would-be on-stage lover, not more than . . . ooh, he can't be more than twenty-two or -three, can he?'

Sofia says nothing. Angelo's comments embarrass her. She has no wish to be sharing these confidences with him but does not know how best to extricate herself. She does not want Beppe to see her in conversation with Angelo, either. Feeling her face burn, she nips the tip of her tongue between her teeth, trying to banish the blush she knows is glowing in her cheeks. Something about Angelo's sculptural good looks and air of experience discomfits her and drags fierce colour into her face whenever he talks to her – though this is much against her will, for it has been many days since she has realized that Angelo da Bagnacavallo is not a kind man.

'I think Lidia makes a lovely Colombina,' she says now, gathering up the red silk skirts. 'If you will excuse me, I must put this away. I'll finish it tomorrow.' And, with a covert glance at Beppe, who is now hopping from foot to foot, bent-kneed and gesticulating wildly at a now furious-looking Lidia, she turns on her heel and scrambles up the wagon steps, pushing her way through into the dimly lit interior. Holding the dress up by the shoulders and shaking out the skirts, she lays it out across the little truckle bed at the far end of the wagon and neatly in-and-outs the needle near the neck of the bodice. She wraps her long length of leftover thread around and around two fingers, then tucks it behind the needle.

It feels good to be earning her keep at last, and her fears of being seen as an unproductive burden – even of being asked to leave – are beginning to recede. These unspoken anxieties haunted her for days as she waited for the hurt finger to mend; she tried not to admit to herself that alongside the genuine fear of being once again on the streets, friendless and grubbing for work, her main worry has been the thought of losing Beppe.

Losing him?

But surely, she says to herself now, you can only lose something which belongs to you. And Sofia can no more imagine Beppe 'belonging' to anyone than she can contemplate picking up a bead of quicksilver in her fingers. The stern little voice in which Sofia argues with herself has been telling her in no uncertain terms, ever since the evening of the *scelta* ceremony, that she is behaving like a child. Yes, it's true that Beppe has held her hand and invited her to sit close to him on numerous occasions – he has even put his arms around her a number of times – and she is sure that she has seen him watching her covertly when he thinks she is unaware. At those moments, her heart lifts and she convinces herself that he might indeed be interested in her – but then she sees him with Lidia and Cosima and the girls who work at the market stalls and the taverns; he smiles and laughs with them too, bending in close to them, touching their sleeves and holding their hands – and Sofia knows he means nothing by it. Nothing at all. He is not trying to seduce – Sofia firmly believes seduction is not in his nature – it's simply as though Beppe needs to touch whoever he's with, to reassure himself that they are really there. As if he wants to prove to himself that whoever it is is not just a figment of his imagination.

She is beginning to wish that she *were* a figment of Beppe's imagination. That way she would belong especially to him.

Sitting down on the truckle bed next to the dress, Sofia thinks through the past days. Two hectic weeks have passed since the day of the *scelta*. Niccolò Zanetti, who travelled with the Coraggiosi as far as Ferrara, has finally headed off, after many fond farewells and promises of meeting again soon, making for the mountains and his much-missed daughter. The troupe has been working hard – they have performed eleven times in the towns and villages of Emilia-Romagna – and not once have they faced a hostile crowd, which is, as Cosima has several times pointed out, something of a departure from the usual. In jubilant mood, Agostino declared earlier this morning that, seeing as the money-bags are now bulging, as soon as the next few secured performances have been successfully completed, a rest may be taken. The Coraggiosi will spend two nights in a comfortable tavern; somewhere, he says, with nothing to do other than eat, drink and sleep. Giovanni Battista has suggested that they go to an inn he knows in the tiny hill-hugging town of Montalbano, a couple of miles north, as the ale there, he seems to remember, is well worth the journey.

Agostino has agreed to this and – after the next few performances – this is where he says they will go.

Everyone has congratulated Sofia on bringing them luck.

Sofia has watched every one of the eleven performances, entranced by the magic the troupe always seems to conjure, and she is slowly starting to unravel the web of complexity that lies at the heart of each show. Each character is becoming more familiar to her by the day. She knows now, for instance, that Agostino's white-faced Pedrolino is almost always sad, often tired and frequently falling asleep; time and again he is on the point of dissolving with remorse at what he perceives to be his many failings. She has learned that Cosima, in her guise of the beautiful *inamorata*, will always walk and talk with elegance and poise, will move like the most delicate of dancers, will never, ever look ridiculous, however much inanity is erupting all around her. Dear Giovanni Battista (in reality, she has discovered, a sweet old man of gentle humour and great affection), once he has been well padded and wool-stuffed around the belly, will portray Il Dottore on the stage: a fat, pompous, arrogant fool in long black clothes and a black skull-cap. His normally lilting voice will parp out like a trombone, he will strut and posture and preen, and will – almost inevitably – fall foul of the machinations of Beppe's mischievous, agile and utterly amoral Arlecchino.

Beppe.

Sofia chews on her thumb. She cannot stop thinking about Beppe.

She dare not make her feelings clear to him. Or to anyone else – though on several occasions she has thought that perhaps she should confide in Cosima or Lidia. What if she were to do so, though, and then discover that her fears are justified – that Beppe cares no more for her than any other of his acquaintance? How could she stay with the troupe if he came to know of her partiality but did not return it? To see him every day after such a revelation would be torture. The others might laugh at her – no, that's probably not true, she admits; but they would almost certainly pity her. She imagines the looks on their faces. She'd have to leave – and even after these short weeks, Sofia feels a dreadful pang at even the prospect of leaving the Coraggiosi. They have been more of a family to her than she can remember having since the death of her mother.

A tinny fanfare from Vico's battered old trumpet sounds outside the wagon, startling Sofia out of her reverie. She climbs back out of the wagon.

Angelo, she is glad to see, has disappeared, as has Lidia.

Beppe is now practising a complicated little piece of nonsense with Vico, with the newly made six-rung ladder. Vico has his trumpet to his lips again and, as Beppe tumbles off the ladder with a startled shout, and rolls neatly to one side, Vico makes a farting noise through the mouthpiece.

Sofia bites her lip, smiling.

Beppe rubs his forehead where he has just banged it on the edge of the ladder. The *lazzo* almost worked that time; he has been wanting the little set of steps to seem as though it is fixed to the floor as he goes up and down, up and over, never reaching the place he is supposed to reach – and he almost managed it that last time. Almost. It is far harder than he thought it would be.

'Oh, shut up!' he says to Vico, who is nearly helpless with laughter. 'I'd like to see you do it any better.'

'Ah, but, Beppe, my boy, I don't need to, do I? I don't even *try* to make the claims to acrobatic prowess that you do, so, luckily for me, no one expects such things of me.'

'That's unfair. I don't make claims.'

Vico's mocking expression softens. 'No – no more you do,' he says, holding a hand out and pulling Beppe to his feet. 'But the claims are made, *amico*, the claims are made, and the expectations are there.' He pauses; then, suddenly still, he adds in little more than a murmured whisper, 'Don't look round, but I think you're being watched.'

Beppe holds his breath. Without moving, or turning his head, he says, 'Who by?'

'Our little newcomer.'

Beppe looks up at the sky for a second, then slowly, casually, as though it just happens to be the way he needs to move, he picks up the ladder and repositions it in such a way that he can affect to see Sofia as if by surprise. He smiles at her. She returns the smile, but looks away quickly, leaning down to fiddle with the fastening of her shoe. Bent double like this, her wild hair obscures much of her face, but Beppe thinks he has seen the colour rise – very prettily – in her cheeks, and wonders if Sofia's apparent discomposure signifies what he hopes it might.

'Gone quite pink, hasn't she?' Vico mutters, grinning. 'You might be in luck there, *amico*.'

Trying to look unconcerned, Beppe raises an eyebrow. 'You think so?'

'Would make a bit of a change for you, wouldn't it? It's been a long time since you ... though mind you,' Vico says now, interrupting himself and pointing at Beppe, 'she was colouring up nicely for Angelo just now, too, now I come to think about it.'

Beppe, who had also seen Sofia in conversation with Angelo, and wished he had not, makes no reply. He too saw Sofia flush at Angelo's appearance and the thought of what that might imply is now making him feel slightly sick. Deciding that he should make the most of Angelo's absence and take this opportunity of talking to Sofia, to try to ascertain ... how the land might lie, he puts down the ladder and, turning to Vico, says, 'I'm just going to—' when Cosima sticks her head out of the largest wagon and calls to Sofia, who stands quickly and hurries away.

'Just going to what?' Vico says.

Beppe stares over at where Sofia has just disappeared into Cosima's wagon. 'Just going to try the business with the ladder one more time,' he says, picking it up again.

11

A fortnight later

The wagons – the largest painted yellow, two of faded blue and one so shabby and paint-peeled that its colour could only be described as 'indeterminate' – are clustered together in an open space near a clump of trees outside the little town of Malalbergo. The horses have been unhitched and tethered to a hastily erected post; they are eating placidly from sacking nose-bags, heads drooping, each with its weight heavily on one leg, rump tilted, the other back foot resting on its tip, like a collection of weary dancers.

Cosima is leaning against one of the wheels of the yellow cart, reading and scribbling notes into a small wood-backed book. Nearby, Agostino and Lidia are deep in conversation on the back step of the smallest wagon.

'Have you asked her yet?' Lidia says.

Agostino shakes his head. 'No, of course not. I wouldn't have done that without talking to you first, *cara*. I have to admit that the thought *has* been sitting at the back of my mind for a little while, but there has been no potential solution at hand up until now. This idea flittered through my mind the moment Niccolò introduced her to us, though I kept it to myself at that point. I do believe she could do it, with a little help. She looks the part, in any case, don't you think?'

Lidia glances over her shoulder to where Sofia is squatting on her heels beside the yellow wagon, sorting through a large basket of costumes. 'Will we be able to adapt the material we already have, to include this new character of mine?' she says. 'Or am I going to end up being thrown out with the rubbish?'

'Oh, Lidia, *cara*, don't say that! It'll be easy to adapt the scenarios. Rosaura – that's who I think you should be playing now – is very like Colombina, only ... only ...' Agostino hesitates, but Lidia grins at him.

'What? Only older? Spit it out, Ago – I'm not stupid!'

Agostino pulls a face. 'It's not just that she's older, Lidia. She's ... well ...' He circles his hands, rotating them at shoulder height, trying to summon the word he seeks. '... more *experienced*, shall we say?'

'What – older and a slut?'

Throwing back his head, Agostino laughs. '*This* is exactly why you will be a delightful Rosaura, *cara*. Rosaura is always very funny, and so are you. So are you.'

'You're very kind, Ago. Can we talk to Vico about it first? See what he thinks?'

'Of course.' Agostino lifts his chin and calls across to where Vico and Beppe are working together to mend a table. The two men are bent over a trestle, across which has been laid the long table-top: Vico is chiselling, while Beppe leans his weight onto the whole to keep it all still.

Beppe's dog is sitting nearby, watching every movement Beppe makes; its hairy eyebrows twitch continually and its tail thumps in the dust every time Beppe speaks.

Hearing Agostino's call, Vico runs a hand through his hair and puts down his chisel. He mutters something to Beppe, before crossing to where Agostino and Lidia are sitting side by side on the steps of the largest wagon. 'Is there a problem?' he says cheerfully.

There is a moment's pause, then: 'Ago believes I've outgrown Colombina,' Lidia says simply.

Vico says nothing, just watches Agostino, who, holding his gaze, draws in a long breath.

'Well, it's true, isn't it?' Lidia says, shrugging. 'I shall be thirty-seven in November, shall I not? And it is getting ever harder to disguise the fact. Beppe's only – what? Twenty-two? Twenty-three? When I play up against him, there's no denying that I'm starting to look more like his mother than his paramour.' Lidia speaks lightly and smiles, but somewhat to her surprise, she can feel tears behind her eyes. She says, 'Ago's been thinking that Sofia might be able to take over Colombina. He wants me to start playing Rosaura. She's like Colombina, he says, but older. And ruder.'

Vico raises his eyebrows and whistles softly as he considers this. 'Does *she* know about this – Sofia?' he says, jerking his head in Sofia's direction.

Agostino and Lidia both shake their heads.

'What if she doesn't want to do it, or if she's no good?'

'We won't know until we ask her, and until she tries, will we?'

Vico looks at Lidia. 'What about you, *cara*? What do you think?'

A shrug. Lidia sighs. 'It's not something I wanted to face, but, looking at her now ...' She glances at Sofia. '... I can just see her playing the part, and doing it well. And ... a new character will be a new challenge, won't it?'

'Call her over, then,' Vico says.

*

'Is something wrong?' Sofia says, frowning slightly as she sees the three of them looking so intently at her. 'Is there a problem?'

'No, no, no.' Agostino pats a wooden chest next to the wagon, inviting Sofia to sit down upon it. 'We've just had an idea, that's all.'

Sofia looks at him enquiringly.

'Well, we thought . . . that is to say . . . we were wondering . . . how you might feel about . . . acting.'

'Acting? *Me?* But—'

Agostino says, 'I've been talking to Lidia, and we're wondering if you might like to consider . . . consider learning how to play Colombina?' He breaks off, watching Sofia for a reaction. She sits without speaking for several seconds. Twice she opens her mouth as though to say something, but closes it again without a word.

'Agostino thinks you might be able to . . .' Lidia swallows. '. . . to take my place as Colombina.'

Sofia gasps. 'What? Take your place? I couldn't do that! You're a *wonderful* Colombina, and—'

Lidia leans forward and hugs her. 'And you are a dear,' she says. 'But look at me!' She hunches her shoulders and stoops, as if elderly and fatigued. When she speaks, her voice quavers. 'I'm just getting too old.' Bobbing into a quick curtsy, she bows her head to right and left, as if accepting applause.

'I don't think you are.'

'Ah, but Agostino does.'

Anxiety begins to flutter inside Sofia's head. 'But I don't know *how* – I've never acted before. I don't have the smallest idea how to do it . . .' she says, '. . . and—'

'We'll teach you everything you need to know.'

Sofia looks at Lidia, who is lifting her eyebrows in smiling encouragement, but, suddenly fearful, she searches the older woman's face for . . . for what? Hidden resentment? Jealousy? Bitterness? She supposes that her future with the Coraggiosi is going to depend upon the answer she gives Agostino now – and the implications of that thought frightens her. What if she agrees to learn to act, and then Lidia decides that – having considered the matter more carefully – she thinks her rightful place in the company has been stolen from her, and turns against Sofia? Or, worse, what if she, Sofia, agrees to learn to act, but simply does not have the capability? Will Agostino allow her to revert to the role of costume mistress, which she has only just begun to fulfil? Or might he just be angry that his time has been wasted, and . . . and ask her to leave?

'What about the costumes?' she says, finding herself unable to put her other fears into words.

'Oh, we all do what we can in and around our acting, don't we? You'll manage perfectly, as we all do,' Agostino says warmly. 'Vico manages the carpentry, Cosima cooks for us all . . . ' He glances over to the yellow cart and coughs. 'Beppe handles all the bits and pieces – the properties – and he and Federico deal with the horses, do they not?'

'Yes . . . but . . . '

'The important thing is: do you *want* to do it?' Lidia says.

Agostino nods vigorously, reinforcing the question.

Sofia bites her lip, looking from person to person as she thinks about this. Does she? She says to Lidia, avoiding answering the question, 'What about you? Will you mind me taking this from you?'

'No, *cara*. No, I really won't.'

'But—'

'I'm a practical person, Sofia, and I know Agostino's right. But you're a dear to be worried about it.'

'How soon would I have to be ready to perform?'

Agostino considers. 'We can easily stay here for a week or ten days – you can practise your skills with the others and we'll work up one of the plays where Colombina only plays a small part, so that you can try out what you've learned in one of the little towns without it being too much for you to manage.'

Sofia nods, but then another thought occurs to her – one which makes her heartbeat quicken. 'Does Beppe know about this?' she says. 'Will *he* mind, do you think? He's the one who has most scenes with Colombina, isn't he?' She glances across to where Beppe, who is now cross-legged on the trestle, is fiddling inexpertly with the chisel and a mallet, his face crumpled with concentration.

Lidia laughs. Taking both of Sofia's hands in hers, she says, 'I can promise you two things. One, I'm very happy about the thought of you playing Colombina – Ago says I'm to be given another character to play; and two, Beppe ... well ... no, he doesn't know, but I'm sure he'll be ... delighted.'

Vico snorts his amusement and shouts over to Beppe, flapping a beckoning hand.

Uncrossing his legs, Beppe swings himself off the trestle. The dog scrambles to its feet. 'What? What is it?' he says as he arrives, the dog at his heels. 'A problem?'

'Why does everyone think that the only things I ever have to talk to them about are problems?' Agostino says irritably.

Beppe leans back, his fingers laced behind his head, elbows winged wide. He looks serious for a moment, then his face splits in a wide smile. 'I think it's a wonderful idea.'

'Well, yes, that's what we think,' Agostino says, 'but Sofia doesn't seem sure she wants to do it.'

Beppe frowns quizzically at Sofia, and sees the colour rise in her cheeks. 'You don't want to? Why not?'

'I *do* want to . . . very much. It's just that . . . that . . . '

'That what?' His voice is soft, encouraging.

'What if I can't do it? What if I'm not very good?'

'Then it'll be our fault for not having taught you properly. But you'll be wonderful – don't forget how easily you invented a verse for our *scelta* poem.'

Beaming, Agostino says, 'Exactly – exactly so! Just what I was thinking, Beppe, you are so right. A natural improviser. Sofia? What's your answer?'

Beppe watches Sofia's gaze move from Agostino to Lidia, to Vico and finally to him.

She nods.

As Beppe smiles at her, the pink spots in her cheeks deepen.

'Marvellous! I'm so pleased! So, can I ask you to teach her what she needs to know in the first instance, Beppe?' Agostino says, eyebrows raised. 'Given that she'll probably have most of her scenes with you.'

'Shouldn't it be me, Ago?' Lidia says. 'As the presiding Colombina?'

'Of course it should, yes, and you'd do it beautifully, *cara*, but you're going to have other things to do. I'd like you to concentrate straight away on working up this new character, with me. There's a lot to learn. Once you're confident, and once Sofia has made a start, then we can begin rehearsing new material. Now . . . ' Agostino frowns as he considers. 'We need to carry on performing in the meantime. So, Lidia, if you would continue with Colombina, while Sofia starts to learn what she needs to know, and then we'll try Sofia out after a week or so here in Malalbergo and then in San Giorgio; and Sofia, my dear, you will be properly ready when we do the big show at the Castello della Franceschina. One of our first truly *prestigious* venues. And that in itself is wonderful indeed – with more venues like Franceschina, we stand a chance of being perceived as being as successful as the Gelosi.'

Beppe is fighting to keep his face impassive, determined not to look too pleased. A knowing smirk is already spreading across Vico's face which he has no wish to encourage. 'Of course I'll teach her, Ago,' he says, deliberately ignoring his friend's unspoken taunt.

Sofia and Lidia prepare the evening meal together. Sofia's head is spinning, and she struggles to maintain her conversation with Lidia as the two of them sit on the wagon steps, peeling vegetables on flat wooden platters balanced on their knees.

'The first performance you'll be involved in will probably be in the main piazza in Malalbergo,' Lidia says, flipping chunks of peeled and chopped turnip into a pot of water and rummaging for another in a bag at her feet. 'We perform there every year about this time. It's always towards the end of the season. Not too many people – just right for your first show. And the audiences have always been very friendly and enthusiastic in Malalbergo. They'll love you.'

Sofia's thoughts begin to jostle. What will Beppe need to teach her? How long will it take? Will she be ready in time? How difficult is it going to be to stand on a stage and remember everything she will have to remember? She has never learned to read – will this prove to be a stumbling block? Will she be the only one who can't? The questions tumble over themselves in her mind until she feels quite breathless.

'Will you be happy for . . . for Beppe to be teaching you?' Lidia asks, looking sideways at Sofia. 'You couldn't have a better instructor. He's good.'

A traitorous flush of colour rises in Sofia's face. Hoping Lidia has not noticed, she nods.

Lidia smiles. Raising an eyebrow, she says quietly, 'Vico says Beppe keeps mentioning you all the time, when the two of them rehearse together.'

'Me?' Her face prickling, Sofia drops the carrot she was about to begin chopping. 'Mentioning me? What has he said?'

'Nothing particular, Vico says. Just your name comes into what he says more often than not.'

Picking up the fallen carrot, and brushing the dust off it, Sofia starts slicing.

'He's been on his own a long time, Beppe has,' Lidia says in a voice softened with affection. 'It really is ages since I saw him with a girl.'

The prickling behind Sofia's face intensifies. 'Has he ever . . . ?'

'He was very much in love once, bless him, three or four years ago, with a girl from another troupe, but it didn't last long. I don't remember why. Don't remember her name, even. She wasn't good enough for him, in my opinion. I remember thinking that at the time.'

'And nothing since then?'

'Not that I'm aware of.'

Sofia tilts the wooden platter towards the pot and knife-scrapes the slices of carrot into the pot with Lidia's turnips.

'But . . . keep an eye out for Angelo,' Lidia says quietly. 'Just a bit of a warning.'

'Angelo? What do you mean?'

'Well, he's got his eye on you, hasn't he? And he and Beppe don't care for each other very much. They never have.'

'Got his eye on me?'

Lidia puffs out her amusement. 'God, yes. With his looks, he's bound to have an eye on any pretty girl that comes his way, isn't he? But I reckon he is a mite more partial to you than he was bargaining on being.'

Not liking the idea of this at all, Sofia says, 'Why do Angelo and Beppe not like each other?'

'Do you know, I'm not sure. I think they knew each other when they were young – but neither of them has ever spoken to any of us about it. Beppe has dropped hints on occasions, but never given any details. There's always a sort of crackling tension in the air between them, though – like a pair of bloody dogs with their hackles up.'

'I'd noticed.'

'Hard to miss it, to be honest.'

Lidia stands up, puts the wooden platter down on the step where she has been sitting, and crosses to where a small barrel, about the size of a melon, has been placed near the brazier. 'Beans,' she says, levering the lid off, drawing out a double handful and lifting them to her nose before she tips them into the pot with the vegetables. 'They'll take a couple of hours in the pot to soften, but they'll fill your belly nicely.' She rolls her eyes. 'They'll make Vico fart, too, but every pleasure has its price, I suppose.'

Sofia giggles.

Late the next morning, Beppe climbs out of the smallest wagon and suggests to Sofia that they make a start on her instruction. 'We can go over to that flat place over by the trees, look, where the grass is greener,' he says, pointing. They walk together to the little clearing, Ippo the dog trotting behind them. Sunlight is filtering through the leaf canopy overhead; it lies in dapples on the grass and, as they reach the far side of the clearing, some small creature skitters in the undergrowth, rustling away from them through the leaf litter. A fallen tree offers a suitable seat, and Sofia sits herself down upon it; the dog curls nose to tail at her feet, one eye on Beppe. Beppe, meanwhile, flips up onto his hands and turns a series of cartwheels around the clearing, over and over, around the perimeter of the flat space. The grass under his palms is cool and slightly damp and the ground is springy. Back once more on his feet, he stands in front of Sofia.

'Right – come on. Up you get! You need to stretch your limbs before we start.' As he speaks, a flood of unexpected images pours into his mind; he tries to ignore them, wishing he had expressed himself in other terms – the thought of Sofia's limbs being 'stretched' is quickly threatening to distract him from his task. He swallows, and puffs out a short breath, fighting not to show his discomposure.

Sofia stands up and faces Beppe. 'You're not going to ask me to stand on my hands, are you?' she says.

'Would you not like to try?'

Sofia laughs. 'No I wouldn't! And I have a very good excuse, don't I?' She holds up the bandaged hand and waggles the fingers at Beppe.

'Don't worry, I shan't ask you to do anything you won't be able to do easily.' He pauses. 'But you do need to loosen up. Like this, look.' He hunches and rolls his shoulders, and tilts his head from side to side.

Sofia tries to imitate him, realizing as she does so that Beppe's fluid, easy movements are not going to be easy to copy. His head and neck and arms seem to move effortlessly, bonelessly, gracefully – she feels awkward and wooden in comparison.

But Beppe is smiling. 'Just right,' he says. 'And now, like this.' He lifts one leg and hugs his knee, then changes legs and hugs the other. Sofia does the same, wobbling wildly on her one foot each time.

Beppe shakes out his arms from shoulders to fingers, the way a wet dog will shake from tip to tail, and his rolled sleeves come loose and fall down over his wrists. 'Now,' he says, re-rolling them, 'before we start, I'll tell you something about Colombina. Some of it you'll know, from having watched Lidia, but there are things you need to understand in a particular way to be able to play the character properly. Does that make sense?'

'I think so.'

Beppe says, 'First of all, you need to imagine Colombina as an animal. What sort of animal do you think she might be?'

'Erm . . . ' Sofia's face flames again as she flounders in ignorance.

Beppe waits. Then he says, 'Think about the name: Colombina.' He pauses. When Sofia did not reply, he says, 'She's usually seen as a dove – a little dove.'

'Oh. Yes, I see. That would make sense.'

'Arlecchino, on the other hand, is most often a cat or a monkey, or sometimes a fox.'

'What, you actually play those animals on stage? I haven't seen—'

'No, not that. It's just that you want to . . . to have them in your mind as you play the character, so you get a feel for the movements and the way they think.'

Sofia nods, picturing Beppe's febrile on-stage agility, hoping that she is going to be able to remember everything he is telling her.

He says, 'Colombina is gentle and sweet, like a dove – but she's much more than that. She's probably the only person in all the *commedia* casts who has nothing wrong with her. She's clever and canny and pretty, and good with money. She *is* a bit of a flirt – she flirts with most of the men in all the plays, in fact, but she never really does anything about it. She's only ever in love with ... Arlecchino.'

Sofia's mouth opens a little and she stares at him. They watch each other for several seconds; then, without taking his eyes from hers, Beppe shrugs and adds, 'Mind you, she might be in love with him, but Colombina does think Arlecchino's a bit of an idiot, and very annoying.'

'Why? Why does she think that? Is he?'

'What, annoying?' Beppe grins. 'Oh yes – he really is the fool that Colombina thinks he is, but somehow he always seems to win through, however many scrapes he gets himself into. Perhaps it's because he's so nimble; that why he thinks he's cleverer than he is.'

Sofia finds that she cannot take her eyes from Beppe, who seems never to be still. Though his gaze remains fixed upon her face, his hands are constantly sketching out in vivid gestures the things he describes, and, more than this, it seems to her that he is somehow lighter on his feet than he ought to be – as though, in fact, he is all but weightless.

'You'll need to get how she stands and walks just right before you can think about saying her lines. Come and stand here with me, look, and I'll show you.'

Tilting forward a little from his hips, Beppe bends one knee and extends the other foot forwards, toe pointed, like a dancer. 'There – try it. See if you can stand like a real Colombina.'

Sofia comes to stand next to him. Looking sideways at him, she tries to copy his stance. As she points the toe of her leading foot, though, she stumbles, then rights herself awkwardly, her face hot.

'Don't worry. Try it again. I'll hold you, look.'

He moves to stand close behind her and puts one hand lightly on each of her hips, fingers forward, thumbs behind. Sofia holds her breath for a moment, feeling her heartbeat quicken. He presses down with his fingers and up with his thumbs, and that pressure suddenly makes it clear to her just how she should bend; she tilts forward a fraction as she has seen Lidia do.

'Perfect,' Beppe says, letting go of her and coming round to stand in front of her. 'Just perfect. Now point that front toe and you have it exactly.'

Sofia now wishes she had not succeeded so quickly – she liked the feeling of Beppe's hands on her – but she does as he says, and this time feels secure in the stance.

'Now, watch me walk like Colombina; watch me and copy me.' Beppe walks across the little clearing, head held high, arms out in a curve in front of him as though he is carrying an invisible basket, pointing his toes on each step. Sofia tries to imitate him, expecting to stumble again, but it is easier than she feared.

'Just right,' Beppe says. 'Well done. You'll have to keep practising that, until it's as easy for you as the way you walk normally.'

Sofia walks twice around the little clearing with Colombina's dainty steps, then stops in front of Beppe, holds her skirts out sideways, and bobs a curtsy. 'She's much neater than I am,' she says. 'I feel quite different when I'm walking like that. As though I'm someone else entirely.'

'Good. That's just how it should be,' he says. 'And it'll get easier and easier. Practise every day. We can practise together. But for now we should do some work as well on how Colombina speaks to Arlecchino. She loves him, like I said, but, most of the time, she really does think he's a bloody nuisance.' He pauses, then runs his fingers up into his hair, elbows out wide. 'And he *is* a nuisance. I suppose he's just *less* annoying to her than all the others, though, in the end. And that's why she loves him.'

Sofia watches him, entranced.

'Let's try something together – a conversation. A typical conversation between Colombina and Arlecchino – the sort of thing that crops up quite often in the different scenarios. Why don't we sit back down over there on the tree, look, and see if you can follow what I start?'

Beppe takes Sofia's hand and leads her back to the fallen tree. Trying not to let him see how very much she is enjoying the sensation of his touch, Sofia sits down next to him. As they sit, the dog lifts its head, its tail scuffing the grass. Glancing down at it, Beppe fondles its ears and the tail thumps more quickly.

'Now,' Beppe says, turning to face Sofia and sitting himself cross-legged on the tree-trunk. 'Colombina often wants to know if Arlecchino really loves her.'

Sofia fiddles a thumbnail between her front teeth. She looks at Beppe's mouth and then back to his eyes, finding it increasingly difficult to concentrate on his words.

Beppe says, 'She's going to ask him if he does, and he will answer by declaring just how much. Colombina will try to match it, Arlecchino will go one better and they'll pile up their declarations, one on the other like a mountain of sweetmeats.' He builds the pile in mid-air as he speaks.

Sucking in a breath, Sofia stares at Beppe's hands.

'So you need to start it off. Go on: ask me whether or not I love you.'

Her skin prickling with self-consciousness, Sofia says in a small voice, 'Er . . . do you? Do you . . . love me?'

Beppe laughs. 'It'll have to be a bit bigger and more dramatic than that, little seamstress. Like this.' He uncrosses his legs and sits astride the tree; then, grasping her hand, he holds it up to his chest, and says, in a voice suddenly husky and trembling with emotion, but still resonant, 'O tell me – and tell me truly, mind – do you *really* love me?'

Sofia stares at him.

'Try it again,' Beppe says, his eyes dancing.

Sofia leans in towards him. 'Tell me, *caro*,' she says, watching Beppe's mouth again, uncomfortably aware of how very much she wants him to move in closer and kiss her, 'Tell me – do you really, really love me?'

Beppe hesitates for a second, apparently holding his breath; his gaze flicks from her eyes to her mouth and back, several times. Then, raising an eyebrow, he leans away from her and says, stoutly, 'Of course – of course I do! How could you doubt me! I love you as much as . . . as doctors love an epidemic!'

Despite herself, Sofia laughs.

'And now, come up with something better than that – bigger than that – to tell Arlecchino how much *you* love *him*,' Beppe says.

Sofia thinks for a moment. 'Well, then, I love you as much as . . . as actors love applause.'

Beppe grins his approval. He says, 'And I love you as much as women love to have their own way.'

Without thinking, Sofia stands up and flings her arms out wide. She looks up into the now cloudless sky, then back at Beppe and, bending down, she picks a little handful of grasses and holds it out to him. 'And I love you', she says, curtsying, 'as much as flowers love the rain.'

Taking the posy from her, Beppe stands too, up on the trunk of the fallen tree. Running along it and back, then jumping down to stand behind Sofia, he puts the grass down, leans around her and, placing a hand on each of her hips again, he says, 'As much as a pickpocket loves a big crowd.' He mimes lifting her purse and rifling through it with a wide-eyed air of covert eagerness, making the chinking noise of the coins as he does so.

Sofia turns to face him. They are very close to each other. Looking up at his face, she says, 'And I love you as much . . . as a blade loves a whetstone.'

Beppe smiles widely and hugs her. 'Oh, you're going to be so good at this.'

'Good at what?'

Beppe whips around and his smile vanishes. Sofia turns to see who has spoken.

Angelo is almost invisible in the darker shade beneath a nearby holm oak. He has discarded his usual doublet; his shirt is untucked at the back and, arms folded, he is leaning against the tree and watching them, his weight on one booted foot, the other crooked up on the trunk. Sofia sees his gaze flick back and forth from her eyes to her mouth and her breasts, and immediately feels as though she is improperly dressed. Her face flames. Fighting down an urge to cross her arms in front of her, she swallows and runs her tongue over her lips, then wishes she had not; to have done so seems to be welcoming Angelo's intrusive stare.

She returns his gaze without smiling.

'Sofia is learning to play Colombina,' Beppe says quietly. His dog scrambles to its feet. 'She's going to be taking over the role. As you'd have known if you'd been there when the decision was taken.'

'Ah. That's what this is all about, is it? I had wondered if I was interrupting a . . . a love tryst.' Angelo raises an eyebrow, his eyes on Sofia. 'But I see it was merely a rehearsal.' He smiles. 'How disappointing.'

'Was there something you wanted?' Beppe asks.

'Yes, as it happens. I want to go through the sword-fight *lazzo* with you and Federico before we start rehearsing in earnest for Ferrara and Franceschina. I don't think we were slick enough in Bologna.'

'Do you not?' Beppe says coldly. He pauses. 'If you really want to, we can work on it a little later – when I've finished what I want to do with Sofia.'

At this, Angelo's eyebrows lift again and he chews down a twisted smile. Sofia sees a muscle twitch in Beppe's jaw, and feels her face grow hot.

'Oh, well, in that case,' Angelo says, 'I'll leave you to ... how did you put it, Bianchi? To *finish what you want to do with her*. I should hate to feel I was intruding. Let me know when you're ready to go through the *lazzo*.'

And, turning on his heel, he strides away towards the wagons; even with his back towards them it is obvious he is expecting his departure to be closely watched.

Sofia looks up at Beppe, who is staring after Angelo. She sees him mutter something half under his breath, but cannot hear his words; clicking his fingers at the dog, he says aloud, 'Let's go for a walk.'

Sofia stands irresolute, fearful that this invitation does not include her.

'Are you coming?' Beppe says. He sees what looks like relief flood Sofia's face as he speaks, and realizes she was afraid he was angry with her. Feeling the muscles tight in his jaw, he knows he is scowling, so, deliberately softening his expression, he relaxes his shoulders and tries to smile. 'Come on,' he says, 'let's get right away from the wagons for a while.' Glancing back towards where

Angelo is now in conversation with a grumpy-looking Vico, he begins to walk with Sofia along the line of trees away from the clearing.

When he sees she is almost trotting to keep up with him, he slows his pace.

'I'm sorry,' he says.

'What for?'

He shrugs. 'I don't know. Oh, it's . . . it's just him.' He jerks his chin back towards the wagons. 'He always makes me . . . makes me want to hit something. Preferably his face.'

Angelo flicks a cursory glance over his shoulder and sees Sofia walking away beside Beppe; the latter is leaning slightly towards the girl, his hands raised, sketching out whatever it is he is saying. The anger Angelo feels at the thought of what appears to be a burgeoning intimacy between the pair of them pushes up into his throat like bile and he stuffs his hands roughly down into his breeches pockets.

His throat contracts as his fingers touch a small glass phial, tightly stoppered with a small cork.

He had quite forgotten it was there – had thought he had none left after he smashed what he had thought was his last bottle in the piazza. God, this must have been in his pocket some time. Pulling it out and holding it up to the light, he sees that perhaps half a finger's depth remains in the little phial. Enough for one small dose. Staring at it for a moment, his heart thudding, Angelo decides to collect his doublet from the wagons and then take himself away for a short walk.

'What's the trouble?' Vico is whittling a short length of wood; he looks up as Angelo approaches and his little knife gleams suddenly bright in the fitful sunshine.

'No bloody business of yours.'

'God, you can be so charming.'

'And you are consistently crass, insensitive, opinionated and ignorant. Keep your intrusive fucking questions to yourself and leave me alone.' His words hang ugly in the late-morning air and, wishing now that he had not spoken, Angelo collects his coat, then strides away from the wagons and off towards a line of scrubby woodland – in the opposite direction to that taken by Beppe and Sofia, ignoring the muttered comments from Vico behind him.

He'll find a quiet place to make use of what little is left in the bottle. There is not much in there, though – thank God, he thinks, that he thought to suggest Franceschina as a possible venue to Agostino; he'll be able to stock up – as long as Sebastiano is prepared to be flexible about payment.

Looking back over her shoulder, Sofia says, 'I'm sorry, but I don't think I like Angelo. I don't know why, but I don't trust him.'

Beppe hears her words and is rocked by a drench of relief. *I don't think I like Angelo. I don't know why, but I don't trust him.* Fighting a strong desire to kiss her, he says drily, 'I'm not sure that any of us do.'

Sofia frowns. She says, 'Lidia . . . Lidia says you used to know him . . . years ago.'

Turning quickly, he looks at her. 'She said that, did she?'

Sofia nods.

'When?'

'Last night, while we were cooking.'

'What else did she say?'

'Just that. No more.'

Beppe hesitates for a moment, wondering whether or not to explain. The painful memories of everything that sprang from that early acquaintance are still keen – too keen. Even after so many years. Shaking his head, he says, 'It was a long time ago. I'll tell you about it some time.'

Ippo, the dog, racing over from foraging in a nearby thicket, jumps up at Beppe, putting dirty paws up against his thighs. He ruffles the creature's ears, then, seeing the wet paw-prints on his breeches, raises a knee and shoves him away.

'The rest of the troupe is so close-knit, and so happy together,' Sofia says. 'I don't understand why you all put up with having someone like Angelo in the Coraggiosi.'

Beppe's past dealings with Angelo blare in his head like a hunting horn. 'Believe me,' he says, 'we've all had this discussion in one way or another so many times it's become predictable. But whatever we all think, Angelo has three things which make us put up with how little we all care for him: his face, his name and his money.'

'I don't understand.'

'Angelo da Bagnacavallo' – Beppe feels the name slick sour across his tongue like phlegm – 'is the only son of a nobleman. His father is a second cousin to the Duke of Ferrara and the family lives in a massive house not far from Bologna. So he tells everyone at every opportunity, he has never wanted to do anything other than act – though his father was always dead against it.' Beppe hesitates, and the hunting horn blares again. 'Apparently, though, a few years ago, sick to the back teeth with his son's determination to join a troupe, the old man agreed that Angelo could be given a portion of his inheritance, so that he could try his luck as an actor. His father probably didn't expect him to succeed. It was a fair sum, I've been told, and Angelo promptly signed it over to Agostino, in return for being kept on as *inamorato* no matter what. It was at a time when the troupe was almost on the point of having to disband because of lack of money, so Ago had no choice, really. The rest of us aren't supposed to know about the arrangement, but we all do – Vico heard Ago talking to Cosima once, and he told everyone else, of course.'

Sofia says nothing.

Beppe scuffs the dry earth of the path with the heel of his boot as he speaks again. 'We're fortunate to have him, but—'

'Fortunate? Why "fortunate"?'

Pulling in a long breath, Beppe sighs it out again. 'It's not just the money – every troupe needs an *inamorato*, doesn't it? And the *inamorati* – both of them – need to be beautiful people if they're to be credible. Cosima's been with the troupe since Ago started it in seventy-five, and she's so beautiful it doesn't matter in the slightest that she's getting a bit too old for the part. But until Angelo came along, the Coraggiosi's *inamorato* was played by a man called Cristoforo Dominio who ... well, he wasn't ugly, I suppose, but he was nothing like our friend back there. And ... Angelo's actually not a bad actor, though I hate to admit it.'

'What happened to him? To Cristoforo?'

Beppe pulls a wry face and shrugs. 'He took one look at Angelo, the day Angelo came to plead with Agostino to be taken on as one of the Coraggiosi, and decided that he couldn't compete. Well, I suppose you would, wouldn't you? He left us within days of Angelo's joining the troupe, even though Ago had promised to keep him on and find him alternative parts to play. And I suppose it has to be said that the crowds have been flocking to look at our *inamorato*'s flawless features ever since.' Beppe raises an eyebrow. 'What with how he looks, and the fact that the word is out that he comes from a family of some standing, he's undoubtedly raised the profile of the troupe. He's put us almost on a level with the Gelosi.'

Sofia still looks puzzled.

Beppe says, 'But we all still think he's a fly-bitten bastard.'

'I'm glad it's not just me that doesn't like him.'

'No, it's not. But there's a lot more to it – I'll tell you another time. Not today.' He forces the memories back into a dark corner, shuts the door on them, and summons a smile for Sofia. 'It's so beautiful out here – I don't want to spoil it talking about Angelo.'

They walk together along the sun-freckled path for several moments without speaking, the only sounds the scuffing of their footsteps in the dusty leaf litter and the spiralling cries of high, distant buzzards. The wooded hills, crisp with gold-, red- and green-leaved trees, soar up steeply to the north, while long feathers of cloud stretch out across the sky, pale and thin, fanning out and wisping to nothing in the light wind. As it turns to the right before it swings around and heads back towards where the wagons are parked, the path narrows – it is only just wide enough here now for the two to walk side by side – and on almost every step Sofia's skirts are snagging on twigs and thorns in the undergrowth and flapping about Beppe's legs.

Their hands brush together as their arms swing.

Once . . . twice . . . three times they touch.

Reaching out, Beppe threads his fingers through Sofia's. As they walk on down the path, he runs his thumb back and forth along the soft skin of the side of her hand, aware that Sofia is glancing repeatedly sideways to look at where their fingers are now clasped. She seems to sense his gaze and looks up at him, and the wide-eyed anticipation in her face sends a sharp shiver of longing down into his belly. Lifting her hand to his lips, he kisses her knuckles, fighting a growing wish to snatch her up into his arms. He is startled by the intensity of the moment, shocked by how very much he wants her – but he won't do it. He won't rush her. He will make himself wait – even though he is not sure why. Something about Sofia is staying his hand – something charming and vulnerable. This, he thinks, flicking a sideways glance at her and trying to ignore his body's protestations, this is something to treasure. If he moves too quickly, it might all spoil and he does not think he could bear that. She has moved in a little closer to him, and has tightened her grip. They walk on together, back round towards the wagons again, and the dog bounds ahead of them, thoughtlessly joyous, tongue lolling, plumed tail up high like a flag.

12

Later that afternoon

Agostino spends a few moments scraping a thick line in the earth with a stick to create the rough outline of a stage. 'Beppe, fetch a couple of the poles from under the yellow cart, will you?' he calls. 'Sofia, *cara*, imagine they're what would be the back hangings. Audience is out that way.' He points. Vico, who is standing in what would be the audience, pulls a face at Sofia and bows.

Nodding at Agostino, Sofia pokes her tongue out at Vico.

Beppe lays two long poles along one of the edges Agostino has drawn in the dust, then, as he goes to step across them, makes everyone laugh by appearing to smack straight into an invisible wall, reeling backwards and rubbing his head, quickly becoming confused by his inability to move forwards. Frowning in anxious consternation, he 'feels' his way along the back edge of the 'stage', palming hand over hand along the non-existent wall until he finds a narrow 'gap', which he then proceeds to squeeze through, sucking in his stomach, pulling himself up onto the tips of his toes and holding his breath extravagantly, puffing it out again in exaggerated relief once he has eased his way 'through' onto the stage area.

Agostino grins at him for a second, shaking his head as though in disbelief, then he snaps his fingers and points over to the far side of the stage. 'Just wait over there, will you, you big idiot? I want to start from *canovaccio* seven, and you need to be in hiding for that one, don't you?'

Beppe crosses to the far side of the stage and crouches like a frog near the front, pulling a large red cloth over himself, fashioning a small peephole from folds of the fabric.

Agostino continues. 'Sofia, *cara*, it's at this point that you need to tell Federico all about Cosima being in love with Angelo – and make it clear to him that he is not going to be able to marry her . . . remember?'

Sofia nods again.

'Remember: voice from down here.' He pats his belly. Bending slightly, he points to a thicket some fifty yards away. 'Speak to the trees over there, look.'

Another nod.

'Right. Federico, are you ready?'

'Aye, I am.'

'Good.' Agostino snaps his fingers and Sofia tilts at the waist and slightly points the toe of her right foot. '*I'm sorry, sir,*' she says stoutly, hands on hips, chin tilted upwards. '*But I know it for certain. She's in love with Signor Oratio, and there's nothing you or I or anyone else can do about it.*' She shakes her head. '*She won't marry you. Whatever you say to her.*'

'*Pah! You're nothing but a chit of a girl and don't know your arse from your elbow,*' Federico says, waving a dismissive arm in her direction.

'A bit more volume, now, Sofia, *cara*,' Agostino hisses.

Sofia flicks him a glance and sucking in her belly muscles, pushes her voice a little harder. '*Hmm. Forgive me if I'm being impolite, signore, but I think you'll find that I'm very well acquainted with both my arse and my elbow, and I know that they are as unlike to be joined in matrimony as are your good self and my mistress.*'

'Good, good, good!' Agostino mutters from the side of the stage. 'Better. Just what I wanted. Marvellous!'

As Federico begins to splutter, a loud sneeze is heard from Beppe's hiding place. Federico stops dead. '*What was that? WHO was that?*'

And, as Beppe creeps tentatively out from under his cloth, trembling extravagantly, Federico begins to harangue him, hurling insults at him and shaking his fist. '*You? Here? Again! How dare you! It's all your fault, you blithering idiot,*' he shouts, '*and if you're not out of my sight in the next couple of seconds, I'm going to—*'

'Creep away now, Sofia,' hisses Agostino, and Sofia tiptoes backwards, step by careful step, as Beppe, arms over his head in counterfeit terror, abandons the red cloth and scuttles away in the opposite direction.

'Lovely!' Agostino calls out, and everyone stops. Cosima, who has been sitting on an upturned barrel, claps softly, and Lidia gives Sofia a quick hug. Giovanni Battista bustles up and pats her on the back, and Federico, from his position on the 'stage', raises his hands above his head and claps twice, grinning broadly. Sofia's face glows with pleased pride and she bites down a smile so wide she can feel it stretching her cheeks.

Angelo, who has been watching the rehearsal from the back steps of the smallest wagon, says nothing. Glancing across at him, Sofia meets his gaze for a moment and, at the expression on his face, her face burns and her smile fades. He raises an eyebrow, then looks away.

'Well done,' Beppe says quietly, taking her hand and squeezing her fingers. She turns to him. 'That was perfect,' he says. 'You remembered everything. 'Now we have to work on the reconciliation between me and you – between Arlecchino and Colombina – that's the last bit Ago wanted to do today.'

Sofia swallows uncomfortably. 'Oh no – that's the piece I messed up earlier.'

'God, we all mess things up a thousand times before we get them right. It's just how it is.'

'Beppe, Sofia, can I have you both, please?' Agostino calls. 'Cosima, Lidia and the rest of you, take a break. Cosima, *cara*, could you possibly find me something to drink?'

Sofia watches as the others wander away. She and Beppe wait together, watching Agostino, who is consulting a small wood-backed book. Frowning, he flips over a few pages. 'Yes, here we are: the reconciliation. It still needs a little polishing, I feel, don't you?'

Sofia clears her throat, and a prickle of embarrassment sends more colour up into her face as she remembers the repeated mistakes of the previous rehearsal. Seeing her discomfiture, Agostino crosses to stand in front of her and puts a hand on each of her upper arms. Shaking her very slightly on each important word, he says, 'Sofia, *cara*, you are doing so very, very well – I am proud of you. You've proved a hundred times already that we have made an excellent decision in asking you to act for us, so you are simply *forbidden* to be downhearted that I want to work further on this scene. Is that understood?' He runs a hand over her hair and strokes along her cheekbone with the edge of his thumb.

His face is close to hers; his expression is so fierce and yet so very kind that Sofia is moved in an instant almost to tears. Unable to answer, she nods, and Beppe leans forward and kisses her cheek.

'There you are, chick, I told you,' he says.

Cosima reappears with a pewter mug. 'Last night's ale,' she says. 'All I could find.'

Leaning towards her and cupping a hand behind her head, Agostino kisses his wife enthusiastically, then drains several long mouthfuls from the mug before handing it back to her. Cosima smiles her slow smile, finishes what is left in the mug and returns to the wagons.

'So,' Agostino says, wiping his face with the back of his wrist. 'Off we go. From *I am truly a fool*, I think, Beppe.'

Cracking his knuckles, Beppe crosses to sit on an upturned barrel and puts his head in his hands in a droop-shouldered attitude of utter dejection. '*Oh my word, but I am truly a fool,*' he says, gazing up at Sofia and shaking his head sadly. '*And you will never forgive me, will you?*'

'*No, now that you mention it, I'm not sure that I shall.*'

'Turn away now, Sofia,' Agostino says. 'You need to be facing out *that* way.'

Sofia flicks what she hopes is a disdainful glance at the miserable Beppe and spins on her heel, folding her arms in front of her.

'Good. Stay that way until he comes up to you, then spin around and walk across away from him.'

Beppe appears, hands clasped in entreaty, but she turns again and takes half a dozen quick paces in the opposite direction.

'And again. Beppe, be quick – get there before she does.'

Before Sofia has reached the designated spot, Beppe is there and he drops to one knee. '*Just one more chance?*'

'Make him wait, Sofia. Make him wait. Just stare at him. Take as long as you want – the audience will wait with you.'

Sofia looks at Beppe, kneeling in front of her, staring up at her imploringly. Her gaze flicks to his mouth, then back to his eyes. Her heartbeat quickens.

'Now your hand.'

Sofia holds out her hand. Beppe takes it in both of his own, very gently, and plants a kiss on the tip of each finger, looking up at her after each kiss. '*Just one more?*' he says. '*One more very small*' – kiss – '*extremely insignificant*' – kiss – '*little chance?*' – kiss.

Sofia pulls her hand from his and pauses for a moment; then, holding it out to him once more, she says, '*Very well. Just one.*' Another pause. '*One last.*' And she allows him to kiss her knuckles before turning away from him again. Behind her, she hears a quiet scuffling sound and knows that Beppe will be dancing from foot to foot in silent celebration. As she has been told to, she flicks a glance over one shoulder and, seeing the dance, she smiles at him indulgently.

'Good ... and go back now, Sofia – you've decided. You're going to let him kiss you properly.'

Sofia holds her breath. She steps back towards Beppe. '*Perhaps I might let you have just one ... proper ... kiss ...* ' she says, raising an eyebrow. Beppe looks out towards the 'audience' and grins, rubbing his hands together in glee, before turning back to her and nodding enthusiastically.

Arms held slightly backwards, Sofia tilts from the waist and leans towards Beppe, presenting him with a puckered mouth. He does the same. Their feet are perhaps a yard apart, but, leaning in towards each other, their lips are almost touching. Almost.

Their faces are an inch apart. They both close their eyes tightly. Their kiss – still with air between the two of them – is vocal and theatrical and Agostino claps.

Sofia's pulse races as Beppe's gaze remains fixed upon hers for several seconds.

'Much, much better. Well done, Sofia, well done both of you.'

'Was that good enough?' Sofia says anxiously, looking from Beppe to Agostino and back again.

'Oh, *cara*, it was indeed. It was perfect. We'll run through the whole show again – twice – tomorrow, then we perform in Malalbergo the following afternoon, and you will triumph, *cara*, you will triumph indeed!' He beams at her. 'But first, you must go and find Lidia, and sort out your costume.'

13

There is no doubt about it: Columbina's pretty grey dress is far too big for Sofia. Standing behind her, Lidia pulls the laces as tightly as they will go, until the fabric between the eyelets begins to pucker, but the bodice still hangs loose and shapeless.

'I knew you were small, but I didn't realize firstly how very tiny you really are, and secondly how fat *I* must be,' Lidia says grumpily. 'Look at it – you could fit three of you in there.' She scowls. 'And it was beginning to feel tight on me.'

'Don't be silly,' Sofia says. 'You're just lovely. It's me that's stupidly little.'

Lidia huffs a disbelieving breath. 'Well, whichever of us is oddly sized, that dress is going to need unpicking and remaking if you're to be seen in it on stage in a couple of days' time.'

'I can do it right away. It's only the bodice that'll need taking in; we can just lace the skirts more tightly at the waist. It won't take me long. Can you pin it in place for me?'

'Where are the pins?'

Sofia points to a small painted chest on the ground near the back steps of the smallest wagon. 'There's a paper of pins in there,' she says. 'I found them in the wagon the other day and put them in that little box with the red flowers on it.'

Lidia retrieves the said box and pulls from it a piece of stiff, waxed paper about three inches by five, folded several times. As she holds it up, it flaps down revealing parallel rows of shining pins, neatly in-and-outed through the paper.

'Lift your arms up again for a moment, then.' Sofia raises her arms, and Lidia takes a handful of fabric on either side of her.

'If you can just pinch the fabric roughly in where it needs to be,' Sofia says, 'and pin it so that the excess cloth is still sticking outwards . . .'

Lidia obliges, then unfastens the laces again and helps Sofia to take the bodice off.

Sofia, in shift and skirt, holds up the pinned bodice and, frowning, examines where the pins have been placed. 'Do you think it'd be possible to set up a table?' she says. 'It'll be so much easier to do this if I can lay it flat.'

'I'll ask Vico.'

A table is found. Sofia, having detached the laced sleeves from the bodice, lays it out flat and quickly repositions Lidia's hastily placed pins so that they mark the line of the new seams-to-be with more accurate definition. Then she turns the bodice inside out.

'Oh, I do wish I still had my scissors,' she says with a sigh.

'Scissors?' Lidia has seated herself on the back steps of the wagon and is eating a torn hunk of bread.

'Mmm. I used to have a beautiful pair of tiny spring-scissors, made of steel. My mother gave them to me when I was a little girl and they were very small, very lovely and sharp as a razor. Just perfect for snipping away even the smallest of stitches. They had belonged to my grandmother before. But thanks to that horrible man in Modena, I left the city in such a panic that I had no time to collect anything – and my darling scissors were left behind.' Picturing her mother, she feels the familiar sharp pang at the thought of her loss.

'We've only got the one pair of shears,' Lidia says, pulling a doubtful face and shaking her head.

'Yes, I know. They're good and sharp, but they're much too big for this job. They'll cut away the excess cloth nicely when I'm done, but this'll take a knife. I'll go and ask Cosima.'

'No, don't worry, I'll get it.'

Lidia returns in a moment with a short-bladed knife with a carved wooden handle. Testing the blade against the ball of her thumb, Sofia smiles her approval.

Pins in place, she sits back down on an upturned barrel. Bunching the fabric of the bodice in her left hand, holding it up so that the sunlight falls on the stitched seams, Sofia fits the point of the little knife under the first stitch and flicks upwards, slitting through the thread with ease; then, working her way down first one side and then the other, she unpicks the two seams.

Repinning the bodice to fit her takes Sofia and Lidia a few moments of twisting and turning, arm-raising and pin-tweaking; once satisfied that it is now snug and comfortable, Sofia bundles it up in her arms and sits down on her barrel. Threading a needle, she tacks the two new seams in place with long stitches; then she takes the pins out and pushes them back into the waxed paper, returning the paper to the little box.

As always when she sews, her thoughts begin to wander. To Mamma, of course. Poor Mamma; Sofia wonders if she will ever lose the images burned into her memory on that last, dreadful day. What would Mamma think of her now: sitting here, stitching a dress in which she is going to walk onto a stage – as an actress? Her heart jumps at the very thought of it. She wishes, perhaps more than ever, that her mother were still here. How very much she would love to be able to tell her about finding Niccolò and being introduced to the troupe, about learning to act – and most of all about Beppe and her fragile, burgeoning hopes. What would Mamma have thought of him, she wonders?

She has been busily stitching for some time, and is now alone, humming to herself. Lidia has gone to help Cosima prepare the evening meal. One side seam is complete, the lining has been cut and fitted and neatly hemmed into place, and she is halfway through the second side, when a soft cough startles her.

She looks up.

Beppe is standing near, watching her intently; she has no idea how long he has been there. Seeing him, her cheeks flame and she puts a hand to her hair, which she knows is tangled and unkempt. She fiddles a curl back behind one ear.

'I've just been into town and I found something I thought you might like,' Beppe says. 'At the market.' He has a paper packet in his hands.

'For me?'

'Yes. Look.' Opening the packet, he shows Sofia the contents: two golden rings of what looks like gleaming and sugared bread. '*Ciambelle*,' he says.

'What are *ciambelle*? They look lovely.'

'You've never had a *ciambella*?' Beppe sounds astonished. 'Put that down for a moment' – he nods at the bodice – 'and we'll have one each. You'll love it.'

Sofia reaches across and lays the bodice on the table. Sitting cross-legged on the ground near her feet, Beppe hands her one of the rings. It is warm, and the sugar dusted over its surface glitters in the sunlight. Lifting it to her nose, Sofia sniffs it; she can smell yeast and butter, a sharp edge of lemon, and another sweet smell she does not recognize.

'Go on – try it!' Beppe says quietly, and she takes a bite.

It is delicious: doughy, softer and sweeter than bread. Smiling as she feels the sugar sticking to her lips, she raises a hand to brush it away, but Beppe leans quickly towards her and catches her wrist. 'No, stop! See how many bites you can take without brushing away the sugar or licking your lips,' he says, and his eyes are dancing. He is watching her mouth. 'I'll do it too. Let's see if either of us can eat a whole *ciambella* without licking.'

Sofia laughs. She takes another bite, and Beppe too begins to eat.

It is an almost impossible task, she quickly discovers. At every bite more sugar clings to her lips and the temptation to lick it away soon becomes almost unbearable. Beppe's mouth, too, is now covered with the stuff, and as she watches him struggling to resist the inevitable, it occurs to Sofia that she would perhaps prefer to lick the sugar from *his* mouth rather than her own.

This thought makes her feel as though her insides are dissolving.

Thus momentarily distracted, she forgets to resist, and Beppe laughs as she licks her lips. 'It's impossible, isn't it?' he says, licking his own, wiping his mouth with the back of his hand and then reaching over to brush the remaining sugar from Sofia's face. At his touch, her smile fades and she holds her breath, her gaze flicking from his eyes to his mouth and back.

Beppe too looks suddenly serious.

They stare at each other for several long seconds.

He moves a little closer and Sofia can feel his breath warm on her face. Tilting his face to one side, he touches her lips with his own, and the grains of sugar are gritty between them. Then a shout of laughter from within the wagon breaks the fragile threads that have quickly spun out between them and Beppe steps back.

Looking down at the remains of the *ciambella* in his hand and holding up the last little piece, he puts it into Sofia's mouth, brushing the crumbs of sugar away with great tenderness.

'Thank you,' she whispers. 'That was lovely.' She is not sure whether she means the *ciambella* or the touch of Beppe's fingers and lips on her face. 'I should finish my seams.'

Beppe nods, his expression still solemn. 'I'll fetch you something to drink. They make you thirsty, do *ciambelle*.' He sucks his fingers and thumb, one by one, still watching Sofia, then turns and walks away towards where Cosima and Lidia are preparing the food.

Her heart beating fast, her thoughts whirling, Sofia wipes her fingers carefully on a cloth, then picks up the part-mended bodice and begins once more to stitch. Her hands are trembling.

14

Malalbergo, not far from Bologna

It is nearing midday when the wagons of the Coraggiosi rumble
up into the piazza in the centre of the little town of Malalbergo,
some miles north of Bologna. The early autumn light is bright
and yellow, and the shadows of the wagons have deepened to
purplish-blue blots, distorting around the wheels and under the
bellies of the horses as they pick their way over the uneven sur-
faces of the roads.

A small but cheerful crowd has come out to greet the new
arrivals: perhaps fifty or sixty people have clustered in groups
along the road leading into the piazza, and the Coraggiosi wave
and smile in acknowledgement of the welcome. Beppe and Vico
are tumbling and clowning out in front as usual, and Cosima and
Angelo, on their pretty ponies, are trotting neatly behind the
wagons, scattering rose petals by the handful. Sofia, much to her
delight, is wearing the newly altered grey dress and walking just
behind Beppe and Vico, waving and smiling, and 'shooing' the two
men away when they double back and try to pester her, much to

the amusement of the watching crowd. Lidia, Agostino, Giovanni Battista and Federico, driving the wagons, are calling out the details of the coming performance.

Every now and again, Beppe catches Sofia's eye and her heart turns over. He is wearing his black mask now, and it is impossible to determine his expression, but the kisses he has blown her and the moment just now when he came close to her and whispered in her ear – '*You look so beautiful*' – have sent her pulse rate soaring and she is finding it increasingly hard to concentrate on staying in character.

There is a little more than an hour until it all begins. The stage is up, the properties are in place and a couple of tables and several benches have been set up in the space between two wagons, where the Coraggiosi have begun to prepare. Lanterns have been lit, for the light is poor this afternoon, and everyone is busy getting ready to paint their faces and put on their costumes.

'You're so lucky with your hair, *cara*,' Lidia says from her place on the bench next to Sofia. 'I wish mine were curly like yours. Then I wouldn't need . . . ' She pats an almost black, tightly curled, brightly beribboned pile of wool which lies limply on the table near to where she is sitting. 'It's so hot and scratchy. Now listen – we do each other's faces quite often, as we only have the one glass mirror. It's Cosima's and she hates to share it.'

Sofia looks across to where Cosima, hair scraped back behind a ribbon, is peering into a gilt-framed looking glass, frowning and poking at her chin with a finger.

'Ago bought it for her in Venezia a couple of years ago.' Lidia smiles at Sofia as she lays out an array of little earthenware pots, glass jars, bowls, scraps of sponge and torn squares of linen. 'All the other mirrors we have are metal, and not much better than useless.' She flaps a small square of polished steel towards Sofia. 'Would you like me to do your face for you? It's not that easy – not until you get used to it.'

Sofia opens her mouth to say yes please, when a noise startles her. She turns around; Beppe is standing behind her. 'I'll do Sofia,' he says, raising an eyebrow.

Lidia smothers a smirk and Beppe shoves her in the shoulder with the heel of his hand. 'Don't you start – apart from anything else, unlike you, I don't have my own face to do, do I?' He raises a hand from which is dangling his black leather mask.

'Do you want to use my paints? I can make room.' Lidia starts to shift along, but Beppe shakes his head.

'Thank you but no; I have some things out in the wagon which will do very nicely.'

Sofia puts her hands to her hair, fingering the untidy braids she made that morning and intending to make a start upon untangling them before Beppe returns, but he says, 'Your hair can wait a minute. Come on, lovely girl, come with me and help me find them. We're on in little more than an hour.'

Her heart jumping as he reaches for her hand, she gets to her feet.

'Things? What things?' Lidia is clearly curious. 'What are you talking about?'

Beppe grins. 'Oh . . . just some things,' he says cheerfully. 'Can I have a couple of your sponges when we get back, though, *cara*?'

Lidia nods, her wish for further information transparently obvious, but, jerking his head as an invitation to Sofia to follow him, Beppe taps the side of his nose with his finger, grins and set off towards the back of the smallest wagon, carrying one of the lanterns.

*

The interior of the smallest and shabbiest of the carts is cramped but neatly appointed. A bunk-like bed runs across the end furthest from the entrance, screened from the rest of the space by a faded curtain, which just now is pulled back and fastened with a ragged cord. Painted cupboards line both sides of the wagon up to about knee-height: these, Sofia always thinks, must once have depicted bright scenes of commedia performances, but after many years the pictures have chipped and scratched, and only the odd arm and hand and the bright splash of an islanded face are visible. Stacked on top of the cupboards are boxes and bags, poles and hooks, waxed paper packets and rolls of coloured cloth. An assortment of costumes hangs on hooks from the roof of the wagon, held back against the sides behind taut-pulled horizontal cords.

Beppe puts his mask down on the nearest cupboard top and Arlecchino's carved leather face grins at them, watching them both with what appears to be a rather lewd curiosity.

'Listen,' he says, breathing quickly. '*Cara* . . . I meant to wait – at least until after the show – but I don't think I—'

Breaking off, he takes Sofia's hands in his. Holding her in close with one hand behind her back, he strokes her hair away from her face with the other. Sofia puts her arms up and around his neck and before she can even draw a breath, his mouth is on hers. Closing her eyes, she breathes in the warm, woody smell of him as, backing awkwardly towards the bunk, still kissing her, Beppe pulls her with him and sits her down next to him on the rustling horsehair mattress. The hanging swag of the pulled-back curtain catches against his head; he pushes it out of his way.

Sofia puts a hand on either side of Beppe's face, pressing herself up against him, and the little sigh of pleasure she makes disappears into the kiss. She feels him stroke around her shoulder, down her back, down and round, down towards her legs, up over her belly and onto her breast; she gasps and he pulls her in more tightly.

Then the wagon jolts sharply as someone climbs onto the back step and Beppe and Sofia jump apart.

'Oh – sorry!' Vico's face is peering through the gap in the wagon's back flap. His attempts to smother a frankly lascivious grin are ineffective. 'Had no idea anyone was in here.' He coughs, to cover a laugh. 'I was, er, looking for my spare doublet; it was in the box under the bunk. No matter – I'll come back later. Um . . . don't forget we're on in an hour or so.'

And he disappears.

'Dear God in heaven,' Beppe mutters, staring up at the roof of the wagon and pulling Sofia in against him. 'Is it not possible to have a single moment's bloody privacy?'

Sofia is breathing heavily. Her lips are tingling and the skin of her whole body is buzzing, as though she has just scrubbed it hard with a rough cloth. Laying her hand back on Beppe's cheek, she lets out a breathy giggle and, at the sound of it, his scowl breaks into the familiar tilted grin and he plants another quick kiss on her mouth.

'Now, if Vico lives up to his reputation,' he says, 'this'll be common knowledge amongst the troupe before we've even left the wagon. He'll be back there this minute, telling them all . . .' Hesitating a moment, he adds, 'Will you mind if he does, *cara*?'

Sofia shakes her head.

'God, I'd been wanting to do that for days. I meant to wait, I really did, but in the end . . . I couldn't.' He holds her face in both hands and kisses her again, neatly and softly, on her mouth. His lips linger on hers for a second or two; then, with a murmur of pleasure, he tilts her face up towards his and looks hard at her, his gaze flicking from one eye to the other and back. 'I couldn't face a whole performance, holding that in. But it's just as well Vico came in; if he hadn't interrupted, I'd most likely not have been able to stop and then we'd not have had time to get your face done properly, my lovely girl. Come on, we have work to do.'

Beppe crouches down and opens a little painted door, reaches inside and picks out a soft leather drawstring bag. Pulling it open, he fingers through the contents; then, satisfied that everything he wants appears to be there, he stands and holds out a hand to Sofia.

Together, they climb back out of the wagon. Hand in hand, Beppe holding both the drawstring bag and his mask, they walk quickly back to the tables and benches, where everyone is now much quieter than usual, each intent on their own personal preparation.

Every head turns in their direction as they cross to the far end of the longer table; the new knowledge blazes clear in every face but no one comments. Sofia holds her breath, waiting for the laughter and the jokes, but no one speaks except Agostino, who says quietly but with great authority, 'You heard what I said just now, Coraggiosi. We have a show to put on in little more than moments. That is what we must concentrate on. Just that. Anything else . . . ' He pauses dramatically. ' . . . *anything* else will wait until the play is over. I'm sure you understand.'

Vico snorts, and Lidia kicks him. Agostino shoots him a look but says no more.

Everyone resumes his or her preparations.

Her cheeks burning, Sofia glances around.

Cosima's face is complete. Huge-eyed and pink-cheeked, she looks more beautiful than ever, Sofia thinks, watching her pull her hair back into a tight knot. The curled wig she will put on in a moment stands on a head-shaped block next to where she is sitting.

Agostino's face looks bleached and ghostly: the thick white paste is in place, but as yet, his features remain undefined. Contrasting with the bright bluish-white of his face, his teeth now appear discoloured. He is fiddling with a small finger-length stick of something black.

Lidia has resumed outlining her eyes, the tip of her tongue protruding as she concentrates, and Vico has gone back to polishing his leather mask with exaggerated care, teasing out its sheep's-wool moustache and checking the leather strings with which it will be fastened. There is something deliberate about the overstated tenderness with which he is running his fingers over its gleaming surface and, as he puckers his lips and plants a noisy little kiss onto the end of the leather nose, Sofia puts a hand over her mouth to stop herself laughing. Vico sees her and raises an eyebrow, but Lidia shoves him in the ribs with her elbow and he assumes an expression of great contriteness and continues polishing with extra vigour.

Federico and Giovanni Battista, who are sitting together on a bench at the far end of the longer of the two tables, are both, like Vico, preparing their masks, lovingly shining and tweaking them. Federico is rubbing up and down along the length of the extended – and unashamedly phallic – nose on his mask with a chamois cloth. Pushing his tongue out into his cheek for a moment, he flicks a quick glance in Beppe and Sofia's direction, then grins and winks, and resumes his polishing.

Beppe shakes his head, laughing silently; taking Sofia's hand, he squeezes her fingers.

Sofia glances across at Angelo, who is pouting into a mirror, turning this way and that as he inspects his face. His eyes too are huge, dark-rimmed and liquid. He has lost weight – he is thinner than he was when she first saw him, Sofia thinks now, though the new hollows in his cheeks merely make him look, if anything, more handsome than ever. He seems preoccupied, edgy, unrelaxed: one leg is twitching and he seems to be chewing at the inside of his lip as he studies his eyes in his little mirror. Something is disconcerting him. As Sofia watches, he pushes a hand down inside the neck of his doublet and scratches, screwing up his face with the effort. He sees her watching him in his mirror and turns to look at her; dropping his gaze to where her hand is still held in Beppe's, a scowl further distorts the perfect features. He turns back to his reflection.

'Well,' Beppe whispers almost soundlessly. 'I told you they'd all know. Vico didn't waste any time, did he? Now sit down, chick, and we'll start. Look, here.' As Sofia sits on one end of one of the benches, Beppe pulls a three-legged stool out from under the table and, sitting himself on this, facing Sofia, he takes from the bag two lidded wooden pots, a small glass bottle, a tiny spoon made of horn, a shallow earthenware dish and a wooden-handled, soft-bristled brush like a fat paintbrush. These he places on the bench beside Sofia. He unfastens the lids of the two pots with studied care, showing each to Sofia in turn. In one is a fine white dust, and in the other a powdery iridescence, which glitters in the lantern light. 'I picked these up in a market in Bergamo, years ago, and I've kept them safe all this time. I've never used them.'

'What are they?'

'This one's nothing special – it's chalk . . .' He picks up the pot containing the white dust. 'But this . . .' His smile broadens. 'This is crushed pearl.'

Sofia's mouth opens.

'I'm not going to do your face thick-white like Agostino's; Colombina doesn't need that – quite often Colombina and the *inamorata* don't make up at all, other than eyes and lips. But I want you pale and pretty, and I want to lift your eyebrows. I want you to sparkle. We'll just put the thinnest, thinnest layer of chalk on – if I wanted it heavy like Ago has it, I'd only put a drop of this in' – Beppe takes the little bottle and waggles it – 'with quite a lot of the chalk. Almond oil. It makes it like a paste. But for you, we'll keep it light. Just a little oil and the smallest, smallest amount of chalk.

Beppe then takes the brush and the little spoon and puts them next to where he has placed the two pots.

'Lidia,' he says, and his voice is loud in the hushed concentration of purpose. 'Can I have a couple of sponges?'

Lidia throws them across.

Beppe pours the oil into the dish; then, picking up the spoon, he adds a small scoop of the chalk dust, mixing it into a paste with his forefinger.

'Here,' he says. 'Eyebrows away first.'

Sofia leans in towards him.

Beppe tilts her face up, holding it still. He smears a little of the chalk paste along the line of Sofia's eyebrow, dips his finger again into the bowl, smears it again. He repeats the process on the other side.

'Good,' he says, leaning back and peering intently at his handiwork. 'Now shut your eyes.

Sofia does what he asks. She feels the pressure of his thumb beneath her chin, his fingertips holding against the side of her head. Then comes a damp softness – it must be one of Lidia's sponges – along the contours of her face, and the earthy smell of the chalk fills her nostrils. She coughs and opens her eyes.

He is very close to her and, thinking of their intimacy just now, she begins to feel as though she is melting all over again. He says quietly, 'Now listen: once I've finished your mouth, which I'll do in just a moment, you're not to kiss anyone until I tell you.'

Sofia whispers. 'But I don't *want* to kiss *anyone*. Only you.'

'Especially not me – you'll only get carried away and make a mess of all this work I'm doing. Why do you think none of the characters ever actually touch lips on the stage? Now pipe down . . .' He kisses the end of his forefinger and presses it onto her lips ' . . . and close your eyes again.'

Sofia bites down a smile and shuts her eyes.

The sponge again: cold and damp over cheeks, nose, eyelids, brows, chin. Beppe's breathing is slow and steady; he whistles softly as he turns her face first to one side, then the other, and his breath is cool against her damp cheek.

'That needs to dry now,' Beppe says. 'And then we'll do the pearl. When the light catches your face, you'll glitter and look adorable. Everyone will love you.'

Sofia opens her eyes. The chalk is tightening on her skin as it dries and she is already fighting an urge to scratch.

'Do you have a mirror? Lidia gave me a metal one, but I don't know where I've—'

'No. Wherever it is, you're not seeing yourself till I've finished.' He pauses. 'Eyes now.'

'What are you going to do with them?'

'Niccolò gave me a tiny pot of this reddish powder the other day: prepared with his usual magic from something he scraped off some stones by a stream near Modena, he said. God knows what it is, but it seems to work well – I've tried it on the back of my hand. I'll do your eyelids with it, then we can black in new brows – higher than your natural ones – and I'll outline your eyes too.'

Sofia cannot help it – she opens her eyes. 'What's the black?'

'Keep them closed. It's burnt cork. But the pearl needs to go on first.'

The brush lightly dusts the contours of her face: over her cheeks and nose, across her forehead, down under her chin and over her neck and collarbones; a faint, faint smell of brine prickles in her nose.

Beppe stops what he is doing and Sofia opens her eyes to see him rummaging in the drawstring bag. He brings out a small ivory pot, some inch and a half in diameter and three inches in length. Easing out the stopper, he takes from it a stick of cork about the thickness of Sofia's thumb, blackened and burnt; then, with a short-bladed knife, he sets to sharpening the end of the stick, nipping away carefully with the tip of the blade until he has honed a sharpish point. He wipes his hands carefully – backs then fronts – along his breeches and checks them, rubbing again until he is satisfied his hands are clean.

'Right,' he says. 'Now I need you to keep very still.' He holds her face again, thumb under her chin, middle finger high on her cheekbone. Forehead furrowed in concentration, he puts the end of the cork stick against Sofia's brow, and, pressing firmly, draws in an arc, high and arched. Crossing hands, he repeats the process with the opposite brow. Stands back. Assesses. Adds to the drawn brow-lines.

'Look up and keep very still. It might tickle.'

Sofia does what he asks. She feels the stick touch her eyelid and flinches.

'Try not to move.'

He tries again. Runs the cork along each lid next to her lashes, first above, then below her eye. Then, 'Look at me now, and let me see,' he says. His smile stretches as Sofia blinks at him. 'Oh that's good. That's very good. Now, a little treat to finish it off. Wait a moment.' He crosses to where Cosima is adjusting her wig. Crouching next to her, he asks her something Sofia cannot hear, and she smiles and nods, and points towards a small raffia punnet. He brings this back over and shows it to Sofia: in it is a handful of dark red berries. Picking one out, he lifts it to her mouth. 'Here – eat this.'

He puts it directly into her mouth, and the tips of his fingers touch her lips. He gives her another. Then, picking up a particularly large berry, he crushes it gently between finger and thumb. 'Lean forward,' he says, and he rubs the crushed berry over her lips. The juice is sweet and sticky. 'Bite your lip between your teeth; work that juice into it,' Beppe says.

Sofia complies.

'God, you look lovely. It's just as well we're not alone,' Beppe says quietly, 'Or I'd be wrecking all the hard work I've just done.' He appraises her face. 'There's one last thing.' He tips a tiny scoop of the chalk into his palm, then adds a pinch of the reddish powder. Mixing them, he dips the tip of the brush into the resultant pink dust and flicks this over the jut of Sofia's cheekbones.

He stands back to admire his handiwork. 'Do you know?' he says almost silently, his gaze flicking from one of Sofia's eyes to the other and back. 'I think I could eat you.'

'Can I see now?'

'No. Not yet – hair first. Here . . . ' Beppe fluffs Sofia's curls up with his fingers, teasing them out and round, fastening them at the back with pins. From his pocket he pulls a couple of ribbons, and makes as if to begin to thread them into Sofia's hair, but, seeing them, she reaches out and takes hold of his hand, saying, 'Wait. Wait a moment.' She hesitates. 'Can I go to the wagon and get something?'

'No, don't move. I'll get it. What is it?'

'In a little box in the patchwork bag under the bunk in the yellow wagon . . .'

'Yes?'

'There are two long dark red ribbons. I was given them just before I met you all – I've kept them safe since then, and I'd like to use them now, I think.'

Beppe raises an eyebrow.

Sofia smiles. 'Don't worry – it was only a boy I'd never met before, selling laces and ribbons and sleeves and things. Nothing more than that. He was just kind. That's all.'

'I'll believe you . . .' Beppe grins. 'Now don't move. I won't be a moment.'

He is back moments later with the ribbons in his hand. He holds them up and Sofia nods. Without a word, Beppe weaves the ribbons in and out of her hair and tweaks them so that the ends lie along the nape of her neck. Then, standing back, he appraises his handiwork. 'Cosima,' he says, 'Can she use your mirror for a moment?'

Cosima holds it out without looking around.

Beppe hands it over.

For a second it lies on her lap, a flattened ellipse, reflecting the sky. Then she lifts it, and the ellipse swells to a circle. A stranger looks back at her: a wide-eyed, surprised-looking stranger with wildly curly black hair. This unfamiliar woman looks oddly beautiful, Sofia thinks, nothing at all like her usual self. She turns to Beppe, whose broad smile of approval suddenly fades. He lets out a low whistle. 'You look enchanting,' he says very quietly, his gaze dipping to her mouth.

Then comes a whoop from Vico. 'Look at our new Colombina,

Coraggiosi!' he says loudly and cheerfully. '*Cara*, you look delicious! I'm not surprised Beppe can't keep his hands off you!'

There is a ripple of laughter. Everyone turns to look at her. Applause breaks out, and a jumble of affectionate praise. Sofia's face burns and she knows she must be colouring underneath the chalk. Her heart swells.

15

Yesterday's final two rehearsals went well, Sofia tells herself as she stands behind the backcloth, listening to the scene unfolding. Very well. She didn't forget a single line, and, according to Ago, did not put a foot wrong. There is no reason why she should not be able to remember everything, and perform as well now as she did then.

But she has reckoned without the noise of the audience: the laughing, the clapping, the oohing and aahing as the story of the play unfolds. From the other side of the backdrop it sounds to Sofia as though a thousand people must have gathered in the little piazza – though Lidia, who has been out there already, says it's perhaps a hundred. Oh dear God – a hundred people – watching *her*! She feels sick. Her heart is thudding in her throat, and her chest – tightly laced as it is into Colombina's pretty grey dress – feels so constricted she wonders that she can get a breath in at all. The chalk and pearl is making her eyes itch and she badly wants to rub them – or at least press against them with her knuckles – but Beppe has already taken her by the wrists twice, and told her firmly not to touch her face at all.

'You look perfect – and you certainly won't look anything like if you smear your eyebrows all over your face.'

Beppe is on stage right now; she cannot see him, but can hear him arguing with Federico. She looks up at the scenario board. Agostino's little *canovaccii* – the scraps of information that remind the actors which scenes are which, in which order – are all pinned in place. Because she still cannot read easily, Beppe has pointed out her scenes to her, marking them with a cross so that she can count the entrances and exits. Her first scene is imminent.

Sofia cannot decide whether the anxiety that is now flooding her head, her chest, her belly and her limbs is pleasant or not. At one moment, it feels horribly like that sickening terror she remembers so clearly as she ran for her life from that wet-mouthed, thick-necked man in Modena; and then the next, the sensation resembles more closely the swooping anticipation she feels in her insides now every time she thinks about Beppe. Is this confusion what the players experience every time they perform?

Cosima lifts the backcloth and steps off the stage, sucking in a long breath and slowly letting it out through pursed lips like a soundless whistle. She waggles her hands and closes her eyes. Opening them again, she smiles at Sofia. 'Any moment now . . . are you ready, *cara*?'

'Yes,' Sofia lies, trying to smile.

'You will be wonderful, my lovely,' Cosima says. 'We are so lucky that Niccolò found you and brought you to us. Enjoy it out there – everyone who is watching certainly will. One moment . . . there goes Vico. Now it's you. Off you go!' And with a swift, light kiss on Sofia's cheek, Cosima lifts the hanging to one side and puts a hand behind Sofia's back.

Not quite pushing her on to the stage, but almost.

Everyone assured her earlier that she would not be aware of the audience as individuals. *You'll hardly see them, in fact – best just to pretend they're not there*, they said. But as she takes her first step through the backcloth and out onto the trestle boards, she can see them all . . . every one of them . . . in minute detail . . . and they seem to suck the very breath from her lungs as she looks around at them.

Beppe has vanished off to the side somewhere. Giovanni Battista with his long black academic gown straining over the big padded belly and Federico in his long-nosed mask and a ridiculously exaggerated military jacket and hat are both staring at her.

'*There's Colombina. She'll tell us*,' Federico says stoutly, pointing at her. '*She'll know the answer*.'

'*Pooh, she's nothing but a green girl*,' Giovanni Battista says with a tut of dismissal. '*How could she know any more than we do?*'

'*That's the point, you fool – she's a* girl. *She'll know*.'

Giovanni Battista shakes his head. '*Very well. Signorina Colombina, tell us. Here is the problem: should a woman marry a military man . . . or an educated man? Brawn or brains? Bravado or wisdom? Which do you think is preferable? Beware – don't jump to any hasty conclusions: a woman's lasting happiness may depend upon your answer.*'

Sofia opens her mouth. For a second she has no idea what to say and she cannot imagine how she is even going to manage a wordless squeak, let alone the lines she cannot seem to remember. An endless moment hangs frozen in the air between her and the two men. And then she knows, and the lines are there, and she says, '*Brawn or brains? Hmm . . . let me think*.' Putting a finger to her lips, she contemplates the conundrum. '*Should I prefer unthinking muscle, or a well-read weakling?*'

Federico and Giovanni Battista take a step nearer as Sofia tries to make up her mind. They stand one on either side of her. She looks from the one to the other, sizing up the phallic nose on the one side and the rotund belly on the other. Then, running the tip of her tongue along her lip she says archly, smiling coquettishly at

Federico and touching his sleeve with the tips of her fingers, '*Brawn. Definitely brawn. A military man would be far more fun, I am sure – at least in the short term.*'

The audience laughs as one, and several people whistle. One man shouts out, 'I'm off to join the army!'

A heart-stopping moment. Sofia is standing behind the backcloth and listening to the conversation unfolding on the other side. She hears her own character's name mentioned: '*Colombina would never have been seen with such a villain!*' Beppe says stoutly, and for a breath-held second, her mind seems to empty completely. She stares at the *scenario* board, and, unable to read the scribbled *canovaccii*, finds that she is entirely unsure of which scene is coming next. Her head hollows and empties and she cannot imagine how she is going to be able to step through onto the stage. It is as though she has not rehearsed anything – she has no idea what comes next. She is about to let everyone down, and they'll never let her act again. Her heart begins to thud almost painfully and she has no idea what she should do.

Footsteps sound on the ladder behind her and she looks around. Angelo has arrived for his scene. Sofia glances at him, then turns back to the (to her) incomprehensible *scenario* board, inwardly cursing. Of all the members of the troupe, he is the last with whom she would wish to share her trouble. She is only on the stage with Angelo three times, it is true, so that narrows down the possibilities of what is coming next, but the three scenes are very different. Much though she has no wish to do so, she realizes she is going to have to ask him for guidance.

'Angelo,' she says in an almost silent whisper. 'I'm ... I'm afraid I'm not sure which *cano* comes next. I'm feeling a little muddled. I'm ... I'm ... ' She tails off, swallowing uncomfortably.

Flicking a brief but uncomfortably obvious glance at her breasts, Angelo taps the *scenario* board and says without smiling, 'Number twenty-three. You hear Cosima crying, start comforting her and then a couple of minutes later, I'll come out and . . .'

Nodding, the scene floods back into Sofia's mind, and, feeling slightly sick, she mutters, 'I'm sorry. I shouldn't have forgotten.'

Angelo raises an eyebrow. 'We've all forgotten things we ought to remember, at some point in our lives.' There is a flurry of applause from out front, and Angelo, listening intently, says, 'That's your cue . . .'

'More than halfway through,' Beppe whispers as he and Sofia stand together, behind the backdrop, listening to Agostino and Federico who are debating passionately on the stage. 'Not long to go and you'll be a fully fledged actress with a completed performance behind her. And a successful one at that.'

Sofia smiles, her lower lip caught between her teeth. Seeing this, Beppe is struck again by a fierce desire to kiss her. He takes her hand and grips it tightly. 'You've done so well, lovely girl. So well. I'm so proud of you.'

'I couldn't have done it without you.'

Considering this, head on one side, Beppe pushes out an appraising lower lip and says, 'No, I think that's a fair assessment – I'd say you're right there. I don't think you could have done.'

Smothering a laugh, Sofia goes to kiss him, but he grips her shoulders and holds her away from him, hissing, 'No! Stop it! You are not to spoil that lovely face. We can kiss all you like afterwards.'

The thought of this eventuality and what that kissing might lead to sends a juddering twist of longing down into his belly; quite distracted, he all but misses his cue. It is only when Sofia says, 'Go on!' and pushes him that he sucks in a short breath, pulls himself together and slips out through the backcloth.

The applause is still filling the little piazza as the actors straighten from their final bow and slip one by one through the gaps in the backdrop. Sofia's heart is racing. She has done it; she has fought her way through a whole performance, and, despite one or two moments of blood-chilling fear, has made no mistakes and has even, she dares to hope, pleased the audience. And, singing through her exhilaration, she hears again in her mind Beppe's words from an hour or so ago: *We can kiss all you like afterwards.*

Being the nearest to the gap in the backcloth, she is first off stage after the cast have all taken their bows. Agostino follows immediately behind her and he hugs her tightly. 'Magnificent, *cara*, magnificent! You were wonderful! Absolutely wonderful! We must celebrate!' He kisses the top of her head, releases her and moves on down towards the ladder.

Sofia stays where she is.

Cosima and Federico appear next, and each of them, too, embraces Sofia as they pass, and both congratulate her. Then Giovanni Battista and Vico push their way through the gap in the hanging. 'Well done!' they both say. Vico adds, 'Told you you could manage it perfectly well, didn't I?'

'You did.'

Vaulting down off the back of the stage, Vico holds a hand out to help Giovanni Battista negotiate the ladder; once the old man is safely on the ground, Vico leans on the ladder, waiting for Lidia. She, however, is busy hugging Sofia. The two stand close-clasped for a moment; then Lidia stands back, holding both of Sofia's hands in her own. 'You did it! You were wonderful, and I'm so happy for you.'

Sofia has to ask her again. 'You're sure you don't mind that I've taken—'

Lidia puts a finger up to Sofia's mouth to silence her. 'Stop it! You make a sweet, clever Colombina, and me? Well, I have thoroughly enjoyed spending the afternoon being a rude and lascivious old trout.'

Sofia laughs.

'Come on, hurry up, we need to get the brazier going and get some ale in.' Vico clicks his fingers and Lidia, smiling widely at Sofia again, hurries to the ladder to join him.

Sofia turns towards the gap in the backdrop.

And then Beppe is there, the last to exit the stage.

He pushes his mask up and off, knocking his black hat to the floor. His hair is damp and tangled, and he looks tired, but his eyes are shining. 'You were wonderful,' he says, putting his arms around her. 'Just wonderful.'

And at last their mouths meet.

Beppe puts one hand behind her head and one in the small of her back; she grips handfuls of the diamond-patterned jacket and presses in as close to him as she can without knocking them both off the edge of the stage.

'Oy!' someone calls. 'When you two come up for air, come and join us, will you?'

Taking his hand from Sofia's head, Beppe waggles his fingers in acknowledgement, but does not break off from the kiss, and by the time he and Sofia finally draw back from each other, the rest of the troupe have gone back to the wagons, the audience has all but dispersed and the piazza is empty.

Only one small boy can be seen, standing in the space behind the stage and staring up at the two of them. When Beppe catches his eye and grins at him, he pulls a face and runs away.

'Listen, lovely girl,' Beppe says now, running his thumb along her cheekbone. 'Tonight is going to be crowded. We're performing again tomorrow, so we won't be dismantling today – we'll be spending the night in the wagons so we can keep an eye on the staging . . .'

Sofia looks at him quizzically.

' . . . and . . . well . . . I don't want the first time we lie together to be in the wagons.'

Lie together? Sofia's heart skips a beat. She stares at him.

'You might have noticed that I always put myself on the far side of any room we've shared, or that I make sure I'm in another wagon to the one you're in . . .'

Sofia says nothing but nods, once. This has been a source of anxiety to her for many days.

'Don't think for a moment it's been because I've wanted to.'

She can feel her pulse racing.

Beppe holds her face in his hands. 'It's been because I've known I wouldn't be able to bear being that close to you if I had to . . . had to keep my hands off you.'

Now imagining Beppe's hands *on* her, Sofia swallows. The melting feeling in her belly intensifies.

'We're off to Montalbano after tomorrow's performance, aren't we? For our little holiday. We'll just have to get through tonight, lovely girl, and then we can find ourselves a quiet place to be alone there.'

Sofia stares up at him.

Behind the wagons, the celebrations are already ebullient. The audience, though not enormous, was generous and the takings were pleasing, so there has been a little more than usual to spend on the ale and food which always follow a show. A big wooden platter of meat and bread, a large round cheese, a bowl of apricots and several jugs of ale have been brought over from the tavern on the far side of the piazza, and the members of the Coraggiosi – clustered now on benches around a makeshift table – are already loud in their appreciation of all of it.

A couple of dozen stubs of candles have been stuck in pots and jars, or directly onto the wood of the table, and the glow from them underlights the faces of every one of the troupe. Wisps of smoke spiral up into the dusk.

Sofia and Beppe slide in next to Lidia on one side of the table, and the rest of the troupe applaud their arrival enthusiastically. As Beppe puts an arm around Sofia, she leans her head against his shoulder, smiling shyly at the exuberant welcome, feeling as happy as she can remember being. Ippo the dog, who has slid out from the yellow wagon, has put himself under the table at their feet. His head is hot and heavy on her lap. She absentmindedly scratches his ears and hears him groan softly – a little husky exhalation of pleasure.

'I say it again, and I will say it *con gusto* to whoever cares to listen, for however long I can hold their attention: you were magnificent, Sofia! Entirely magnificent!' Agostino has already consumed a fair amount of ale, even in the few short moments that Sofia and Beppe were otherwise occupied on the back of the stage, and he is now gesticulating widely to emphasize his words. On each *magnificent* he thumps the table with a fist and ale slops from several cups onto the scrubbed wood.

The others clap and Lidia leans across and gives Sofia a quick kiss on the cheek. Beppe's arm tightens around her.

'Was it as terrifying as you had expected?' Cosima says, and her face is full of affectionate pride.

Sofia bites her lip, smiling. She nods and everyone laughs.

'But you rose to the occasion, like a consummate professional, and conquered your fears!' Agostino proclaims. 'I'd like to propose a toast, firstly to Sofia – the newest and certainly the bravest member of the Coraggiosi – in fact a true *coraggiosa* herself! And then to our dear and absent friend, Niccolò Zanetti, for bringing this little girl to us in the first place.' He raises his cup, and everyone follows suit.

'How about a song?' Vico suggests.

There is a murmur of agreement.

Scrambling out from his place at the table, Vico disappears, returning a moment later with his guitar. He spends a few seconds fiddling with the tuning pegs and picking at the strings, then pats the rounded end of the instrument and looks enquiringly around the gathering. 'Well? Any suggestions?'

'How about "I Didn't Dare Say It"?' Federico suggests. 'Or that one about banking?'

'Banking?' Beppe asks, frowning.

'"Hor Vendut'ho la Speranza", I think it's called,' Federico says. 'You know – where the man says he's invested heavily in the hope of being loved, but his investment has gone down the drain.'

Beppe shrugs. 'Don't know that one.'

'Oh no, that sounds *far* too miserable for such a *joyous* occasion,' Agostino says. 'Vico, let's have "I Didn't Dare Say It" and we can all enjoy some good honest cuckoldry.'

Everyone laughs.

Vico picks at the strings of his guitar and, in his clear, carrying tenor voice, starts to sing. Lidia soon joins him. The song is tuneful, easy to pick up and delightfully rude, and before long the rest of the troupe – and half a dozen passers-by who have heard the celebration and come to share in it – are joining in the refrain.

'Where are you all staying tonight?' somebody booms as the song draws to a close and a sustained bout of applause breaks out.

Sofia turns and sees a big, cheerful man with his arm around a woman not much smaller than he is.

'Here in the wagons, signore,' Agostino says, waving his cup of ale in the vague direction of the cluster of carts behind him.

'But I have a room you can use! Can't have such extraordinary artists camping out in their carts! Not in our town – it would be a disgrace!'

'We do it all the time, signore,' Cosima says, smiling her wide, slow smile and looking, Sofia thinks now, more beautiful than ever in the low and flickering candlelight. 'We think nothing of it. And besides, we need to be here to keep an eye on our belongings.'

'All of you? Surely not.'

Agostino considers. 'No, now you mention it, perhaps not all. Perhaps some of us *could* take you up on your kind offer. In fact,' he says, his frown breaking into a wide smile, 'I think it's fair to say that you are generosity personified!'

'I can fit – oh, say, four of you comfortably in my downstairs chamber.'

Agostino looks around the troupe. 'Sofia, you deserve a warm night. And you, Cosima, *cara*, and Lidia. Giovanni Battista, as our elder statesman, go too, and try to keep the girls under control.'

Giovanni Battista gets to his feet and bows solemnly to Agostino, his face set in an expression of mock determination. 'I shall, signore,' he says in a ringing voice, 'do my very best – or shall perish in the attempt!'

A spatter of laughter.

Sofia turns to Beppe, having no wish to be parted from him. But he squeezes her hand and says quietly into her ear, 'Go and get a good night's sleep, lovely girl. Make the most of it. We'll . . . find a quiet corner to be alone tomorrow.'

16

The little hill town of Montalbano

'Just the two rooms I have free this evening, my friends,' the ale-man says, jerking his head towards the stairs. 'And you're welcome to both of them. Don't worry, you'll all fit in – all my beds are wide – well known for their generous width in and around Montalbano, I think you'll find. There's two beds in the bigger of the rooms. And I have blankets a-plenty, so you certainly won't be cold. It's indeed a pleasure to see you all again, signori and signore, if I may say so. It must be several years since . . .'

'It's a pleasure to be here. We're all most grateful, signore – and of course particularly delighted to hear about the width of the beds – which, I have to tell you, are legendary across Emilia-Romagna,' Agostino says, inclining his head in decorous thanks. Vico doubles over, coughing to hide the laughter he cannot prevent, and Lidia kicks him in the leg. Sofia, though, is not laughing. She has caught Beppe's eye and, at his quick smile, she is thinking of the 'quiet corner' he said he would try to find for the two of them and of what they might do there. Not one word of Agostino's conversation with the ale-man has she taken in.

The little tavern is crowded and noisy, and a pleasing savoury smell – some sort of stew, Sofia presumes now – hangs in the air above the tangle of conversations, luckily stronger than the acrid odour from the various animals in the room. Several chickens are pecking hopefully at fallen food on the rush-strewn floor, a couple of cats have perched on top of a crumbling *credenza*, their paws neatly tucked in under their chests, and, over by the wide hearth-stone, a large and very hairy black pig lies flat, its eyes closed, the only sign of life the rise and fall of its belly and the occasional twitch of a sharp-toed trotter.

Many heads turn and watch as the Coraggiosi cross the room together and seat themselves at one end of a long table near the fire. Beppe's dog sniffs briefly at the pig, but backs away hurriedly when it raises its huge head from the floor and opens a baleful little eye to glare at the intruder.

The troupe is loud in its enjoyment of the food, the ale, the warmth, the company, and, within minutes, the attention of every-one in the room has focused itself upon the Coraggiosi's table, and other conversations have died to a mutter. Sofia wonders what these hill-dwellers must think of their exuberant, brightly col-oured, voluble visitors. She can imagine what she would have thought of them herself, had she been sitting here in this room, watching them – can imagine the curious envy that would have filled her, looking at such high-spirited camaraderie. She smiles like a cream-fed cat to think that she is now a part of it, that she belongs to them, that she is now an actor, that she has been soundly kissed by the anarchic and irresistible Arlecchino – and that he, Beppe, has promised her that the two of them will spend some time alone together this very night. Squashed in between Beppe and Giovanni

Battista at the table, Sofia looks sideways at him as he throws back his head and laughs at a joke of Vico's; a hot little thread wriggles down into her belly at the thought of what the night might hold.

Beppe catches her eye. Smiling, he grips her thigh under the table and the hot thread tugs. She lays a hand over his, her fingers falling into the gaps between his and his grip tightens for a second.

'Giovanni Battista, this was a *tremendous* suggestion of yours. I, for one, cannot think of a more congenial place to spend our well-earned days of rest,' Agostino says, his booming voice interrupting Sofia and Beppe's moment of intimacy. Giovanni Battista smiles and nods as he takes a long draught of ale.

Vico leans across the table and says, 'Beppe, how do you fancy doing a bit of nonsense to earn a few extra *baiocchi*?'

'Like what?'

'I don't know . . . we could do the juggling *lazzo* from *The Other Doctor* – you know, where you juggle and I keep pinching one or other of the bits and pieces you're juggling with.'

Beppe's gaze shifts from Vico to Sofia. His raised eyebrow is eloquent: *Are you happy if I do?* She nods and smiles. Beppe says to Vico, 'Do you have anything to juggle with? The bag of balls is out in the wagon and I can't be bothered to—'

'Bound to be something. Wait a moment.' Glancing around the room and jumping up from his seat, Vico reaches up to the shelf above the fire and takes down an age-shining knot of wood the size of a child's fist and a tin cup. Beppe picks a couple of fat plums from a bowl and lifts a bread roll from a nearby dish. 'Shall we announce it, or just start?' he says.

'Oh, just start, I think, don't you?'

Beppe runs a covert hand along Sofia's thigh below the table before getting to his feet and edging out to stand in an empty space on the tavern floor. Sofia touches his fingers as he goes. Vico passes

Beppe the wood and the cup, and Beppe begins to flip everything up into the air and catch it again deftly.

The room falls silent.

Beppe sends the objects up one by one, then in pairs, flips one higher than the rest, passes one behind his back. Vico, meanwhile, having seated himself cross-legged on the table nearby, now swings his legs around and stands. Affecting to look unconcerned, and whistling softly between his teeth, he edges nearer and nearer to where Beppe is standing, casting deliberately shifty glances in his friend's direction; then, so swiftly that a blink might have hidden his movement, he darts out a hand and snatches one of the plums from the whirling circle.

An old man claps loudly, and several other drinkers murmur their admiration. Somebody whistles.

Beppe manages to continue juggling with the rest of the objects, though with a wild look of aggrieved annoyance on his face – as though it's impossible for him to stop, despite Vico's pilfering of his plum; as though the things are sailing through the air of their own volition. He chatters nonsensically at Vico, who now holds the plum up before a wide-open mouth, as if about to bite into it; he admonishes Vico, gesturing with jerks of his head to ask for the return of his fruit. Vico refuses, plum still held up ready.

The tavern drinkers are laughing now.

Beppe demands again more loudly, and this time Vico shrugs and, turning away, flips the plum over his shoulder back to Beppe, who incorporates it immediately into the cascade of thrown objects, with a nod of smug satisfaction.

More laughter and a spatter of applause. A couple of drinkers bang their mugs on the table.

'He's very clever, is he not?'

Sofia starts as Angelo seats himself in the space next to her on the bench, vacated by Beppe.

'Yes, he is,' she answers politely, inwardly cursing as she feels her colour rise. She flicks a glance at him before turning once more to watch the performers.

'You seem to have been spending a great deal of time with him recently.'

Sofia glances sideways at Angelo again. 'Yes, I suppose I have. But then you know that Beppe's been teaching me what I need to know for playing Colombina,' she says, uncomfortably aware of the way in which Angelo's gaze is continually flicking downwards to the upper edge of her bodice.

'Of course.'

A moment's heavy silence.

Angelo speaks again. 'And much of that teaching has had to take place in private, in the backs of wagons, so I understand.'

Sofia grits her teeth and says nothing. Her heart is beating faster.

'It's probably not the best idea to get too close to him.' Angelo runs the tip of his middle finger along Sofia's wrist and down the back of her hand.

She snatches her arm away, fully intending to ignore this remark, but a little cold wire of anxious curiosity winds itself around her until she cannot bear to remain silent. 'Why do you say that?'

Angelo twitches down an unpleasantly satisfied smile. 'Ah, well, I shouldn't wish to affect your work with such an effective . . . *teacher* . . . but . . . ' He tails off.

'But *what*? What are you trying to say?'

Raising both hands, palms forward, as though to pacify her, Angelo says, 'Oh, just that it has to be said that one cannot ever fully escape one's parentage, and—'

'Parentage? What do you mean?' Sofia stares at Angelo. His expression is calculating, and his eyes are unnerving her. Close to like this, the whites seem reddened and the pupils huge – he looks ill, she thinks now. His breath, too, is stale and sour, and his hands, still raised, are trembling slightly.

'Has he not told you?' Angelo says.

'What? Told me what?'

A volley of applause from the watching drinkers drowns Angelo's muttered reply. As Vico and Beppe come back to sit once more with the troupe, Angelo stands up, wincing as he does so. Bending towards Sofia, he says softly into her ear, 'I knew his father, years ago. It was not an acquaintance I valued – Signor Bianchi was not an admirable man. I just think you might one day come to regret your choice, that's all.' He pauses. 'If you ever do – regret it, that is – let me know, won't you? I wouldn't hold it against you.'

Open-mouthed, Sofia stares at him. Angelo raises an eyebrow; then, edging his way sideways between the jumble of tables, he leaves through the door to the upstairs rooms. Sofia cannot tear her eyes from where he has vanished.

Beppe sits back down on the bench seat next to her. Reaching out, he picks up a large cup of ale and takes a long draught. 'What did you think?' he says, smiling and taking her hand under the table. '*A bit of nonsense*, as Vico said, don't you think?'

Sofia has no idea what to say.

'What? What is it?' Beppe is frowning, clearly aware of the change in her demeanour. 'What's happened?'

Sofia looks back towards the tavern door, unsure what to say or do. She feels the pressure of Beppe's fingers on hers, sees the newly anxious look in his eyes. 'I . . . er . . . it was . . . it was Angelo. He . . .'

Beppe's expression darkens. 'What's he said?'

'I don't really know . . . but . . .'

Beppe stands. 'Come with me.'

He leads her out of the tavern, out through the side door, past the big barn where the horses have been stabled and on into the sudden silence of a steep lane which leads away from the town up into the heavily wooded hills beyond. The night air is chill on Sofia's face and the road is treacherous with loose stones which turn and scuff under their shoes as they walk. A fox barks into the stillness. Turning to look at her, Beppe stands with both her hands enfolded within his own. 'Now: what has he said that's so upset you?'

'Something about you – about your father . . . He said he knew him. Years ago.'

Beppe says nothing.

'I didn't know what he meant by it.'

Staring up into the branches of the nearest tree, Beppe mutters, 'God, he must be very drunk to bring that up.'

'Please, Beppe, what is it? What was he talking about?'

Beppe lets go of Sofia's hands and runs his fingers up into his hair. He stands there for several seconds, elbows winged wide; then, suddenly dropping his gaze to his boots, he folds his arms over his head for a moment, each hand holding the opposite elbow. The gesture gives him the look of a frightened little boy, and Sofia is struck by a fierce desire to hug him. But she stands still and waits.

After several endless seconds, Beppe straightens and starts to speak in a flat voice quite unlike his own. 'My father used to work in the kitchens in the great house owned by Angelo's family. The Castello dei Fiori, a few miles outside Bologna. He and I lived in a couple of rooms on the estate with some of the other kitchen staff. It was just the two of us – my mother died when I was little.

Angelo and I were not far off the same age and – God, it's hard to believe now – we liked each other. We spent most days together. We'd fish in the streams, set traps for rabbits, try to teach the estate dogs tricks, practise tumbling . . . things like that.' He looks up at her for a moment. 'Angelo's father knew nothing about our friendship, mind. He'd have forbidden it if he had – wouldn't have wanted the son of the second cousin of the Duke of Ferrara messing about with the . . . the unwashed offspring of a widowed kitchen drudge.'

Sofia stares, saying nothing.

Several long seconds pass.

'My father drank pretty heavily. He'd always been partial to his ale, but it got much worse when my mother died. He'd get into easy rages when he had had a few too many, and he was a big, heavy man. I became used to dodging out of the reach of his fists. He never meant anything by it, but after he broke my nose one time, I decided it was safer just to keep out of his way when he was in his cups. It eventually reached the point where Papa was sodden with ale more often than not. I don't know how he managed to keep his job, to be honest.'

He pauses again, and examines his hands for a moment. He is breathing deeply with long, slow, measured breaths. He looks up at her. 'Angelo and I were in the kitchens one afternoon. I was about twelve, he a year or so older. We'd been out all day and were hungry and I had suggested that we try to wheedle some food out of my father rather than wait until the evening meal. He would often find stuff for us. We were lurking in a corner together, laughing at nothing, waiting for him to cut us some slices from a leg of ham, when a fight broke out. This other man – no one I knew – said something derogatory about Papa's drinking – as well he might have done, to be honest – and Papa swung round and lashed out at him. Caught him hard on the jaw. It must have hurt – he staggered backwards, but stayed on his feet. And, even as Angelo and I stood there and watched, he hit back. He was clearly a capable fighter – far better than Papa. Papa tried to keep his end up, but he was very drunk and before long the other man was wasting him. It was awful. Everyone in the kitchen was shouting and yelling, spurring the fight on, goading them both as if it was a bloody cock-fight or something – and then the other man pulled a knife.'

Sofia's hands are over her mouth.

'They both fell to the ground and rolled over and over and that knife was flashing in the torchlight, and then it got dropped and picked up again, and I don't know exactly what happened, but someone cried out – this terrible, animal howl – and I thought it was Papa. I thought he'd been stabbed. But it wasn't. It was the other man, and Papa had knifed him.'

Beppe swallows and draws in a long, trembling breath.

'He died – that other man – died in a lake of his own blood. There in the castle kitchen. And they took Papa away and said that he had murdered him.' He shakes his head. 'But he wasn't a murderer. He was trying to save his own life. I saw it all.' His voice cracks as he adds, 'And Angelo saw it too, and he knew what the truth of it was, and he could have spoken up – I still think he could have stopped what happened. I couldn't do a thing, but him, with his father being who he is, he could have stopped it. He didn't, though. He said nothing.'

'Oh, Beppe.' Sofia's voice comes out as a cracked whisper. 'What did happen?'

'They locked Papa up. There was some sort of trial, I suppose, but it was all behind closed doors and I had no idea what was said. First I heard, they were talking about hanging him, but right up until the last moment, the rumours were rife that they were planning on commuting the term to banishment. A couple of other people had been banished instead of hanged, and I thought it would be the same for Papa. I had our bags packed and I was ready to meet him and leave the area. I didn't know where we'd go – I just wanted to get us both away. But whether they changed their minds, or whether it had been planned that way all along, the moment came and . . . rather than release him, they hustled him out, past where I was standing waiting, to the outskirts of the city where they'd scrambled together a makeshift gibbet. And they hanged him there. In front of me. They didn't do it very well . . . and he took most of the morning to die.'

Beppe looks upwards and swallows. The undignified jostling of the howling crowd as they pushed and barged along the short road to the gibbet is as clear in his head as the day it happened: his father all but insensible with terror in their midst, panting and whimpering, his feet dragging in the dust. Beppe clutches the bags he has packed, watching helplessly from the side of the road. And then come those terrible, sickening jerks and twitches as his father hangs, pissing and shitting himself, his face darkening, his neck stretching out beyond the believable – on and on for what seemed like hours.

'I struggled to reach him, pushing at the crowds, trying to get through. God, it sounds so terrible, but I wanted to tug down on his legs to finish it all quickly, but they fought me back, kept me away from him. I was only twelve – there wasn't much I could do. I couldn't bear to look but couldn't make myself turn away. And Angelo was there. He stood there and watched it all. I saw him, a little way off. I know he could have stopped it. He could have gone to his father.

'They left his body up on the gibbet . . . for nearly three weeks,' he says to the sky. 'Food for crows, they told me he'd be. An example to everyone. And they grinned at me when they said it. He stayed there until finally he was unrecognizable even as a human being, and then – only then – did they let me cut him down.' He hesitates, trying to push from his mind the truly unbearable image – the worst one of all. This one he cannot describe aloud.

Nausea is thick in his throat and he retches as he climbs onto an upturned barrel he has dragged from a nearby tavern. The body turns slightly in the breeze – this thing that was once his father – and the eyeless, shredded, dark red face glares at him for a moment, sighing out a smell of rotting meat. His breath coming in short, sickened gasps, Beppe screws his eyes shut and reaches up above the body, grabbing hold of the rope in one hand. He holds a short-bladed knife in the other, and with this he begins sawing at the rain-stiffened rope. It takes several minutes, longer than it might because he has to keep stopping and turning away to breathe, not wanting to inhale the foul odours of the body, but after what seems a lifetime, several strands of the rope give way at once and the body lurches downwards.

Beppe smothers a sob.

Crying openly now, he resumes his work with the knife; the final strands are severed and the body drops to the ground, flopping against the side of the barrel and almost knocking him backwards.

He wipes his eyes and nose with the heel of one hand.

'Poor Papa. He had many faults, but he didn't deserve to die like that.'

Her face now glazed with tears, Sofia puts her arms around him and holds him tightly. His cheek on her hair, they stand close-clasped for several minutes.

'I had had to leave the castle, of course, as soon as my father died,' Beppe says into Sofia's hair. 'There was no job there for me – God, I wouldn't have stayed if there was! I couldn't wait to get away from the place.'

'What did you do? How did you live?'

'I stayed nearby until . . . until. . . until they let me have the body. One of the castle groundsmen let me stay with him. Felt sorry for me, I suppose. I went every day to the *podestà* to ask if I could cut Papa down – I hardly ever dared go near the body, though. I'd look from a distance, feeling sick, apologizing to him, telling him I loved him. Then . . . after . . . I took myself back to Bergamo. We'd lived there before, and my mother's parents were there and I went to them. I didn't see Angelo again for years – not until the moment I realized just who our new and handsome *inamorato* really was when he presented himself to the troupe a couple of years ago. The recognition was as unpleasant for him as for me, I reckon.'

Sofia's mind is teeming with horrible images she cannot banish, and Beppe's description of his father's last appalling moments is ringing in her head. She says, 'How long after your father . . . died . . . did you decide to be an actor?'

'Not long. The Gelosi came to Bergamo that summer and that was the first time I'd ever seen a troupe perform. I'd always been able to tumble and juggle and that, and the moment I saw their Arlecchino, I knew that was what I had to do – who I had to be. It'll sound strange perhaps, but after everything that had happened, I wanted to laugh. Wanted to make other people laugh. I needed to be funny. And – there's another thing. I liked the fact that I would be able to hide behind that mask.' He pauses. 'I asked them straight out if I could join them, but they said no.'

'Why?'

Shrugging again, Beppe says, 'I knew before I asked that they'd refuse. I didn't want to play any other character than Arlecchino, so I knew there'd be no place for me.' He smiles ruefully. 'I asked anyway though, just in case their Arlecchino – he's still with them: a brilliant man called Simone da Bologna – might have said he was thinking of leaving. But of course he wasn't.'

'And what happened then?'

'Nothing – till the following year. The Coraggiosi came to the town, and I went to three of their shows – followed them right out to Brescia in fact, pleading with them a dozen times a day to take me on.' He huffs a short laugh. 'I must have looked so pathetic: demonstrating my juggling and dancing and tumbling for them right there in the street, over and over again. I think they took me on to shut me up, in the end.'

Sofia presses in against Beppe's side, relishing the weight of his arm across her shoulders. 'But what about their old Arlecchino? What did he think of you being taken on?'

'It was a bit like with you and Lidia, I suppose. He was out-growing the role, getting too old to manage all the *lazzi*, and I think he was really glad to go, in the end. He lives in Ravenna now; we see him from time to time when we pass through.'

'But when Angelo turned up and you realized who he was, what did you think? What did you do? Did you tell Agostino about him? Why did Angelo stay when he realized who you were? Did you think about leaving?'

Sucking in a long, long, shivering breath, and speaking through it as it sighs out again, Beppe stares back up at the sky. 'I had no idea it was him at first. We'd both changed so much since we had last seen each other – I'd only been twelve, and he thirteen or so when I left the Castello dei Fiori. He had already signed over his money to Ago before we found out each other's names and he realized who I was. Lidia told me she'd heard him pleading with Ago to take him – he was so desperate to join a troupe and had apparently tried several, including the Gelosi, but no one had had room for him. We didn't either, really, but we were so short of money it seemed like a godsend, Ago said later. I suppose after making such a fuss, Angelo would have felt ridiculous saying he wanted to leave again straight away.'

Sofia nods, believing this. 'Why didn't you tell Ago though? Why didn't you say what had happened?'

Beppe pushes his fingers up into his hair. 'You want the simple truth? I was afraid to. I hadn't been with the troupe that long myself. I was afraid Ago might tell *me* to leave rather than the son of a cousin of the Duke of Ferrara, who had just given him a dirty great bagful of *scudi*. I could imagine him not wanting the scandal of a murder to affect the troupe's reputation. So I said nothing.' He pauses. 'I've never told anyone any of this in fact.'

Tears are slick on Sofia's cheeks, and she is shivering. The night air is chilly. Realizing how cold she is, Beppe stops. Unfastening the laces of his old doeskin doublet, he takes it off and wraps it around Sofia's shoulders. 'Come on,' he says, 'let's go back. You're frozen.'

Relishing the quiet intimacy of the tree-lined pathway, though, Sofia is reluctant to return to the bustle of the tavern. 'Do we have to? I'd rather stay out here with you.'

Beppe stares at her. 'God, I'm so glad you ran into Niccolò that day, little seamstress. I don't know what I'd do without you now.' He tilts his head sideways and kisses her, putting his hands inside the doublet, which hangs oversized, sleeves dangling. Sofia presses up against him, wrapping her arms tightly around him, and the doublet slips off her shoulders and falls to the ground. His mouth is on hers and he is stroking her hair, her neck, her shoulders, her arms, kissing her as though he cannot get enough of her – and then he slides one hand around onto the tightly laced, stiffened front of her dress. He stops. Looks at her. Runs a finger along inside the top edge of the bodice, pulling it gently outwards. He swallows. 'We do really need that quiet corner I mentioned before,' he says softly. 'We can try and find somewhere when the others go to bed.'

Sofia's eyes widen.

Vico and Federico are both smirking when Beppe and Sofia appear in the doorway to the tavern a little while later, their grins widening as the pair cross the tavern: she and Beppe have clearly been the subject of recent discussion. Sofia sees Lidia nudge Vico hard with her elbow and frown at him. Squeezing her fingers, Beppe says quietly, 'Go and sit with Lidia and Cosima, will you? I'm really not in the mood for Vico's jokes. We'll find our private place later, when they all go to bed.'

'Been taking the air, have you, *amici*?' Vico says loudly, the tip of his tongue pushing a bulge out into the curve of his cheek.

Beppe answers flippantly as Sofia edges in behind the far end of the table, and Lidia shifts along to let her sit down. She raises an eyebrow, and Sofia can feel herself blushing, but Lidia says nothing.

The evening has stretched into night, the tavern fire is no more than cooling ashes and all but a couple of the drinkers have left the building. The Montalbano ale-man is wiping his tables with a grubby grey cloth and an air of detached fatigue. As the room has emptied, the Coraggiosi have quietened and their conversations are now little more than muttered asides. Giovanni Battista is asleep at the table, snoring, his grizzled head on his arms.

Beppe is watching Sofia. She is leaning against Lidia, her feet curled up under her; her eyes are dark-rimmed and heavy-lidded with tiredness, and her cheeks have pinked up from the earlier heat of the fire. She has been watching him covertly ever since they came in from outside and every time she has caught his eye, his guts have turned over on themselves. She looks very young, very sweet and very pretty, he thinks – and he wants her very badly. Her tenderness as she clung to him after his terrible admissions earlier on has moved him, and his wish to wrap himself around her and make her a part of himself is becoming almost painful in its intensity.

He cannot wait to be alone with her; he is longing for this endless evening to end and for everyone to leave the two of them in peace. The familiar jumble of bodies he knows there will be in the tavern rooms upstairs when they all go up will be unbearable to him tonight – like tight-pressed puppies in their dam's nest, they'll be at least three or four to a bed, breathing, snoring, rustling, fidgeting – and on top of that he doesn't know in which room Angelo may already have settled himself. His company would be particularly unwelcome. He and Sofia will definitely have to search out some quiet space where they can be alone.

He does not think he can wait much longer.

In all the nights that Sofia has been with the troupe, as he told her after the show in Malalbergo, he has deliberately not lain next to her, wherever they have been staying, be that wagon or tavern or stable. To be in close proximity to her and not reach out for her, to feel the warmth of her body next to his and not respond: it would have been impossible. And so he has resisted, he has avoided temptation and kept away, not wanting to rush her, not wanting to make her anxious, not being sure how she felt until the other day. But now . . . now that they have kissed so intensely, now that he has learned what her small and pliant body feels like in his arms, now that he is certain that Sofia wants him as much as he wants her ... that has made everything feel very different.

It is getting ever harder for him to sit still – one leg is twitching, he has chewed the skin around his thumbnail until it is sore, and has shredded at least three pieces of bread into crumbs which now lie scattered across the table in front of him. Somehow managing to join in the various conversations which are still quietly buzzing, Beppe sweeps the crumbs up into little piles, scatters them again, re-forms them; then he swirls a shining pattern of spilled ale around them with his finger, glancing over at Sofia every few seconds.

Finally, after what seems to him like hours, the troupe get to their feet, shrugging on doublets, hitching crumpled breeches and skirts, rubbing tired eyes and smothering yawns. Seeing Sofia watching him, Beppe raises his eyebrows at her and, with the smallest jerk of his chin, asks her to wait for him. He sees her nod once and, as she comes over to him, he strokes down the back of her hand, hooking her index finger up with his own. His heart thudding uncomfortably, he is about to tell her to go up with the others, and then to make some excuse to return back down here to the tavern room, when Vico, coming up behind her with Lidia, puts an arm around Sofia's shoulders and scoops her away from him, starting to shepherd her towards the door to the stairs. 'Come on, *cara*,' he says, 'we'll find you a comfortable spot. Place like this, with decent beds, it's always worthwhile getting up there quickly so that you can choose where you sleep. Isn't it, Beppe?' He turns to him. 'Coming?'

Breathless with flaring irritation, Beppe sees the smirk firmly in place on his friend's face and notes the startled anxiety on Sofia's. He hesitates. If he openly challenges Vico now, squashes him with a joke, as he knows he could; if he were to snatch Sofia away from Vico and tell him that the two of them are planning on finding a place to sleep elsewhere . . . alone . . . then he is almost certain that Sofia's embarrassment will smother any desire she might be feeling: it would no doubt put paid to any . . . any *intimacy* they might have in mind. It will spoil everything. Bloody Vico. Fond as he is of him, Beppe would like nothing more than to floor his friend with a well-aimed punch right now, but, swallowing down his frustration, he manages a semblance of a grin and, reaching out, he takes Sofia's hand. Squeezing it, in what he hopes will feel like reassurance, he says, 'He's quite right, *cara*. We don't want to let Federico or Giovanni Battista take all the best places. Come on.'

17

Sebastiano da Correggio stares down at Maddalena, who lies curled on the floor at his feet, her arms wrapped protectively around her belly. 'You have to be mistaken.'

Maddalena does not reply.

Sebastiano kicks her hard in the hip with the flat of the sole of his boot. She cries out, but he takes no notice. 'Get up!' he says, his voice cracking. 'Grovelling on the floor like a stricken bitch won't achieve anything.'

When Maddalena neither moves nor speaks, Sebastiano kicks her again, then grasps her by the wrist and pulls her to her feet. She hunches her shoulders, crossing her arms in front of her, curling her body in upon itself, and the sight enrages him. He slaps her across one cheek and the sound rings out into the quiet of the room. 'For God's sake, stand straight! You look pathetic, hunched over like that.'

'What do you want me to do?' Maddalena finally manages to mutter, one hand now flat against the side of her face, where the skin is already crimson. The other remains splayed protectively over her belly. 'Please – tell me what I should do.'

Sebastiano strides across to the credenza and pours himself a glassful of grappa. He swallows it in one, wincing, then flings the glass into the empty grate where it shatters. 'What should you do?' he snarls. 'What do you think? Get rid of the bastard, that's what. Like every other whore who finds herself in the same situation. Find yourself someone who'll show you how to dispatch it.'

Maddalena begins to weep.

'Oh, for God's sake, don't stand there snivelling! What the hell do you think your impotent cuckold of a husband is going to say when you tell him the news? And what will happen to me when he discovers who has fathered the brat? Which will no doubt be only a matter of time, as you seem to have no ability whatsoever to keep even a shred of information to yourself.'

The weeping intensifies.

'Find a way to get rid of it, Maddalena, or . . .' Sebastiano hesitates, then he says, ' . . . or I might just have to find a way to get rid of you.'

He turns from her and strides out of the room, slamming the door behind him. His boots are thunderous on the wooden staircase. Running down from the *sala*, he grabs a leather doublet from a chair by the door, pushing his arms down into the sleeves and roughly fastening it as he leaves the house. His thoughts race, dizzying him as he walks. Dear God, on top of everything else, this new discovery is terrible. That final threat was carelessly uttered, perhaps, but from the drop-jawed expression of naked terror that flashed across Maddalena's face as he spoke, it is clear that she believes that he has every intention of carrying it out.

So perhaps it would be a solution. If all else fails. *Cazzo!* – his standing in the city is precarious enough as it is, without another new scandal to push him nearer the edge. But he has more pressing problems before then. He must find his cousin. He needs the money from Marco if he is to pay – oh God, how many creditors are there now? Seven? Eight? To say nothing of the mounting unpaid costs at Franceschina? If he cannot widen the net of buyers for his laudanum – buyers whom he knows will almost immediately become entirely dependent upon him to continue replenishing the stocks they cannot get from anyone else (thank God for his Swiss contact) – then his future at Franceschina will be precarious indeed. *Merda!*, the shame of having to sell the place and move away would be catastrophic – he cannot imagine it!

If he is not careful, word will spread, some other broker will step into his place and he will lose his edge of exclusivity.

The commedia show he has commissioned will be happening any day now – and if he is honest with himself, he is increasingly desperate for the event to be a success. Even if it is only in truth one more glittering layer of deceit, lying like a golden filigree over the cesspool of his financial disasters, it will provide 'evidence' to his neighbours – for another few months at least – that his coffers are better-stocked than they really are. And a good impression is all it should take to keep the pretence alive for a while.

That angel-faced addict, Bagnacavallo, will be one of the visiting actors, of course. One of Sebastiano's few regulars – though sadly not, so he has discovered, one whose money he can rely on. He, Sebastiano, has three or four bottles Angelo can have when he and the troupe come to Franceschina, if Angelo has the money. He won't give anything away on trust any more – no, he won't make that mistake again! His previous leniency, based largely on now all-but-faded hopes that the handsome and noble-blooded Angelo would provide him with a stream of new and well-heeled customers, now seems sadly misguided, and Sebastiano realizes that he simply cannot afford to subsidize such an unreliable payer.

'I'll have the money up front, or the exquisite Signor da Bagnacavallo can go away empty-handed, however desperate he says he is and however prestigious his bloody forebears.'

But now he must find Marco — another bloody unreliable payer — and one who owes him one hundred *scudi*. A hundred! He cannot remember when his cousin last paid him a single *baioccho*. Marco will most likely be in his favourite tavern.

He'll try there first.

18

Sofia glances around the upstairs room. It is bigger than she was expecting – much bigger than any other room the troupe has shared since she has been with them – but the two low beds still take up much of the floor space. One of the beds is enormously wide, the other a little smaller. The low ceiling is heavily raftered; it must once have been painted, Sofia thinks, though what were probably bright colours have long since faded. The shutters on the single window have been closed against the chill of the October night air. Rushes cover the otherwise bare floorboards. A wooden chest, its once vividly-coloured panelling now chipped and inde-cipherable, sits along the foot end of the smaller bed.

Sofia glances around at the Coraggiosi readying themselves for the night by the light of several candle stubs. They have far more room here than they are used to. With the self-contained ease of long-accustomed travellers, Agostino and Cosima have already tucked themselves under a couple of blankets on one side of the smaller bed, leaving space for one other person, and are still and quiet. Their heads lie close to each other on the pillows. Vico is squatting on his heels beside the larger of the two beds, unfastening Lidia's laces for her; he has one eye on Beppe, who has sat down on the opposite side of the mattress. Vico might well be watching Beppe, but Beppe has eyes for no one but Sofia and his eyes are huge and dark in the candlelight.

Sofia has shared tavern rooms and the wagons – and occasional borrowed bedchambers and *salas* – with these same people on numerous occasions now, and their cheerful banter and comfortable camaraderie has always been a comfort to her. She has up until this moment loved the claustrophobic bustle of it; has felt included, wanted, liked – even loved – by them all, and their warmth and unselfconscious friendship has sustained her over the weeks she has lived among them. But now, tonight, they are suddenly nothing more than intruders – intruders upon hers and Beppe's new-found need for privacy – and she wants to grab Beppe's hand and run from the room. To get away from them. But she cannot: tonight her friends are effectively paralysing her. She knows she could no more let them see her leave this room with Beppe to go to some private place than she could dance naked in the piazza, and, somewhat to her surprise, an unfamiliar feeling of resentment begins to settle itself like a lump of uncooked dough high in her chest.

She walks around the end of the larger bed and seats herself next to Beppe. He puts a hand over hers and shifts in closer so that his hip is pressing up against hers. 'I'm sorry,' he says in an almost silent whisper. 'Vico took me by surprise. We'll find a place to be alone tomorrow. I promise.'

Sofia nods, heeling off her shoes.

'Turn around and I'll undo your laces for you,' Beppe says. He fiddles with the wispy curls on the nape of her neck for a moment, then his fingers move down the ridge of her spine to the fastenings of her dress; she draws in a soft breath, closing her eyes as she fights not to turn around. Agostino and Cosima might be well on their way to being asleep, but Vico and Lidia are still awake and the candles are still lighting the room; she does not want either of them to see her kiss Beppe – any mockery just now would be too dreadful – so she sits still, aware of a faint trembling in her arms and legs, and listens instead to the flip of the laces slipping through their eyelets as Beppe unfastens her dress. Sliding out of her sleeves, she eases the bodice off, folding it in two and laying it on the floor next to the bed. The knot at her waist takes a moment to unpick; then she pushes her skirts off, and these too she folds roughly and places on top of the bodice. Clad now only in her much-creased chemise, she takes the far edge of the two blankets Beppe is holding out towards her; he hutches across to put himself next to Vico, leaving space for her. Her heart thudding, Sofia swings her legs around and lies down beside him.

This is the first time she has lain next to him – the first time she has been in such close proximity to him with so little clothing on. Her limbs continue to tremble.

Over on the far side of the bed, Lidia reaches across and pinches out two of the candle flames. One last stub, on the chest at the foot of Agostino and Cosima's bed, still flickers fitfully.

Beppe spreads out their two blankets; turning his back on Vico and shifting as far from his friend as he can, he pulls Sofia in close to him. Draping an arm over her, he tucks his legs up behind hers. His breath is warm on her neck. She struggles with herself for a moment, but despite her awareness of the others, she finds she cannot help but turn, and is just sliding around under the blankets to face him when the door to the chamber opens.

The light from the last of the lit candles wobbles in the draught. Sofia holds her breath.

A familiar voice, though slurred now and strangely toneless, says, 'Oh, *merda*! I'm sorry. Didn't realize you'd all gone to bed.'

'God, that's all we need,' Beppe mutters between gritted teeth.

'Everyone *does* look comfortable,' Angelo says. 'Other room's full, though – Federico and Giovanni Battista are crammed in with a couple of other travellers. Any space in here?'

Agostino grunts and shifts across, nearer to Cosima, making room.

Muttering to himself, Angelo edges between the two beds, stumbling past where Sofia is pressing up against Beppe, to sit heavily on the unoccupied edge of the second mattress, next to Agostino.

'Any spare blankets?' he says. Nobody answers, but somebody – Sofia thinks it must have been Lidia – throws a blanket across the room. It lands with a muffled flop. Angelo murmurs thanks and, untidily heeling off his boots and shrugging his arms out of his doublet sleeves, he rolls himself in the blanket without further comment. The chamber falls silent.

Only the sounds of breathing can be heard.

Even the quietest whisper would be clearly audible now.

Sofia does not dare say anything to Beppe; she curls herself against him and he wraps his arms – and the blankets – tightly around her.

She can feel his pulse beating against her cheek and knows she will not sleep.

Beppe dares not do more than hold Sofia against him. Vico is still awake and listening – Beppe can tell by the sound of his friend's breathing – and, worse than this, Angelo's presence is now filling the room like a noxious gas. The pent-up desire for Sofia he has been feeling all evening is turning now into a painful restlessness:

one of his legs is twitching, and he has started winding strands of Sofia's hair around his finger – round and round, tightening it until he can feel a throbbing in his fingertip – then unwinding and beginning again.

She has turned towards him and has curled against him, her knees bent up over his legs, her head in the crook of his shoulder. Her unruly hair is tickling the side of his face. The hand which is resting on his chest is stroking his skin, softly, gently: she is doing no more than contracting and spreading her fingers but each little movement is making his need for her worse. He is longing to kiss her but holds back; once he starts, he knows it will be impossible to stop.

19

Sofia and Beppe have passed the hours since they rose this morning in a haze of frustrated longing. The Coraggiosi have been in a determinedly cheerful mood – this is a hard-earned rest, after all, and Agostino has, since everyone came downstairs this morning, been exhorting his troupe to make the most of the break from routine. He has been resolute in his intention to involve everyone in his ideas for relaxation, and, despite their best efforts, Sofia and Beppe have been unable to extricate themselves for more than a few minutes at a time since first light.

Back in the crowded tavern room for the second evening of the troupe's little holiday, Sofia thinks through the day's events. She awoke many hours ago wrapped in Beppe's arms as the morning light began to filter through the ill-fitting shutters, stiff and uncomfortable from having been some time unmoving, and momentarily confused by the unfamiliar sensation of being held. Opening her eyes, she saw – too close to focus clearly – the side of Beppe's still-sleeping face next to hers, and, laying a hand on his cheek, kissed his mouth very gently.

He tightened his hold on her.

Then Vico coughed.

Beppe opened his eyes. Smiled at Sofia.

Vico sat up, yawned and stretched. 'Good morning, Coraggiosi,' he said cheerfully, kissing Lidia and ruffling Beppe's hair. 'No work today. What a treat. What shall we do?'

'Why don't you shut up and let other people sleep?' came Lidia's voice from the far side of the bed, thick with morning drowsiness.

'Because, my little cherub, on a day with no work, it seems a crime to waste it lying here doing nothing.'

'Hmm. Lying here doing nothing sounds like a perfect plan to me. Shut up.'

Laughing softly, Beppe murmured, 'Shall we get up, lovely girl?'

Nodding, Sofia kissed his mouth once more, then sat up, hunching and rolling her shoulders, pushing her fingers up into the now tangled mass of her hair. As she did so, Beppe stretched, cracking his knuckles above his head.

Turning sideways to pick up her skirt from where she had laid it on the floor, Sofia caught sight of Angelo's perfectly profiled head on the other side of the room, on the pillow next to the still-sleeping Agostino; his eyes were wide and he was staring at her. Suddenly acutely aware of the flimsiness of the lawn of her chemise, she pulled the bundle of her skirts up off the floor and held them bunched in front of her. Holding Angelo's gaze for a moment, she stared back without smiling and then looked away, turning her back on him.

'Do you want me to do your laces?' Beppe said.

'No – not here. Not in front of him.'

'What? Who? Oh. I see.' Beppe's voice was almost soundless. 'Come on, take your dress and let's go. Somewhere else. Anywhere else.'

In a corner of the little space just outside the door, Beppe held Sofia's skirts out for her to step into, and, standing behind her, neatly fastened the laces at her waist; he tucked the long loose ends down inside out of sight. Sucking in a breath, Sofia closed her eyes as his hands moved around and upwards – but before he could do more than run a flattened palm against one breast, the door banged open, knocking into him. Lurching forwards, he bumped against Sofia and threw her off balance; scooping her up in his arms before she fell, he and Sofia both turned to see who had opened the door.

'Oh. Sorry,' Lidia said, catching her lower lip between her teeth to smother a smile. 'Sorry to be in the way.'

And so, as the tavern room bustles around Sofia in the half-light of the evening, it seems to her that thus has the day unfolded: since dawn, today has been nothing but a series of interruptions and obstructions to every attempt she and Beppe have made to find a moment's peace and privacy. Or – she corrects herself – almost every attempt. Her heart is beating faster now as the end of the evening approaches, for despite all the interruptions, she and Beppe did manage to make a discovery this afternoon.

Out behind the tavern is a large hay-filled barn.

'I'll not let Vico ambush us again tonight,' Beppe said as they stood hand in hand at the barn door just after lunch. 'If we wait until they are all noisy and busy drinking, we should be able to slip out, one at a time, and come out here. I'll bring a couple of blankets. Will you like that idea?'

Sofia did not answer, but nodded.

Beppe runs a hand along her thigh now and grips just above her knee. 'We might nip out to that barn soon,' he says very quietly into her ear. 'I think they're all happy enough now not to notice us going.'

Sofia glances around. Agostino, smiling widely, has both arms raised as he declaims with great energy; cloth and jug in hand, the ale-man is watching him, round-eyed and fascinated, ignoring his other customers. Cosima is curled against Agostino, moving slightly with every one of his enthusiastic gesticulations, and Vico has his arm over Lidia's shoulder. He is pointing with his other hand to where Federico and Giovanni Battista are busy arguing about nothing, their affectionate quarrel well lubricated with ale. Lidia's head is resting against Vico's but her eyes are closed. Angelo sits apart, slumped in his chair, his head resting heavily on one palm; he is watching the proceedings sideways on, through half-closed eyes. He is, Sofia thinks now, looking at his slow blinking and the slackness of his exquisite mouth, very drunk.

'You nip out now,' Beppe says. 'Go out to the barn and wait for me. I'll get a couple of blankets from upstairs.'

A bright moon is rising. Papery-white and just off the full, it is hanging low above the treeline and is bathing the old barn with a soft greyish light. Though somewhat ramshackle, with strips of moonlit sky showing through gaps in the wooden-plank walls, the barn is fragrant with the smell of cut hay; as Sofia's eyes adjust to the gloom of the interior, she can see that this hay is piled untidily throughout the building. High above her, the underside of the roof is swathed with little swags of dust-heavy cobweb and, even as she stares, something tiny scutters along a beam, no more than a fragment of shifting shadow. Several sleepy hens croon softly as she takes a rustling step in from the door towards where a half-height wall supports a section of upper floor. A ladder leans up against this little wall, and an elderly mule is asleep on the far side of it, head down, spine sagging, ears drooping. Nearby, the Coraggiosi horses, too, are dozing. One of them, sensing Beppe's presence, nickers softly and tosses its head.

Ippo, Beppe's dog, is curled in the hay by the horses. He scrabbles to his feet as soon as they come in, and barks once, but Beppe hisses at him to lie down, to be quiet, and he obeys at once, his tail thumping softly.

'Shall we go up?' Beppe says quietly.

Sofia nods, and puts a foot on the bottom-most rung. It feels sound. She begins to climb, Beppe right behind her; she clutches the side of the ladder in one hand and an awkward bundle of her skirts in the other. Crawling carefully across from the top of the ladder onto the loosely boarded floor of the upper level, a sudden movement makes her gasp and start back – a white-winged owl, disturbed by the two intruders, sweeps silently past her – close enough for Sofia to feel the draught from its soundless wingbeats; it soars out through a gap in the wall on the far side of the barn.

'Will this be enough for a bed for you?' Beppe says, dropping his armful of blankets and pulling off his doublet. He stands in front of Sofia, stroking her hair back from her face. 'Or would you rather go back indoors and share with the others again, on a proper bed in the warm? We can wait for somewhere more comfortable, if this is—?'

Sofia silences him with a kiss. He murmurs incoherently into her mouth, but the words dissolve and Sofia does not listen to them. 'Stop it,' she says. 'No, I don't want to wait – not one moment longer. Do you?'

Beppe coughs a short laugh. 'God, no! I'm not sure I could have lasted more than another few seconds, to be honest.' Dragging armfuls of hay together to make a thick mattress, and flapping out one of the blankets, he sits down on it, patting it with the flat of his hand. 'Come here.'

Sofia sits neatly beside him, feet out in front of her, back straight, hands in her lap, like a child on its best behaviour.

She is not at all sure she can remember how to breathe.

Turning just his head, Beppe kisses her again, quietly and chastely; for a moment it is only their mouths which connect, and then Sofia finds herself lying back on the blanket, and the hay is scrunching beneath her, and Beppe is searching for her breast, but the stiffened front of the dress seems determined to thwart his attempts. Fiddling with the top edge of the bodice, he tries to pull it aside – once, twice, three times – and it stubbornly refuses to allow him access.

'Undo my laces – quick,' Sofia says, sitting up and turning her back towards him. Beppe fiddles with the knot of strings at the nape of her neck. Knot undone, he flips the laces through hole after hole and the tight pressure on her chest and belly lessens as the dress unfastens. Shifting around, she leans towards Beppe and he eases the bodice and sleeves from her, throwing them to one side, leaving her in skirt and shift. Then, reaching around behind her back with trembling fingers, she unfastens the laces at her waist herself, and kicks her heavy skirts down and off her legs.

Now she wears only her shift.

They look at each other for a long moment, saying nothing, not moving. All at once aware of her body and how very much it wants – needs – to be touched, she finds herself staring at Beppe's mouth.

'What was it we said that time – *as much as a blade loves a whetstone*?' he says quietly, and Sofia's insides leap.

'Take your shirt off,' she says, and Beppe sits back, crosses his arms, and tugs his shirt over his head in one fluid movement. Sofia reaches for him; he rolls with her until she is on her back and he is sprawled above her. Then his mouth is on hers; crooking one leg up and over her thighs and pushing a hand under the loose-fitting chemise, he at long last finds her breast. She arches towards him, gasping, as his fingers close around it.

'Mmm,' he murmurs, trying to push the folds of the chemise out of his way, 'I think this needs to come off ...'

Sofia sits up and pulls off the shift.

'God, you're so beautiful,' he says almost inaudibly, reaching out and running his fingers around the swell of both breasts. Moving in close, pulling her in to him with a hand in the small of her back, he kisses her. 'And you smell and taste as good as you look.'

'Beppe,' she says.

His face crooks into its tilted smile. 'What? What is it, little seamstress?' Taking her by her upper arms, he lays her back on the blanket, pulling the other rug over them both.

She strokes the skin of his chest with the tips of her fingers. 'I ... I'm not sure I know how to do this properly. I've ... I've never—'

Beppe stops her question with another kiss and then returns his attention to her breasts, making her squirm with pleasure. 'Don't fret, lovely girl,' he says, '*you* may not know, but just look at you – your body knows well enough, doesn't it?'

'Am I doing what I should, then?' Sofia says, gasping again as Beppe's mouth finds her nipple.

Beppe lifts his head. 'What do you think?'

She does not answer, and for a while they say no more but content themselves with wordless exploration: searching and learning and discovering the secrets of each other's bodies with fingers and lips and tongues, and the exploration is a revelation to Sofia, who quickly discovers that her body does indeed seem to know very much more than she ever believed it might.

Then Beppe hutches across and slides on top of her, and Sofia sucks in a breath as she feels his weight settle. He pauses. The quiver of anticipation that runs down through her belly is part-way between excitement and trepidation – she is not sure which it might be – but she crooks her knees and wraps her legs around him, finding that now the moment has come, she wants him very much more than she fears the unknown. Her hands lie fisted on either side of her head for a moment, until Beppe uncurls her fingers and links his own through them, pressing her hands down onto the blanket. She can feel and hear the hay scrunching under the pressure.

'Are you ready?' he says.

Sofia cannot answer, but manages a murmur of assent and a nod.

Murmuring her pleasure as Beppe kisses her, she frees her hands and strokes around the back of his head, down his back and onto the curve of his buttocks, pulling him in towards her. She feels him reaching in between her legs; his touch makes her gasp once more and she pushes her hips up against his, gripping around his back, wrapping her legs more tightly around him. He hesitates for a second . . . and then Sofia's mouth opens in an O of surprise as he pushes gently into her and a jolt of exquisite pain melts quickly into a wave of sweetness.

Their bodies move rhythmically together; through the narrow gaps in the wooden-plank walls, fitful silver stripes of moonlight fall in flickering lines across legs and arms, backs and buttocks, and the breathy gasps and sighs of their loving are the only sounds in the night-still barn.

The first greyish light of dawn is filtering through the gaps in the barn walls sending dapples of silver across where Sofia is curled against Beppe beneath one of the blankets. Below them, the mule stamps a hoof and snorts softly. A barely-audible skittering scratches on the wooden floor somewhere nearby as some tiny creature moves somewhere beneath the hay, and the wood of the barn creaks as though it is stretching and yawning. The scent of the hay is strong in Sofia's nostrils; within the circle of Beppe's arm she lies with her head against his chest and her knees bent up and over his legs. Her face moves gently with the rise and fall of his breath.

With his free hand, Beppe strokes her hair away from where it has tendrilled across his face, blowing from a jutted lower lip to clear the last wisps away from his nose. Turning his head, his face is right up against hers; he gives her a soft, slow, squashed kiss, and she nips his lower lip between her teeth.

Pulling it free, he lays a hand on Sofia's cheek, and, stroking it with the edge of his thumb, he says, 'I told you your body would know what to do.'

'Only because you taught it well.'

She cannot see his face – he is too close – but a stretching of his skin against her cheek tells her he is smiling. She contemplates her body as a separate thing from her*self*, a *thing* which knows how to perform tasks she had presumed she could not do – and she starts to take stock of each part of it as it lies drowsily in Beppe's arms. Her lips are tender and swollen with kissing and her skin is tingling. Her hips feel ... stretched out. Flattened. There is a stickiness between her legs and down along the tops of her thighs; it has puckered and stiffened on her skin as it has dried. Putting a hand down under the blanket, she runs her fingers over the dried place, scratching at it. Within her loins an unaccustomed weight lies heavy, too, not unlike the monthly aches she so often experiences, and all this should, in the normal run of things, be discomfort, Sofia thinks, but somehow it is not; she finds she is cherishing every part of it.

She draws in a long, slow trembling breath, and lets it out again.

'That was a big sigh.' Beppe has opened his eyes. 'Not a sad one, I hope.'

Sofia curls against him more tightly. 'Oh, no. Not sad at all. Not in the least part.'

'Then what?'

'Just thinking.'

'About what?'

'My body.'

'That's funny,' Beppe says, reaching for her breast under the blanket. 'So was I.' He pauses. 'What were you thinking about it?'

'Just about the things it has just done. Things I wasn't expecting it to do.'

'Were you not? I was expecting it to do just what it did.'

Sofia laughs.

Beppe strokes her hair away from her face. 'Trouble is, I know your body better than I know you, now. Tell me about you. God – I told you all those terrible things about ... about my father yesterday. Tell me something about you now. About your family.'

The lazy warmth of the moment chills in an instant.

Sofia holds her breath, trying to think how to tell him. Surely, she thinks now, of all people he will understand. He will know how hard it is to tell something like this.

'It's difficult,' she says, wanting more time to think as a memory – her father's voice, rough with fear – flashes into her mind.

'For God's sake, what's the matter, Giacinta? Are you ill? What's happened?'

Mamma will not look at him, though he holds her face in his hands and tries to force her to do so. She pulls her head away from him and stares instead at the still-open front door; the only change in her that

Sofia can see is a further widening of her eyes — she can see white all the way around the brown iris. Papa takes her by the upper arms and shakes her, his voice louder now and more urgent. 'Giacinta, please! You're frightening me. Stop it! You're frightening Sofia — look at her! Tell me what's happened!'

'Worse than my story?' Beppe says softly, stroking her hair back from her face.

Sofia nods. 'I think it might be.'

'Can you tell me any of it, lovely girl?'

'I'll try.'

Beppe puts a hand on the side of her face and kisses her mouth. She responds, turning to him, pressing in against him, and, in an instant, their need for each other ignites again; for a few moments the urgency of their bodies absorbs them too intensely to think further of tales of past grief, but then, moments later, as Beppe shudders to a halt and Sofia clings to him, breathing as heavily as though she has been running, she says, in between gasps, 'My mother was a healer.'

Beppe holds her tightly and her breathing slows.

'She used to take curatives of her own making to sick neighbours and friends — she grew herbs and flowers, and made tinctures and salves and lozenges — and over the years she began to build a reputation. People would seek her out.'

'And your father?'

'Papa was a baker.' She hesitates. 'One day — I was about six or seven — Mamma came home from seeing one of her neighbours. It was as if she had lost her reason. She burst into the house, gasping for breath, wild-eyed, her hair loose . . . I was terrified. I couldn't understand what she was saying.'

*

'Sofia! Sofia! Quick! We must pack — we must pack as many of our clothes and belongings as we can carry. We have to leave, now, straight away!'

Mamma's eyes are wide and blank, and a thin and shining line of spit has slid from one corner of her mouth and trickled down towards her chin. Her hair looks, Sofia thinks, as though she has not brushed it for days.

'What's the matter, Mamma?' she says in a small voice, hoping her mother will smile at her and reassure her. But she does not reassure Sofia; she shouts at her in a hard voice that sounds as though her throat is tearing.

'Just do it — don't argue! Put your things into a bag. We have no time to lose. We have to go now.'

'But what about Papa?'

Mamma stares at her and says nothing.

'Papa,' Sofia says again, beginning to cry. 'We have to tell Papa.'

'No. We have to go. There's no time. We can't wait for him.'

Beppe is sitting up now, watching Sofia intently. One of her hands is in his, and he is stroking it with the side of his thumb.

'Then Papa came back and he couldn't make sense of what she was saying either — not for ages. Finally, she came out with it. A woman she had been treating had died, and the woman's husband had accused Mamma of poisoning her.'

'I went there just now and she was dead.' Mamma's voice drops to a whisper. 'He called me a witch, Paolo, and he says he will make sure they have me burned for what he insists I've done. I think he means it.'

'What were you giving her?'

'Lavender and barberry. For sickness and the flux.'

'Nothing else?'

Mamma shakes her head. In a whisper Sofia can hardly hear she says, 'It was the right thing to give her – I know it was. I don't know why she died.'

'I didn't understand what she was saying. *Have her burned?* I thought she meant like the time I'd burned my arm on a hot pan. I couldn't understand why someone would want to do that to another person deliberately.'

Beppe says nothing, but his eyes are huge and unblinking and his gaze is fixed upon Sofia's face.

'Papa agreed that we should get away – even if it was just for a short time – so we packed a bag with essentials and left the house.' Sofia pauses. 'Of course, we had no idea of what was to come, but—'

She is about to continue when the barn door crashes open, morning sunlight floods in and disturbs the hens; they flap their wings and scold the intruder with a barrage of irritable clucks and croons. Beppe's dog barks. One of the horses snorts. Startled, Sofia clutches her blanket to her chest; her heart is racing. She is in a stranger's barn and she is naked. Beppe puts a finger to his lips and shakes his head. 'Don't move,' he mouths soundlessly.

Sofia's memories hang fragmented in the air as the newcomer moves about below them.

Whoever it is begins to whistle. Tuneless and lilting, his song jolts and jerks as he works noisily: banging and thudding, then grunting with exertion as, so it sounds to Sofia, he lifts something heavy and shifts it across the barn.

'Hey, hey, hey . . . good morning, good morning, good morning . . . up you come . . . come on then . . .'

Sofia thinks she recognizes the ale-man's voice.

'Ooh, but you are one lazy, ill-smelling, bad-tempered pile of old dog-meat,' he says, in a tone far more affectionate than his words might imply. 'Come on, out you come – good girl. That's it. I'm not shifting twenty-five barrels on my own – come *on*.'

Beppe and Sofia glance at each other.

A scuffle of hoofs, a jingle of harness buckles, a half-hearted mumbling attempt from the mule at a discordant bray; several indistinguishable, muttered comments from the ale-man. Then Sofia hears man and mule cross the barn floor, and the great door closes behind them.

And opens again a second later.

A familiar voice. 'Beppe? You in here?' Sofia cannot see him, but Vico sounds as though he is grinning. 'We're moving on, Ago says, and we need to get the wagons hitched up straight away – thought you might have sneaked out here last night. You weren't in the upstairs room and half the blankets were missing and – well, you had to be *somewhere* . . .' He clears his throat. '*Er hem*. Both of you. I've looked everywhere else.'

'We'll be down in a moment,' Beppe says, and Vico laughs. Sofia closes her eyes, inwardly shrivelling with embarrassment.

'Glad to see my instincts are as fine as ever, *amico*,' Vico calls cheerfully. 'Hope you had a . . .' He clears his throat again. '. . . had a . . . er . . . a good night.'

And, whistling loudly, he leaves the barn.

'Tell me the rest of your story later, lovely girl,' Beppe says. 'We're going to have to get up and it's too important a tale to rush.'

Thoroughly disconcerted now, Sofia nods.

'A few more minutes more won't hurt, though . . .' Beppe adds quietly, pulling her on top of him, running his hands over her buttocks and kissing her once more.

20

Bologna

Marco da Correggio – slight, dark, hollow-cheeked and brown-eyed – is indeed in the tavern, sitting on a low seat near the fire, a large tin cup of ale in his hands, but as soon as he sees Sebastiano, he scrambles to his feet and does his best to leave by the little door at the back of the downstairs room, knocking the cup onto the floor with a clatter. The ale splatters dark across the dusty flags. Elbowing his way between drinkers, he mutters thoughtless apologies as he bangs into shoulders and backs, slops drinks and knocks chairs; grabbing for the latch, he struggles to open the door, but, unfortunately for him, it catches on the uneven floor below and refuses to open wide enough to allow him to squeeze out.

Sebastiano, shoving past the same disgruntled tavern-goers – ignoring their protests – reaches Marco before he can wrestle the door any further, snatching at his cousin's arm and tugging him back into the tavern's room.

'Come with me,' he mutters. 'Just come outside with me now, and—'

'*Vaffanculo!*' Marco says. 'I haven't got it, Sebastiano, and there's nothing you can do about it.'

Sebastiano drags him by the wrist, bending his arm acutely to pull him in close, and hiss-whispers into his ear: 'You know you don't have a choice, Marco. I'm having that money.'

'Piss off! Let go of me – I haven't bloody got it, and I don't have a chance of getting it either.'

Sebastiano has brought Marco right across to the entrance door now, and, yanking it open, he hauls his cousin out into the street; every eye in the tavern is upon the pair as they leave the room. Marco now snatches his arm out of Sebastiano's grip, but Sebastiano grabs him by the front of his doublet and slams him up against the outside wall of the tavern. 'I have no intention of falling foul of my creditors, Marco. You know what will happen if you don't pay.'

'You'll have to give me time.'

'I don't *have* time. Let me spell it out to you – just in case you've forgotten any of the details in the fog of the ale you've clearly been downing back there – I lent you one hundred *scudi* last year, did I not? After you proved how indubitably poor your gaming instincts really are and lost most of your inheritance within a few hours.'

Marco says nothing.

'Make no mistake, that was a hundred *scudi* I could ill afford. I only gave it to you because you are my father's brother's son and you promised to pay it back within two months. What a fool I was. That was eleven months ago – and you've given me ... what is it now?' Sebastiano scratches his head and screws up his face as though trying hard to remember an evasive fact. After a pause for effect, he says, in a voice thick with contempt, 'Nothing. Not one single stinking *baioccho*. I've waited and waited, been more patient than I would have thought possible, but things have changed. I *need* eighty-five *scudi* – for reasons I have no intention of going into with you. And I need them now. This week. I intend to have what you owe me, one way or another.' Taking a handful of Marco's doublet, he continues, 'Now you listen to me ... My cousin you might be, but you are also a vicious little ponce who's been discovered one too many times with his cock inside the breeches of an underage *bardassa* with the morals of a tomcat. And – dear God, how grubby this becomes! – this particular underage and amoral *bardassa* just happens to be someone to whom we are both closely related. Our other delightful cousin Fabio – that unprincipled disgrace to the family name – is worryingly well known to the authorities, I think you'll agree ...'

Marco swallows uncomfortably, wincing as though Sebastiano has spat at him.

Sebastiano continues, ' ... and I think you'll remember I'm now armed with written testimony from several of Fabio's other ... *friends* ... even if ' – he shrugs and pulls a face – 'even if that evidence might perhaps have been extracted under some ... duress. I have acquaintances in high places, as I'm sure you're aware, and one or two of them are acquaintances who would pay handsomely for the sort of evidence of debauchery in this city that I could give them – in sumptuous detail.' He pauses. His voice drops to a cold and expressionless whisper. 'It would probably be the *strappado*, don't you think? For the pair of you. For the decidedly indelicate, if titillating, combination of sodomy and incest.'

Marco looks stricken, clearly imagining the agonies of broken arms and dislocated shoulders. Sebastiano and Marco have both witnessed the horrors of public *strappado* punishments. 'I'll fucking kill you,' he mutters, white-faced.

Grinning unpleasantly now at his cousin's discomfiture, and ignoring the threat, Sebastiano says, 'I'll have that eighty-five – either from you, or from my high-ranking acquaintances. It's up to you.'

Pushing his fingers up into his hair and gripping a fistful, Marco stares at his cousin. 'I'll find it for you by the end of the week,' he says in a voice flattened by defeat.

Sebastiano smiles, and when he speaks again, his voice has lost its menace and now sounds bright and conversational. Reaching out, he pats Marco twice on the cheek with the flat of his palm. 'Marvellous! I knew you'd see it my way. Bring it with you to Franceschina, why don't you? The travelling players are coming to the castle in a couple of days – come and see the show.' He grips Marco's shoulder. 'Stay for a few days – it's going to be spectacular.'

Marco says nothing.

'Have you seen them yet? They play regularly in and around Bologna. The Coraggiosi, the troupe is called.'

A mute shake of the head.

'I saw them in Ravenna last year – they were magnificent. That's why I've asked them to come to the castle. They're quite something. To be perfectly honest, I'm hoping they'll go some way to preserving my reputation amongst the great and the good. A reputation *you*'ve gone quite some way to bring down, what with one thing or another. I'll see you at Franceschina.' He turns to leave, but checks and adds, 'Or perhaps I won't, on second thoughts – you being neither great *nor* good. You might be a little preoccupied collecting me what you owe, anyway, might you not?'

Marco stares after Sebastiano, breathing heavily, shaking his head. 'God, you are a bastard,' he whispers, pressing himself back against the wall and feeling sick and light-headed. He has no more chance of scraping that amount of money together than he has of flying. What few coins he ever manages to put aside, Fabio spends without a second thought, and what Fabio doesn't spend on himself, he, Marco, spends on Fabio. An image of his young cousin's exquisite, feline smile comes into his mind and his guts turn over. He knows he is ruining himself for the sake of that boy: pointlessly, stupidly – but inevitably.

Would Sebastiano really do it? Really hand him and Fabio over to the authorities, knowing what the result would almost certainly be? At the prospect, Marco slides down the wall to sit in the dust at the edge of the road; a hissing has begun in his ears and he can feel sour spit gathering at the back of his mouth. *I have acquaintances in high places, as I'm sure you're aware – and one or two of them are acquaintances who would pay handsomely for the sort of evidence of debauchery in this city that I could give them – in sumptuous detail . . .* Evidence. Evidence. His thoughts buzz pointlessly for several long moments, and then he draws in a sharp breath and opens his eyes wide. He will have to find evidence of his own – lacking the means to pay Sebastiano what he wants, that, surely, must be the only way to stop him. If he, Marco, can find – or fabricate – evidence of some sort of equally heinous activity taking place under Sebastiano's own roof, then he'll use it like a counterweight to stop his cousin before his cousin stops him . . . permanently.

21

The Castello della Franceschina, a few miles outside Bologna

Standing alone, the red-brick castle looms squat and square, two storeys high with a stout, castellated tower at each corner, uncompromising and simply designed, like a child's toy fortress. A clump of trees stands bulwark behind the mass of the building, but other than this, the land around is uninterrupted farmland, stretching away towards a barely undulating horizon.

The wagons scrunch to a halt, and everyone climbs out onto the wide dusty space in front of the castle, looking around them, taking in the beauty of their prestigious surroundings.

'There you are, Beppe, my boy,' Agostino says cheerfully, arms outstretched. 'I told you that our venues are becoming ever more exalted, did I not? Look at this! And performing indoors for once. Luxury! Our most highly prized competitors would be congratulating themselves on having secured such a place.'

'I'm sure you're right, Ago,' Beppe says, coming up to stand beside him, 'and it's an impressive building, I agree. But it's the audience that matters, though, isn't it?'

Raising his eyebrows and pushing out his bottom lip as he considers this remark, Agostino nods. 'Yes, of course you're right . . .' His smile returns as he adds, ' . . . but Signor da Correggio has assured us that our audience will be both numerous and enthusiastic. He's invited prestigious friends, local dignitaries, all the nearby nobility – we couldn't ask for a more exalted collection!'

Heaving a bag from the back of the smallest wagon, Vico grunts as it hits the ground. He says, 'Yes, fine. That's all very well – just so long as they laugh in all the right places, eh?'

The wide main door of the castle opens with a resounding bang. Three men scurry out towards the Coraggiosi. Despite the fine quality of their dark doublets and breeches, it is clear from their demeanour that they are servants: there is an indefinable air of obsequiousness about them. They are smiling, however; the oldest and stoutest of the three, who has a cloud of grey hair like dirty thistledown, raises a hand and begins to speak in a breathlessly excited voice even before he has reached them.

A warm welcome is offered, genuine delight at the prospect of the performance to come is declared, the wagons are led off around the back of the castle to be placed neatly side by side, and the horses are unharnessed and led away to a nearby patch of pasture, where they express their pleasure in bucks and rolls and snorted whinnies. The troupe is hustled into the castle to see the grand reception room which is being prepared for the evening's show.

'This, signori and signore, is the Southern Banqueting Chamber. The largest room in the *castello*,' says the oldest and stoutest servant, his arms held out wide, palms upwards, fingers spread.

Her mouth dropping open, Sofia gazes up at the ceiling: barrel-vaulted, richly corniced and elaborately frescoed, it is divided into painted sections, each of which seem to depict some form of traditional story, where satyrs, nymphs and mythological creatures play out their adventures amongst wreaths and ribbons and sprays of flowers. The colours are sumptuous and vivid and, Sofia thinks, absolutely beautiful. She has never set foot in a place such as this.

'This is quite something, isn't it?' Beppe says quietly, his mouth near her ear. 'Makes a bit of a change from the corner of a rubbish-strewn piazza.'

Still wide-eyed, still gazing around her, Sofia nods.

Agostino declares his approval with verbose extravagance and the servants exchange smug looks of proud proprietorship. Extra hands to help build the staging are offered but politely declined. The Coraggiosi have the construction of their stage well organized, and neither need nor wish for assistance with it.

Some two hours later, Sofia is underneath the trestles, checking that the last of the securing pegs are in place. This is a job for which she has happily volunteered, and Beppe has equally willingly offered to help her. The pair of them have been hidden away under the stage for far longer than the job really requires them to be, and, after some fifteen minutes, are both perhaps somewhat more dishevelled than might have been expected given the simplicity of the task.

Crouched awkwardly beneath the boarding, which is sitting lower than usual – the indoor trestles being shorter than the outdoor ones – Sofia is fiddling with a final peg which seems reluctant to slot into its allotted hole, and Beppe is reaching around her. She runs her fingers back and forth along his forearm as he fixes the peg with ease, then sucks in a soft breath as he pulls her in towards him. Turning within his arms, she holds his face between her hands while she kisses him. Here in the dust-smelling darkness of the understage, those glowing embers, not yet cooled since the previous night, ignite again and even the pressing reality of the imminent performance recedes in the face of their hunger for each other.

But their moment of intimacy does not last long.

'Oy!' Federico's face appears at the back edge of the trestles a moment or two later. 'Stop that, you two – there's work to do!'

Beppe and Sofia pull apart. Smothering a giggle, Sofia turns onto hands and knees, preparing to crawl out, but Beppe holds her by the hips. 'Just a moment,' he says, pulling her back towards where he is kneeling so that her buttocks fit in snugly against the front of his breeches, 'Listen, lovely girl,' he says, curling his body over hers, 'You started telling me about your mother yesterday . . .'

Closing her eyes, Sofia turns her head so that her cheek rubs softly against Beppe's. 'Not now – I don't think I can—'

'No, chick, I didn't mean now. But we must find time. It's important.'

Sofia says nothing.

'This afternoon is going to be extraordinary,' Beppe says. 'This place is beautiful, the audience are going to love you and you're going to be the perfect Colombina. And then afterwards – well, there'll be time for . . . all sorts of things afterwards, won't there?'

Pushing back against him, Sofia feels as though she is dissolving all over again. 'Oh yes,' she says. 'Yes, there will.'

'Beppe!' Federico's voice is louder now and sounds irritable.

'Come on, *sartalina*,' Beppe says, running a hand over Sofia's bottom. 'My little seamstress. It's time to go.'

As they scramble out from under the staging, Sofia sees that they have been joined by a stranger: a heavily built man of about thirty-five, dark-haired, dressed in an elaborately slashed doublet, with white frilled linen at neck and wrists. He is ruggedly handsome, clearly wealthy and, Sofia thinks, probably rather arrogant, judging by the slight edge of disdain apparent in his expression. The corners of his mouth lift in what looks like amusement, as she and Beppe get – a little awkwardly – to their feet.

'Beppe, Sofia, this is Signor da Correggio,' Agostino says, looking harassed. 'Our host. Signore, this is Beppe Bianchi, our Arlecchino; and Sofia Genotti, who is playing the role of Colombina.'

As Beppe nods a greeting, and Sofia bobs a quick curtsy, Signor da Correggio rakes the pair of them with a glance. Beppe he dismisses in an instant, but his gaze lingers on Sofia; she sees him looking at her breasts, and moves a little closer to Beppe. Beppe takes her hand.

His eyes still on Sofia, Signor da Correggio says, 'You are all most welcome: I'm very much looking forward to the show. People will be starting to arrive in a few hours, I should say, so I'll leave you to your preparations. I'll make sure to come and find you after the performance . . . to congratulate you.'

A soft cough comes from the other side of the room. Turning, Sofia sees Angelo stepping forward to intercept Signor da Correggio as he heads towards the door. The latter checks and Angelo, flicking a quick sideways glance over towards where Agostino and Cosima are busily overseeing the last of the stage preparations, says something to his host which Sofia cannot hear. Signor da Correggio shakes his head. Angelo, his expression tense and his jaw twitching, mutters some other inaudible comment. Sofia frowns: the two men clearly know each other far more intimately than she has presumed. It is Angelo's acquaintance with da Correggio that secured them the performance here at the *castello*, that much she knows from everything Agostino has told them all, but until this moment, she has imagined the connection between the two to be tenuous – something of a formality.

'Oh, very well. Come with me now, then – five minutes, no more,' she hears the signore say, a bite of irritation in his voice; then he turns on his heel and strides out of the room, Angelo a couple of paces behind him.

Vico whistles as Angelo reaches the door and Angelo rounds on him. 'Can you not ever keep your fucking mouth shut?' he snarls, and Vico pulls an open-mouthed face of exaggerated indignation as the door shuts behind him.

'But I have no other means of getting hold of it – you *know* that, Correggio. You *promised*. I don't have time to find another source, before ... before I ... look, I just need it now, for God's sake!'

There is a petulant whine in Angelo's voice and Sebastiano feels a frisson of contempt for such dependence. He barks out a short laugh. 'To be honest, I doubt there *is* another source. The stuff has only been in existence a few years – it's not easy to come by. My contact in Switzerland is probably the only ready source there is. An apothecary might be able to sell you a few drops every now and again, if he can get hold of any – and if you persuade him you're in desperate need of it, I suppose ...' Putting a hand on the wall over Angelo's shoulder, he leans in close to his face. 'I, on the other hand, have three full bottles upstairs you can have, as soon as you hand over the money. It's as simple as that.' He pats Angelo's cheek.

Angelo closes his eyes and says nothing. The muscle in his jaw twitches again. From his silence, it is clear to Sebastiano firstly that Angelo has indeed failed to raise the necessary money, and secondly that he is struggling to invent yet another lame suggestion for how to wheedle a bottle out of him gratis. He is unsurprised and unimpressed when Angelo finally speaks. He almost laughs.

'Perhaps I can offer you something in lieu of the full payment.'

Sebastiano snorts. 'Suggest something, then.'

He is shocked, however, by what Angelo says next. The suggestion leaves him speechless.

'I saw you eyeing up our Colombina back there . . .'

Pausing for a moment, his pulse quickening, Sebastiano says quietly, 'The little girl with the curls? The one who was under the stage just now?'

A brief nod.

'What of it?'

'I could . . . steer her your way, after the performance . . .'

Sebastiano runs his tongue along his lips and swallows visibly. 'She seems to be . . . somewhat intimate with the boy with the black hair. How will he feel about this? I don't want any ugly scenes. The house is full of guests I should not wish to embarrass.'

'I'll get him out of the way. He needn't know. Not till later, anyway.'

Sebastiano considers this, feeling his cock shift in his breeches. The girl is exquisite – the ripe mouth and the peach-round breasts are crying out to be kissed and, more than this, there is something particularly enticing about the prospect of fucking her while Angelo detains her lover elsewhere in his house. And he'll make sure Maddalena knows what he is doing, too, and with whom. That will only add to the spice of it. He says, 'And what about her? The girl? Will she co-operate?'

Angelo raises an eyebrow and his mouth twitches into a mirthless grin. 'You can be very persuasive when you want to be, Correggio.'

Sebastiano laughs. 'Very well. You get the boy out of the way, and make sure I have at least an hour with the girl, and then you can have one of the bottles.'

'How about letting me have a dose from it now?'

'Before the show? Are you joking? You'll fall asleep on the bloody stage and spoil the play for my guests. No – you can damn well wait.'

'But—'

'Get the boy away after the show, give me an hour with the girl and it's yours. Not before.'

And, striding away, he heads towards the staircase which leads up to his bedchamber. He wants to make sure it is fit to receive . . . an unexpected guest a little later on.

Sofia smiles up at Beppe, who is staring appraisingly at her face, the little pot of crushed pearl in one hand and the wide brush in the other. 'I'm going to put a little more of the pearl on than before – the stage will be lantern-lit and you'll shimmer beautifully,' he says.

'Give me your mask, and I'll give it a polish while you're doing my face.'

Putting the brush between his teeth, Beppe reaches behind him, grabs the mask from the hook from which it is dangling, and passes it over. Sofia takes a square of linen from the table, folds it over her fingers and begins to stroke the already gleaming black leather, working the cloth into the folds over the brows, the creases under the eyes, the smooth bulge of the cheeks.

'Whoa, stop it! Don't look down – do it by feel,' Beppe says, putting a finger under her chin and tilting her face upwards again.

Sofia takes hold of his wrist, stroking up onto his palm with her thumb. 'Can we do some other things . . . by feel . . . later on, after the show . . . ?' she says, biting her lip.

Beppe puffs a breath. 'Stop it – you'll make me forget my lines.'

The chalk and pearl creases around Sofia's eyes as she smiles at him.

'Has anyone seen my handkerchief?' From the other side of the room, Giovanni Battista sounds anxious, but Cosima is already holding it up between finger and thumb and flapping it out to him — as she does at least three or four times every performance.

'Sofia, *cara*,' she says quietly, 'next time we have a moment, make Giovanni Battista a dozen or so of these, will you? Gio, Sofia will make you a pile of handkerchiefs, and we'll keep them for you, safe and sound.'

Sofia glances across at Giovanni Battista. He catches her eye and she blows him a kiss. Pretending to catch it, he tucks it carefully into his breeches pocket with the handkerchief, then turns back to squint into the tiny steel mirror.

The lanterns, candles, torches and rushlights have been lit and the great banqueting hall is buzzing with a dozen conversations. Sebastiano gazes around, delighted with the unfolding evening. The effect of it all is even better than he hoped it would be. Everyone seems to be enjoying themselves so far, and the atmosphere in the room is positively glittering. The peacock-bright dresses and doublets echo the colours of the frescos, filling the room with a dancing display of colour and shimmer as some three dozen men and women cluster in groups, conversing. Some are already being shown to their chairs by the castle servants, for, unlike the usual jostling, shoving, fidgeting audiences in piazzas and market squares, here at the Castello della Franceschina Sebastiano has made sure that every one of his invited guests will be comfortably seated. Almost every chair, stool and bench in the building has been drafted into service. The elderly servant with the dirty-thistledown hair is beaming as he extends an arm to shepherd a couple of new arrivals into the room.

'Ah, da Correggio, so good of you to invite us!' A reedy voice cuts through the hum of conversation, unpleasantly familiar to Sebastiano.

Breaking from his contemplation of the room, he snaps around. '*Buon giorno*, Signor di Maccio – and the lovely signora. It's a pleasure to see you both here at Franceschina . . . after far too long.' Sebastiano pecks a bow towards a gaunt-faced man with sparse, almost colourless hair. Taking the man's wife's hand, he lifts it to his mouth; Maddalena says nothing as his lips graze her knuckles – though he feels her arm stiffening, and she snatches her hand back, avoiding his eye. Her other hand, he sees now, is starfish-splayed over her belly – the swelling there is more obvious now, far more obvious even than the other day, and he wonders briefly how even a man as obtuse as Paolo di Maccio can have failed to notice it – and then an idea comes to him. An idea so simple he is astounded he has not thought of it before.

He almost laughs aloud.

He has threatened Maddalena with exposure of her infidelity on so many occasions, never really intending to do so, enjoying the taunting, but *now* is the perfect time to do it. Now, as he contemplates the encounter he is planning with the little actress later on this evening, he realizes that he can enjoy putting a suitably theatrical end to his increasingly troubled liaison with Maddalena. He'll be rid of her at last. Biting down a grin, he imagines how the conversation might unfold: *I can only think that you must have noticed your wife's . . . erm . . . recently altered physique, signore,* he will say in an intimate whisper, deliberately politely, an arm around di Maccio's back. As friend to friend. He practises the smile, now, and Signor di Maccio – unwitting – returns it. *I wonder, though, if you have surmised the cause.* He will stand back then. Harden the look. Tighten the smile. No doubt the old man will frown, Sebastiano thinks. He will bluster out his lack of comprehension, and into this confusion Sebastiano will drop the truth. Still smiling. *You won't know this, but she's carrying my bastard – that's the reason she's the shape she is. I've been fucking the little whore for months – seeing as you are entirely incapable of doing so yourself – and what is inside that swollen belly is the result of the ... er ... entertainment I've been offering her. Don't worry, though, sir: I'm as tired of the games we've been playing as I think she is – and you're welcome to have her back – her and the brat.*

He looks over at Maddalena, his gaze on the rounded protrusion of her skirts. Maddalena stares at the floor.

I very much doubt, though, he will continue, *you will wish society to know either of the ever-flaccid contents of your breeches, or of the whoring promiscuity of your opium-quaffing wife, will you now?* He will pause then, enjoying the effect. *Oh? What's that? Did you not know about her need for the latest medicaments either? Oh, I'm so sorry; I thought you must have done. But don't worry –* his smile will broaden here – *nobody need know anything about any of it. I have no intention of disseminating the news. In fact, you can pass off the bastard chit as your own if you should care to – to silence the whisperers. Under ... certain conditions, that is.* And then he will drop his smile and in a cold, hard voice he has used to great effect on many similar occasions, he will name his price.

He glances from Maddalena to her husband, delighted with himself. At the sight of his satisfied smirk though, Maddalena's eyes widen and she looks, Sebastiano sees now, positively terrified.

'Do take your seats,' he says, swallowing down smug relief and gesturing towards where a variety of benches and chairs have been placed facing the stage. The latter is now complete and colourful, with its brightly painted street scene stretched taut over the back ropes; a large basket, a couple of chairs, a barrel, a travelling bag, and a stuffed dog have been placed strategically ready for the performance to begin.

The room looks vivid and gaudy in the light from at least two hundred candles, and a dozen pitch-soaked torches are burning in brackets along both side walls. The fifty or so seated guests are murmuring happily amongst themselves – their anticipation shimmers in the air above them like a heat haze – and around the edges of the great banqueting room the servants have gathered in quietly chattering clusters – those of the Franceschina household and those who have travelled here with the various invitees.

Hunching his shoulders and carefully avoiding eye contact with any of the castle underlings, Marco da Correggio walks closely behind a party of half a dozen loudly conversing guests as they make their way in through the great entrance doors of the Castello della Franceschina, and is shown with them through to the Southern Banqueting Chamber. Edging past a pair of elderly women seated on the end of a row of chairs towards the back of the room, he seats himself next to a dapper little man in a brightly embroidered doublet, sliding down low in his seat and folding his arms tightly across his chest.

From here, Marco can see the back of Sebastiano's head. Up at the front of the room, his cousin is talking to someone – Marco thinks it is the husband of Sebastiano's latest paramour. Leaning in towards his companion, Sebastiano is gesticulating with animation and seems in surprisingly good spirits. Presumably, though, given everything he was saying the other day, he is acting, Marco thinks.

He swallows uncomfortably. The plan he has been working on since that last encounter with Sebastiano in the tavern seems now, in the face of this glittering collection of his cousin's friends and acquaintances, pitifully inadequate. Childishly simplistic. It smacks of desperation. His confidence in his idea is rapidly swirling away. If this evening's event is a façade, constructed by Sebastiano to convince those around him that his finances are in better shape than they really are, then it's a bloody effective one, Marco thinks now. Looking up at the stage, and seeing the busily painted backcloth depicting an almost-believable receding street scene, it occurs to him that the room is in fact positively buzzing with artifice. Will the invited guests be more convinced by Sebastiano's false proclamations of affluence, or by the actors' imminent performance? Or is the one necessary to the other for the credibility of either? He cannot work it out.

Pushing a hand into his breeches pocket, he runs a finger along the creased edge of a folded letter: the letter that he hopes will be enough of a lever to get Sebastiano off his back once and for all. If it works, it will end up as a stand-off between the two of them: each of them will be dangling a rock over the other's head.

Marco doubts that any serious criminal charges would be brought against Sebastiano should the adultery come to light. Sebastiano is unmarried, so he, Marco, cannot follow Sebastiano's idea and use the threat of the *strappado* or a gibbet as a deterrent. The sterner punishments would no doubt be meted out to the various women involved, and Marco doubts that that would trouble his cousin excessively. No – Marco's only hope of release from Sebastiano's tyranny rests solely on the distinct possibility of his cousin's social exclusion. If Signor da Budrio were to hear of Sebastiano's behaviour, Marco is almost certain that his cousin's hopes of maintaining any sort of position in Bolognese society would be in ruins – for the governor of Bologna is a fanatical moralist.

It is quite certainly his only hope. He cannot raise the money, and knows he cannot outrun Sebastiano and his heavies for ever. He will just have rely upon his cousin's desperation to maintain his social standing.

Wiping his nose with the back of his wrist, he slumps lower in his chair as a masked figure, wearing what looks like a couple of flour sacks cinched in at the waist, steps bent-kneed onto the stage, carrying a guitar. Staring out at the audience for a moment, the odd-looking man crosses the boards and seats himself on the barrel; he begins to play and sing, and the audience falls silent.

22

From his seat in the front row, Sebastiano is enjoying himself. He has just heard Maddalena cough quietly; she and her husband are just a few seats behind him. He does not turn to look at them. He would prefer not to let her know he is thinking about her. He is finding it hard to contain his delight in his new idea, and his gnawing fear of his creditors is, for the first time in weeks, beginning to recede. It is, he reasons with himself now, unthinkable that di Maccio will allow his, Sebastiano's, revelation of his wife's infidelity and corruption – and of di Maccio's own impotence – to leak out into society, and the old man is easily wealthy enough to give Sebastiano everything he means to ask for, without really depleting his own coffers. It's a perfect solution. He will whisper his intentions to him when the performers stop for a break in the middle of the play.

He is tired of Maddalena – he realizes that now. It's true that she's beautiful: God yes, her body is undoubtedly luscious. In fact even the thought of it now – ripe and rounded and splay-legged beneath him – is making him stiffen, but there's no doubt that she's a damned liability. She makes him so angry, so often – she can be an unthinking fool – and he will be glad to be rid of her. She can pass off the bastard she's carrying as her husband's child – di Maccio should be pleased, Sebastiano thinks. In fact, he'll be providing the impotent old fool with an heir he would never have been able to create for himself. Generous, really.

The gorgeous woman in the red dress leaves the stage and – Sebastiano's mouth opens slightly – a new character appears from behind the backcloth. Slight, dressed in grey: it is the girl with the wildly curly black hair. God, she is exquisite, Sebastiano thinks, stiffening further as he begins to contemplate exactly what he intends to do with her when Angelo introduces her after the performance.

Hands on hips, the girl tilts her chin and scowls in disapproval as Arlecchino falls at her feet, grinning up at her and blowing her a kiss. A kiss? He, Sebastiano, will blow her more than a bloody kiss. He puffs out a breath – God, look at her! Angelo da Bagnacavallo's wholly unexpected suggestion is going to be worth considerably more than the single bloody bottle of laudanum he has promised him. The man would probably make far more money as a pimp than an actor.

'*Oh, shut up, you idiot! This will wipe the smile off your face*,' Sofia says, and Beppe scrambles to his feet. '*Listen!*' She flaps a hand, beckoning to Beppe to come closer. '*Listen to what I heard Rosaura say just now – it's so dreadfully shocking.*'

Beppe's face is of course inscrutable behind his mask, but his body radiates curiosity. He sidles closer, head tilted to one side. '*What?*' he says, taking Sofia's fingers in his. '*What is it?*'

And, free hand cupped around her mouth, whispering in the loud hiss she has been taught to use – a hiss that she knows will carry right to the back of even a busy piazza – Sofia tells him of the terrible treachery of Angelo and Vico's two characters. How they have knocked out the long-nosed character, Il Capitano – played by Federico – and left him for dead in a ditch.

Beppe's mouth opens wider and wider as she speaks, and his hands illustrate the shock his mask conceals. '*But . . . but . . . that's t-t-terrible!*' he stutters. '*In a d-ditch! Like a . . . like a . . . dead dog? Or a . . . a . . . pile of yesterday's leftover pasta?*'

Laughter from the audience. Beppe starts to stagger about the stage, drunk with shock, and Sofia trots after him, hands clasped, eyes wide. '*I'm sorry,*' she says. '*I didn't know you'd be so upset to hear about it . . . I always thought you didn't like him very much.*'

Beppe stops suddenly and straightens. Shaking his head and pushing his hands down into his breeches pockets, he shrugs and says in a much stronger, more cheerful voice, '*I don't. Can't stand him, the stupid old fool – but he's my master! I have to be sad. It's . . . it's obligatory.*' And he reverts to the shocked staggering.

The laughter from the audience is louder now. Turning to them, Beppe shrugs again, lifting his shoulders far higher this time, and the corners of his mouth turn down. Somebody catcalls.

Sofia, meanwhile, nods, pulls a small square of embroidered linen from her sleeve, wipes her eyes delicately and blows her nose.

The show is nearly over. Sebastiano is contemplating slipping out just before the end, to ensure he can find Angelo and the little creature with the curly hair as soon as she emerges. But no, he now reasons with himself, he should stay, as he wants to make sure she sees him clapping enthusiastically. He is intending to use his enjoyment of the show as his ostensible reason for opening a conversation with her, and that gambit would appear decidedly unconvincing were he not to be seen applauding with the rest of the audience. He'll make sure she catches sight of him before she leaves the stage. He will need, too, to be seen by the rest of the guests: the illusion of him as magnanimous host must be maintained through to the end of the evening.

Marco da Correggio, from his seat near the back of the great chamber, glances at his dapper little neighbour in the fancy doublet, then returns his gaze to the front of the room, and the back of his cousin's head. He can feel the letter, crisp-cornered and bulky in his pocket. Not long now.

'Mind your face,' Beppe says quietly as Sofia struggles to unfasten and take off the grey dress in the cramped space behind the stage. 'Don't smudge anything. We're nearly there – and you've done so well! You've been wonderful.' He tilts her chin upwards with the tip of one finger and kisses her mouth. 'Quickly, get this on. We'll hang the dress here, look.' Beppe pushes a heavy wooden hanger into the bodice of the grey dress and hooks it onto a loop of rope. 'Here.'

Standing in front of her in his hose, he holds out the diamond-patched breeches he has just taken off. They are still warm with the heat from his body as Sofia steps into them. Her fingers are trembling as she pushes her chemise down inside the breeches and pulls in the drawstrings at the waist as tightly as they will go. Even drawn in snugly, though, and with the bulk of the chemise padding them out, the breeches hang on her hips. 'I look like a sausage,' she mutters, scowling down at her rounded belly and hips.

Behind his black mask, Beppe is grinning. 'That's just what I was thinking myself,' he says. 'A very appealing sausage, though.' Holding out his jacket, he gives it a little shake. 'Quick – we're back on stage in a few seconds, and I've got to get this bloody dress on.'

Sofia pushes her arms down into the jacket sleeves, and begins to fasten it as Beppe takes an identical – if considerably larger – version of the grey dress from another hanger. Scrambling into it, he tugs the front fastening laces tight and knots them. He pulls the black woollen hat from his head and hands it to Sofia who winds her unruly curls into a knot and crams the hat onto the back of her head.

'Here!' Vico is standing at the bottom of the backstage steps. 'You've forgotten this.' He is holding a black half-mask on a stick. Sofia smiles her thanks, crouches down and takes the mask from him.

Beppe, meanwhile, is adjusting a black curly wig, pushing wisps of his own hair up and under the front edges. Seeing Sofia biting down a smile, he puts a hand to his cheek and simpers at her, bobbing down into an arch curtsy. Sofia climbs up onto a wooden crate, reaches out and – as Beppe has just done to her – tips his face upwards with her forefinger under his chin. 'Oh, you do look pretty, signorina,' she says, kissing him and sniggering.

'Stop it, you two – and get on that bloody stage,' hisses Vico from below.

Raising a hand in acknowledgement, Beppe scoops an arm around Sofia and lifts her off the crate. Grabbing a handful of one of her chemise-padded buttocks for a second and grinning at her smothered squeal, he then jerks his head towards the gap in the backcloth. 'Come on – last scene.'

The players bow and the applause rises up, filling the big banqueting chamber with a noise that sounds to Sofia like roaring flames. Holding hands, they all bow yet again, and the noise goes on, spreading up towards the painted ceiling, filling Sofia's ears. She cannot stop smiling – she's succeeded. She has performed again, in this most prestigious of venues, without any major mishap, and the audience seem to have enjoyed what she has done. She feels Beppe's grip on her right hand tightening and looks around at him. His tilted smile is so wide that his mask is being pushed off-centre. 'You did it again,' he whispers. 'Well done! We'll be able to call you a seasoned professional soon.'

Looking back at the cheering audience, Sofia sees their extravagantly doubleted host, on his feet, his clapping hands raised to head-height. His gaze seems to be fixed upon her.

The Coraggiosi push one by one through the backcloth, then jostle down off the back of the stage, down the steps and out to the back of the chamber, where they are met by a dozen or more people, all eager to talk to them, to share their happiness, to be a part of the magic. *Thank you, all of you – that was wonderful! . . . When is your next show? I want to make sure I'm there . . . Is it dreadfully hot behind those masks? . . . How did you do the scene with the ghost? I loved that . . .*

Sofia is giddy with it, exhausted, ecstatic. She is hot and tired, and the chalk and pearl on her face is now itching so badly she wants to scrub it away, but it feels to her now – even more than it did after her very first performance – as though some unknown force in her is elbowing past the fatigue and the discomfort. She could run and jump and sing and laugh, she thinks. In fact, she is almost sure she could manage one of Beppe's somersaults.

He is beside her, mask now pushed up onto the top of his head, displacing the ridiculous wig. Hugging her, he swings her around, lifting her feet a little off the floor. She looks up at him, her smile stretched wide, her eyes shining; lowering his head to hers, he reaches forward to kiss her.

'I must congratulate you,' says a voice behind them, and Sofia's head snaps around to see who has spoken. Sebastiano da Correggio is holding out a hand towards her. 'Your performance was quite delightful, signorina,' he says, and Sofia smiles. 'Quite the most striking part of the evening for me.'

'You're very kind, signore,' she says, feeling her face burn.

'No, not at all. Not kind at all. Merely expressing a heartfelt opinion.'

Sofia begins to protest, trying to explain that her part in the play was merely a small fraction of the whole, but Signor da Correggio is having none of it. 'My dear signorina, as your host for the evening, I believe it's entirely acceptable for me to be outrageously partisan in my appreciation of the entertainment I've just witnessed. *I* think you were the best thing in the show – certainly quite the prettiest – and I'm happy to say so to anyone who asks.'

Federico and Giovanni Battista edge past, carrying one of the long wooden poles between them. Federico gives her and Beppe a meaningful look and jerks his head towards the stage.

Sofia glances back at him. 'Thank you, signore, you're very kind, but if you will excuse me, I must help pack away.' She gestures to where everything is already being taken to pieces. 'The dismantling has started – we always do the dismantling together . . . all of us.' As she takes Beppe's hand, she sees a shadow cross the signore's face, but his expression clears quickly.

'Of course,' he says with a brief bow. 'But I should like you to drink with me later.'

Sofia does not reply, but smiles briefly; she hopes the slight twitch of her head she feels herself make did not look too much like a nod.

That was not her intention.

'Here, Beppe!' Vico calls from under the stage, holding up a coil of rope. 'Catch this, will you?'

*

'Just piss off, Marco.' Sebastiano flicks a dismissive glance at the letter in his hand, then looks back at his cousin.

'You need to listen to me, Sebastiano.'

'No. No I don't. *You* need to listen to *me*. You owe me one hundred *scudi*. I don't care what is in this pathetic scrawl of a letter – I don't give a two-*scudi* shit if you send it to da Budrio this week, next year or tomorrow morning. If you do, I shall merely refute the charges and point out to the signore that they have been pressed by someone who is wilfully withholding from me a considerable sum of money owed.'

'The women concerned will bear witness . . .'

Sebastiano laughs, hoping that the cold thread of terror that has flashed over his scalp at the thought that this might in fact be the case will not show in his expression. 'You really think they would? You really think they would condemn themselves like that – just to revenge themselves on *me*? Are you mad?'

Marco does not reply.

Turning his back on his cousin, Sebastiano screws the letter into a ball, throws it onto the floor and strides away without looking back. He hears a soft sound of rustling paper as he goes, and is sure that Marco has picked the paper back up and is trying to smooth it out again.

In an unlit corner of the smaller banqueting hall, Paolo di Maccio is holding his wife's wrist in one bony hand. 'Is what he says true, Maddalena? You are with child?'

She does not reply.

Di Maccio's gaze drops to her belly. 'Dear God. How could I not have seen?' he mutters. Looking back at her, he says in a voice constricted with anger, 'You hardly need to confirm it, but is it really true that it is *his*? Is this da Correggio's child?'

Maddalena again says nothing, but the slight lift of her shoulders is enough of a reply for her husband. His face whitens. 'God in heaven, have you any idea what you have done? That man could ruin us completely.'

In the smaller of the two banqueting halls, the remains of a sumptuous meal lie scattered across an expanse of linen-draped table. Four many-branched candlesticks have dribbled yellowish wax onto the cloth, and these fast-hardening spatters lie untidily amongst the debris of torn bread, part-empty bowls of fruit and sweetmeats and glittering glasses. The earlier plates of roasted capon with orange sauce, of fresh egg pasta stuffed with pumpkin and flavoured with sage and of crisp-skinned grilled bream have long since been collected and taken away by the dozen or so castle servants.

The wine is still flowing freely and the Coraggiosi, along with the dozen or so other guests, have eaten well. 'Probably one of the best meals we've ever been offered after a performance,' Agostino says, wiping his mouth with the back of his wrist. Getting to his feet and lifting his glass, he turns to Sebastiano da Correggio, who is sitting at the head of the table. 'Signore, this has all been entirely delicious. An extraordinary meal! You have far, far exceeded your remit as our highly esteemed host, and we are all enormously grateful, I promise you, every one of us – are we not, Coraggiosi?'

A murmur of heartfelt agreement and a patter of applause buzz around the table.

Sofia is truly exhausted. The euphoria she felt immediately after the end of the show has evaporated and she now just feels heavy and woolly-headed with the wine she has drunk; her eyes are itching and the skin on her face – scrubbed clean now of the chalk and the pearl – is dry and tight. She leans wearily against Beppe, who puts an arm around her shoulders.

'We can go to bed soon,' he says, and Sofia smiles up at him. 'Together?'

Beppe says quietly, 'Yes. Why not? The others are all taking up the offer of the two big castle rooms which have been decked out for us, so that'll leave the wagons empty. Might you prefer to . . . ?' He does not complete the question, but Sofia nods.

'Yes,' she says, smiling. 'I think I might.'

'Come on then – shall we go now? I think it's late enough for us not to look rude if we leave.'

Beppe and Sofia both make as though to stand, but before they have even pushed back their chairs, Angelo, who has just come back into the room, edges behind several chairs and says quietly into Beppe's ear, 'You need to go out and see to your dog.'

'What? What do you mean? What's the matter?'

Angelo flicks a glance up the table towards where Sebastiano is sitting. Sebastiano is watching him. He nods once, then says, 'I just went for a piss a few moments ago, nipped out to fetch something from the wagons and found several of the servants out there. The dog must have got loose and gone after a rat or something, they said – he has quite a cut on his leg.'

'Where is he?' Beppe is on his feet. Sofia stands too.

'They said they'd take him into the kitchens . . .'

'I'll come with you,' Sofia says. Beppe nods, but as they turn to leave the room, Agostino calls down the table, hand raised. 'Sofia! Wait a moment – don't go! *Cara*, come here and talk to Signor da Correggio before we all go off to bed. He says he's been waiting all evening to have a chance to tell you how much he enjoyed your performance. I've just told him that you've only ever been on a stage a couple of times, and he says he is struggling to believe me. Come and tell him all about it!'

Sofia's heart lurches, and she looks at Beppe, who shrugs.

'Go and talk to him. I'll find Ippo,' he says. 'I'll bring him back up here, and then we can go to the wagon.'

Sofia nods. Scraping back her chair, she sidles along behind the other members of the troupe, up towards the head of the table. Signor da Correggio stands as she approaches, and snaps his fingers to one of the servants, who immediately hurries over with an extra chair: a delicately carved wooden folding stool. Da Correggio flaps it open and places it immediately next to his own seat.

'Signorina, come and sit,' he says, patting the stool.

Sofia follows instructions.

Leaning towards her, Signor da Correggio puts an arm around her shoulders. His breath is sour with the wine he has been drinking and Sofia swallows uncomfortably.

'Signorina,' he says quietly, his mouth close to her ear, creating an unwanted intimacy between them, 'it simply has to be a blatant falsehood that this is only your third performance, that you are in fact a . . . not far from being a *commedia* virgin. Signor Martinelli' — he nods towards Agostino — 'is quite obviously telling me a pack of lies. You have been acting for years!'

'No, signore,' Sofia says, more confidently than she feels. 'I promise you, he's quite correct.'

Da Correggio's other hand goes to Sofia's chin: she tries not to flinch as he tilts her face up towards his and studies it for some seconds. Then, turning to a frozen-faced woman some seats away, he says, 'There, Maddalena, what do you say now? I told you she was exquisite, did I not? Quite exquisite!'

The woman makes no response. Her features might have been carved in stone.

'What about you, signore?' He is now addressing a thin man with sparse hair, seated next to the woman, and seems, Sofia thinks, to be goading him deliberately. 'Well, Signor di Maccio, do you not agree with me that this child is quite lovely? And did she not perform well? Was her pretty little Colombina not a triumph? Does the sight of such a perfect creature – seen close to – not *arouse* you, sir?'

Her skin prickling with embarrassment, Sofia's gaze flicks from the woman to this Signor di Maccio – a sparse-haired, finely dressed nobleman – who, she sees, is eyeing her with what seems worryingly like distaste rather than admiration. Signor di Maccio turns back to da Correggio and Sofia is shocked at the naked rage in his sunken-cheeked face. The atmosphere around this end of the table has tautened and stiffened, as though the signore is somehow paralysing everyone around him with his heartily cheerful words – rendering his guests oddly lifeless. It appears to be calculated, and he seems to be thoroughly enjoying the process.

Turning to Agostino, seated a couple of seats down on her other side, Sofia widens her eyes, pleading silently with him to be rescued. But Agostino's big face is flushed and his goblet is empty, and he merely smiles widely at her, enjoying his host's admiration and not registering Sofia's distress.

'Ago, sort out a dispute for us!' Federico says then in a truculent voice from further down the table, and Agostino turns away. 'Giovanni Battista says we should be thinking about performing some of Lombardone's scenarios but *I* say the man can't write.'

Agostino opens his mouth to reply, and at this, da Correggio lays a hand over Sofia's. 'Signorina,' he says in little more than a whisper, 'if your friends will excuse you, I have a mind to show you a treasure. A tapestry – one of the Correggio heirlooms, which I am sure will interest a gifted needlewoman such as yourself. Come with me now and I promise you you'll be astounded ...' Taking her hand, he stands.

'Oh ... Signore, forgive me, but ...' Sofia tries to excuse herself, tries to pull her hand from his, but da Correggio seems not to hear her and his grip is strong.

'Ago—'

But Agostino is now engaged in vociferous debate with Federico and Giovanni Battista, and the three men, their voices raised, are distracting Vico and the two women. Nobody seems to hear her and she dares not speak more overtly. Beppe is still nowhere to be seen. Angelo is the only other member of the troupe she can ask to help her; staring hard at him, she wills him to say something, but he is picking at the skin on the side of his thumbnail with his teeth and seems to be deliberately avoiding her eye.

Gripping her hand almost painfully, Signor da Correggio leaves the banqueting hall and hurries Sofia through two other large and beautifully appointed rooms towards a flight of stairs. He appears to be about to climb them, when a deep voice sounds out from above, and he checks.

'Servants,' he says. 'Damn them. Perhaps we'll have a look at my study first.' He looks hard at Sofia and runs his tongue over his lips. 'We can go back upstairs later.'

Sofia's eyes widen. 'Later? But, signore, I have to—'

'We don't have much time,' he mutters, more to himself than to her. 'Come on!'

They walk fast together, and the signore is now gripping Sofia's wrist, rather than her hand. Through another painted room, out into a plain, brick-floored corridor, where both she and Signor da Correggio stop dead. A liveried servant – young and slightly built and with a heavily laden tray in his hands – backs awkwardly out of a door and starts at the sight of them, gasping audibly. The stump of a candle he has in a candlestick on the tray sends wobbling shadows up and around his face, and even in the almost-darkness, Sofia can see that he is flushing deeply. She wonders whether she should call to him to help her, but before she can speak, da Correggio snaps at him.

'What the hell are you staring at? Go on – get lost!'

The boy pushes back through the door without a word.

'Damn them! Damned servants, getting in the way wherever I turn.' He takes hold of the handle of yet another door a few yards further along. 'Here. In here – you'll like this. My study. The walls are hung with silk my father brought back from a trip out east many years ago.'

The room is unlit, but moonlight is flooding in through a wide casement, and as Sofia gazes around, she sees that it is richly furnished. A set of deep shelves is busily filled with books, rolls of paper, pots, rows of bottles of different sizes – several of them very small – a feathered hat and a number of painted wooden boxes. A long, ornately carved table stands in the centre of the room; it too is littered with many smaller objects Sofia cannot determine in the darkness and a heavy iron candlestick stands, unlit, at each end. A ladder-backed chair sits neatly in front of the table, a doublet draped across the upright. Several other chairs have been pushed back against the wall with the door in it; over on the far side is a small bed, hung with drawn-back curtains.

A bed.

At the sight of this, her heart now thudding uncomfortably, Sofia is rocked by a wave of nausea. Muttering to herself, breathing heavily, she tugs once again at her hand. The signore, however, holds fast. Putting his other arm around her back, pressing in flat-palmed, he draws her in close, and his sour wine-breath is strong in her nostrils. She feels him take hold of her chin again with his finger and thumb; he tilts her face up towards his. Straining backwards with both palms on his doublet-front, gritting her teeth, she struggles to push him away from her, swearing under her breath.

'What's this? Well, well, well! Not quite the lady I took you for, it seems. Did the actors teach you that language or did you know it before? What's the matter, *carissima*? I just wanted to show you my study. I thought you might like to . . . ' He ducks his head, takes a handful of her hair, and puts parted lips onto hers before she can get away from him, probing into her mouth with his tongue, sliding his free hand up and onto her breast, but Sofia twists her head away, feeling her scalp burn. His mouth slides wetly across her cheek towards her ear.

Taking her by the upper arms then, pulling her upwards, almost off her feet, he starts walking her backwards towards the bed. 'What's the matter?' he says as they stumble together across the room. 'Not just a stage virgin, then, but *virgo intacta* in the bed-chamber as well? Is that it?'

'Let go of me . . . ' Sofia mutters through her teeth, trying helplessly to twist her arms out of his grip. 'You bloody bastard, let go, and . . . '

'Oh, I *am* disappointed . . . very disappointed. I had thought you might have relished the idea of spending tonight with me,' da Correggio says indistinctly, and his wine-sour words are hot against the skin of her face. 'It'd be a night you'd not forget in a hurry. I had thought actresses in general had fewer moral scruples than you seem to possess . . . but no matter—' He interrupts his own sentence, tugging Sofia in close again. Pushing her down onto her back and covering her mouth with his own, he silences her protests, but she twists her head away once more, and a ragged scream spills out of her – hot against da Correggio's cheek.

The door bangs open.

'Hey! You! Leave her alone!'

Beppe's voice.

Da Correggio is blocking her view of the room; Sofia cannot see Beppe, but she hears him banging past the furniture, hears Ippo's scrabbling claws and panting breath.

'Get off her, you bastard!'

And then he is there, pulling at da Correggio, dragging him to his feet, knocking him off balance so that he releases Sofia's arms. She scrambles out from under him. Ippo is snarling and barking. 'What the hell do you think you're doing?' Beppe says, squaring up to da Correggio, tugging him around, grabbing fistfuls of the embroidered doublet and pulling him away from Sofia. Stumbling backwards, she almost trips over a chair; gasping, she throws her arms out sideways to keep her balance.

'Keep your hands off her!' Beppe's voice cracks. He shoves at da Correggio's chest with the heels of both hands.

Da Correggio staggers, then rights himself. 'What the hell—?'

Beppe stands square now between da Correggio and Sofia, who begins edging backwards towards the study door. 'I think you'll find . . . *signore*,' he says, his voice thick with anger, 'that the lady has no wish for your company. Perhaps you'll be good enough to stand away and let her – and me – go back to our wagon.'

'You fucking little reprobate, how *dare* you!' Da Correggio's face is distorted with rage. Jaw jutting, his cheeks blotched darkly, he raises clearly practised fists, elbows angled, but Beppe stands his ground, his hands balling too.

Sofia's gaze flicks from one man to the other, breath held, wide-eyed.

Da Correggio takes a step towards Beppe, who does not back

away. '*I* think *you*'ll find, you ignorant little shit,' he says in a carrying whisper, 'that this is *my* house, and that I can invite whom I choose into my bed – and when.'

'It's usually thought to be good manners to accept a refusal after issuing an invitation, though, isn't it?'

Da Correggio swears and punches out at Beppe, who ducks nimbly; straightening, he lets fly with a fist. The blow cracks hard against da Correggio's jaw, and the nobleman grunts and staggers backwards, tripping over a wooden chest and sprawling on his back onto the floor.

'Quick!' Beppe turns, grabs Sofia's arm and drags her towards the door. 'Before he gets up again!' Half running, half falling, the two of them – followed by the dog – stumble across the room and out of the door; da Correggio slurs out another vitriolic oath, then slumps back to lie groaning next to the bed.

Beppe's hand is tight around Sofia's wrist as they bang the door shut behind them; they run together, with the dog, back through the castle and out, out towards where the wagons have been parked near the meadow at the back of the building. Both gasping for breath, chests heaving, they lean against the side of the yellow wagon for a moment; Beppe hugs Sofia and holds her close, then stands away from her, a hand on each of her arms. 'We have to get out of here, *cara*,' he says. 'Right away from here. He'll be after us as soon as he can alert the servants, I'm sure of it. I'll run in and tell Agostino and Cosima. I think we're all going to have to go – tonight. The whole troupe.'

'Oh God, Beppe, what have I done? I've ruined everything . . .'

'*You?* You've done nothing, my lovely girl, nothing at all! It was that fucking whoremonger out there!'

Sofia is startled by the vehemence of his words, but he pulls her into a tight hug, then holds her face and kisses her, saying, 'Get into the smallest cart and hide while I go and tell the others, then we'll hitch the cart up and get ourselves out and back on the road to Bologna.'

'But what if he—?'

'I'll not be more than a moment. Ippo will stay here with you.' Beppe kisses her again, orders the dog to stay and guard, then turns and runs back in through the door.

23

An hour later

Stumbling across the room and crouching next to the sprawled figure, the young black-clad servant reaches out towards the back of his master's blood-soaked head; as his trembling fingers touch a sticky wetness and he feels the softened sag of a shattered skull, he recoils with an open-mouthed gasp, retching and wiping his hand quickly on his breeches.

He pushes himself back upright and backs away from the body; the ground sways unsteadily under his feet. 'Quick!' he shouts out, his voice thickened with shock, stumbling backwards, scrabbling like a monkey out into the corridor. 'Quick! Somebody get help! The signore – oh God, quick!'

'What? What is it?'

'What's the noise about?'

'What's going on?'

Three, four, five people appear from different doors, every face wearing the same expression of fatigued bemusement – it is well past midnight. The oldest and largest of the new arrivals frowns at the boy, shaking his head in irritation. 'Giuseppe Palmieri, what on earth are you doing, boy, making such a commotion so late at night?'

Giuseppe, leaning now against the wall, closes his eyes as the floor beneath him continues to buck and heave. He flaps a hand out sideways, muttering, 'In the study – go and look. It's the sig-nore.' And then he bends double and splatters vomit onto the brick floor.

It is clear from the outset firstly that Signor da Correggio is dead, and secondly that the bloodstained iron candlestick by the side of the body was the weapon responsible. As the shocked gaggle of servants raise lighted torches and look with horror at the sight of their master sprawled face down across the crimson-blotched floorboards, the candlestick lies, clearly visible, some few feet to one side of his head – where it has apparently been dropped by whoever wielded it with such devastating effect. The shadows from the torches shift about it, bobbing and wobbling as the torch-bearers move; the flamelight has the curious effect of making the iron sconce appear to dance with an entirely inappropriate sense of levity.

One man feels for a pulse. Finds none. Seeing enquiring faces, he shakes his head. Several people gasp; others cross themselves. One man falls to his knees, his lips moving in silent prayer.

'We should alert the authorities,' the oldest and largest servant says. 'Whoever did this can't have got far – the body's hardly chilled.'

'Someone ought to search the castle – or get out on the roads and see if they can see anyone.'

Two men hasten to volunteer, looking around at their companions, cheerfully smug at the thought of the importance of their new role in the impending adventure. Seeing this, another, younger man offers to accompany them, and, clapping him on the back and nodding their approval, the two volunteers accept.

They hesitate by the door as a thin boy says timidly, 'I saw something earlier. A girl. Here in the corridor, she was with—'

Somebody interrupts. 'Who was it, Piero?'

'One of those bloody actors, I expect,' comes another voice. 'They're the only strangers here tonight. Nothing but criminals, they are, in general, actors. Was it, Piero? An actor?'

'How should I know?' Piero says. 'I hardly caught more than a glimpse. It was a girl, that's all I know. Just a girl. A curly-haired girl. In a yellow dress. She was with the signore. And then—'

He is interrupted again. 'We need to wake them all up. The actors. Find out if anyone's missing.'

A thickset man with a twisted face says, 'But they've already gone.'

'What?'

'Heard them out the back by the stables, not half an hour since. Harnessing up their horses. Thought they'd just decided not to stay. Didn't think to talk to them.'

'One of them . . .' Piero tries to speak, but nobody listens and, shrugging, he closes his mouth again.

'Oh dear God, we must hurry,' the oldest servant says now. 'This early departure has to be significant. We must find them. You three' – he points to the three volunteers – 'you set off straight away, and you too, you can go with them.' A young man in castle livery starts at being thus singled out, but nods his acceptance of the task. The oldest servant turns and points to a red-faced man in stableman's clothing. 'Franco, take one of the swiftest horses now and rouse the *podestà*!'

Franco puts his hands on his hips, his expression outraged.

Jabbing a finger against his chest, he says, 'Me? Why me? Quite frankly, in my opinion, they've done us a bloody great favour: the opium-soaked bastard had it coming to him one way or another before long.'

There is a clotted mutter of agreement amongst the gathered servants, but the oldest servant's mouth has dropped open in shock; his several chins are wobbling and his thistledown hair stands on end. 'Franco! How dare you! You are a Franceschina servant, and as such your loyalty should be—'

Franco snorts. 'Loyalty? Stuff loyalty – he had no loyalty to us. Bernadino was dismissed only last week over nothing, wasn't he? Nothing! After – what? Twenty years' service? And little Caterina . . . well, we all know why *she* left, don't we? Poor bitch – carrying his bastard and far too many bruises, and—'

'No! No! Stop, stop, stop!' The oldest servant now looks near to tears. Pointing to the body with a stubby forefinger, he says in a voice distorted with distress, 'Look at him! Our master is lying dead at our feet – we should all have more respect. And every minute we stand here insulting his memory, the further away will be those responsible.'

The three volunteers and the young man in livery clear their throats. 'Er . . . should we get going?'

The oldest servant turns to them. 'Yes! Go quickly!'

'Which way?' one of the volunteers asks. 'Bologna? Verona? Where do you want us to go?'

The October night air is dank and cold – a scribble of ragged clouds has partially obscured the moon, and the chill feels to Sofia as though a thin sheet of uncooked pastry has been draped around her shoulders. She can see almost nothing in the fitful darkness; the lantern they have lit and hung to one side of the cart is illuminating little more than a few feet in any direction and the light from the moon is intermittent as the clouds scud. The bigger, yellow wagon shows only as a square block of denser darkness in front of them, with a faint, dirty glow to one side of it, while the third wagon – some way out in front – cannot be seen at all. The endless jumble of scrunching hoof-beats sounds oddly like last night's applause. With Beppe on one side of her and old Giovanni Battista on the other, Sofia wishes she could find a way to banish the fears of the night; she cannot determine, though, whether this trembling she cannot prevent is because of the cold, or fear. As she presses in against Beppe, he gathers the reins into one hand and puts an arm around her shoulders.

'Eh? What's this?' he says. 'Oh, my lovely girl, you're shivering. Here, take these a moment . . . ' Handing her the reins, Beppe scrambles back over the seat, through the little door-flap and into the interior of the cart. Sofia hears a box being opened behind her, and several small objects being dislodged and tumbling noisily onto the floor of the cart. Beppe swears several times as yet more things fall. Then a moment later he is back up next to her, flapping out a couple of blankets. 'Here,' he says, 'here's one for you, Giovanni, and now – stand up, little seamstress . . . that's it . . . ' Tucking the blanket under her bottom, he folds it neatly around her legs, while Giovanni Battista grunts and shifts his position as he wraps himself in his.

'There. Better?'

'Much. Thank you.' She hands the reins back and leans in close; Beppe's arm is around her again. He kisses the side of her face and she turns to him, offering him her mouth, ignoring the proximity of the old man. Beppe kisses her as the horse walks along in the blackness, the wheels of the cart scrunching and clattering on the rough ground.

The tears Sofia has been holding back begin to fall then, hot on her skin between her face and Beppe's. As they touch his cheek, he pulls back, wiping them gently away with the edge of his thumb. 'Hey, hey, hey, don't cry, *cara* – we've left the place now. It's all over. We don't ever have to go back.'

'But . . .' Sofia begins. '. . . but what if that man . . . what if he wants to have you charged with assault? You hit him so hard . . .'

Beppe snorts. 'I'd have hit the snivelling bastard a bloody sight harder if I could have done.'

'But . . . but he might not care about that, he might—'

'Oh, I reckon he'll be too embarrassed to do anything about it at all. An arrogant sod like him, admitting he was floored by a draggletail actor? I don't think so, do you?'

'Oh God, Beppe, I hope not.' Sofia puts her hands over her face. Speaking through her fingers she says, 'It's all my fault. I've wrecked everything.' She looks up at Beppe. 'You're all going to wish you'd never met me, and—'

'Now you stop it. Right now! I said before: none of this is your fault. You've done nothing – nothing at all. No one is angry with you.'

'And Ippo – his leg . . .'

'Look, that's not your fault either, is it? Daft dog got out and must have caught that leg on something. It's a nasty little cut, but it's strapped now and he'll do. He's not even limping. So stop worrying.'

'Beppe's right.' Giovanni Battista, perched uncomfortably on Sofia's other side, pats her knee, then grips it briefly in reassurance. 'None of us is angry. None of us is blaming you for anything. Why on earth should we?' His voice is warm and slow.

'I'm just sorry you had to be frightened like that,' Beppe says. 'I should have guessed that . . . that stinking pile of offal would try something of the sort – it was written all over his face at that table. If it's anyone's fault it's mine. I should have been with you.'

'We all should have seen it coming,' Giovanni Battista says quietly. 'We've been in the company of men like him often enough.'

'And thank God that boy saw you with him and spoke up when I was searching for you. I'd not have known where to look otherwise.'

Sofia leans in against Beppe and puts her head on his shoulder, jolting back and forth with the movement of the wagon. Pulling her in close, he grips her arm, tipping his head sideways to rest it lightly against hers. Her hair tickles his cheek. Giovanni Battista draws in a long, uneven breath and puffs it out again.

The blackness is still almost absolute; beyond the dirty little patches of light from the wagons' lanterns, to either side of the road and out behind them all is impenetrably dark; only far ahead does the low line of the approaching city show like a pale smear on the horizon.

'Not long now,' Beppe says.

As if in echo of this sentiment, Sofia hears Agostino's voice far ahead, calling back to them. 'That's Bologna ahead. We should be there in about an hour.'

Two men on a pair of heavy Franceschina horses head north towards Verona, two take the Modena road while another three make their way towards Bologna.

One of the three on the Bologna road kicks his horse and increases his pace, muttering darkly about the inconvenience of being forced out onto the road in the small hours of a cold morning (though significantly failing to hide his excitement at the thought of a possible imminent arrest). His companions speed up too, to maintain their position abreast. The light from the little lanterns hanging from each pair of stirrups flickers over the stones beneath the three horses' feet and the fitful moonlight throws the road ahead into piebald relief.

'Where do you reckon they've gone?' the first horsemen says, his voice jolting in rhythm with his gelding's gait.

'God knows.'

'Do we even know what we are looking for?'

'Three big wagons. No idea other than that. Piero said he saw a girl in the corridor outside the study with the signore, and—'

'Bloody hopeless, if you ask me. Waste of time. Hardly any moon, no chance of seeing anything – added to which, we don't even know what they look like. We could be riding right past them all and we'd be none the wiser. I hate bloody riding in the dark.'

'I'd say anyone out on the road at this time of the morning needs to be stopped and questioned,' the youngest of the three says. 'But Leonardo says it's the girl we need to take. Very young, Piero says. Load of curly hair. He saw her clearly. The dirty old lecher had her by the arm, he said – I'm not surprised she whacked him one, to be honest. She's the one we are to pass on to da Budrio, if we catch them.'

The first horseman shakes his head, screwing up his mouth as he considers the situation. 'Poor bitch won't stand a chance against da Budrio. The man's a bloody Tartar. Doesn't have a compassionate bone in his body, so I've heard.'

'You're not wrong.' The second horseman puffs out a breath. 'He's been in power too long, I reckon. There was bloody nearly a riot last month when he had that poor boy sent off to the galleys. Remember?'

'What – the one who was supposed to have raped that farrier's wife?'

'That's the one.'

'I know the boy's uncle. He said there wasn't a chance the lad was guilty – just in the wrong place at the wrong time with a face that fitted for some reason.' He trots on in silence for a few seconds, then adds, 'Bastard. Da Budrio, that is.'

'Bastard he may be, but he's a fool, I reckon. If he goes on like that for too long, they'll not stand for it – the Bolognese. There's a lot of bad feeling in the city right now. Very bad. People don't like being kicked around and it's been going on for years. And it's only getting worse.'

The first horseman nods agreement. Setting his jaw and tightening his reins, he kicks on again, hoping more than ever that it will be he and his companion who encounter this unknown killer. Then a thought strikes him: a killer? They are in pursuit of a murderer. He might be in danger himself. They all might, he and his friends.

'What if they turn on us?' he says, reining in a little. 'What if this girl goes for *us*, like she's done to him – the signore?'

The second man glances across, slowing his pace. 'Do you think . . . ?'

The third man shrugs. 'We've got our orders, haven't we?'

'That's as may be,' the first man says, his expression mutinous. 'I do what I'm told, like we all do, but I'm not prepared to die for him, the foul-tempered son of a strumpet. I say if we see them, we keep quiet and get the *sbirri* on to them. We'll do better to leave it to that bunch of bloody thugs to arrest them.'

'The *sbirri*?'

The first man shrugs, picturing in his mind Bologna's black-clad, law-enforcing heavies: always intent on achieving arrests, and rarely concerned with the rights and wrongs of the methods they employ to achieve them. 'Why not?'

The three men trot on, silent now, each immersed in their own thoughts. The horses' hoof-beats fall into and out of time with each other and the darkness gradually becomes imperceptibly thinner and paler as the minutes slip past.

The word comes back from Agostino and Cosima at the front of the line. 'We're almost at the city walls. We should pull in and stop for a rest.'

'Is it safe to stop?' Sofia says, anxiety thudding back up into her throat again.

Beppe pushes his fingers through his hair. 'Safer than going on. All the marketeers and the travellers will start coming and going in and out of the city soon, and then we can slip in unnoticed. If we go in now, someone will be sure to remember us. We'll be safer in the city centre in a crowd. We can take the wagons out to the space behind that big piazza where we put them after that performance before.'

'I'd jump down and stretch your legs, my dear,' Giovanni Battista suggests. 'And if you can give me a hand, I'll do the same.'

Fastening the reins, Beppe vaults down onto the ground and hands first Giovanni Battista and then Sofia from the cart. The old man frowns in discomfort as he eases the tension of the journey from his back and shoulders; in this grey dawn light the lines and creases in his face are deeply shadowed, the hollows in his cheeks more pronounced than usual and he looks almost ancient, Sofia thinks. She stretches too, yawning, hunching and rolling her shoulders, twisting her head from side to side, spreading and curling her fingers.

Agostino comes hurrying towards them. 'Beppe,' he says, arms slightly raised, his face a mask of compassionate concern. 'Are you all managing back here? Sofia, my dear ... oh, come here, you poor girl! I haven't had a moment to tell you how sorry I am that you had to endure something so terribly and unreasonably unpleasant . . .' He throws his arms wide and pulls Sofia into a hug which quite knocks the wind from her. 'I'm so sorry. We should never have chosen that venue. It quite threw you into the way of that man, and—'

Sofia pulls back. 'Don't be silly – you couldn't have known,' she says, shaking her head.

Agostino sighs. He lifts Sofia's hands to his lips and kisses her knuckles. 'Maybe not, *cara*, maybe not . . . but we all should have noticed when he took you away from the banquet, and we all feel horribly responsible, and—'

He breaks off at the sound of approaching hooves. Sofia gasps. Grabbing her hand, Beppe pulls her close, wrapping an arm around her shoulders; she grips a handful of his doublet. Three men on horseback are slowing their pace. Their stares are frank and appraising as they walk their mounts between the wagons and the roadside ditch, looking down on the huddled group standing quietly in the half-darkness.

'Broken down?' one of them asks; all three have slowed to a halt. 'A problem with a wagon? Need any help?'

'No, no, no, no,' Agostino says, with a creditable pretence at cheerful levity. 'Thank you, but no. We're heading into the city – just giving the horses a moment's break and stretching our legs. We've been on the road some time.'

The man raises his eyebrows and lifts his chin in acknowledgement; then, gathering up his reins, he and his companions walk on past without further comment.

Sofia puts her hands over her face.

Beppe pulls her into a hug. 'God,' he says. 'I thought they were from—'

'So did I,' Agostino says, wiping his forehead with the back of his hand. '*Santo Çielo*, so did I! Let's get on into the city straight away – I don't feel comfortable being out in the open like this.'

Beppe helps Giovanni Battista back onto the wagon as Agostino walks away, then turns to Sofia. 'Get into the cart now, will you?' he says. 'I think I'd rather you weren't seen. Just in case.'

Sofia nods. Climbing up into the cart, skirts hitched inelegantly in her arms as she scrambles over the tailgate and edges across the interior of the little wagon to the untidily piled bunk, she pushes aside several baskets, a couple of brightly coloured doublets and a bag full of hose and laces to make room to sit down.

The wagon jolts and creaks, and Sofia hugs her knees, feeling her heartbeat thudding against her bodice-front. Ippo, curled in his basket, lifts his head and rests his muzzle against the edge of the bunk. Reaching out, Sofia scratches him between his ears, sightlessly staring at the far wall of the wagon.

The patch of ground behind the piazza is perhaps some fifty feet square, surrounded on all sides by the blank back walls of buildings; one narrow entrance leads on to the piazza, just wide enough for the largest wagon. Underfoot it was probably once a neat arrangement of cobbles, but now most have broken and cracked, weeds have pushed up between the uneven stones and the whole area has a dilapidated and neglected air. Though last time the troupe had parked here it had been stacked with barrels and boxes, today it is virtually empty and there is room aplenty for all three of the Coraggiosi's vehicles. Beppe steers the little cart up to sit beside the others and pulls the pony to a halt. Jumping down, he helps Giovanni Battista down from his seat, then hurries around to the back. Sofia is already climbing out.

'Come on,' Beppe says, taking her hand. 'We need to get the

horses unhitched, at least for now, then we'll all have to discuss what best to do – where we should go.'

Cosima and Lidia appear as Beppe begins to unbuckle the first of the harness straps, both their faces taut and pinched with anxiety. Cosima pulls Sofia into a hug and murmurs her apologies; Lidia too embraces Sofia and Beppe is touched at the sight of the tenderness in both women's faces. Watching intently, he sees them lead Sofia away to one side of the little patch of ground, where they all sit down, Sofia in between the other two, on a broken section of wall. He can no longer hear what they are saying, but Cosima's vehement gesticulations and Lidia's frowning nods illustrate clearly their sense of outrage at their erstwhile host's behaviour. Sofia, Beppe can see, looks exhausted. He doubts she slept at all on the journey. Her eyes are bigger and darker than usual; pinkish-brown shadows stand out beneath them, and her hair has tendrilled into a tangle of wild ringlets. She looks from Cosima to Lidia and back, nodding again and again, though saying not a word.

Every few seconds, she glances over towards where he is still unhitching the pony, as though to reassure herself that he is still there, and every time he catches her eye, his heart turns over, and fury at da Correggio's treatment of her blazes again in his guts.

Holding the mare's reins up under her chin, Beppe clucks his tongue at her as he begins to encourage her out of the shafts. She is tired and tetchy, though, and, tossing her head irritably, baulks at being moved, scraping her hoofs on the cobbles and stamping. Tightening his grip, Beppe walks slowly backwards, edging the pony out, murmuring endearments and encouragements. With one final angry toss of her head, the stocky little mare consents to being moved.

But as she steps forward, several things happen at the same time.

A group of perhaps half a dozen men, dressed in dirty black doublets, bursts wordlessly through the entrance to the patch of waste ground, brandishing heavy wooden sticks. Several paces behind are three anxious-looking men in servants' livery. They look vaguely familiar.

A blade flashes in the light.

Beppe's horse shies, going up onto her back legs and tugging the reins almost out of his grip.

Sofia cries out.

Agostino shouts, 'No! What in heaven's name . . . ? What do you think you are doing?'

Both the other horses, startled, bang noisily against the wagons as they swing around sideways.

One of the liveried servants points and shouts, 'That's her!'

Three of the men shove their way past Beppe; two of them knock Cosima and Lidia out sideways, the third grabs Sofia by the wrists, pulling her to her feet.

Sofia screams.

'No!' Beppe lets go of the horse's reins and runs around behind the wagons, launching himself at the man holding Sofia. 'No! Get off! Get off her!'

But even as he drags the man's arm backwards, one of the other new arrivals swings out wildly with his wooden club: it catches Beppe across the side of his head. Lights flash in front of his eyes and a pain like a whip-crack shoots through his head down into his neck. He crumples to the ground, hearing Sofia scream again – screaming this time for him – and is only dimly aware of a chaotic confusion of dark-clad limbs, incomprehensible shouts, and a jumble of patches of colour and dancing light.

24

Sofia presses herself back against the stone wall of the small room, wrapping her arms around her bent knees. Her eyes are swollen and hot, stiff with shed tears, and the skin around them feels puckered and tight. Wisps of hair which stuck to her soaked cheeks while she was sobbing earlier have dried there – scratching them now, they peel away, like tiny shreds of woodshavings. She tucks them behind her ears. One wrist is burning from where it was held so roughly by the man who pulled her from where she was sitting next to Cosima and Lidia, and, though it is too dark in this room to see clearly, she is sure that she has a sizeable bruise on her upper arm. It hurts even to touch the place where she fell against the table several hours ago.

But all she can think of is Beppe.

The image of him, staggering back and falling, hands clutched to his head – the sight of the wooden club swinging – fills her mind now, terror at the thought of what might have happened to him blotting out any fears she knows she should be feeling for herself. Signor da Correggio is dead – they shouted as much right into her face as they dragged her down the steps and pushed her in here, shoving her so hard that she tripped and fell against the table.

He is dead, and they think her responsible.

They think her a murderer.

As they did her mother.

A murderer.

Did Beppe's punch kill the signore? Dear God, it can't have done. She is sure that the signore had been moving – she is sure she heard him swearing profusely – when they ran back up those steps, and, though Beppe did hit him very hard, Sofia cannot imagine it was the kind of blow that kills. She curls up more tightly on the narrow straw mattress, clasping her bent legs with a fierce intensity, trying not to cry out, pressing her face down onto her knees until her forehead aches and bright patterns swirl in front of her eyes.

The big club swings – with a crack horribly like Arlecchino's noisy wooden *batocchio* – and Beppe falls again and again, over and over in front of her eyes. The sound that the club makes against the side of his head echoes in her mind. A low, animal moaning fills her ears and only when she looks up and her mouth is open does she realize that it is she herself making the noise.

Beppe winces as he pulls on Arlecchino's mask; the leather is pressing painfully against the swollen lump on the side of his head. Grabbing at his black woollen hat, he climbs – more gingerly than usual – out of the wagon. Though he is trying his hardest to ignore it, he is feeling dizzy and sick.

Outside, the rest of the troupe are already assembled. Costumed and with faces painted and masked, they are a bright splash of colour on this sunless October morning.

Agostino beckons them all in to stand close to him as he issues instructions. 'Cosima, *cara*, and Lidia, just wander through the crowds and point them in our direction. We want as big an audience as we can muster. Angelo, you, Federico and Giovanni Battista begin on the far side of the square with that argument from *The Desperate Doctor*, will you? And Beppe, Vico: I want the juggling *lazzo* you did at Montalbano, to start with. It went down so well there, and it's eye-catching. Beppe, *caro*, that's if you can manage it . . . after . . . ?'

Swallowing uncomfortably, trying to move as little as possible, Beppe gives one brief nod. 'I'll just get the bag of balls,' he says, climbing back into the wagon and reappearing a moment later with a mesh bag filled with small reddish leather balls.

'Ready?' Agostino says.

Everyone nods. Another swirl of nausea rocks Beppe as he moves his head. He closes his eyes and breathes slowly through an open mouth for a moment; then, patting the place where his wooden *batocchio* is tucked through his belt, he follows Vico, Lidia and the others out into the piazza, the mesh bag bumping against his leg at each step.

It takes perhaps ten minutes for the beginnings of a crowd to collect. Cosima and Lidia charm passers-by, taking them by the hand and batting their eyelashes, assuring them that they are unlikely to see skill of this magnitude this side of Rome. Within moments, Beppe and Vico are at the centre of a jostling ring, and if Beppe is fighting at every moment not to vomit from the pain in his head, not one of the laughing onlookers has any inkling of his discomfort. Not for the first time, he blesses the anonymity of Arlecchino's mask.

Just as Vico over-arms a ball back into the whirling ring between Beppe's hands, and as a loud spatter of applause fills the piazza, Agostino holds up his hands for quiet. Beppe catches the balls, one by one, then stands motionless. Vico turns too; Lidia and Cosima grasp hands. Angelo, Federico and Giovanni Battista stop the improvised conversation they have been having on the far side of the piazza and hurry across, bringing with them the two or three dozen men and women who have been laughing at their antics.

'We have something to tell you . . . ' Agostino's voice rings out across the piazza and the last murmurings die to silence. 'And we tell you this now, because we need your help.'

He hesitates for a moment, then, in the same carrying voice, says, 'Last night, we performed our play for a nobleman. It matters not a jot who he was. It matters even less where he lives. What *does* matter a great deal is what he *did* when the show was finished.'

Several people murmur amongst themselves, but Agostino silences them with a look.

'He chose,' he continues, louder still, one hand now raised like an avenging archangel, 'after having enjoyed our offered entertainment, to try to seduce our youngest troupe member – and then, when she proved unwilling, he deemed it acceptable to use his superior strength and social standing to . . . to attempt to force her to act against her will.'

Somebody mutters, 'Bastard.'

Agostino hears. 'A bastard indeed, signore. A most apt description. And a most despicable way to behave.' He gazes out across the crowd for a moment, then continues. 'Our lovely little Colombina – who is nothing more than the victim in this crime – is languishing now in a locked room in the building behind the Palazzo Communale, unaccountably accused – of *murder*!'

A shocked intake of breath. The word is repeated in hissed undertones around the piazza.

'Yes, murder,' Agostino says gravely. 'The "bastard", it seems, is dead. Though not by Sofia's hand.'

Mutters of 'Who killed him then?' and 'Lecherous son of a pox-scarred *puttana* – they're all the same' can be heard in the crowd.

'We don't know who killed him,' Agostino says now, his voice carrying clearly. 'But we *do* know that Sofia did not. We want her out and back with us again. And we need your help.'

The crowd's rumbling intensifies.

'How many of you have ever attended a Coraggiosi performance here in the past?'

By the sound of the rumbling affirmation and the spatter of applause, a large proportion of the crowd are seasoned audience members. Agostino smiles and his eyes glitter. 'Then,' he says, his voice ringing clearly across the piazza, 'if you have ever enjoyed our offered entertainments, come with us now – come to the *palazzo* and help us. Get our girl released. With just the eight of us, we stand little chance of being heard against the stony deafness of the authorities – despite the significant carrying qualities of our voices . . .'

A buzz of muted laughter trickles through the crowd.

Agostino continues. 'But with the might of the people of Bologna behind us, they *have* to listen. So please, please, come with us now and protest with us.'

'I want her back,' Beppe says now, pulling off his mask, his voice cracking. 'I need to get her back. Please help.'

The crowd begins to clap. Several people whistle. Talking amongst themselves now, people begin to move forward and, with the eight costumed Coraggiosi performers at their head, they start to stream across the square towards the Piazza Maggiore.

Passing an open window, her hand held tight in her father's, Sofia overhears a rough voice saying, 'Which poor sod are they after this time?

They're down the Via San Marco, Mario said. At least a dozen of them. Don't fancy the chances of whoever it is, poor buggers.'

'Oh, God . . .' her mother breathes. 'What do we—?'

'We walk, that's what.' Papa's grip tightens. 'We keep walking.' He takes a long breath. 'The moment we run, we're finished.'

'But—' Mamma is breathing heavily, and every now and again she staggers, putting out a hand to steady herself against the walls of the houses they are passing, as people do when they have had too much ale.

Papa pulls her hand up to his mouth and kisses her knuckles. 'We must get out of the city – as fast as possible. Not far to go now. The Porta Romana is only just down the end of that street and along a short way and then as soon as we're out, we'll get over to the far side of the river, and then do our best to pick up a boat. The river will be the quick-est . . . come on.'

Mamma stares at him but seems not to see him.

Grabbing her fingers and squeezing fiercely, Papa holds her hand until she gasps. 'Stop it,' he says. 'Pull yourself together, cara. Think of Sofia. Walk – and walk fast!'

Sofia starts, and the pictures fade, as the key clacks in the lock and the door to her room bangs open. Still sitting on the straw mattress in the furthest corner of the room, where she has been, immobile, for the past hour, she hunches her shoulders and stiffens, feeling her heartbeat thud up into her throat as a bald man in a threadbare brown doublet comes in. His lumpy head, Sofia thinks dully, looks like a shiny kneecap. He is carrying a metal tray, on which are an earthenware jug, a plate, a bowl and a tin cup; there is a hunk of dark bread on the plate and the bowl is steaming. He bangs the tray down on the table and the cup falls over on its side with a clatter. A trickle of something that looks to Sofia vaguely like vomit slops over the side of the bowl.

'They said to bring you something to eat.' The man in the threadbare doublet glances at her and jerks his chin towards the meal he has brought her.

Sofia does not reply and does not move.

'Soup,' the man says.

Sofia remains silent.

The man clicks his tongue at her, shaking his head as he turns to leave. '*I*'d make the most of it, if I were you,' he says, sounding irritated, as though she has already refused to eat.

The door closes and the key clacks once more in the lock.

Sofia hears the man's footsteps for a second or two, moving away; then the suffocating silence of the room falls over her again. She looks at the bowl – the unappetizing trickle of brown liquid has pooled around the base – and realizes to her surprise that she is hungry. She will do better, she thinks now, to try the soup while it is at least hot – for, judging by the smell, she doubts it will taste good. Releasing her grip on her knees, she slowly unfolds her legs. Wincing at the stiffness, she stands and crosses to the table. There is a stool tucked underneath the table; she pulls it out and sits on it.

Close to, the soup smells like – and probably, Sofia thinks, was made from – musty vegetable peelings, but she nonetheless tears pieces from the lump of bread, dips them into the bowl and eats, though without really registering what she is doing. The bread is sour and tough, but Sofia finds that she is grateful to have something to do with her hands, and she begins to tear the pieces into smaller shreds, wanting the process to last for longer.

The earthenware jug contains water. Sofia pours and drinks. This, at least, is fresh and sweet, and she refills the cup twice.

It is not long, though, before the inevitable consequence of all this becomes increasingly insistent and finally unavoidable: her bladder is full. Sofia falls to her knees and feels under the bed with her fingers; she pulls the table away from the wall – but she can find no receptacle of any description other than the jug, bowl and cup on the tray. She bangs on the door with her knuckles, timidly at first, then louder and more insistent.

'Please! If you please, can somebody come?'

Her pleas are met with silence.

She calls again and again for several minutes. Then a male voice says roughly, 'Quiet! You be quiet! You'll be seen later.'

'But I need . . . ' Sofia begins to remonstrate, then stops. If she insists, she reasons with herself now, she might be made to relieve herself in front of this unknown man. Tears – of shame, of fear, of despair – begin to leak from the corners of her eyes again, and, taking herself to the furthest corner of the room from the bed, she gathers her skirts and underskirts up into her arms and squats.

As they reach the north-east entrance to the Piazza Maggiore, the crowd jostling in behind Beppe, Agostino and the rest of the troupe has more than tripled in size. Perhaps a hundred, perhaps a hundred and fifty people are streaming in through the gaps between the stuccoed buildings, and as Beppe glances behind him, he can see that the atmosphere amongst them all is febrile: some are laughing and excitable, as though they are preparing to see a show; others look mutinous, dangerous, unpredictable. Most are men, though perhaps a couple of dozen women and a handful of children can be seen.

'I hope to God you know what you're doing, Ago,' he mutters.

'What?'

'I hope you know what you're doing – this lot look as though they might start a riot.'

Agostino puts an arm around his shoulders. 'That's exactly what I hope they will do, *caro* – or at least, what I hope the authorities *fear* they'll do.'

'But—'

'Trust me. I want her out as much as you do.'

Doubting this, but grateful for the support, Beppe draws in a long, shaky breath, squares his shoulders and marches on, his head pounding, his stomach still heaving. The crowd behind him swirls and shifts out into the piazza like a flotsam-filled dam-breach, noisy and untidy and crackling with energy.

Agostino points and shouts. 'Over there – that's where we are going. Can you see, everyone? The door to the left of the *palazzo*.'

Murmurs of assent, cries of 'Hurry up then', 'What are we waiting for?' and 'Bastards!' can be heard throughout the throng. Beppe feels a surge of bodies pushing up against him. He grabs Agostino's wrist. 'Ago, I don't like this. Don't let them get out of hand. Tell them what to do. Stop them boiling over, before it's too late.'

Agostino nods.

Jumping up onto a low wall, he holds up both hands and the crowd slows, stills and quietens. Feet shuffle; several people cough, clear their throats, a few murmur and then fall silent.

'Thank you, all of you,' Agostino says, in his clear, ringing voice. 'Thank you for your support. We are all very, very grateful.' He looks around at the rest of the troupe, who are nodding in agreement. 'Now, we need to play this very carefully. Very carefully indeed. Please – let *me* speak with them in there. I know what I want to say, and I know *how* I want to say it. You don't need to do anything – just be here. Be with us. Be the threat lying silently behind my words, build yourselves up behind me like a bank of thunderclouds, ready to break; like a—'

A spatter of applause runs through the crowd and someone shouts, 'Sod thunderclouds, we'll fucking flatten them if they won't let her out!'

Beppe's heart turns over. Scrambling up onto the wall next to Agostino, he shouts, 'No! Please! Please stay calm. Just do what Agostino tells you. We'll never manage if you start a fight. They'll arrest you all and I'll never get her back. Just do what he says – please.'

His voice breaks on the final plea; the crowd hears it and quietens.

More slowly now, with Agostino and Cosima, Beppe, Vico and Lidia, Federico, Giovanni Battista and Angelo at the head, the crowd moves along the northern edge of the great piazza and swarms out around the door to the smaller, darker building to the left of the Palazzo Communale.

Agostino clicks his fingers at Beppe, his hand outstretched. Beppe passes him the wooden *batocchio*. Agostino holds it tightly in his fist and hammers on the door with its leather-bound handle. The sound rings out loudly across the piazza.

For a count of more than twenty, nothing happens. Beppe wonders if he might actually be sick. Agostino bangs on the door a second time and, before he has completed the final thud, a voice from inside can be heard, saying angrily, 'All right, all right, all *right*! I'm being as quick as I can.'

The crowd seems to press more tightly together. Beppe looks around at them all; perhaps three hundred people are there now: far too many to count. Their very silence seems menacing.

The door has opened a crack, and a thin man of some forty years is peering out of the gap between the door and the jamb. At the sight of the throng of people, his mouth drops open, and his fingers tighten around the edge of the door.

Agostino says loudly, 'You have a girl in here accused of murder.'

The man frowns, mouth still gaping.

'Her name is Sofia Genotti – and she is innocent.'

A murmur spreads through the crowd; Agostino holds up a hand without looking around, and silence falls again behind him.

'The only evidence you have for her guilt comes from one of the dead man's servants. That servant is partisan. And he is lying.'

The man in the doorway shakes his head and shuts the door.

Agostino hammers on it again. The crowd joins in, shouting for the man's return. Shouldering his way past Cosima and Vico, Beppe too bangs on the wooden panels with a clenched fist. 'Open the door!' he shouts, his mouth close to the wood, both hands now flat against the door. 'Please! We have to talk to you. We have proof! She can't have done it!'

The door remains resolutely closed.

'But, signori, there's hundreds of them!'

'What do you mean? Where?'

Looking around the candlelit room at the seated group of dignitaries, the thin man gestures wildly with both arms in the vague direction of the Piazza Maggiore. 'Out there! In the piazza – *hundreds* of them. The man says she's innocent.'

'Who is?'

'That girl who's just been brought in, I think that's who he's talking about.'

'The traveller bitch who killed ... what's his name? ... da Correggio?'

The thin man shakes his head. 'I tell you, they're saying she didn't do it.'

A heavy, corpulent man, almost bald apart from a thick fringe around the back of his head at ear level, pushes back his chair with an audible scrape and stands. 'Of course they want us to think she didn't do it, but I don't care a damn what they say. I've been told there's an eyewitness and I'm having this girl. I've been waiting for a clear-cut case like this to make plain exactly how well we intend to deal with scum, and I'm not letting it slip away.'

'But with respect, Signor da Budrio, you need to talk to these people – there are *hundreds* of them out there!'

'So you say.' Da Budrio raises an eyebrow. 'And I expect they'd like to think themselves an effective insurrection. Well … we'll see about that.' And, lifting an elbow high and screwing up the side of his face as he scratches behind an ear, Signor da Budrio strides from the meeting room.

He nears the bottom of the second staircase, and realizes that from outside in the piazza, a slow, rhythmic, throbbing chant is pushing its way through the heavy doors, each word ponderous and measured: '*Let – her – out! Let – her – out! Let – her – out!*'

Da Budrio pauses, hand on the door handle; then, sucking in a deep breath, he opens the door.

Beppe starts. As the door opens wide, a heavy, red-faced man with a fringe of white sheep's wool hair around the back of his head stands square in the doorway. The chanting increases in volume as he appears. Beppe is not chanting himself; he cannot: his mouth seems set closed, but the words the crowd are howling reverberate in his head as a plea – a prayer. *Let her out: please, please, let her out.* He has pressed a fist against his lips and is chewing at the knuckle of his thumb. Lidia and Cosima are standing right behind him; he can feel their breath on the back of his neck.

'*Let – her – out! Let – her – out!*'

273

At the sight of the new arrival in the doorway, Agostino holds up both hands for quiet, and word of his request ripples through the crowd; they fall quiet section by section, from the front through to the back.

'Are you responsible for this rabble?' the man with the sheep's-wool hair says to Agostino in a voice thick with dislike.

'I would not address them as such, but I asked them to come here with me, yes.'

'Why are you here?'

Agostino's voice deepens, thickens, becomes louder. 'We are here because you are holding a young woman in that building there' – he points – 'on a spurious charge, for which there is no reliable evidence, while we here have proof positive that she could not have committed the crime of which she has been accused.'

The heavy man raises an eyebrow. 'You sound very certain, signore.'

'That would be because I am. And these good people here are too.'

The crowd shifts silently as the sea will move against a rock face: not breaking, just lifting and swelling massively.

The heavy man eyes them all without a word.

Agostino says, 'Sofia Genotti is a member of my troupe of actors: the Coraggiosi. She is innocent of any crime, and—'

'I have an eyewitness acc—'

'If you have an eyewitness, then you also have a liar!' Beppe blurts out, interrupting him, moving to stand shoulder to shoulder with Agostino. 'Sofia was with me last night. I know she didn't do anything to touch this man even, let alone hurt him. He was quite certainly alive when we last saw him.'

The man in the doorway stares at him and the crowd seems to tauten. People move in a little closer to each other, pressing forwards, drawing in and focusing their attention on the man in the doorway.

He, however, unabashed, draws himself up to his full height. 'My name, should you not know it already, is Signor Antonio Giovanni Lorenzo Bellano da Budrio,' he says loudly. 'I am the governor of the city of Bologna, and I am ultimately responsible for the arrest and detention of anyone who breaks the law within the area of the city's jurisdiction, though of course I rarely have direct contact with those detained. I do not take kindly to anyone attempting to interfere with due process.' He pauses and gazes out imperiously across the still-growing crowd. 'However many of them there might happen to be at any one time.'

Beppe looks in desperation at Agostino, whose gaze remains fixed upon da Budrio. Cosima takes his hand. Beppe glances at her. 'Ago will do what's needed,' she says quietly into his ear. 'Trust him.'

Agostino draws in a long breath. 'Signore,' he says and his voice carries more clearly across the piazza than did da Budrio's. 'You seem not to understand. I fully accept that you are responsible for what happens to those who break the law. But Sofia Genotti is not one of them. She need not concern you. She is innocent.'

Beppe nudges Cosima. 'Don't let him mention Correggio's attack on Sofia, for God's sake. That'll give them a motive,' he says, feeling the sting of tears in the corners of his eyes.

Cosima gives him a tight little smile and shakes her head. 'He won't. He knows that.'

The crowd begins chanting again. Low and menacing, the three long syllables roll around and around the piazza and Agostino's voice rings out above the growl of it. 'I appreciate the importance and dignity of your position, honoured signore,' he says. 'As do my friends here.' He gestures grandly at the crowd and a spatter of applause ripples through it. 'But please believe me when I say that we do not intend to leave until we have justice. Sofia is innocent and we need to have her back with us again.'

Beppe sucks in a shocked breath: Angelo has stepped forward, his exquisite chin raised in arrogant disdain. Before Agostino can speak, he says loudly, 'Signor da Budrio, I am Angelo Francesco Giuliano Cesare da Bagnacavallo – son of Signor Giuliano da Bagnacavallo of the Castello dei Fiore. Second cousin to the Duke of Ferrara.'

Da Budrio's face certainly twitches at the mention of Angelo's prestigious parentage, but he makes no other response. Angelo continues, and there is now an exaggeratedly aristocratic drawl to his voice, 'Perhaps we might be allowed to discuss a situation which my father would undoubtedly wish to have resolved without . . . how shall I put it? . . . *undue unpleasantness*.'

Beppe's visceral dislike of Angelo fights now with a surge of hope.

Several other faces appear in the darkness behind da Budrio – faces creased with anxiety and anger – and someone puts a hand on da Budrio's shoulder. He turns away to face into the interior of the building. The door remains open and the chanting continues.

Curled in a ball on the uncomfortable mattress, with a thin blanket tucked around her, Sofia's nose is prickling now with the acrid and shameful smell of urine; her skirts are chill and damp around the back of the hem, where she failed to hold them properly clear, and her face is sticky with half-dried tears. Her thoughts have tumbled and jostled for so long she can now no longer make sense of anything – her skull just seems to be filled with an unidentifiable buzzing.

She is locked up. A prisoner. They never locked Mamma up all those years ago – though she is certain they intended to – poor Mamma never even reached a trial. Sofia and her parents had thought themselves safe in the salt marshes of Comacchio: far from Ferrara, far from their accusers, in that beautiful wild expanse of nothingness so many, many miles from anywhere; they had thought no one would ever bother to search that far for them.

The sky is enormous. A clear grey-blue, it soars over the landscape like the inside of a vast silver dome and, given that much of the area over which it arches is water, that dome seems to plunge downwards too, falling away in a vertiginous swoop beneath their feet. It is like being held somehow in the centre of a measureless glass bubble. She imagines some Olympian god, holding up a transparent sphere and peering curiously into it, failing to see her and her family; to a god they would be no more than minute specks: tiny flaws in the transparent perfection of his globe. She looks about her: here and there, thin dark smudges of low-lying land break up the otherwise unremitting silver, and dotted along these sparse lines is the occasional squat building, reflected exquisitely in the unmoving water. The odd clump of marshy grass lies like an inkblot on the great grey sheets, but other than these unimportant interruptions, there is little to see but air and water.

'Look! Mamma, Papa, look!' Sofia points out across the water. 'What are they?'

Papa and Mamma turn to see what has startled her. At least thirty or forty extraordinary – and enormous – birds are standing in shallow water a few hundred yards from them. A soft pink, they have long, stilt-like legs, some straight, some bent at an acute angle halfway down. Gracefully curving necks lead to heavy heads, with enormous, angular, black-tipped beaks. A small blot of shadow lies on the surface of the water beneath each bird, shifting over the rippling surface as they move. Some of the birds have dropped their heads to the water and are

277

dabbling in the shallows, while others appear to be keeping watch: necks stretched upwards, the heads swivel from side to side almost comically, Sofia thinks.

Something startles them then, and as one they take off, honking, spreading wide wings and trailing the long crane-fly legs out behind them. They swirl up and around and down, landing again within seconds and resume the dabbling and watch-keeping.

'What are they?' Sofia says again, her voice not much more than a whisper.

'I've no idea, cara,' Papa says. 'But they seem to live here, don't they? Perhaps we'll learn about them from someone when we settle down and find a house.'

'We're going to live here?'

'Yes.' Papa is looking at her carefully. 'I'm fairly certain that we are. What do you think of that idea?'

Sofia gazes about her for several seconds before answering. 'I think,' she says slowly, 'I think I shall like it. It will be like living in the middle of the sky. And there's nowhere for the bad people to hide here, is there? If they come after us, we'll see them coming a long way away.'

'But we didn't. We didn't see them coming – not then, and not now,' she says aloud, and her words hang like dead things in the musty air of the cell. And at the thought of her mother's terrible final moments, her father's slow decline and death the following year, and fearful for what might lie ahead, she wraps her arms over her head, and curls up more tightly, clutching handfuls of her hair. A sob swells in her throat.

She has been crying for so long that she has no tears left. Sightlessly staring at nothing with eyes that feel as though they are lidded with leather, Sofia lies on the hard straw mattress, listening to the mute nothingness of the inside of the cell, when a sound filters through: a low, throbbing, repetitious sound – like chanting. Sitting up and frowning, she strains her ears to try to hear more clearly.

It's a long, three-beat chant, whatever it is they are saying. Three thudding words, repeated over and over again. Sofia gets to her feet. Dragging the table over to the wall beneath the window, she scrambles up to stand on it: from here she can just see out. Much of the piazza outside is hidden by part of the building next door, but from what she can see in the little gap between the two walls, it's clear that the square is teeming with people, and it must be they who are making the noise. Sofia screws up her face, trying to make out the words they are saying.

'*Let – her – out! Let – her – out!*'

She holds her breath. Shuts her eyes, listening even more intently.

'*Let – her – out! Let – her – out!*'

Da Budrio turns back to face Agostino and Angelo. 'You wait here,' he says. 'I shall return.'

And before either man can do more than open his mouth, the door closes once more. Beppe leans against the wall by the door, his forehead pressed painfully against the brick, trying to swallow down the rising wave of panic that is fast threatening to overwhelm him. Lidia and Cosima both step close and put arms around him.

'He said he'd be back,' Lidia says. 'He's not just walking away from us.'

Cosima nods. 'It looks as though they might be thinking seriously about what we've said ... what Angelo said.' She puts a hand around the side of Beppe's head, drawing him in close; he leans against her for a moment; then, gripping her fingers, he stands straight again, turning back to look at the crowd.

The people in the square start singing.

One lone voice begins it – a clear, ringing tenor – then more and more join him, and the sound rapidly fills both the piazza and Beppe's head. He has no idea what the song might be – though he thinks he has heard it before, perhaps in a tavern, perhaps in the street – but here, issuing from two, three, four hundred mouths, it has a haunting power and the hair on the back of his neck prickles.

The Coraggiosi stand in a tight group by the door. Agostino and Cosima, Lidia and Vico, Federico, Giovanni Battista and Angelo – and Beppe, a little to one side now, right by the architrave of the door, leaning against it, waiting, waiting.

Just as the crowd's song builds to a ringing crescendo, the door opens again and the sound quickly fades. The thin man from earlier looks at the troupe and says, 'Signor da Budrio wonders if you would care to come in.'

Agostino nods and takes a step towards the door. 'Thank you.'

The thin man shakes his head. 'No – you misunderstand. The signore would like to see *him*.' He nods towards Angelo. 'Just him.'

Agostino clutches at Angelo's sleeve. 'Please, Angelo, don't agree to this. Take us all in with you.'

Angelo stares for a moment at Agostino, his expression impossible to read. His gaze moves to the women, to the two older men, to Beppe. Beppe's heart races. Then, after several long seconds, Angelo shakes his head. 'It'll be better if I go alone, I think,' he says. And without a backward glance, he follows the thin man into the darkened entrance, and the door closes once more.

25

They have been living in the house on the edge of the salt marsh for just less than a fortnight. Long and low, red-roofed and brick-walled, it sits near the edge of a wide expanse of water; scrubby bushes cluster around two sides of the house and, away to the left of the building, a long strip of land curves away like a protecting arm around the edge of the marsh.

The furthest of the three rooms holds two straw-filled mattresses, one wooden chest and a broken chair; in the middle room a table and several folding stools give the family somewhere to sit and eat, and the small fireplace over on the far wall provides the means to cook and keep warm. And in the outermost room, a long low table and a bench fill most of the space.

Mamma has already begun collecting leaves and roots to dry and turn into her special tinctures and powders: bunches and piles lie neatly along the whole length of the table on shallow, sand-filled trays.

The light in all the rooms is dim and indistinct: rather than glass in the windows, they are lined in a thick parchment, which gives an odd, filtered light: as though, Sofia thinks, the house were underwater.

She stands by the low table in the outermost room and fingers the dozen or so bunches of drying leaves and flowers lying on the sand-trays. Picking one up, she holds it to her nose, then, grimacing, puts it back down quickly: woundwort. A bunch of starry-white bogbean flowers catches her eye and she reaches out to run a finger over their ragged, frilled edges; they are already beginning to turn brown. Several bunches of cudweed lie in piles at one end of the table, and Sofia straightens them to lie more neatly. What was it Mamma said about cudweed as they picked these leaves a few days ago? *It'll make you sweat,* she said – *good for fevers. It can turn a man . . . into a devoted lover, too,* she added, smiling at Sofia.

'Does Papa like it?'

She saw a smile on Mamma's face for the first time in days. 'Oh, Papa doesn't need it. He never has.'

She fiddles the fading white flowers with the tip of her index finger for several more seconds, pleased with the silky fringed feeling of the petals against her skin, then turns back towards the middle room. Mamma asked her to keep an eye on the fire while she was out getting food from the market in the town, and Sofia is determined to show her how well she can manage the task. Squatting down in front of the little hearth, she jabs at the mound of glowing logs with a short iron poker. A burst of red sparks spits out at her and a log crumbles and falls; several nut-sized lumps bounce out, white hot, onto the stone surround and Sofia, standing quickly, kicks them back into the blaze with the toe of her shoe. She adds another couple of logs, then sits back on a low stool to wait and watch her charge, making sure it behaves and works hard until Mamma's return. Or until Papa comes back from his search for work.

Sofia and her mother cross one of the many bridges which up-and-over Comacchio's myriad canals. This one is of stone: neatly built, shallow, merely for foot passengers. Some are bigger, strong enough for a laden cart; others are flimsy, ramshackle, poorly built affairs, which wobble *each time someone crosses from one side of a waterway to the other. Sofia does not like these wobbling ones; there are several she fears will collapse beneath her each time she sets foot upon them. Sofia and Mamma make their way down one long waterside street, cross another bridge – a sturdy stone one – and turn down a narrow alley towards an open space in the centre of the town where Sofia knows the bustling market regularly takes place.*

They are hand in hand: Mamma is walking quickly with the basket of herbs over her arm, and Sofia skips by her side. 'And the crayfish's claws are tied tightly – like this . . . ' Mamma bunches the tips of her fingers and thumb together and points them at Sofia. '. . . because they're very, very cross about having to become our supper . . . ' She jabs the fingers forwards to pinch the end of Sofia's nose.

Sofia laughs.

'The nice market man has promised us three crayfish in return for these . . . ' Mamma shakes the basket. 'And the other man has given us cheese and asparagus – he didn't really want to, but the crayfish man told him he should.'

'What does asparagus taste like?'

'Delicious! You dip those long green fingers into melted butter and bite off the tips – like this . . . ' She takes hold of Sofia's free hand and holds the end of her daughter's small index finger between her teeth for a second. Sofia squeals happily. 'And they taste green and lovely.'

'What does green taste like, though?'

Mama frowns, thinking. 'I don't know – just green. Fresh, like the smell of summer.'

'Poor crayfish,' Sofia says. 'They have no idea what's just around the corner for them.'

And neither had we, Sofia thinks now, sitting up on the thin mattress and hugging her knees. Neither had we. Not then, not now.

26

Nearly an hour has passed since Angelo strode away into the darkness of the house beside the Palazzo Communale in the company of the formidable Signor da Budrio. Beppe has been pacing the length of the façade of the building like a caged animal ever since, back and forth, pointlessly, wordlessly, counting his steps – twenty-two each way – hands deep in his breeches pockets, staring down at his feet as he walks, scraping and scuffing the dust. His head is still pounding.

The crowd became restive some moments ago, and seemed on the point of abandoning their defiant support and slipping away bit by bit, but Agostino, Cosima, Vico and Lidia, Federico and Giovanni Battista, almost without discussion – merely by sharing a flicked glance and mutter and a couple of nods – began to perform. Quickly adapting the final scene from *The Three Loyal Friends* to remove Arlecchino from the proceedings – Beppe was clearly beyond any involvement – within a couple of minutes, they had the crowd hooting and catcalling, clapping and laughing.

Beppe hardly heard them.

Each time he passes the door now on his relentless paced way from one end of the building to the other, he glances across at it, willing it to open, feeling in his chest wild, suffocating, smothering surges of hope and despair pushing up like silt into his throat.

The scene concludes and the crowd applauds wildly. Agostino, standing now up on a low wall, shouts out above their noise, 'Stay with us! Please! It can't be long now – and if . . . if . . . if it has gone badly . . .'

Beppe's heart twists painfully but Agostino's voice rings out again. 'If it has gone badly, then we will need you. We might even need to storm the building. We'll have her out, come what may!'

The crowd cheers and claps, people stamp their feet and whoop. Beppe knows in his heart that this can only be Ago's wild words; he imagines the crowd pushing through, past the wool-haired man, da Budrio, surging into the building like rats, barging their way along corridors, up staircases, banging on doors and breaking windows, knocking down anyone who stands in their way in their search for Sofia. It couldn't happen. Why has Ago said it?

'But . . .' Agostino continues. 'But we must wait patiently a little longer, please, my friends. Just a little longer.

Murmurs of agreement. The clapping and whooping dies away.

Lidia now begins to sing – a haunting, lilting love song, which Vico normally accompanies on his guitar – and Beppe feels tears pricking sharp in the corners of his eyes. Lidia's voice rises up above the mutterings of the crowd, and the whole piazza falls silent to listen. The sound is pure and sweet, laden with longing and love, and redolent with a heart-touching comprehension of the pain of loss.

Beppe feels Cosima's arms around him. 'Oh, don't cry, sweet boy,' she whispers. 'We'll have her back soon, I'm sure.'

Wiping his eyes with the back of his wrist, Beppe nods at her, nipping the end of his tongue between his teeth.

Lidia's voice lingers on a high note, then falls back down to resolve the melody into its final bars.

The crowd claps, cheering and stamping once more, and, distracted by their energy, deafened by their noise, Beppe does not hear the door to the dark building opening at last and he is watching Lidia as it swings wide.

But someone shouts out, and he whirls around.

The crowd has begun to clap and the sound is echoing off the walls of the piazza. Several people whistle.

Flanked by Angelo and a grim-faced Signor da Budrio, Sofia is standing in the doorway. Small and white-faced and dirty, her hair tangled and flattened on one side, her eyes are wide and dark-rimmed and she is looking out at the crowd, her mouth dropping open a fraction at the sight of the packed city square.

Beppe steps forward, breath held, his heart racing. Some dozen people are standing between him and the doorway, but he edges through, turning sideways, arms raised, muttering apologies as he shoulders his way past.

Suddenly aware of the movement, Sofia turns and sees him. She stares at him, and he cannot take his eyes from her face. Someone is speaking – a deep voice – but it takes Beppe several seconds to realize that it is da Budrio and that he should listen.

'And so,' da Budrio is saying, 'following a frankly revelatory discussion, we have come to the conclusion that it will perhaps be advisable – given the circumstances laid out to us so forcefully here by Signor da Bagnacavallo . . .'

He inclines his head to Angelo, who lifts his chin, smirking out at the crowd, a scroll of paper in one hand.

' . . . it will be advisable to presume that the killer of the unfortunate Signor da Correggio is regrettably still at large. Our forces and moneys will henceforth be put into attempting to discover the real culprit.'

The crowd mutters and someone shouts, 'What are you actually going to *do* about it, then?'

'Aye – what's to be done?'

Several more people call out *their* wish to know more about proposed plans, and da Budrio holds up a hand for quiet.

Sofia and Beppe are still gazing fixedly at one another.

Beppe is struggling to breathe.

'I have men departing for the Castello della Franceschina as we speak,' da Budrio says pompously, and, putting a hand in the small of Sofia's back, he pushes her gently out, away from the door. She moves like a sleepwalker towards where Beppe is standing, until she is no more than a pace in front of him. For a second he stands immobile; then, with a rush of exhilarated relief that leaves him light-headed, he throws his arms around her and holds her tight. She clings to him, crying now, grasping handfuls of the back of his doublet, pressing herself against him, tilting her face up towards his.

Beppe cups the back of her head with one hand and kisses her, and the crowd applauds enthusiastically, shifting in to stand closer to the two clasped figures, who are entirely unaware of being the centre of such rapt attention.

'But ...' Da Budrio's voice booms out above the surge of clapping and Beppe and Sofia pull back and turn to look at him, arms still wound around each other. 'But I am nonetheless extremely angry. Yes,' he says, holding hands up to quieten a rumble of sulky murmuring. 'Yes, I accept that doubt may have been cast upon the reliability of the evidence offered for this crime, but public order has been threatened. Public calm has been disrupted. Public safety has been put at risk – at the instigation' – he points at Agostino

with a fat and accusatory forefinger – 'of this troupe of repro-
bates.'

Beppe holds his breath, pulling Sofia in more closely to him.

'And so I have no choice.'

The crowd is entirely silent now. Nobody speaks, nobody mutters; only a cough is heard, somewhere at the back of the piazza.

'You actors will not work here in Bologna again.'

Every member of the troupe gasps audibly, and the crowd shifts
and murmurs.

Da Budrio continues, 'I do not wish to hear of any performances by this troupe – not one, however small, however
impromptu – within the area of the city's jurisdiction, for the next
two years. Two years, do you hear? And know that that area of
jurisdiction extends to Reggio in the west, to Ferrara in the north
and out to Ravenna in the east. Signor da Bagnacavallo has the
details of the agreement we have drawn up. Have no doubt about
this' – he glares at the Coraggiosi – 'any breach of my injunction
will result in summary arrest and detention and I will not look
upon the matter with any sense of leniency again. My reputation,
built over decades, has always been one of stringent rigour and I
see no reason for it to change now.'

Glancing round at Agostino, Beppe sees his face is drawn and
tight. He has Cosima by the hand.

'And you, city-dwellers,' da Budrio concludes loudly, turning
once again to the crowd. 'I am aware that you were encouraged
and drawn into this ... this ... *insurrection* at the instigation of a
persuasive and highly skilled bunch of deceptively convincing
rogues, but the fact remains that you did, by your own choice,
agree to gather together here today and to threaten the calm and
order of the city of Bologna. And that, I cannot and will not tolerate. Do anything of the like again – any one of you – and you

will find me considerably less accommodating than I have been today. Do I make myself clear?'

'All too fucking clear!' A rough male voice from somewhere in the crowd shouts out distinctly. 'You've cocked up and someone else is going to have to pay for it. It won't be the first time.'

A rumble of muttering.

Da Budrio's colour is rising. 'I will not endure such insubordination!' he shouts and his voice is thick and raw with anger.

Several others in the crowd rally in support of the heckler and a flurry of jeering jibes can clearly be heard.

'What d'you plan to do about it then, you pointless, two-*scudi* despot?'

'You've treated us like dirt for long enough, you bastard!'

'Justice! None of you knows the meaning of the bloody word!'

A dozen or so black-clad men are clustered in the doorway behind da Budrio; turning his head over his shoulder, he mutters inaudibly to the tallest of them, who snaps his fingers. The whole bunch strides out into the piazza, pushing a brutal way through the jostling crowd to where the heckler and his friends are still jeering. Staring, horrified, Beppe watches as three of them round on the protester, flooring the man with several well-aimed punches. The others, a few of whom have drawn short-bladed knives, have their backs to the fight, as though daring anyone to object, and the crowd pulls back, clearing a circle around the combatants.

Nobody tries to intervene. It seems, Beppe thinks, that the Bolognese desire for justice is perhaps not as passionate as their words have implied.

The men in black drag the heckler to his feet – he sags in their arms – and they pull him half-conscious through to where da Budrio still stands in the doorway of the town hall.

'Take him away!' da Budrio thunders. 'As I said: I will not tolerate insurrection.'

No one speaks or utters a sound as the black-doubleted thugs half carry, half drag the protester out of sight through a nearby open doorway.

The piazza is still and silent.

Da Budrio glares around at them. 'Be gone, the lot of you! And you, you actors – you too will be gone from the city's walls by sunset. I have no wish to lay eyes on any one of you again.'

The crowd swirls quickly away, like dirty water down a drain, and within minutes, the Coraggiosi are alone in the piazza, standing awkwardly, looking at each other and not speaking. Beppe has reluctantly relinquished his hold on Sofia, but has her hand gripped tightly in his; they stand side by side, pressed against each other, and Beppe can feel Sofia trembling. Her face is streaked with tears and dirt.

Agostino speaks first. His voice is tight and his face, Beppe thinks, looks somehow shrunken and older than it did even this morning. 'Angelo,' he says. 'Thank you for what you've done. Thank you for getting her out.'

A murmur of agreement buzzes between the other members of the troupe. Angelo, however, looks deflated. His face too has altered. The arrogant aristocrat of a few moments ago has wilted, and his high-chinned, disdainful confidence has vanished, leaving a surprising air of anxiety and discomfort hanging about him like dirty rags. When Agostino says, 'What did you say to him? How did you do it?' Angelo merely shrugs and mutters, 'I don't know. There are just times when it is useful to have exalted antecedents, I suppose.'

Cosima moves across and gives him a hug, which Angelo does not return. Looking a little affronted, she stands back and puts a hand on his shoulder, saying, 'Well, we are all very grateful, whatever you said.'

Federico clears his throat. 'But we had better move, hadn't we? However grateful we are.' He nods towards Angelo. 'Or we'll all be in trouble.'

'Oh, heavens, yes,' Agostino says. 'Sofia my love, we are so, *so* happy that you're safely out.' Striding across towards her, he pulls her away from Beppe and into an embrace; then, standing back and putting a hand on either side of her face, he stares down at her, a furrow of concern between his eyebrows for a second or two. Then he looks around at them all. 'But Federico's right. You heard what the man said ... and you saw what's just happened. We're going to have to leave Bologna fast!' He clicks his fingers. 'I suggest we head down to Firenze.'

'Firenze?'

'Yes. We need to get out of Emilia-Romagna – away from da Budrio's influence – and apart from anything else it will be warmer going south. We might be out in the open rather more than we had anticipated before now.'

Sofia looks at Beppe. 'I'm so sorry,' she starts to mutter. Her lip trembles and tears begin to swell in her eyes, but Beppe shakes his head.

Turning to face her, he runs a hand over her hair. 'No. Stop it. You've done nothing to be sorry for – just don't say it.' Lifting her hand to his mouth, he kisses her knuckles. 'I'm just glad you're safe. We all are.'

Two small boys are standing beside the yellow wagon when they arrive at the patch of waste ground: glancing repeatedly from side to side, they are shifting their weight from foot to foot, blowing on their fingers. As the troupe approaches, their eyes widen – one leans towards the canvas cover and hisses loudly, before scrambling up and over a wall; the other ducks into an impossibly small gap between two buildings and vanishes, while the three horses start at the disturbance and pull on their tethers, their scraping feet kicking up dust and pebbles. A grubby little face peers out from inside the wagon and Beppe, Agostino and Vico all shout and break into a run. The third boy – smaller than the other two – vaults out of the wagon, a canvas bag in his hand, making for the wall over which his friend disappeared seconds before, but Vico grabs for and catches his ankle. 'What the hell do you think you're——?' he begins, tugging downwards.

The boy kicks out and Vico falls back, swearing and covering his eye with his hand, but, snatching at the boy's shirt, Beppe catches hold and pulls; the child falls at his and Vico's feet, dropping the bag.

'Piss off! Let me go!' the boy says, spitting at Vico, who, one hand still clamped over his eye, has hold of the child's leg again.

'Piss off yourself, you little thief!' Vico tugs at the child's foot, pulling him further down onto his back. 'What the hell were you doing in our wagon?'

The boy spits again but says nothing.

Pushing past Vico, Cosima bends down next to the boy and grabs at the collar of his oversized and tattered doublet: the jacket rucks up, covering the bottom half of the child's face. Yanking him upwards, out of Vico and Beppe's grasp, her normally passive face colours with anger and her eyes flash. 'Tell me: what were you doing in that wagon?' she says, now holding his upper arms and shaking him. Her voice cracks. The boy glares at her, but at least refrains from spitting a third time.

Agostino shouts, 'Go on, tell us! What were you doing, you little——?'

His voice is thick with anger but Cosima looks up at him and shakes her head. 'No. Leave this to me, Ago,' she says, turning back to the boy. 'What's your name?'

The boy says nothing.

'As soon as we know who you are and why you were in our wagon, you can go.'

'I'm not saying nothing – bloody murderers!'

'What?' Cosima loosens her grip on the boy's arms and he jerks himself free.

Scrambling back from her, the boy glances from one shocked face to another and spits one last time into the dust at their feet. He begins to run. 'That's what they're saying in the city,' he says thickly over his shoulder. 'Bloody murderers!'

Within seconds he has disappeared and the Coraggiosi stand staring at the place where he has vanished.

'So,' Vico says, touching his eye with the tip of one finger and grimacing. 'That's what Bologna thinks of us now. A bunch of assassins.'

Sofia puts her hands over her face.

Beppe glares at Vico and mouths, 'Shut up,' as he puts his arms around Sofia. Raising his hands in apology, Vico turns away, bending and picking up the canvas bag the child had let fall. Opening it, he peers inside. Frowns. His frown deepens as he reaches inside and pulls out a small brown corked bottle.

'What the hell's this?' he says, pulling the cork with a little high-pitched 'pop' and sniffing curiously. 'Smells awful.'

Nobody responds. Then Angelo, turning and seeing what Vico is holding, strides over, elbowing past Beppe and Sofia and snatching up both bag and bottle. 'Keep your bloody hands off!' he says in an odd, distorted voice. Clutching bottle and bag close to his chest, he edges between the wagons, and climbs up into the smallest cart without another word.

'Well . . . what the . . . ?' Vico says, shaking his head.

'Let me see that eye.' Lidia is looking determinedly at him, chin lifted, frowning in consternation.

'No, leave it. It's just a black eye. It'll mend itself.'

'The skin's split. I'll wash it for you.'

'It's fine. I don't need you to bother with it, and—'

'I don't care what you think you don't need.'

As Vico and Lidia begin to bicker, Beppe turns to Sofia, who has seated herself on the bottom step of the smallest wagon. She has her face in her hands and the ends of her fingers are hidden in her hair. He sits next to her, edging her along the seat with his hip. Putting his arms around her, he holds her close.

'What will the troupe do now, if we're not allowed to perform in Bologna?' she says, leaning against him, her face still covered. Her voice is distorted by her fingers.

Trying to ignore the cold lump of anxiety which lodged itself in his chest as da Budrio made his announcement, Beppe says, 'Don't worry – we'll just find new territory, that's all.'

'God, everyone is going to hate me for making this happen. If Niccolò had never introduced me to you all, then—'

'Then I would never have met you. And I wouldn't . . .' He tails off, rocked by the enormity of the notion of chance, and says no more, contenting himself with tightening his hold on her.

Agostino strides around the end of the wagon, his expression still set and serious. 'We have to go. Beppe, help me harness Topo. She's in a state and you're the only one she won't bite when she's like this. I want to be out of here within the hour.'

Beppe nods. He squeezes Sofia's shoulders and stands, following Agostino around to the front of the wagon.

'I can't deny it, Beppe,' he mutters almost soundlessly as Beppe begins fastening the mare's buckles and patting her neck as he bends to pass the girth-strap under her belly. 'This is a dreadful blow. I'm not sure the troupe will survive it.'

His voice equally quiet, Beppe says, 'Oh God, don't say that,

Ago! You can't mean it! What's to stop us starting again further south – like you suggested?'

The mare tosses her head and snorts angrily. Beppe shushes at her, scratching between her eyes, and holding fast to her bridle.

Agostino's voice is now little more than a whisper. 'You know as well as I do that it takes *years* to build up the sort of following we have along the route: people are waiting for us at each city now, crowds form in expectation of our arrival, word spreads ahead of us. That doesn't just *happen*, does it?'

'No, it doesn't, you're right, but that doesn't mean we can't try to make it happen a second time. We're good, Ago. Thanks to you, we're really good. We'll succeed again.'

Agostino wipes his eyes with the back of his wrist and Beppe, touched by the older man's sudden air of vulnerability, reaches out and takes his hand. Agostino tries to smile, but all he can manage is a tight twitch of his cheek muscles. Cosima, appearing now, sees the look pass between the two men and checks. Standing squarely in front of Agostino she puts a hand on either side of his face and stares into his eyes. 'Now, you listen to me, Agostino Martinelli,' she says softly. 'You and I started this troupe – God knows how long ago – and we've made it into something wonderful, and neither you nor I nor any other member is about to give up on it now, just because some pompous old oaf of a man has given us a bloody great boot up the backside.' She puts her arms around him and hugs him. 'And don't you dare let that little girl see how worried you are. She already feels totally responsible for what's happened, and you are not to make it worse.'

Agostino shakes his head.

'Beppe,' Cosima says over Agostino's shoulder. 'You go back and help Sofia get cleaned up and changed as we get the wagons going. Ago, take the yellow wagon, Federico can take the blue and

Lidia and I will manage this one – Vico can walk alongside Topo until we are out of the city, in case she starts getting silly.' She kisses Agostino tenderly. 'No more of this fretting. I want to hear you loud and blustering and stuffing far too many words into every sentence, exhorting us all to better things – just as you normally do. The troupe is not called I Coraggiosi for nothing, is it? We need you to be *brave* – come on, *carissimo*.'

As he turns to go back to Sofia, Beppe sees Cosima and Agostino embracing again. Tipping his head back and staring up into the sky for a moment, he runs back round to where Sofia is still huddled on the wagon step. 'Listen, lovely girl, we need to get you tidied up and fit to be seen again,' he says, taking her hands and pulling her to her feet. He holds her face tenderly and kisses her mouth, and feels her arms sliding around his waist.

'Oh, Beppe,' she says into the stuff of his doublet, clinging tightly. 'I don't care how uncomfortable it is, but stay next to me. And wherever we sleep tonight, be with me. Please?'

'I'm not sleeping anywhere other than where you are, little seamstress. Not ever.'

The three wagons rumble away from Bologna a little while later, the iron-clad wheels and the horses' hooves loud on the cobbles as they go. A scattering of people along the route wave to them and shout their goodbyes, and the Coraggiosi wave back. One small figure, though, makes no gesture of farewell. One small boy in an oversized doublet, from his vantage point on top of a wall near the southern gate to the city, merely stares after them, tearing moodily at a hunk of bread he stole from a nearby market stall some moments ago. 'Bloody murderers,' he mutters to himself, spraying breadcrumbs over his tattered breeches.

27

That evening, in an upstairs chamber at the Castello della Franceschina, a number of people have gathered to stand vigil over the body of Sebastiano da Correggio. His bloodied head has been washed, and his clothes have been changed. The badly stained shirt has already been burned. Now, lying on his bed in the grandest of the bedchambers at the *castello*, dressed in his most expensive embroidered doublet and breeches, da Correggio looks peaceful: his hands are folded on his chest; his eyes (which were wide and staring when they picked him up from the floor of the study) have been closed; candles burn at the head and foot of the bed and a dozen silent figures are keeping watch. Da Correggio's cousin, roused from his bed less than an hour after he returned home from watching the play, stands in the shadows near the head of the bed. Marco's eyes are stiff and heavy with lack of sleep and he has been trying for the best part of an hour to avoid looking at where a seeping stain has darkened the linen on which his cousin's head is resting. Glancing across the room, he catches the eye of his elderly uncle, who is seated in a carved wooden chair near one of the tightly shuttered windows. His uncle stares at him without comment for several long seconds; then, shaking his head a fraction, he drops his gaze to his clasped hands. His lips begin to move in silent prayer.

Marco looks from his uncle to a row of Franceschina servants, standing stiffly and smothering yawns, then to a couple he recognizes from the performance last night – the paramour and her husband. The man is thin, sunken-cheeked, with sparse hair and a beaky nose. He is finely dressed and clearly wealthy, and his rather beautiful wife is – Marco flicks a glance downwards – expecting a child by the look of her. She is silent and upright, staring fixedly at Sebastiano's face. By rights, Marco thinks now, she should be crying out – falling to her knees as she weeps and clutches at her hair; in circumstances like this, Marco feels sure that his cousin must be feeling the lack of an appropriate display of feminine grief to mark his passing and he wonders briefly why the usual group of hired women have not yet been brought in – it seems almost shameful that none is here to bewail his cousin's passing. Sebastiano had no time to prepare himself for death, after all; he left the world unshriven, which, Marco thinks now with a pang of fear, bodes ill for a man such as his cousin as he faces Judgement laden down with so heavy a burden of wrongdoings.

As he does himself.

He shivers at the thought.

This woman is no paid mourner: she stands still and quiet. Her face is set, her mouth no more than a compressed line in her face. One hand caresses the slight swell of her belly.

It seems to Marco, watching her now, that she is concealing some unspoken truth behind that mask-like expression as she is concealing the child beneath her skirts. He cannot determine what it might be – unexpressed love, perhaps? If she were actually in love with his cousin, she could hardly declare it in front of her husband, though of course the counterfeit wailings of most mourners are rarely anything other than an expected exhibition and a woman hiding such a covert passion might well wish to take advantage of the custom to give herself the freedom to howl and tear her clothes in what would be in reality a genuine display of grief, performed under the nose of her unsuspecting husband.

Presumably the child she is carrying is Sebastiano's.

Looking at her now, though, Marco thinks, he is not sure that it is love she is concealing. There are no tears glittering unshed; her jaw is set and her mouth firm. She looks more as though she is trying not to spit.

28

The road up and over the mountains between Bologna and Firenze is often steep and at times it twists and turns to such an extent that manoeuvring anything like a heavy wagon around the tight bends can be a genuinely hazardous experience. The Coraggiosi have spent much of the last few days struggling with their three unwieldy carts along narrow roads which have at times crumbled alarmingly when anyone has been unwary enough to stand too near the edge, sending rubble and dust tumbling downwards in scurrying puffs.

At times the drop is enough to turn the stomach.

The October weather has begun to disintegrate. The wind on the slopes has been colder than anyone expected and the wagons offer little in the way of genuine shelter when exposed like this. Even the yellow wagon, whose canvas cover is by far the newest and most robust of the three, seems to be made of little more than paper when hit broadside with biting gusts from the east, as it has been for the last couple of days. Everyone – well wrapped in their warmest clothes – is looking forward to reaching lower ground.

It is not only the weather which is deteriorating, though: Sofia has been uncomfortably aware for the last day or so of a worrying change in atmosphere among the troupe members. The high-spirited banter which normally buzzes between them all – the witty, affectionate bickering, the re-enacted extracts of recent perform-ances, the loudly voiced and highly opinionated criticisms of rival actors in other troupes – has all but dried up. Agostino, whom Sofia has rarely known to be silent on any subject, has hardly spoken at all since the troupe left Bologna; he and Cosima have talked quietly between themselves but have shared little with the others, while old Giovanni Battista, feeling the autumnal chill, has largely remained within the smallest wagon, wrapped in a blanket and dozing on the little bed.

Angelo has ridden on his dark pony a few paces behind the wagons since Bologna, stony-faced, saying almost nothing, and merely shrugging dismissively at mealtimes and in the evenings, when anyone has tried to raise the subject of what was discussed between him and Signor da Budrio. When they stopped overnight in the little town of Borgo Tossignano, he disappeared completely, re-emerging only the following morning as the troupe readied themselves to resume their journey, looking drawn and pale and heavy-eyed. No one has yet asked him where he went.

Sofia would have liked to share her worries with Beppe, but he has been on foot most of the way, walking with the horses – he has had much of his time and energy taken up with helping them nego-tiate the treacherous mountain roads. Sofia knows that he is only doing what has to be done, but the inevitable result of it all is that while he has kept his promise of never sleeping away from where she is, in daylight hours he has hardly spoken to her. Over the past couple of days he seems to have become increasingly tense and withdrawn, and Sofia is beginning to dread that some unspoken barrier has arisen between them. She dares not ask Lidia or Cosima what they think, so as the jolting, chilled and monotonous days have passed, she has swallowed down her fears and tried to immerse herself in the myriad little tasks that fall to her lot. But Beppe's words keep coming back to her, words uttered as he stared up into the sky on the lane outside Montalbano: *I could imagine Agostino not wanting the scandal of a murder to affect the troupe's reputation.* And that scandal was a murder supposedly committed not by a member of the troupe, but by his long-absent father, years before. Is this why they are all withdrawing from her? Is this why everything seems to be falling apart – because of the *scandal of a murder?*

Early in the morning of the fourth day of the Coraggiosi's journey south, Lidia has been making herself useful, repainting small items of scenery, and Sofia has been glad to keep her company; she has been stitching and darning damaged costumes, thankful for the comforting warmth of the piles of fabric on her lap.

'We'll be down on the plains soon,' Lidia says, frowning as she struggles to keep a small gilt-framed picture still on her cloth-covered lap, a paint-laden brush held out sideways as the cart jolts across yet another uneven piece of road.

Gasping and swearing softly – she has just jabbed herself with her needle – Sofia says, 'Have you been down this far south before?'

Lidia shakes her head. 'No. I'm not sure any of us have. We've always kept to our territory – along from ... oh, I suppose Piacenza in the west, down across to Ravenna on the coast.'

Her face burning, Sofia stares down at the cloth in her hands: Beppe's diamond-patterned jacket. Resisting the urge to pick it up and press it to her face – to breathe in the smell of him – she fiddles a little section of seam between finger and thumb as she says, 'I feel so responsible for all this.'

'You mustn't. And I know Beppe's said the same to you over and over again. You simply mustn't. Because—'

'But I do. If I had made more of a fuss about leaving the banqueting room – if I had refused to go with da Correggio – we'd be in Bologna today, wouldn't we? Getting ready to set off for Ravenna.'

Lidia pauses. 'Well, yes, I suppose we would. But you could just as easily say that if Ago hadn't agreed to perform at bloody Franceschina, it would never have happened. Or if any of us had stopped you leaving the room with that man. Which we all should have done.' She waves a hand in the air and paint spatters across the floor of the wagon. 'Or if Beppe hadn't gone down to the kitchen to see about Ippo when he did, then da Correggio would never have made his move and . . . oh, you could drive yourself *mad* thinking like this. You'll have to stop it.'

Sofia nods.

'We'll over-winter somewhere – getting work where we can, preparing new material, rehearsing, performing indoors if we can secure a commission or two – and then we can start touring again properly in the spring, trying to establish ourselves in Toscana. Cosima suggested that we could go and present ourselves at the Villa Cafaggiolo – that's down on the other side of the mountains. With Angelo's family connections we might get ourselves a performance there and that would be a good start.'

'Angelo's connections? What do you mean?'

'Cafaggiolo's the summer residence of the Medicis, and the Duke of Ferrara married one of the Medicis a few years back. Angelo's father is a second cousin, if you remember.'

Sofia puffs a breath in surprise. 'The Medicis? Surely not! Do you really think a family that prestigious would be interested in a little troupe like—?'

'Like us? Oh, I do hope so. Ago's hopeful, anyway, Cosima says.'

The scandal of a murder. Dreading the thought that the scandal might reach Cafaggiolo before the Coraggiosi and that everyone will blame her if it does, Sofia sighs and picks the jacket back up. Pushing her hand down inside one of the sleeves, she spreads her fingers out, holding the cloth tight across them so that she can begin to darn where the sleeve has worn thin over the elbow, a patch about the size of a large coin. She weaves the needle in and out of the remaining worn threads, back and forth, creating a fine mesh, then ducks into and out of this soft web, over and over, keeping the threads taut across her fingers. Slowly the patch starts to feel thicker and stronger.

They stop for the evening on the edge of the pretty town of Castel del Rio. Beppe volunteers to try to find some food and Sofia offers to go with him. They leave the rest of the troupe settling the huddle of wagons and the disgruntled horses on a patch of waste ground, and, with a woven straw basket looped over Sofia's arm, they start to make their way through a number of narrow streets and down several sets of steps towards where voices and bustle can be heard.

'Sounds as though there might still be a market in the main square,' Beppe says.

Sofia bites down the question she fears will irritate him. *What do we do if there isn't?* She knows what he will say if she asks: *We'll find something. We always do. Don't worry*. But she *is* worrying – she is worrying all the time. Her squirming anxiety is eating away at her. Every day she watches Beppe to see if she can read any reason for his new distance from her; every day she searches the faces of the troupe, covertly waiting for them to reveal what she is sure they must be concealing; waiting for them to say what she dreads hearing: that she has brought them bad luck, that she should go, should leave them to repair the damage she has caused.

She contents herself now by glancing up at Beppe and flicking him a quick smile when he catches her eye. He grips her fingers for a moment and smiles back, but his face is tense. His normally wide, tilted grin is tighter than usual and the skin around his eyes is dark, she thinks, almost bruised-looking. She tries to convince herself that this must be simply because he has walked much of the way from Bologna and must be exhausted.

'There, look,' he says now, pointing down the length of the little street. 'Let's go and see what we can find.'

A cramped square is filled with stalls. Several are displaying collections of knives, whose steel blades glint in the low light of the afternoon sun. Another is laden with vegetables: brightly coloured piles of *melanzane* and beans; asparagus; bunches of thin, finger-like carrots – yellow, dark red and orange; while one smaller stall has dozens of *finocchiona* sausages hanging from a stand, as thick and long as a man's forearm and, even from several paces, redolent with the soft smell of fennel.

'Shall we get one of those?' Beppe says, pointing at the sausages.

Sofia nods. 'One should be enough for all of us, shouldn't it?'

'Easily. And if we get a good load of vegetables, Cosima or Lidia will make a stew.' He flashes her a quick smile. 'Let's hope it's Lidia.'

Approaching the *finocchiona* stall, which is being tended by a girl not much older than Sofia, and nodding towards the dangling sausages, Beppe suggests a price for one which makes the girl laugh. At her laughter, he seems to shrug off his fatigue, and feigns taking offence, his hands on his hips, his mouth an irritable O, shaking his head in counterfeit annoyance, but the girl's eyes dance and she starts fiddling her thumbnail between her teeth; she is,

Sofia sees with a twinge in her belly, very much enjoying Beppe's performance.

'How about', he says then, reaching across to the vegetable stall and picking up a handful of walnuts which click together in his palm, 'a moment's entertainment to make up for the ... er ... lack of *baiocchi*?'

He flips the nuts into the air and juggles with them for a few seconds. The girl – along with the owner of the vegetable stall – smiles widely and claps enthusiastically. Nodding his appreciation of the applause, Beppe puts the nuts back on the stall display and makes an extravagant, swaggering bow.

'You win,' the girl says. 'After that, you're welcome to it – even at that ridiculous price. Thank you!'

'And come here,' the vegetable man says. 'You and your girl: come here and let's see what we can do for you to go with that old sausage.'

Sofia smiles at him –a little comforted by his presumption of her connection with Beppe – and she moves in closer to the displays of vegetables.

'What would you like?' the stall man says. 'You could make a nice warm potful with some of these ...' Picking up three turnips and a green-fronded bunch of carrots, he waves them at Sofia. 'And some beans, and a couple of ...' The turnips and the carrots go into Sofia's basket, and, reaching out, he takes up two large aubergines. 'How would these do?'

'How much?'

'For a pretty thing like you? Ooh, now let's see ...' He names a very reasonable price.

Sofia looks at Beppe, who nods. 'Thank you, signore. That will be lovely.'

'Thank you.' Beppe pecks him a quick bow.

'Just do that again, will you – with the nuts?'

'What about with the turnips instead?'

'Even better.' He puts his hands to his mouth and shouts out across the square, 'Hey! Giovanni! Lisabetta! Stefano! Come here and see something special! Not to be missed!'

Several people come from their stalls, arms folded, curious frowns in place between raised brows. Questions are asked, but the vegetable man shushes them and nods at Beppe, who quickly obliges with the turnips. The newly formed small crowd murmurs and gasps and finally applauds as Beppe flips the turnips up high and catches them for one last time in neatly cupped hands. He replaces them on the stall, then bows with a flourish.

Sofia claps too.

Coins are clinked in pockets, but Beppe says, 'No, please, I wasn't expecting anyone to pay anything. Only . . . if anyone has any bits of food they might not be needing, perhaps you can spare those instead.'

Lidia's stew is thick, hot and filling and everyone eats well that evening. Huddled around the two braziers, warming their hands around their bowls, the troupe consumes the stew in hunger-driven silence, wiping out refilled bowls twice with hunks torn from the two big flat loaves given to Beppe and Sofia by a delighted baker after the juggling performance.

Normally, Sofia thinks now, after a good meal, Vico would be getting out his guitar, and he and Lidia would sing. Federico might tell a humorous story or two and everyone would laugh and add to it, turning it and twisting it, building it up into something which might one day become a fully-fledged scenario. Sofia knows of at least two of the Coraggiosi shows which began life as nothing more than a piece of after-supper silliness.

Tonight though, as there has been every evening since the departure from Bologna, there is a quietness about the troupe. Almost a melancholy. It is like being in a ship becalmed. The sails hang slack and useless and the water around them is glassy. She looks from face to face and sees the same expression on each – a flat, weary lack of enthusiasm – and it frightens her. Whatever Lidia says, whatever Beppe has repeated over and over, she feels responsible, and here, faced with this new and unprecedented apathy among her new and much-loved friends, a probing wire of guilt begins to needle her. She sits quietly next to Beppe for a while after the meal; his arm is around her shoulder, but, whereas even a few days ago, he would most likely have been fiddling with her sleeve, stroking her arm, squeezing her in close to him at intervals, planting a kiss every few minutes onto the top of her head, now his hand hangs still, fingers bent into a graceful curve. Sitting stiffly within this newly unenthusiastic embrace, she glances around at the others: Vico and Cosima are smiling; Lidia is now on her feet, collecting up the dirty bowls and spoons; Giovanni Battista is leaning in close to the brazier to warm his hands – all this should feel familiar and comfortable, but there is a detachedness about them all that is unnerving her badly.

Nobody speaks for several minutes and it seems to Sofia that the air between them all is thickening and stiffening, becoming harder to breathe, and suddenly she knows that she needs to get away from it – to be on her own for a while. Muttering to Beppe that her head is aching and that she needs to lie down, she slides out from under his arm, hoping that he will protest and follow her. He does not, but as she walks alone towards the oldest and smallest wagon, Ippo, the dog, scrabbles to his feet and trots after her, tail swinging slowly; he jumps up into the cart behind her. As Sofia flaps out a blanket and wraps it around herself, Ippo leaps up onto the little truckle bed with her and curls into the crook of her knees. Feeling tears stinging in the corners of her eyes, she scratches his fur, grateful for his company.

The voices of the rest of the troupe carry across the still evening air; much, but not all of what they say is clearly audible, and she holds her breath, desperate to hear more, dreading hearing some damning criticism of her part in their troubles.

Beppe stares into the flames in the brazier. Leaning forwards, he holds his hands out, aware of how much warmer his front is than his back. His feet are cold: heeling off his boots, he rubs each foot between his hands for a moment, then pulls the boots back on. A flat, damp weariness is making him feel frighteningly heavy and stale; he can see the same feelings reflected on every face around the brazier and, with a pang of trepidation, wonders, if this is the new reality for the troupe, how they are ever going to rally themselves out of this lassitude.

The loss of the territories has hit them hard.

Harder, Beppe thinks, than even Agostino predicted it would.

He realizes now how used the troupe has become to the comfortable familiarity of the towns and cities of Emilia-Romagna; how they have all – perhaps complacently – come to expect the cheering welcome offered by audiences who await their arrival with undisguised delight and make their enjoyment of the performances so abundantly clear time after time. The prospect of playing to possibly three-quarters-empty piazzas, of being run out of strange towns by unfriendly authorities and – perhaps worst of all – of having to research endlessly into the new territories to try to make any new material relevant to new audiences, is terrifying, and Beppe is sure that all the others are feeling the same.

Only Sofia will not understand the extent of what has been lost. Thinking of her now his heart turns over; he knows she feels responsible for it all, and knows too that he has been distant from her these past few days – he has been so wrapped up in his worries. He has not been fair to her. A rush of love for her sweeps through him, and, straightening, he determines to go to the wagon and tell her so right away, but—

'. . . and apart from anything else, God knows how long it's going to take to re-establish ourselves down here,' Angelo is saying to nobody in particular in his aristocratic drawl, and Beppe pauses to listen.

Vico and Federico speak at once. Federico nods at Vico and repeats his comment. 'Just keep your mouth shut, Angelo, if you have nothing constructive to say. We don't need reminding.'

'And who the hell do you think you are, telling me when to speak and what to say?'

Cosima raises placatory hands and begins to reply, but Vico interrupts her. 'No, Cosima, Federico's right. Shut up, Angelo. Cramming our problems down everyone's throats all the time is only going to make it worse. We need to—'

'I know you will all only shout me down,' Angelo says, louder than before, 'but I'm going to say it. I'm laying the blame at Sofia's feet. If we hadn't had her with us in Franceschina, we'd not be in this bloody predicament now, and—'

Beppe jumps to his feet, hands raised in incredulous anger. His soup bowl drops to the ground, cracking into two pieces. 'What? *You* were the one who got her released in bloody Bologna! What were you *thinking* of, if you're saying she—'

'I did what I had to, nothing more.'

'*What you had to?* What's that supposed to mean?'

'I hardly think I need to explain it to you.'

310

Beppe's hands have curled into fists. 'Well, I think you do. What did you mean: you did *what you had to*?'

Angelo raises an eyebrow and shakes his head almost pityingly. Taking his time before he answers, tracing around the outline of his mouth with a finger, he says finally, 'She didn't kill him – I'm not denying that. And I don't care to see innocent parties wrongly convicted—'

'What? *What* did you say? You bloody hypocrite!'

'Beppe – what—? What in heaven's name . . . ?' Agostino's face is crumpled with concern and lack of comprehension but Beppe takes no notice of him.

'You fucking hypocrite, how you can stand there and say . . . after everything that . . . ' Anger closes his throat, and he tails off.

'What are you *talking* about?' Agostino says.

'He knows.' Beppe does not take his eyes from Angelo's face.

'She was clearly innocent,' Angelo says, staring back fixedly at Beppe, speaking as though there has been no interruption, 'so I was happy to intervene. I'm just saying that despite her innocence, it is thanks to her that *we* were implicated in the whole unpleasant business, and that we've now been thrown out of Emilia-Romagna.'

'No it bloody is *not*!' Beppe's voice cracks.

'You go too far, Angelo,' Agostino says. 'Sofia is blameless – both of the murder and of any part in what followed. She's nothing but a victim.'

'You cannot deny, though, can you, that nothing seems to have run the way it used to since she arrived. And *you*'ve probably exacerbated it' – Angelo points accusingly at Beppe – 'by throwing yourself at her the way you have.'

Beppe's mouth falls open, but he can think of no response.

Cosima says, 'Angelo, that's enough! We're grateful to you for whatever you did back there which got our lovely girl released, of course we are, but I cannot sit by and listen to you speak to other troupe members like that, and—'

'What are you saying?' Beppe says, his voice little more than a whisper now. 'Why should I not have got close to Sofia? Why should *you* care one way or the other? Jealous, are you?'

Angelo laughs. It is a sneering, mirthless little puff of air, no more, but Beppe tightens his fists. 'Or is it just because it's me? You just don't want *me* to have her. What did I ever do? I was your friend. All those years ago I was your friend – and you turned your back on me and I've never known why.'

Vico, Agostino, Federico and Lidia all start to question Beppe at once, but he takes no notice of them, and then Angelo's dismissive comment cuts through their clamour.

'You're pathetic,' he says, getting to his feet. 'I'm going to bed.'

'What is it that you'd like to hear? What do you want me to say?' Beppe's voice is still quiet, but rises as Angelo flicks him a sneering glance. '*Oh yes, you're right,*' he says loudly, '*I made a mistake. I hate to admit it but she's trouble. I should never have got close to her – I had a feeling it was going to end badly right from the start.*' He pauses, then hisses, 'Something like *that*?'

'Beppe . . .' Lidia reaches out to take his hand, but Beppe shrugs his arm away from her. He is still staring at Angelo.

'I've never said anything to anyone about what happened when we were lads. Never. Never told Agostino or anyone. Only Sofia, the other day.'

Agostino has stood up. 'Beppe, what are you—?'

'What am I saying?' Beppe finally turns to look at Agostino, then around at the rest of the troupe. Everyone is staring at him, open-mouthed with bemused concern. He flicks a glance at

Angelo, whose sneering glare seems, Beppe thinks, to be daring him to speak, daring him to reveal their shared past. He opens his mouth to explain, then closes it again. 'Nothing,' he says in a small, flat voice. 'Nothing. It was a long time ago.'

Cosima shakes her head, her expression stricken.

Agostino's gaze flicks from Beppe to Angelo and back, his mouth slightly open, a frown puckering his brow into deep ridges. 'Angelo, what is Beppe talking about? When you were lads? Did you two know each other before? What is this?' His voice tails off.

Angelo glances dismissively at Beppe and then turns to Agostino. 'I have no idea what he's talking about,' he says. Picking up his dirty bowl and spoon from where it has been sitting at his feet, he walks away towards the wagons without another word.

Turning to a nearby tree, Beppe smacks out hard at the trunk with the palm of his hand. The impact stings wildly and he smothers an oath; then, leaning against the trunk, pressing his cheek against its cold roughness, he closes his eyes and tries to steady his breathing. He senses someone next to him, feels an arm about his shoulders. Wanting Sofia, he opens his eyes, but it is Lidia who has come to comfort him.

Her face is lined with concern. 'What is this all about, Beppe? What's going on between you two?'

Shaking his head, Beppe says nothing.

'You knew each other before, didn't you? I've always thought so.'

'Yes. We did.'

'When? Where? Why have you never said? Either of you?'

Beppe cannot look at her, or at Vico, who has joined them. 'It's difficult,' he mutters, shrugging. 'I'll tell you some time. Not now.'

'But . . . ?'

'Please, Lidia, I just can't.'

She hugs him. 'I'm sorry. Whatever you want, sweet boy. Tell us when you're ready. We're all badly rattled by everything that's happened. It's going to take a bit of time to settle, that's all.'

Beppe nods.

'I said the same to Sofia a few hours ago. It'll just take a bit of time.'

'Here.' Vico, his eye still swollen and bruised, is holding out a mug of ale. 'Have this. I'm having one.'

Taking it from him, Beppe returns to the brazier and, sitting back down on the little stool, he leans forward, cradling the mug in both hands, his arms resting heavily on his thighs.

'Tell you what, though, there is one thing I'd like to know,' Vico says, sitting down next to him, swallowing a mouthful of ale and wiping his mouth with the back of his hand, 'and that's where our handsome friend goes when he disappears – which he does considerably more often than anyone else. It's not always in the same town, so I don't think it's a woman. Though there would be enough takers, I reckon.' He snorts softly. 'And – now I'm thinking about it – what was he so worked up about with that brown bottle the other day, when that little bastard urchin tried to ransack the wagons? What was that all about? Beppe, do you know?'

'Brown bottle?' Cosima asks.

Vico nods. 'Mmm. Just before we left Bologna. The scabby little boy had pinched a bag from one of the carts – he dropped it when he ran off. I picked it up after he'd gone, and there was this brown glass bottle in it. Pulled the cork. It smelled of … oh God, I don't know … rancid spices or something. I was just sniffing it when Angelo saw me. Snatched it off me and barked at me to keep my hands off it. Thought he was going to throw a punch.'

'Spices?' Cosima is looking puzzled.

Vico nods again. 'Mmm. Spices. Sickly, though. Really strong. Made me feel a bit light-headed just sniffing the stuff.'

Agostino's expression is serious. 'Oh *cielo*, I don't like the sound of that at all,' he says, more to himself than to Vico. 'Not at all.' He sighs deeply. 'Oh dear, what on earth is happening to us all?

'*Do* you know, Beppe? Does whatever has happened – whatever it is that you don't want to talk about – does it explain this little bottle? And Angelo's absences?'

'No. I know nothing about any of that – truly, Ago. I'd tell you if I knew.'

Agostino pats Beppe's shoulder and turns to Cosima. 'What do you think, *cara*?'

Compressing her lips, Cosima sighs. 'I've always had my worries and doubts about Angelo. He's always been ... oh, I don't know ... *detached* from the rest of the troupe, hasn't he? On his own, in a way. He doesn't have a close friend amongst us, after all, does he?'

Agostino frowns. 'Oh dear, I'm not liking the sound of all this at all. It all seems very troubling and uncertain. And spices? Goodness knows what's in that bottle. I think I need to go and talk with him. I'll go now, before he goes to sleep. Or disappears off again somewhere. Stay here, the rest of you, will you? I don't want Angelo to think that we are stacking ourselves up against him.'

'Even if we are ...' Vico says drily.

Agostino flashes him a look. Striding away from them over towards the wagons, arms tightly folded in front of him, head ducked forwards, he stops in front of the blue wagon. Beppe sees him shake his head; then, squaring his shoulders, Agostino reaches up and draws back the hangings, leaning in for a moment; he climbs up onto the wooden step and disappears inside.

A lump of wood shifts in the brazier and a shower of fat red sparks spatters out towards where Beppe, Lidia and Vico, Cosima, Federico and Giovanni Battista are sitting. One lands on Lidia's skirts and she pats it away hastily. A silence has fallen amongst them all. Apart from a long sigh from Cosima and a phlegmy cough from Giovanni Battista, no one makes a sound. Only the hissing crackle of the fire breaks the stillness of the night air.

They sit wordlessly for several minutes; Beppe finds himself holding his breath, and realizes how fiercely he is straining to hear what might be being said in the blue wagon. Glancing at the others, he sees the same expression of taut concentration on each face that he can feel upon his own.

Then, standing, he says, 'I'm going to Sofia – she said she had a headache. Do you have anything I can give her for it, Cosima?'

'Look in the blue box in the smallest wagon. Niccolò left me some feverfew – take a cup of hot water and steep some of the flowers in it for her. It might help.'

Beppe nods his thanks and, scooping up a cup full of water from the iron pot on the brazier, he makes his way back over to the smallest wagon, where he and Sofia have been sleeping for the past few nights, curled together on the cramped truckle bed, sleeping fitfully, grateful for the warmth of each other's bodies as the autumn nights have chilled.

Vaulting up over the tailgate, smiling in anticipation, he is surprised to see that the wagon is empty. His smile vanishes.

It takes no more than a couple of seconds to cross to the blue cart. Standing on the bottom step and leaning in through the hangings, he sees Angelo on his feet, one hand up on the canvas roof-cover, pointing an accusatory forefinger at Agostino. Agostino is shaking his head, mouth open as he tries to interrupt the angry flow.

'You have absolutely no right to—' Angelo breaks off and snatches his head around as Beppe clears his throat. 'What the hell do *you* want?'

Seeing in an instant that Sofia is not there, Beppe makes no reply but draws back out of the wagon and runs, a little thread of anxiety beginning to tighten around his throat, towards the only place Sofia can be. The yellow wagon.

But it too is empty.

29

Maddalena stares out of her bedchamber window. A fluttering tremor in her belly startles her, and she presses a hand to it, tucking her chin down and staring at the place where the child has just kicked. Then, lifting that hand, she gazes at the palm, curling and uncurling her fingers, frowning at it, breathing a little faster as she contemplates what it has done. She has washed her hands a hundred times since, but they still feel dirty.

30

'Go back! Go back, Ippo – please!' Sofia bends and points back down the path, the tears hot in her eyes and suddenly chill on her cheeks. Her voice cracks as she says again, 'Please, *caro*, go back!'

But the dog stands square, staring at her, tail slowly wagging and tongue lolling.

'Go! I don't want you!'

This last, though, is a lie. Sofia hisses at the dog once more, to absolve herself of guilt; then when Ippo still refuses to turn back, she crouches down, fondles his ears and hugs him, burying her face in the thick fur of his neck.

With the dog at her heels, she strides on, swallowing more often than is comfortable, breathing through an open mouth, for her nose is congested with crying; every few seconds she wipes her eyes with the back of her wrist. It is very dark, though a fitful moon is shining at intervals through untidy clouds. She has no idea where she is going – but the thought of staying a moment longer after what she has just heard is entirely impossible. *Oh yes, you're right, I made a mistake. I hate to admit it but she's trouble. I should never have got close to her – I had a feeling it was going to end badly right from the start*. That's what he said. She heard it clearly. *She's trouble. She's trouble. She's trouble.* Beppe has been distant and different for days; ever since she was released from that dreadful place, he has been . . . not unkind, not unloving, but just different. She knew something was wrong right from the start, and so even if she is horrified and miserable at the thought of what she has just heard him say, she has to admit that she is not *surprised*. Such a sentiment is, after all, what she has half expected – and dreaded – ever since she first kissed him. Nothing that felt so wonderful could be allowed to last. She knows that she would not be able to bear seeing open rejection in his face, so leaving the troupe like this – before he can pretend to her that he wants her to stay – seems to be the only option.

But where will she go?

What on earth will she do?

She would be unwise to go back into Bologna, and Modena would be no less foolish – it seems to Sofia now that false accusations are beginning to dog her every step, and a sense of anger begins to rise in her. The foul-breathed man in Modena – an accusation of theft; the authorities in Bologna – an accusation of murder, for God's sake! They thought her a murderer. And now Beppe has accused her of being *trouble*. Perhaps though, she thinks now, he at least is justified in his accusation. Perhaps she *is* trouble, for complications certainly seem to follow her wherever she goes.

It's like poor Mamma.

The three men walk slowly towards them.

'Leave the brat,' one of them says. 'It's you we want, you murdering bitch.'

'No . . . I've done nothing . . . ' Mamma says, and her voice is high and thin.

'Nothing? Only poisoned my wife.'

Mamma shakes her head. 'No. No, I didn't. I tried to make her well.'

The man sneers at her. 'I think not.'

'You have to believe me – I tried my best for her.'

For a moment, Mamma presses back against Sofia, crushing her against the wall, then at the last moment, she breaks away and starts to run. Sofia screams. Ignoring her, the men race after Mamma. Mamma runs fast, and reaches the bridge before they do. It is a flimsy wooden bridge – one of the wobbling ones that Sofia is frightened to walk on. And as Mamma runs onto it now, there is a terrible tearing noise of breaking wood and two of the supporting struts collapse. Mamma shrieks. Sofia's mouth opens and she tries to scream again, but no sound comes out as Mamma falls with the breaking bridge, down onto the stone coping of the canal and into the water.

The men are looking at where Mamma is in the water. She is not moving.

'There's blood in the water.'

'Fuck. Let's get out now.'

'Roberto, come on! What are you waiting for? It's what you wanted, isn't it?'

And they run. Heavy-footed, swearing as they stumble in their haste to get away, they run.

Mamma doesn't move. Sofia is on the edge of the canal now, lying on her belly, reaching out to Mamma.

'They've gone, Mamma! You can come out now! Mamma!'

She touches her mother's shoulder with the tips of her fingers but Mamma just turns silently and floats a little further away from the bank. She is face down in the water and now Sofia cannot reach her at all.

*

The clatter of hooves startles her.

'What the——?'

A small and shabby cart has pulled sharply across to avoid her, and the hooves of the two harnessed horses skitter on the loose-stoned ground. Ippo whines and scurries around the back of her skirts.

Gasping, she takes a step back off the path into the shadows. She won't go back. If Beppe no longer wants her, then to be in their company and to have to see him and be near him every day would be a torture she cannot bear to contemplate.

But it is not the troupe.

'What the hell are you doing? D'you want to get yourself killed?' An unknown male voice, sharp with fright.

Sofia cannot see his face. 'I'm sorry,' she mutters.

Another voice, a woman, says, 'Giorgio, stop, will you? It's just a girl. What in heaven's name is she doing out here in the dark like this?'

Sofia hears the man click his tongue against his teeth. He sounds irritable. 'No doubt she has her own reasons. Come on, we have to make up time. We're out in it ourselves, after all, and your father—'

'No, Giorgio, wait. Signorina, are you in need of assistance? I see that you're heading away from Castel del Rio and it's a most dreadfully long way to the next tavern. Are you—?'

'Oh, for God's sake, Maria, leave the girl alone. We can't afford to delay.'

Sofia does not know how to answer.

The woman – Maria – says, 'I'm sorry, but I can't believe you're happy to be out here alone. Can we take you on to the next tavern or town? You could travel up in the cart with Giorgio and me.'

'Maria, I—'

'No, Giorgio, we can't leave her out here. Enrico was robbed only last month, and he's a man *and* handy with a sword. They took everything he had. Look at her: she can't be much more than sixteen.' Maria pauses. 'There's more than robbery a girl like her needs to fear. Go on – get down and help her up.'

Giorgio sighs. 'Very well.' He puffs a breath. 'Should you care for a ride to the next tavern, signorina?'

His tone clearly declares his irritation and doubt, but, silently offering a brief prayer of thanks, Sofia nods. 'If it's not too much trouble, signore, then yes, I should be most grateful.'

'Good.' Maria sounds pleased. 'I knew you would. Help her up next to me, Gio. Can you manage, signorina?'

Sofia mutters a yes. Giorgio hands the reins to Maria. Clicking his fingers to summon Sofia over to where Maria's horse is fidgeting and tossing its head, he bends and places his hands together, making a step. Sofia places one foot onto his palms and feels him shove firmly upwards. Grabbing at Maria's proffered arm, she slithers one leg over the edge of the rough wooden side of the cart and pulls awkwardly at her skirts, freeing them from where they have caught and crumpled beneath her. She sees the man wipe his muddied hands on his breeches.

Maria shuffles across the seat to give Sofia more space. 'Is that enough room for you? I'm sorry, it's not a very pleasant cart, but we had to—'

'Maria, that's enough.' Giorgio's voice is clipped and irritable. 'There's a dog down here. Is it yours, signorina?'

'Oh yes, yes he is.'

'Here – take him.' With an inelegant scrabbling of paws, and a fair amount of frantic grunting, Ippo is handed up to Sofia, who holds him tightly on her lap. He is too big to sit there comfortably, and his claws dig into her legs as she tries to settle herself on the cramped seat; she can feel him trembling as she holds him in close.

Sofia, finding herself pressed against Maria, smells clean wool and freshly washed linen; this woman's travelling clothes are obviously well made and expensive. She hopes fervently that her own smell, by contrast, is not too unpleasant to her fragrant new companion.

'What's your name?' Maria asks as Giorgio climbs back into the cart, takes the reins and clicks his tongue. With a scrunch of pebbles under the iron rims of the wheels, they move off.

Sofia tells her.

'Why are you out in the middle of nowhere in the dark?'

'It's hard to explain.'

'Oh, so is our story – you simply *cannot* have as terrible a situation as ours!' Maria says, sounding far more cheerful about her circumstances than her words would imply. 'We're determined to marry, we two, but Papa has refused. He has never cared for anyone in Giorgio's family and the thought of being joined to them for good if we marry is threatening to send him into a permanent decline ... He's refused to let it go ahead, so we've run away. We stole Papa's woodsman's cart and horses and left two hours ago. We're going to travel right through the night. We're on our way to Ravenna.'

Sofia does not know what to say.

'They won't come after us as far as Ravenna, I'm sure, will they, Gio? We'll be right out of Toscana and I can't begin to imagine them following us that far. Just a few days – that's how long we think it'll take to get there – and then we'll marry. Won't we?'

Her companion makes a noise of assent in his nose.

'What about you, though? What brought you to be out here like this? All on your own. You must be terribly brave ...'

'I'm not,' Sofia says quietly.

'Oh, you must be. I'm sure I should never have been able to walk alone like that in the middle of the night . . .'

'Let the poor girl be, Maria,' the young man says with a trace of affectionate amusement in his voice.

'No, I must ask her all about it. Do tell – why are you out here by yourself?'

Sofia pauses. Trying to explain what has happened in a few words seems impossible, and she has no wish to divulge details. She says, 'I . . . I found out that . . . that I was wrong about how someone felt about . . . Well, I . . .' She cannot finish the sentence. 'I wanted to get away,' she ends in a very small voice, feeling tears thickening in her nose.

'Oh . . .' Maria says. 'I'm sorry. I should not have pried.'

'No, Maria you shouldn't have. I'm sorry, signorina, she's as greedy for other people's gossip as a starving dog for yesterday's soup bones.' The young man's words may be harsh, but the affection still obvious in his tone softens the criticism.

Maria wriggles her fingers up into one sleeve, and pulls from it a small square of lawn, which she hands to Sofia. 'There – dry your tears. I didn't mean to upset you.'

The grey dawn light comes upon them slowly, unnoticed by Sofia who has in fact managed to doze briefly a couple of times over the past hour or so, her head drooping onto Maria's shoulder. Ippo is now sitting at her feet, his head in her lap.

The roads have been steep and winding, though on this more easterly journey Sofia thinks that the various tracks seem to have been less precarious than those taken by the Coraggiosi wagons on the trip down from Bologna.

An image of Beppe's face, smiling its tilted smile, looking back at her from his place at the front of the line of wagons, holding the tetchy mare's bridle, comes into her mind and a pain, sharp as a knife-cut, stabs into her chest. She might never see him again. The thought leaves her almost breathless. A little sound like a sob escapes her.

'Signorina?' Maria turns her head, trying to see Sofia more clearly. Sofia feels her companion's fingers searching for, and holding, her own. 'Is something distressing you? We're nearly at ... what is the name of the place, Giorgio?'

'Lugo.'

'That's it. Nearly there. You'll be able to get a much more comfortable ride – perhaps in a decent-sized wagon – from there.' She shifts position, clearly stiff from sitting still and cramped for so long. 'And Giorgio and I'll be in Ravenna within a couple of days, I should think.'

Sofia cannot help it: at the thought of these two lovers running together to find a future, the tears she has been holding back begin to fall. Silently she weeps and, not wanting to draw attention to it by wiping her face, she tips back her head and lets the tears run. They catch in the corners of her mouth – she opens it to breathe as her nose begins to block – and the salt taste is strong on her tongue. Ippo senses her distress and lifts his head, sniffing the air and scrabbling up trying to reach her.

'Signorina?' Maria's voice is thick with fatigue. 'What is it? What's the matter? Oh *cielo*, you're crying again. Giorgio, she's crying ...'

'I'm sorry,' Sofia says through her tears. 'Perhaps ... perhaps I should walk now. It's nearly morning and it won't take long to reach the town – I can see it from here.'

Maria begins to protest, but Giorgio says, 'No, Ria, let her go. She's said she wants to walk.'

'But—'

'You've been so kind, both of you. I'm very happy to be on foot again. Thank you.'

'But . . .'

Seemingly keen to be rid of her, Giorgio climbs down from the cart, helps Sofia and the dog down; then, retaking his seat, he clicks his tongue once more, slaps the reins on the horses' rumps and begins to trot away from her. Maria, however, stares over her shoulder at Sofia for several minutes as the cart picks up speed along the path towards the tiny smudge of darkness up ahead, which Sofia presumes is the outskirts of Lugo, and only as the distance becomes too great does she turn back and put her head on Giorgio's shoulder.

'Oh God, I can't find her anywhere . . .' Beppe has been back to each of the three wagons; he has searched twice through all three; he has crawled underneath them, climbed into them, pulled open cupboards – even those he knows are clearly far too small to conceal Sofia; he has stripped back blankets and then, leaving the wagons, has battled his way through nearby undergrowth, shouting for her, fearful that she may have wandered and slipped, injured herself, be unable to answer him. Vico, Lidia, Agostino and Federico have searched too and the air has been thick with their calls. Cosima, however, has remained by the brazier with her arm around Giovanni Battista: the old man's distress at the news of Sofia's disappearance has rendered him breathless and light-headed. Other than Angelo (who appears to be drunk and who has flatly refused to join in the search, declaring that if Sofia has taken the wise decision to leave the troupe, that decision should be respected), they have all shouted themselves hoarse and have soaked and muddied their clothes as they have crawled through gaps in hedges, waded along ditches and walked around the perimeters of several fields.

Exhausted and baffled, they sit back down by the now ash-filled brazier. Cosima has taken Giovanni Battista and seen him into the bed in the smallest wagon.

'Where's the dog?' Vico says now as Cosima reappears.

Beppe looks up, realizing that he has not seen Ippo for hours.

'She must have taken him.'

'No,' Beppe says. 'He must have followed her.' The cold and hollow space behind his eyes seems to chill further, to push its way deeper into his skull. Breathing fast through an open mouth, as though fighting physical pain, he winces as unwanted images pour into his mind: of Ippo pawing at Sofia's inert body in a ditch; of the dog barking as Sofia is bundled into a wagon by a faceless stranger; of her face, tear-streaked and frightened – and worse, of her face being flushed with relief at having left.

He is at a loss.

He cannot imagine why she is not here.

'We'll start searching properly at first light.' Agostino puts an arm around Beppe's shoulders and shakes him gently. 'We might be able to see footprints – it's been raining and there should be something.'

'I just don't understand why.'

There is a long pause.

Federico says, 'None of us does, Beppe. None of us does.'

The little town of Lugo is just waking up. Shutters bang open; sleepy-eyed workers stumble out into the early-morning chill, pulling coats and doublets tight about them and running hands through tangled hair. Two little boys scurry out through a cracked wooden door, squealing with laughter; the smaller of the two is carrying a carved wooden pig which he brandishes above his head. Making thick snorting noises through his nose, he runs after his companion, who squeals in mock terror, then laughs aloud.

Sofia stares about her, one hand on Ippo's head, scratching the fur behind one of his ears. She is very hungry. She was too tense and miserable to eat much of the meal last night, and now, after that long night's riding and walking, her belly is griping and uncomfortable and she feels a little light-headed. Reaching for the small bag fastened to her belt, she chinks the coins within through the thin leather. There must be a dozen or so *scudi* in there, perhaps more: money earned over the weeks she has been with the troupe and carefully hoarded. Thanking providence that she at least has the wherewithal to feed herself for a while this time, she wanders along several streets until she sees a row of covered shops.

She buys bread, two slices of sausage and a small bunch of grapes. A corked bottle of ale is the only drink she can find. Sitting down on a bench at the corner of a small piazza, she gives one of the sausage slices to the dog, then wraps a torn piece of bread around the other and eats it. The ale proves to be sweet and nutty and she drinks it gratefully, but then, draining the last mouthful from the bottle, she feels tears prick sharp in her eyes and nose. She is homeless again – and this time it's immeasurably worse. Before, although she was frightened and cold, and had no idea what she was going to do, she had had no real sense of loss. Her rooms at Signora Romano's had been cheerless enough and her friends there had not been close ones. Apart from a few once-treasured possessions, she has never really missed what she left behind.

But now . . .

While searching for food, she has managed to avoid thinking about Beppe, but now, sitting here on the edge of the ever more bustling piazza, try as she might, he elbows his way back into her mind and she sees again his tilted smile; she pictures him with head thrown back, eyes dancing as he looks up at a whirling blur of juggled objects. Beppe on stage: masked, black hat on the back of his head, brandishing his whip-loud *batocchio*, cracking it against a thigh as Arlecchino tumbles across the stage, chattering inanely to Agostino or Vico or Federico. Beppe walking on his hands across the little green clearing where he first began to teach her to act. And then come the images she cannot bear to allow herself to picture, pouring in like swirling water through a breached dam: herself lying in Beppe's arms, warm in the wagon beneath crumpled blankets, happily chilly together in the hay barn in Montalbano; Beppe's hands on her skin, running over her arms, her breasts, her back, her buttocks – oh God, she cannot bear to think of it! She bends forward and puts the heels of her hands over her eyes; pressing hard, bright patterns erupt and swirl.

Something cold and wet touches the back of her hand and she looks up. Ippo is at her feet, nosing her fingers, whining softly. He scrapes at her skirts with one paw. Leaning further forward, her face now glazed with tears, she fondles his ears and pats his side, murmuring unthinking endearments.

Beppe shakes his head. 'No, I'm going after her. I have to.'

His face creasing with concern, Agostino stares at him. 'But . . . but you have no idea where she might have gone, Beppe. North, south, city or village or open land – how on earth will you begin to look?'

'She won't have gone south – I know it. She's never been down on this side of the mountains before . . . I think she'll be heading back to places she knows.'

'But, Beppe,' Lidia breaks in, 'she's been banished. Da Budrio made it quite clear that she won't be tolerated back in Bologna. She knows she can't go back.'

Beppe shrugs. 'There're plenty of places other than Bologna.'

'Exactly! How do you think you're going to manage to search the *whole* of Emilia-Romagna – or further afield? On your own?'

'My dog is with her. He'll find me – or I'll find them both.' Feeling his face stiffening into a scowl, Beppe turns and strides away to the wagons, where, grabbing at a leather sack, he rummages through his belongings, roughly stuffing into the bag a spare pair of breeches, hose and a shirt, the half-dozen leather juggling balls and a purse in which is a chinking handful of coins.

Cosima's face appears at the door. She is holding out a sacking-wrapped parcel. 'Here, my lovely. That should keep you going for a while. Cheese, bread, some slices of that lamb from the other night, and a few plums.' In her other hand is a bottle of ale. 'And this might help, too.'

The concern in her face moves him. Without a word, he takes the food and ale from her and puts it into the bag, then he puts his arms around her and they stand close for a long moment. She says, with her head on his shoulder, 'Find her, Beppe, and bring her back. It doesn't feel right here without her any more.'

'No. It doesn't.' He swallows uncomfortably, then stands back from Cosima. 'I'll find her. I have to.'

A few streets down from the little piazza where Sofia bought her bread and sausage is a long narrow street which leads right down to the edge of the town. It has no opening at the far end: a featureless, windowless, stucco-fronted house blocks right across the thoroughfare, along the length of which runs a trickle of dank water which disappears into a tiny ditch at the far end. Washing is strung on dozens of lines across the street, flapping in the slight breeze like festival flags. Several shops open out onto what is, in fact, little more than a wide alleyway; at one window Sofia sees meat: fresh and smoked. Some half-dozen bloodstained rabbits hang heads down, their ears drooping, their front paws daintily together. A large pig's head on a slate slab glares, mouth agape, a furious grimace still etched across its lardy face as though daring anyone to recoil in disgust, and, Sofia sees now as she peers further in, a cluster of grease-whitened sausages dangles from a row of hooks on the back wall, like a bunch of long-since-severed arms.

Not finding the contents of the shop at all appealing, Sofia wanders on, Ippo at her heels.

A door opens just ahead, and a large woman wrapped in a voluminous white linen apron steps out backwards into the street, leaning away from the weight of several large baskets. Thick white cheese rinds show through the gaps in the weave.

The woman nods cheerily to Sofia as she passes. 'Mind now,' she mutters. 'Shouldn't want to trip over you.'

Smiling, Sofia steps back out of the woman's way.

'I've some lovely sheep's cheese new in this morning, *cara*,' the woman says over her shoulder as she walks on. 'Fresh in from Faenza. Pop in and have a look. Can't do better than a nice piece of cheese, I always say.'

Faenza. Why does that name sound familiar? Sofia knows that she has never been there – why should it chime in her mind so significantly? And then a memory: *A pretty little place called Faenza. It overlooks an ancient landscape, thick with old oaks and sweet chestnuts, with beech trees and conifers.* Niccolò. Niccolò Zanetti. He lives in Faenza. He said he was going back there when he left them a few weeks ago.

She will go to Faenza and try to find Niccolò.

31

Even though it is chilly this morning, the sun is bright on the dew-glittering field in front of him; turning to look back over his shoulder, Niccolò Zanetti puts a hand up to shade his eyes. Far ahead, a long line of now-leafless oak woodland stretches up and over the hills. A scatter of rooks swirls up and around, cawing harshly before they sink back down into the treeline.

A small, dark shape comes out of the trees and moves across the edge of the field.

Niccolò whistles and the shape stops dead for a second, then begins to run. A moment later is it is at his side: a skinny, rough-coated creature with a long thin tail, which, until a month or so ago, was owned by an elderly and increasingly frail old man in the town – an old man who had often had recourse to Niccolò's ministrations over the years.

'Take Bacca when I go, Niccolò, won't you?'
'The dog?'
A nod. 'He likes you. And you'll be good to him, I know that.'

'I'd be honoured, Eduardo, you know that.'

'You'll be able to take him along when you go back out on the road —
he'll enjoy travelling.'

Niccolò reaches out a hand and the dog noses his palm, flecks of
drool spattering out as it pants and shakes its head. Yes, he thinks:
Eduardo was right. Next spring, when he ventures back out, he'll
be pleased to have company. Next year might well be his last on the
road, though; it's a life for a younger man, really. The poor sleep,
the lack of comfort, the heckling crowds and the constant threat of
being run out of town by officious authority figures: Niccolò has
loved it in the past and has relished the fun of the shows he puts on,
but he is not sure he has the heart for it any longer.

'Come on,' he says and Bacca pricks his ears. 'Let's go back.'

Bending and picking up a short length of stick, he throws it
ahead and the dog bounds after it, joyfully splay-legged and
ungainly. It is no more than a short walk back to the little house
where his daughter and her husband have lived for years now —
modest, it is true, but still a warmer and far more welcoming home
than the two-room hut he and Anna rented for so many years until
Anna married at the tender age of sixteen. That, of course, was
when he, Niccolò, took to the road.

He puts a hand to his eyes again, gazing over to where Anna and
Franco's little house stands set into the hillside. Smoke is rising
from the rough chimney stack and a row of freshly washed shifts
and shirts hangs on a long line between one of the outer walls and
a tall pole some thirty yards away.

Niccolò checks.

Beside the pole is a figure he does not immediately recognize.
He frowns, trying to focus in the sharp light. It appears to be a
young woman and a dog — too slight and with too much wild-

looking hair to be Anna. His daughter always keeps her hair neatly tucked away under a linen cap, these days.

Bacca slows and the hair on his neck rises, but, reaching down to the dog, Niccolò scratches between the creature's half-pricked ears. 'Who's that, then?' he says softly, staring across at the motionless figure. 'Who's come to see us up here at this time of year?'

Bacca glances up at him, then returns his gaze to the new-comers.

'Stay close,' Niccolò says and the dog keeps pace as he walks towards the house and the girl.

A resigned shake of the head. 'No, signore, I'm sorry. I've not seen anyone of that description.'

Beppe does not bother even to try to smile now. He just turns away, muttering thanks, puffing a sigh and pushing his hands through his hair. He has asked perhaps a hundred different people, perhaps two hundred – in villages and towns, taverns, farms, along roads and at the doors of outlying houses – and at every place he has stopped he has received a negative answer to his questions. In every face at which he has gazed he has seen only blank ignor-ance – some have been kind, some dismissive, but however sympathetic they feel towards him, every face has been ignorant.

All except one. One person not far from Castel del Rio thinks he might have seen someone of Sofia's description, in a cart in the small hours, a couple of days ago.

Heading north.

The immensity of his task is beginning to weigh upon him, and the certainty he felt on leaving the troupe that it would be only a matter of days before he tracked Sofia down is beginning to seem little more than ridiculous. But, he reasons with himself now, it cannot be impossible – she only had a matter of an hour or so on him. She cannot have been on the road any more than a couple of hours at most before her disappearance was discovered. If she'd been on foot, he would have caught up with her by now, he is sure of that. He ran almost without stopping for the first hour of his journey.

She must somehow have found a lift of some sort.

In a cart, it would seem.

Sitting down on a boulder at the side of the road which leads into the little town of Lugo, Beppe puts his head in his hands and closes his eyes. Where can she have gone? There has to be logic to this. He has only to think with Sofia's mind, to try to work out where she would think to go. It must be possible.

He is missing his dog badly. Normally, Ippo would be here at his feet, aware of his master's distress, pressing up against him and whining softly. Oh God, he hopes that the dog is with Sofia.

Where now? Where on earth should he look now? Italy is beginning to seem like a limitless, featureless desert, and the task ahead of him entirely impossible to achieve – but he cannot conceive of not continuing to search. Even the thought of not finding Sofia makes him feel physically sick. But what if he has missed her, and has left her somewhere behind him – or what if that one witness is wrong? What if she has done what he has been so sure she has not: what if she has gone south? Here he is, sitting outside Lugo, and she might, even as he thinks this, be walking across a piazza in Firenze, or even further south – heading for Roma? Feeling his breathing quickening and his thoughts beginning to fragment, he snatches at his leather bag and pulls it towards him; unfastening the strings, he pushes his hands down inside it. Right at the bottom is the little mesh pouch in which are his five leather juggling balls.

Standing, he begins to juggle.

Beppe has always been calmed by the utter absorption this takes. And, as the balls now start to circle, his breathing does indeed slow and the tight band of tension which has been gripping his head like a garrotte for hours loosens its grip. For some ten minutes he juggles, evenly to begin with, then flipping one ball up higher than the rest each time, then passing another behind his back and into the circle again. For some ten minutes he remains unaware of anything but the rhythmic flipping of the whirling circle between his hands, then, throwing each one high, he catches them all, and sits back down.

To his astonishment, there is a spatter of applause.

'That was clever.' Three small boys are clapping, their eyes wide with admiration.

Beppe nods his thanks.

'Do it again, will you?'

On the point of shaking his head and walking away, he sees the longing in their eyes and, with a resigned grin, obliges, throwing in a couple of extra tricks for good measure. The boys are as delighted with the reprise as with the original performance and their applause is, if anything, even more enthusiastic.

'Could you teach us?'

Beppe shakes his head. 'No, I'm sorry. I don't have the time, I'm afraid. I'm glad you enjoyed it – but it takes a fair bit of time to learn to do this. And I'm . . . I'm very busy. I'm looking for some-one.'

'Who?'

'A girl.'

'A *little* girl? What does she look like?'

A flicker of hope flares again in Beppe's chest. 'Not little – she's a grown-up girl. About that high.' He holds up a hand, palm down, at about the height of his own chin. 'Thin. Dark hair – very curly.'

He holds his hands up a few inches out from either side of his head to indicate the bulk of Sofia's wild hair. 'And she might be with a dog. Scruffy brown and white dog.'

The boys look at each other.

One of them says, 'Does she have a yellow dress?'

Beppe holds his breath as he nods.

The boy shoves his hands deep into the pockets of his breeches. There is a certain swagger to his stance as he scuffs at the dust with one foot and says, 'Mmm. Saw a girl with big curly hair and a dog like that – brown and white – day before yesterday. In a yellow dress.'

'Where?'

'Market.'

'What time? Where is the market? What was she doing?' The breathless questions pour out, tumbling over each other.

'Early. Market's that way.' He points. 'She bought sausage and bread. If it was her, that is.'

Beppe stuffs the juggling balls back into their pouch and pushes the pouch back into the bag, which he swings up onto his shoulder. Reaching out, he clasps a hand on either side of the boy's face and kisses the top of the child's head. Then, grinning at the boys, one of whom is now rubbing his hair with a look of astonished disgust on his face, he pulls a few coins from a pocket and presses them into one grubby and nail-bitten hand. He starts to run in the direction the boy indicated, calling out thanks. Overwhelmed with excitement at the thought that Sofia might even still be there, in the market – that he might see her within minutes, he cartwheels over into a handspring, turning head over heels in mid-air. The leather bag falls to the ground; he scoops it up as he rights himself and runs on.

The three small boys whoop and clap behind him.

*

'But you must be mistaken. I cannot imagine Beppe ever saying such a thing – or even thinking it! I know how he feels about—'

Sofia interrupts. 'I heard him, Niccolò. I heard him as clearly as I'm hearing you now.'

Niccolò frowns and shakes his head, tutting with his tongue as he considers this. 'Tell me again about what happened at . . . where did you say it had happened?'

'The Castello della Franceschina.'

'Yes, yes . . . Franceschina. Oh dear heavens, this is all so terrible. I can't believe all this has been happening whilst I have just been ambling about here picking plants and thinking about nothing.'

Sofia explains it all for the second time. ' . . . and now the troupe has been banished from Emilia-Romagna, and they've lost all their territories and I'm responsible for ruining everything for them. I'm not surprised he wishes he'd never met me.'

Niccolò's daughter Anna is sitting quietly on a chair by the fire, a loose bundle of wool fibres in her lap; she is picking at it, teasing the threads out and straightening them, feeling her way across it, thread by thread. Her gaze is on her father and Sofia. The latter is uncomfortably aware of being watched, and flicks a glance across towards Anna every now and then; Anna has not spoken to her yet, but the watchfulness in her gaze does at least seem, Sofia thinks, to be kind. There is something of Niccolò in her face: a certain gentleness in her eyes.

Niccolò says, 'And you have no idea who actually killed this man?'

'Of course not. I don't think anyone has. He was definitely alive when Beppe and I ran away from him.'

Even the phrase *Beppe and I* hurts to utter.

Anna clears her throat.

Both Niccolò and Sofia turn to look at her.

'I'd want to know.'

'To know what?'

'Who did it, Papa. I'd want to know who did it.'

Sofia stares at her. 'What are you saying?'

Sofia glances across at Niccolò, but he is staring at his daughter.

'Too many people are accused of things they haven't done and nothing is ever done about it. Go and find out who did it. Make somebody do something about it.'

'Perhaps you're right, *cara*,' Niccolo says quietly. 'Sofia, we could go together. To Bologna.' He pauses. 'Anna, what do you think? Will you mind if I leave again so soon?'

There is no sign of her in the market. Beppe's soaring hopes have fast receded, leaving him feeling faintly nauseous. But she was here, he is certain of it. Several marketeers seem to recall serving a girl of her description.

'With a dog, you say? Black curly hair?'

'Yes. Very curly. Wild, really.'

'Brown and white dog 'bout that high?' A palm held out a couple of feet from the ground.

'Yes.'

A nod. 'Saw someone of that description – ooh, perhaps day before yesterday. Sweet girl. Pretty smile.'

'Is she still in the town?'

A sceptical grimace and a shake of the head. 'I wouldn't know, my love, I just wouldn't know. She'll know, though – that woman over there.' The stall-owner points to a bread stall nearby. 'See her? Short woman with a cloth wrapped round her head? She knows everything that happens around here.' A snort. '*Everything*. Interfering old besom. No one in Lugo can so much as fart without *her* passing comment.'

Beppe raises a hand in thanks and makes his way over to the bread stall. He repeats all the now too-familiar questions.

The bread-stall owner confirms a sighting.

'Would you know if she is still in town, signora?'

He watches, his heart racing, as the woman shakes her head slowly.

'No, my lover, I don't think she can be. That was day before yesterday, and I've not seen her since. I particularly noticed her – had a look of my daughter – and I'd have remembered seeing her again. If she needed food, she'd have been here – only place to get decent food around the town, this market. And I sell bread, do I not? So she'd most like have come to me. My guess is she was just passing through. Most strangers do. Not much to keep them here, in Lugo.'

Beppe stifles a frustrated sigh. 'Where might someone go from here, do you think?'

The marketeer puffs her ignorance and shakes her head. 'Oh my word, I can't imagine. Ravenna, perhaps. Ferrara. Or Bologna.'

Trying to force a smile of thanks, Beppe steps back from the bread stall, but the woman purses her lips in concern. Quickly stepping out from behind her heavily laden table, she puts herself in front of him and, somewhat to his surprise, she grips him by both upper arms, her fingers splayed like bunches of fat little sausages around his doublet sleeves. 'Bless you, boy,' she says, looking up into his face. 'I hope to God you find her. Here.' She reaches out, snatches up a small loaf, and presses it into Beppe's hands. 'A little something.'

Touched, Beppe mutters his slightly confused thanks, and moves on, his thoughts in turmoil. Where now? She has been here – that's something. He was right to have been certain she would not have gone south, so perhaps, he reasons, he should trust to his instincts again, and just try once again to think through the possibilities – to think with Sofia's mind and work out where she would choose to go. Sitting himself down on a piece of broken wall near the edge of the market square, he starts to tear small pieces off his loaf, pushing them into his mouth and chewing with no real awareness of taste or texture.

She might want to go home, he says to himself. To Modena. Whoever it was who accused her of theft that time will no doubt have forgotten about it by now. She might well be thinking it's safe to go back. He tries to order his thoughts, laying them out in front of him on the dusty ground as though they were a pack of *tarocchini* cards. He stares down at his boots. 'She ran away for a reason. What was it?' Thinking through everything that happened that evening, the argument with Angelo comes back into his mind. A drench of cold sweeps down through him as he remembers his own words, almost shouted at Angelo in his anger – *I made a mistake. I hate to admit it but she's trouble. I should never have got close to her.* What if she had heard that? What if she believed it? He says aloud, 'Oh dear God, what if she thinks I've stopped loving her?' Swallowing uncomfortably, he closes his eyes for a second. Thinking through the things he had said and done over the day or so before Sofia's departure, and imagining her perception of his manner, Beppe squeezes what remains of the little loaf tightly in his fist; a flurry of flakes of the crust break away and fall over his knees and around his feet. Leaving aside this all-but-unbearable thought, he tries a more practical slant. 'She knows that the authorities in Bologna still probably believe she killed that man. So why would she go there, when they put her in prison and then told her she'd been banished? No. She'll not go there. She'll go to Modena. I think she'll go to Modena.'

Beppe pulls his purse from his breeches pocket. Tipping the contents into one palm, he counts his coins. Fifteen *scudi* and a handful of *baiocchi*: enough to get him to Modena. He could hire a horse. Perhaps even buy one.

The mare is stolid and stout, but her eyes are gentle and the long forelock which hangs from between her ears gives her a pleasing air of calm femininity; Beppe takes to her instantly. Scratching her between the eyes, he watches as she puckers her muzzle and half closes her eyes, showing her teeth.

'Aye, she likes that. She likes you.' The old man pats the mare's neck, his gaze on Beppe's face. 'She'll do well for you – but don't take her more than thirty miles in a day. Her legs won't stand for it.'

'I won't. I'll take good care of her. Thank you.' Beppe hands over the coins, and the old man nods without comment as he pushes them about on one palm with the forefinger of the other hand, counting them. He looks up. 'I'm sorry I have no saddle for her, but—'

'It's no trouble. I'm just as happy without,' Beppe says. Checking the straps and buckles of the mare's bridle, he winds the straps of his leather bag around his shoulders so that it hangs on his back, then turns and vaults nimbly onto her back. With the reins gathered and tautened, he turns her and, hand raised in farewell to the old man, he kicks the mare on. She begins to walk away, head nodding back and forth in rhythm with her steps.

32

Outside the walls of Bologna

A young woman is standing near the back of a large and beautifully painted wagon, on the steps of which is seated a man of some thirty years. He is in shirtsleeves and breeches, with a flute held loosely in one hand; she is in shift and skirt. She is holding a bunch of paper flowers clasped close to her heart, and her eyes are shut, her face tilted up towards the sky.

'Once more, Isabella, if you will,' the young man says, pointing at the woman with the flute. 'I need to hear that edge of *desperation*. This is *eating* at you from the inside out and you're in *agony*.' He makes an impassioned gesture with both arms, fingers splayed on one hand, the flute clutched tight in the other. 'Let us feel it with you.'

Opening her eyes, Isabella smiles at him and nods. 'From the beginning?'

'From the beginning.'

Sucking in a long breath, she says, '*And the more deeply I am in love, the more fiercely am I jealous.*' She stares for a moment at the flowers. Then, throwing them from her and clenching a fist, she says, '*My jealousy burns inside me every moment, like the very embers of hell – those fires of love which have blazed so brightly for so long have been entirely consumed by the ravaging flames of distrust and suspicion. Like a furious fever, it rages hot within, whilst I am frozen without.*' She looks over to the young man and smiles sweetly. 'Better?'

'Perfect.'

'And then Francesco will come in, unsuspecting, and I shrink back into the shadows and watch as he crosses the stage. Yes?'

'Exactly. I want them to fear for what you might be tempted to do. They'll know, won't they, that you still have the little knife?'

Isabella smiles and nods. 'They'll just have seen me tuck it up my sleeve, Flaminio, as we arranged.'

'Good girl. We'll work on the next scene – the mad one – this afternoon.'

'Food now, though, I think, don't you?'

'And an ale or two, I'd say.' Flaminio puts the flute to his lips. As he and Isabella walk over towards where a dozen or so others are clustered around a brazier, on which a large iron pot is steaming, he starts to play a merry dance tune, and Isabella's steps fall quickly into a three-beat rhythm to match it. Arms in the air, she twirls on her toes and her skirts bell out around her.

'Come here! Sit down and eat, *cara*,' calls a man in a brightly embroidered doublet, raising a hand to beckon Isabella over to where he is seated near the brazier. 'Prudenza has made a stew worthy, I would hazard the opinion, of public acclaim.'

A plump girl of about twenty, noticeably pregnant, smiles and shoves the brightly embroidered man in the shoulder. 'It's a pot full of mutton and turnips, as well you know, Francesco.'

'Aaah! But what kingly turnips, Prudenza, what kingly turnips.'

Isabella kisses Francesco as she sits down next to him, accepting a bowl of stew and a large hunk of bread. 'Thank you, Prudenza, you're a wonder. I'm *so* hungry, I shall probably end up eating the bowl as well.'

Prudenza pulls a face. 'Might be tastier than the stew.'

'Mmm – it's lovely. Thank you,' Isabella says thickly, wiping a stray drop of gravy from the corner of her mouth with the tip of her ring finger.

Putting his flute down carefully on an upturned barrel, Flaminio Scala helps himself to a bowlful and, standing facing the rest of the assembled people – seven men, three women and two small boys – and pointing at them with his spoon, he says, 'Well, Gelosi, we perform in two days' time. I'm delighted with you all. Since our sojourn in France, we have improved beyond all expectations, and I confidently expect *Arlecchino Goes to the Moon* to be the raging success it deserves to be.'

Someone starts picking at the strings of a guitar. The tune he plays is haunting and sweet and, before more than a few notes have rung out, a girl begins to sing along with him. Two others join in, and the tightly harmonized song spirals up into the crispness of the October air like tendrils of smoke. A dog begins to bark, as though in competition with the song, and one of the assembled men pushes it with the toe of his boot to quieten it.

33

'Do you think Anna is upset not to have been able to come with us?' Sofia asks.

Niccolò shakes his head. 'No, no, no, no. Franco needs her, and she wouldn't want to leave him on his own, anyway. They've divided up their working tasks between them so well now, it would be hard for one or the other to take over the whole, I think. And I've left Bacca with them, too, haven't I? They were pleased to have him. He's a good little dog, and I think he'll like the life there better than whatever cramped old journey we're about to have in the cart. I'd planned to take him with me next time I went on the road, but two dogs might have been difficult to handle in such a small space, don't you think?'

Scratching Ippo's ears, Sofia nods. 'I liked Anna very much.'

'And she you.'

'Oh, Niccolò, do you think so? I couldn't help thinking that she resented my being there and then taking you away.'

'You didn't take me away, child. I chose to come with you.'

Niccolò smiles and pats Sofia's hand. 'There is not a chance I could possibly have let you set off on your own.'

The donkey's long ears are pinned back, and her steps are staccato and prim, ringing out against the hard road. The little cart jolts and squeaks.

'You remind me of Anna,' Niccolò says now. 'You reminded me of her that first day I met you in Modena. Strong and independent and determined.'

Feeling at that moment frightened and tired and tremblingly unsure of herself, Sofia does not know what to say to this.

'That's why I wanted to help you so much, I suppose,' Niccolò says, smiling. 'I imagined how I would feel if it was Anna – how much I'd hope that someone would do for her what I was able to do for you. She's a good girl. I brought her up alone, and she's made me very proud.'

Touched, Sofia nods. 'I liked her very much.'

Niccolò pats her hand again and they travel on for several minutes without speaking. Violetta has put her ears forward now and picked up speed; she is trotting with purpose, it seems, and they cover the ground quickly. They stop for an hour or two in a little town, but Niccolò is determined to make as much progress as Violetta will allow.

'I'd like us to get to Castel San Pietro by nightfall.'

'Castel San Pietro?'

'The tavern-owner there is a good friend of mine. After a night's sleep, with luck we should make Bologna by tomorrow evening.'

Sofia glances across at him. 'If the authorities find out I'm there . . .'

'Why should they? You won't be with the Coraggiosi . . .'

Sofia bites her lip.

'. . . and it's the troupe they'll be watching out for, isn't it?'

'I suppose so. What are we going to do when we get there?'

Niccolò frowns. 'Do you know, I'm not sure. But I know how these things work. If you trust to the good Lord – or to fate, or to whatever you believe to be most trustworthy – something usually turns up. We need to ask around, find out what people are saying about what happened at Franceschina – delicately, of course. We don't want to draw attention to ourselves.'

It is Sofia's turn to frown. 'But what if we do this – ask around – and we find out that no one knows anything? Then we will be none the wiser, and I shall be . . . ' Tailing off, thoughts of Beppe flood into her mind again. She pictures him first in shirtsleeves and grubby breeches, barefoot, practising his tumbling, over and over until the move is perfected. Then she sees him on stage, masked and wearing his wild, diamond-patterned jacket and trousers, declaiming some spouted piece of nonsense, flipping head over heels in frustration when whichever character he is haranguing fails to understand him. And then, as this second image of Beppe plays itself out in her head, an idea occurs to her – a startling idea which makes her draw in her breath. Though how she will accomplish it alone, she cannot begin to imagine.

'Is something troubling you, child?' Niccolò asks.

Sofia shakes her head. 'No. But I've just thought . . . Listen, tell me what you think?' And she explains the idea. By the time she has finished, Niccolò is smiling – the widest and happiest smile she has seen on his face since the day he introduced her to the Coraggiosi.

'That is a brilliant idea. We'll have to find a way, child,' he says. 'A way will most definitely have to be found.'

*

There is a small piazza in the centre of the little town of Pianoro; it is cramped and overlooked on all sides by buildings in varying stages of dilapidation, but on the east side is a well. Fed by a spring, the sweet water bubbles up into a squat, square stone basin and trickles out again through a hole in one corner. Squatting in front of it, Beppe cups his hands and scoops up palmfuls, over and over, till he has quenched his thirst. Giglio, the mare, dips her muzzle into the water too, and sucks noisily, splashing a great deal of water over the sides of the basin and onto the cobbles.

Beppe waits for her to finish; then, patting her neck, he walks her around the edge of the piazza towards where an archway leads off towards the north.

'Only about ten miles to Bologna. We'll stay there a day or so, give you a bit of a rest, then move on to Modena. Are you up to that, chick?'

Giglio tosses her head and snorts.

Gathering up the reins, Beppe pulls the mare in close to a low wall. Scrambling up onto the wall, he vaults onto her back again and, clicking his tongue, gives her a soft kick. She breaks easily into a shambling trot.

As they make their way northwards out of the town and turn onto the long road which leads directly up to Bologna, Beppe is thinking of Sofia. The thought that he might not be able to find her flaps about him like a lime-trapped bird. Modena is where he thinks she will be; he begins to plan the quickest route there. A thought strikes him. 'Now I have you,' he says to the mare, 'it'd be possible to cut across country to Vignola and go directly up to Modena from there – it'd certainly be quicker than heading north now, going through Bologna and then going off west past Castelfranco.' He pats the mare's neck. 'What do you think, chick? Would you be happy to go over the hills? Get off the roads?'

But, as though in answer, even as he speaks, the mare stumbles over a loose stone and pecks forward. Without a saddle, Beppe lurches up onto her neck, and it is only with luck and by clutching inelegantly at a fistful of mane that he manages to remain seated. 'Or maybe not,' he says, patting the mare's neck again. 'Perhaps it would be foolish to move away from the roads. I need to be where Sofia is most like to be. I can't imagine her setting off across the hills on her own. I hope to God she'd not think of doing it, anyway.'

They trot on for several miles, largely in thought-filled silence, broken only spasmodically by brief conversations with fellow travellers, until the road splits into two. One branch – the wider, better-maintained of the tracks – wends slightly northwards, heading towards Bologna, while the other – in fact little more than an untended path – heads more directly west.

'Modena?' a young traveller told him just now. 'Oh yes ... I doubt it's much more than a day's ride. If you go down to – look, can you see, *amico*?' He points. 'That stunted-looking tree down there? Go left there, that'll set you on the right path for Modena.'

Beppe and the mare stand where the road divides.

It takes a moment to make up his mind which one of the two paths he will take.

34

Bologna

Sofia sat on this very bench with Beppe, less than a fortnight ago, she realizes as she looks about her. She can almost feel him there still, almost sense the weight of his arm around her shoulders. She runs her fingers over the wood, and a great sigh shudders in her chest as she breathes it out. Ippo lays his muzzle on her lap and his tail thuds softly on the stone floor. Sofia strokes his head.

The tavern is almost empty. A small group of clearly inebriated but cheerful men has clustered by the fire – they are laughing together at something Sofia cannot hear – but apart from them, the place is deserted, and the under-worked ale-man has a distinct air of irritation about him as he busies himself ordering his barrels and bottles, and rinses glasses in a large wooden bucket. Lit by a couple of dozen stumpy candles, the room flickers and bobs in the shifting light, seeming almost to breathe as the flames move in the many draughts.

'So where do we go now?' Sofia says. 'What do we do?'

'We rest for tonight,' Niccolò says. 'That's for certain. Then we can start wandering in the morning, and talking to people. We'll start in the Piazza di Porta Ravegnana – there's always a crowd there. Leave it to me to start with.'

'Ravegnana? But – that's where I first met . . . '

Niccolò nods.

Swallowing uncomfortably, Sofia says, 'And what about . . . '

'What – your splendid idea?'

'Yes.'

'Ah, well. That will all depend on who we meet, will it not? On who happens to be in town at the moment? We might be lucky – I hope to God that we are. In fact,' Niccolò says, patting the back of Sofia's hand, 'I feel the Almighty *owes* us a crumb of good fortune. We have both had a surfeit of the opposite up until now, I feel.'

The following morning dawns crisp and clear; the sun has a clean white brightness about it, and the sky is the colour of damascened steel. Seeing that Niccolò has already left the upstairs room, Sofia dresses quickly. She has only the yellow skirt and bodice in which she left Castel del Rio so hurriedly; it was pretty once, but now, after so many days on the road, it is starting to look distinctly worn; the hem, she sees now, is filthy and stiff with spattered mud and dust. Picking up a double-handful of the skirt, she holds it to her nose, and grimaces at the sharp, unwashed smell. She is quite as dirty as the day she met the Coraggiosi.

Running her fingers up into her hair, she starts to pick at the tangles in her curls, teasing them out wisp by wisp, wishing she had thought to put a comb into the bag of belongings she snatched from the box beneath the truckle bed in the smallest wagon, for her hair is badly knotted in several places now. She eases the bag open, and tips the contents out into her lap: a spare shift; the two long crimson ribbons, tied together in a now-crumpled bow . . . and

Beppe's old black woollen hat – the spare, the one he no longer uses. She holds this to her nose too, and tears spike sharp in the corners of her eyes; it still smells of him and, as she closes her eyes, it is as though he is there in front of her.

'But he wishes he'd never met me, doesn't he?' she mutters. 'He says I'm trouble.' Clutching the hat in both hands, she holds it against her mouth for a moment, then stuffs hat, shift and ribbons back into the bag. Adjusting her bodice so that it sits more comfortably, she leaves the upstairs room. Her soft footsteps are accompanied by the click-claw scrabbling of Ippo's paws as she hurries downstairs to where Niccolò is sitting by the now extinct fire. Only ash and a strong smell of woodsmoke remains.

He pushes a basket of bread and a bowl of apricots across the table towards her. 'Eat, child. We might be a long time on our feet today. I have bought milk too. Here, look.' He slides a tin mug of milk towards her.

Sofia tears off a piece of bread and dips it into the milk. 'Do you think there might be some scraps for Ippo?' she says as the dog noses against her knee.

'Let's see, shall we?'

Niccolò raises a hand, and the ale-man stumps over. He does not answer Niccolò's request – he merely shrugs and walks away – but within seconds, he has returned with a pewter bowl half filled with torn scraps of meat, bread, cheese rinds and a marrow-bone, shiny with glistening red shreds, which he places on the floor near Sofia's chair. Ippo, tail wagging furiously, drops his head and begins to eat.

'Violetta had oats last night,' Niccolò says now. 'The ale-man says she may stay here at the tavern until tomorrow. She will be glad of the rest. Ippo can stay in the stable with her.'

Sofia nods, her mouth now too full of bread to answer.

*

The Piazza di Porta Ravegnana is indeed crowded, even at the early hour at which Niccolò and Sofia arrive there. Market stalls have been crammed into every available space and the crowd is busily pushing its way from place to place, haggling, laughing, arguing, shouting; spending money and making it in equal measures.

Sofia watches as Niccolò begins to search for information. Staying close, she says nothing as he charms his chosen targets as effortlessly as she remembers him doing back in Modena the day she first met him.

'Busy here today, is it not, signora?' he is saying now to a large lady in a richly embroidered blue dress.

'Oh, indeed it is, signore. I have to say I cannot be doing with it for much longer.'

'I heard that there was something of a riot here in the city not long ago.'

'A riot, signore?' The woman sounds shocked.

'So I was told – perhaps you know more than I do. Over in the Piazza Maggiore.' Niccolò jerks his head in the direction of the piazza, lowering his voice to something of a thrilling whisper. 'An accusation of ... murder, someone told me.'

'Murder? A riot? Oh *cielo*!'

Sofia sees Niccolò smile sweetly at his companion's ignorance. 'My dear signora, please do not trouble yourself! I have clearly been misinformed.' He bows neatly and turns away, leaving the large lady staring after him.

A few seconds later he tries again – with no success.

And again.

And again.

And then ... 'Yes,' he says, 'so I heard. In the Piazza Maggiore.'

His new friend – a young man in a leather jerkin and dirty

canvas breeches – is nodding vigorously. 'You heard right. I was there. At the back of the crowd.'

At this, Sofia's eyes widen and she takes a step back. What if she is recognized? But the young man seems not to notice her; his attention is firmly on Niccolò.

'Do tell me about it, signore.'

The young man grins and begins to expound upon the events of that day, gesticulating wildly, enjoying the effect that his narrative is having upon his listener – for Niccolò is making sure to encourage him, with nods and smiles and sucked-in shocked breaths. 'And then . . . then that fat old pile of offal, da Budrio, God rot him, as good as *admits* that he'd got it wrong and that the little bitch is innocent, and he tells the lot of us to bugger off.'

'And did you all do as you were told? Did you – bugger off?'

'You're damned right we did. After some poor sod spoke out and got himself roundly thumped and dragged off by the bloody *sbirri*. I wasn't hanging about there to get picked up and thrown into the cell they'd just booted the girl out of, was I?'

Niccolò again lowers his voice to the thrill-soaked stage whisper. 'And did you . . . did you ever find out . . . who did the deed? If the girl didn't?'

Sofia holds her breath.

The young man leans in towards Niccolò. 'I heard tell', he says in a sibilant hiss, 'that they've searched the castle where it happened – from top to bottom – and have found nothing. Nothing at all.'

Disappointment floods down into Sofia's belly.

'Never mind, *cara*,' Niccolò says, his arm now around Sofia's shoulders. 'Never mind. You didn't think we would discover what we came searching for on the first morning, did you?'

'No, of course not.' Colour floods into her face at the lie.

'We'll just keep trying.'

A sudden flurry of movement shifts the crowd around them, and a blare of loud and joyous music pushes its way into the piazza. Thinking of the Coraggiosi, Sofia is suddenly awash with confusion, as a desire to see Beppe – so strong it all but knocks her over – fights with a dread of meeting him and seeing the rejection she knows will be clearly visible on his face. She stares about her, searching for the origin of the sound.

A pair of pretty white ponies with bright ribbons fluttering in their manes and tails, ridden by two young boys, struts ahead of a procession – a procession of characters so familiar to Sofia that seeing them here, she holds her breath. Two masked men – the phallic-nosed and ridiculous Il Capitano and the white-eyebrowed, huge-bellied Dottore – stride along in front, arguing vehemently, and deliberately ignoring the clapping of the fast-gathering crowd. Behind them, their steps so light and delicate they might almost be dancing, come the Lovers. The woman is younger than Cosima: fair-haired and sweet-faced, with tiny hands and feet, while her companion is older, taller, broader-shouldered than Angelo; he is good-looking, though not, Sofia thinks, as startlingly handsome as Angelo. As Cosima and Angelo have done so often, though, these two are smiling out at the crowd, throwing flowers and sweetmeats towards reaching hands, acknowledging the many cheers and whistles with flourishes of their elegant hands. Several other *zanni*-masked figures stumble along behind them, and then there he is: Arlecchino.

Sofia's heart turns over.

But of course it is not Beppe. This man is shorter, stockier than Beppe. He wears his hat further forward, pushed over to one side. Despite the instantly recognizable diamond-patterned leggings and jacket, despite the familiar crack of the wooden bat, there can be no confusion: this man's movements, though agile and funny, are nothing like Beppe's wild, fluid, weightless tumblings.

Beppe or not, Sofia cannot take her eyes from him.

'Oh my good Lord . . . this is the Gelosi,' Niccolò whispers in her ear, his eyes shining. 'We've spoken about them often, have we not, the Gelosi? Probably the most successful troupe in Italy at the moment. That's Isabella Andreini, and that' – he points to the broad-shouldered Lover – 'that's her husband, Francesco. The one at the front – Il Capitano – I think that must be Flaminio Scala. He writes all their material. My word, we're lucky to see them.'

'Do you know them, then?' Sofia says, tearing her gaze from where Arlecchino is now hopping along on one foot, clutching the other, with his mouth wide open as though in agony.

Niccolò shakes his head. 'Not in the way I know the Coraggiosi,' he says. 'Not as friends. I met Francesco Andreini once, a couple of years ago, that's all. A good man, I thought.'

'Oh, Niccolò, do you think they might . . . ?'

'What? Your idea?'

Sofia nods.

'You'll have to ask them, child. I simply couldn't say. This is the Gelosi, not just any troupe. But if they agree, then you could have no one better to help you accomplish what you want to do.'

'Will you come with me?'

'Of course, though I'm going to leave everything to you – it will come better from you. We can follow them now – it looks as though they are intending to perform here in the Porta Ravegnana, doesn't it? Best venue in the city – as we know.'

'Come on then, we'll need to talk to them before they start to prepare for their performance.' With her hand tightly grasping Niccolò's, Sofia begins to push her way through the crowd, pulling him along behind her, towards where the last of the troupe's four big bright wagons is now entering the piazza.

'Yes, this afternoon. We will start as the clock in the piazza chimes three, signore. Not a moment before and not a moment later! But if you will excuse me, we have a stage to set up, and preparations to make. I'll look forward to seeing you at three!' And Signora Isabella Andreini kisses the tips of her fingers and blows the kiss neatly towards an eager-faced man, who pretends to catch it; he holds it in a fist against his lips, grinning broadly.

Her wide smile fading to a practical determination as she turns away, Isabella Andreini pushes her fingers up into her hair. 'Francesco, where exactly do you want to set the stage?' she says.

'Over there.' Francesco Andreini points to a spot almost exactly where the Coraggiosi pitched their stage a few weeks before. 'Just in front of the taller of the towers. Where we set last time – I think it worked well, don't you?'

Signora Andreini nods.

Sofia watches as she walks back to the wagons.

Niccolò nudges her. 'Go on, ask!' he says, almost under his breath.

Sofia glances at him. 'Are you sure I should . . . ?'

'Yes – go on!'

Sucking in a breath, Sofia follows the woman and stops near her as they reach the wagon. The woman turns, inclining her head curiously as she sees Sofia.

'Signorina? Are you hoping to come and see the show?'

'No – oh, I'm sorry, I mean yes, of course . . . but that's not why . . . ' Sofia finds herself stuttering, and stumbling over her words, but the sweet-faced woman smiles.

'What is it, signorina? Can I help you with something?'

'Oh dear God, I hope so.' Sofia holds Isabella Andreini's gaze steadily.

Signora Andreini frowns briefly, then reaches out a hand. 'Come with me,' she says, stepping up onto the first step of the wagon. 'Come in and tell me whatever it is that you very clearly need to say. I'll need to be quick – we have a stage to set – but I can see that whatever it is, is important.'

Inside the wagon, another young woman, visibly with child, is seated on an untidy pile of blankets on one of three narrow truckle beds. She too frowns curiously at the sight of the stranger.

'Prudenza, do you mind if we talk in here?'

'No, of course not. Do you want me to leave?'

Signora Andreini shakes her head. 'No, no, stay.' She points to a painted stool, inviting Sofia to sit. 'Now, signorina, tell me what you want.'

Drawing in a long breath, Sofia says, 'Until a few days ago, I was playing Colombina with the Coraggiosi.'

She sees Signora Andreini flick a glance over to where the girl called Prudenza is now intently staring at the two of them.

'Until a few days ago?' Signora Andreini says. 'Are you . . . what was the name?' She clicks her fingers, trying to summon the information. 'Genotti? That's it. Are you Sofia Genotti?'

Startled, Sofia nods.

'I've heard of you.' As Sofia frowns in incomprehension, Signora Andreini adds, 'Word travels fast in our profession. News of a new talent in particular spreads quickly.'

'Oh.' Sofia stares at her, not knowing what to say.

'So, what was it you wanted to say, signorina?'

'Oh. Oh, yes. Er – I don't know if you heard about what happened at the Castello della Franceschina a few days ago . . . ?'

'Yes, I had heard – as I say, news spreads quickly. Though of course I don't know if I have been told an accurate version of events. The Coraggiosi have been . . . sent away from Bologna, is that right?'

Sofia nods, her cheeks flaming. Hesitating, she says, 'Because of me. I was accused of . . . of murder, signora. God, that sounds so terrible – I didn't do it.' She looks up at the roof of the wagon for a second. 'Of course I didn't do it. They accused me, but they had to let me go, because there was no evidence. Agostino and the troupe had collected an enormous crowd, back in the Piazza Maggiore, to demand my release – really enormous, hundreds of people – and I think it frightened the authorities into letting me go. But I know that they still think I did it, and that's why they sent the troupe away.'

Signora Andreini and the girl called Prudenza are both staring at Sofia now. 'We had heard something of this – battered over the head, wasn't he, the man?' Isabella says.

Sofia nods. 'With an iron candlestick, they told me.'

'How dreadful.'

'Yes. He was not a good man – but yes, it's terrible. Oh, signora, I want to know who really did do it!' She pauses. 'Because if they find out the truth, they might lift the banishment order and allow us back into Emilia-Romagna.' She hears in her head what she has just uttered, and amends her sentence. 'Allow *them* back.'

'What do you want from me? Why are you telling me this? Why do you say "them" like that? Have they thrown you out – the Coraggiosi?'

'No!' Sofia hesitates. 'It's not as simple as that, but—'

A voice shouts outside the wagon, interrupting her. 'Isabella! Prudenza! We need you! Are you coming?'

A look of frustration flickers across Signora Andreini's face. 'Come back here after the show, signorina. We will talk then.'

*

Beppe stares up at the city walls, glad now that he made the decision to travel this way. The mare is tired – she is beginning to drag her feet – and, sliding off her back, he gathers the reins up in one hand. Putting the other up under her muzzle, he fiddles the soft skin of the horse's whiskery lower lip with the tips of his fingers and, pulling her head in against his shoulder, he stands with her for a moment. The mare's hot breath clouds up in front of him. 'Good girl,' he says quietly. 'You've done well, really well – we'll rest now.' He pauses, staring up at the sky. 'I hope to God I chose the right route.'

'They're good, aren't they?' Niccolò says, turning to Sofia as the players take their bows, to cheers and whoops and a storm of wild applause from the enormous crowd. 'You can understand how they've earned their reputation.'

Sofia nods. She is still riveted by the Gelosi's Arlecchino. She knows, of course, that it is not Beppe, but how can she look at that costume, see someone in that mask, playing that role, and not think of him? To her, this man is nowhere near as accomplished a tumbler as Beppe, but his timing is perfect, she thinks now; he is clever, and funny, and his performance was wonderful. She wipes her eyes with her sleeve. 'Niccolò, I need to get back to Signora Andreini's wagon, now the show is over. She seemed willing to listen to me, at least. It's a start, isn't it?'

Niccolò hugs her. 'It is indeed, child, it is indeed. Get along with you. I'll go back to the tavern and wait there with Violetta and Ippo.'

Sofia nods and, without another word, turns from him.

She eases through the crowd of people now leaving the piazza; the place is loud and joyous with that unmistakable buzz that comes only from a satisfied audience.

As she approaches the wagons, Signora Andreini beckons her over, and Sofia quickly finds herself once more up inside the largest of them, seated on the painted stool again. Signora Andreini is now accompanied not by the pregnant Prudenza, but by a man Sofia does not fully recognize, though she knows who he is by what he is wearing. Dressed still in the richly embroidered doublet and breeches he was wearing just now on the stage, he is perched on the end of one of the truckle beds, his shoulders slightly hunched in the cramped space.

'Signorina,' he says. 'I am Francesco Andreini. My wife tells me you wish to talk to us. About something . . . of import.' He inclines his head, and gestures around the wagon with a flourish. 'Well. Our show is at an end. The floor is now yours – tell all!'

Sofia swallows uncomfortably. She clears her throat. Looking from Francesco Andreini to his wife and back, she again begins to explain.

Both Francesco and Isabella Andreini listen intently; Isabella's mouth opens as Sofia describes Signor da Correggio's assault upon her in the study, and Francesco shakes his head, frowning and tutting his tongue against his teeth.

'We all ran from the place,' Sofia says, 'and travelled back here to Bologna, fearing that Beppe would be arrested. Da Correggio was alive when we left. Quite definitely alive. He was groaning and swearing, and struggling to get up.'

Both the Andreinis are gazing fixedly at her.

Sofia tells them of being arrested, of Beppe's being so brutally knocked down by the black-jacketed thugs who had dragged her away from the troupe; she describes the filthy cell and her sickening fear, then her relief at being released – a relief quickly drowned by a smothering guilt as the troupe is banished from their beloved Emilia-Romagna, and left to face an uncertain, unfamiliar future elsewhere in Italy. 'Everything seemed to change when we left the territories,' she said. 'All the life went out of the troupe – all the sparkle. But if,' she says, 'if I could discover who really did it, perhaps they might be persuaded to lift the banishment order, and . . . '

'How do you propose to do that?' Francesco does not sound incredulous – he wants to know. 'Do you know?'

Sofia pulls in a breath. 'I had an idea. I wanted to find a troupe – I wasn't expecting for a moment that it would be you, the Gelosi, but I hoped a troupe might be here in the city.' She hesitates. 'Might it be possible, do you think, to put what happened into a performance – to act it out – and then for one of the characters to complain about the injustice of it all? Directly to the audience? Might an audience somehow be . . . oh, I don't know . . . *nudged* into remembering . . . or *admitting* what they know but perhaps don't want to accept?'

Isabella looks at Francesco and mutters something Sofia cannot hear. He nods and answers in an equally inaudible undertone. They converse quietly for several seconds. Then Isabella turns back to Sofia. 'You played Colombina?'

'Yes.'

'We'll have to ask Flaminio,' Isabella says to Francesco, 'but I'm sure Prudenza wouldn't mind. In the state she's in at the moment, she'll be grateful.'

Sofia does not understand.

Seeing her confusion, Isabella says, 'Look, I don't know whether or not your idea has any chance of success, but I'm happy to try for you. We're all road-dwellers, aren't we? All of us. Like a massive, disparate family. I think you've been shabbily treated and, well, perhaps . . . perhaps Genesius and Vitus have had a hand in bringing you to us, and I'm sure they would be . . . *displeased* if we didn't act upon their introduction.' She takes Sofia's hands in hers.

Feeling the prickling threat of tears, Sofia says, 'You're very kind.'

Isabella Andreini squeezes her fingers. 'No, not kind at all, just angry on your behalf.' She glances over at Francesco, who nods. 'Here's how we'll do it. We'll put you in as Colombina for a day. Prudenza is beginning to get too heavy to perform now – she'll be glad of the rest, to be honest. We can work together to write it into tomorrow's show, and after your Colombina has poured it all out to Arlecchino, I'll make him address the audience. Simone – he plays Arlecchino – is so good at that, it'll probably be best coming from him.'

'Tomorrow's show? But that's so soon.' Sofia shakes her head in consternation. 'How can you—? Will you be able to—?'

Francesco Andreini throws back his head and laughs. 'So soon? Ha! We have about twenty-two hours. This is luxury, child – *hours* more than we often allow ourselves for the preparation of new material.'

'But—'

Isabella Andreini raises a hand. 'I think you – and the rest of the troupe – have been treated shabbily by the authorities – and by the aristocracy. We want to help.' She stands and begins to gesticulate theatrically as she adds in a suddenly more carrying voice, 'Because, after all, what does our profession stand for, if not to demand a voice for the little man, if not to puncture the tough and ugly bubble of self-regard so often presented so unthinkingly by the wealthy and the powerful?'

Sofia stares at her.

'We'll do it. Why not? We'll try to find your murderer for you.' She stops and stares at her husband for a few seconds. Then, her eyes glittering, she turns back to Sofia. 'And then, here's a thought: stay with us for a while. After we move on from Bologna, come too. It'll be an adventure – we'll be going to France in the New Year. We've been asked to visit the French court. If what they are saying about you is true, you might be able to help us out. Prudenza won't be able to work much longer – it will be weeks and weeks before she is fit to be back on stage. Come and play Colombina with us – at least while Prudenza approaches her confinement. If you don't feel you can return to the Coraggiosi, then you are going to need work – and right now, we need a Colombina. Such a coincidence shouldn't be ignored, should it?'

Sofia stares, unable to think of an answer, but Isabella Andreini smiles. 'Francesco,' she says, 'go and find Simone, will you? We'll need to work together.'

Arriving some moments after the show had begun, Beppe found the Piazza di Porta Ravegnana so tightly packed with eager and enthusiastic Bolognese, all struggling to see what was transpiring on the stage, that he quickly realized any hope of getting any nearer the front was out of the question. Scrambling up onto the pediment of a large and crumbling pillar, he watched – amused, despite his grinding anxiety – as the Gelosi's Arlecchino flipped and tumbled as he had so often done himself. But Arlecchino then took his Colombina in his arms, and, Beppe, his smile vanishing, turned away and stared up at the roofscape of the piazza, swallowing down a drench of longing so fierce it made him feel physically sick.

The show is over now though, and the crowd is dispersing. Beppe cannot help himself: as the piazza empties, he wanders up to the edge of the staging and stares critically at the intricately painted hangings draped across the back of the trestles. They're good, he admits now, running his fingers along the edge of the trestle boards and examining the street scenes. The perspective works perfectly – they're lovely.

Two young boys appear – each about eleven or twelve years old – looking self-consciously important. Standing back a pace or two, Beppe watches as they begin to collect props and carry them off the stage, away to where four large and beautifully painted wagons stand side by side a little way to the left.

'Yep, Simone's in with them now,' one of them says. 'So Francesco said. And *God* knows what changes they're planning. It'll be *us* that'll have to remember a thousand new things by tomorrow, of course. Same as usual.'

'But who *is* she?' The other boy is frowning. 'This girl. Why are they making changes? When did all this happen?'

'*When?*' The first boy puffs a laugh. 'Not "when *did* it happen?" It's happening *now*, Bernardo, it's happening *now*. I don't know – some girl turns up, spouts some story or other, and all hell breaks loose.'

'Who? That girl who came through just now? She was pretty,' Bernardo says. 'She smiled at me.'

The first boy laughs. 'Ha ha! You think she'd be interested in you? It's not only Arlecchino who's gone to the bloody moon – you have and all.'

A few paces away, unnoticed, Beppe is staring at them, hardly breathing.

'What story, anyway?' Bernardo says. 'What's she saying?'

'Not sure of all of it. Francesco didn't say much ... which makes a change. Just that she's an actress, anyway, according to him. Er ...' He pauses, frowning as he recollects Francesco's proffered snippets of news. 'Er ... he said that ... she didn't do a murder they said she'd done – well, thank God for that, I suppose,

367

seeing as she's over there in the wagon with the Andreinis – but someone else thought she had, and . . . what was it? Oh yes. Some man she was in love with said he didn't want her any more, so she's come here instead. Or something like that. They'll be at it all night, I reckon. And, tell you what, I'll bet she comes with us when we go to France. If she's any sort of actress, I'll lay a wager they'll want her. They need someone fast – Prudenza's not far off the size of a buffalo now, isn't she?'

Beppe's heart is racing so fast now he feels almost light-headed.

35

The early-morning light is pushing its way in around the edges of the shutters in Marco da Correggio's bedchamber, its silvery bleakness contrasting with the yellow glow of the single candle on the table by the bed. Marco is on his knees, roughly folding a second doublet; he pushes it into a large leather saddlebag, into which he has already stuffed two shirts, a tangle of hose, a spare pair of boots and a bag of coins; then, muttering to himself, he opens another chest and rummages through the contents, pulling out pieces of clothing and discarding them higgledy-piggledy across the floor.

'Bloody thing – why do I never seem able to find a damn thing I'm looking for?' he says, slamming down the lid of the chest.

Abandoning his search, he snuffs the candle and grabs the saddlebag by the straps, rough-fastening it as he leaves the room. Closing the door to his apartment, and taking the stairs two at a time, he leaves the building by the street door. His horse, stabled nearby, is saddled within minutes without recourse to the elderly stable-man, who remains deeply asleep in his little bed above the stalls, unaware of the activity below him, and before many people are awake in Bologna, Marco is on the road, heading north towards Verona, with his breath hanging in clouds around his head in the chill early air. The horse's hoof-beats ring out clear in the stillness.

Over in the Villa Castellino, Maddalena di Maccio is lying on her back beneath heavy woollen blankets, staring up at the canopied cover of her bed, her hands splayed protectively around the swell of her belly. Beside her, old Paolo di Maccio is asleep, his mouth agape, his breath harshly regular. She turns her head to look at him; the jut of his beaky nose and the wet gleam of his sagging lower lip, just visible in the early light, repulse her. Staring at him with nauseous dislike for several long seconds, she then turns away from him, drawing her knees up and wrapping her arms around them, pressing the side of her head into her pillow.

She will not think of it.

Cannot.

She cannot think of much, anyway – the yearning need for a dose is beginning to overwhelm her again. Her skin is crawling and her mouth is dry as she contemplates the flooding relief she knows even a few drops will bring. That part-empty bottle – the one she took from Sebastiano's bloodstained pocket – is within reach in the small chest in the ante-room. She would be unlikely to wake Paolo. Once he is snoring like this, he is hard to rouse, thank God.

The child within, roused perhaps by Maddalena's now wildly racing heartbeat, pushes softly at the wall of her belly with some indeterminate limb, but Maddalena ignores it. Her mind is fixed now upon the little bottle. Edging towards the side of the bed, careful not to lift the blankets, in case the influx of cold air should rouse Paolo, she slides out from under the covers and pads across the rush-strewn chamber floor towards the ante-room.

Under the window in the ante-room is a painted wooden chest; Maddalena lifts the lid. The bottle is in a box, hidden beneath several dresses. Her heartbeat now filling her throat and thudding in her ears, she pulls out the box and removes the bottle, holding it up to her lips and pressing it there a moment. The child in her belly stirs again, but she once more ignores it.

Back in the bedchamber, Paolo di Maccio is still deeply – and loudly – asleep. From a table near the window, Maddalena picks up one of several small red Murano glasses, each of them no more than twice the size of a large thimble. She pours water from a silver pitcher into the glass; she is careful, but the jug is both large and full, and a glittering splash of it slops out onto the front of her night-shift. Gasping at the cold, she flashes a panicked look across to her husband, fearful that she will have woken him, but the noise of his ragged breathing rasps on.

The tiny cork makes a faint, high-pitched, musical 'pop' as she draws it. She has no spoon to measure the dose, but, reluctant to wait any longer, she holds the bottle up for a moment, before slowly lowering it first to the horizontal, then downwards, and letting what she intends to be a spoonful fall into the little red glass. Her hand slips, and she fears that more of the liquid than she had planned might have fallen into the glass; it is too dark to see clearly, however, and she is not prepared to waste any by throwing out the dose and beginning again.

It will have to do.

Will it banish the memories she is beginning not to be able to bear? The sight of Sebastiano ogling the little actress after the performance that night and the knowledge that her time with him was truly at an end. The sickening shock of seeing him dead. The sickly-sweet iron smell of the curdled clots of blood in his hair, the dark-stained doublet collar, his hand – still warm when she touched it – outstretched on the wooden floor. Her own voice, muttering to him: *So someone's finished you off, you bastard. Don't fool yourself – I'm glad. But I'm having the bottles. I know where they are and I'm having them.* Her heart races as she remembers holding her breath, then pushing beneath the inert mass of his body, burrowing into his pocket, to find his key. She touched his hair by mistake as she pulled her hand free with no key, too nauseated to have searched properly. There was blood on her fingers. Then, turning, she had seen the three bottles on the study table, one tipped onto its side.

Deliberately slowing her breathing now, with both hands cradling the little glass, she stares down at it, breathing in the spice-scented tang of the laudanum; then, holding her breath, she tips the contents of the glass into her mouth and swallows it in one. It tastes much stronger than usual. Restoppering the bottle, she tucks it deep under her pillow.

She cannot have been out of the bed for more than a few minutes, but the sheets are already chilled as she slips back under the covers. Turning her back determinedly upon her still-sleeping husband, she draws her knees up again, feeling the warmth of the dose spreading through her. For the first time in days, the racking tension that has been gripping her begins to loosen its hold, and she closes her eyes. The faintest ghost of a smile twitches at the corners of her mouth.

A few minutes later, though, her eyes snap open again, as an unexpected wave of nausea grips her. Holding her breath, she waits to see if it will pass, but the giddiness grows more intense and the room begins to move around her as though she were at sea. The child within her begins to kick frantically as though in a panic and she sits upright. 'Paolo,' she says, and her voice sounds like a stranger's. 'Paolo, help me . . .'

36

'And then, after that, I'll turn to the audience and start haranguing them, yes? But only at *that* point,' Simone da Bologna says, stabbing down with a finger onto the paper where the new lines have been roughly scribbled down. 'There, look: after Colombina has said, "*Someone has the truth festering within them like a tumour, I'm sure of that.*" I'll make some sort of foolish remark, as though I haven't listened to a word of what she's been saying, then I'll—'

'Then you'll drop the idiocy and do your best to unearth the truth.' Isabella smiles at Simone, then, turning to Sofia, says, 'Is that the sort of thing you were hoping for?'

Sofia cannot answer. She nods.

'Shall we run through? Here, in the wagon – I don't want the risk of anyone overhearing before we are ready to unleash this at the performance.'

'Good thought, Bella.' Simone stands and, linking his fingers, stretches his arms out before him, cracking his knuckles. Wincing, he hunches and rolls his shoulders. 'God, it's only when you try to move that you realize just how long you've sat still in a cramped wooden box like this bloody wagon. I'll need to sleep for a bit before we perform. We all will.'

Sofia stands too. Privately surprised at Simone's complaint, as to her, this wagon is luxuriously large, she eases out the stiffness from each arm and leg.

'Here,' Simone says to Sofia. 'Come and sit here. I'll read over your shoulder.'

Sofia can feel colour flooding into her face. 'I . . . I, er . . . ' she stammers. 'I don't read very well, but I remember what's been put together. I'll . . . I'll say it from here. If I may.'

Neither Simone nor Isabella show any sign of surprise at Sofia's admission.

Then the back flap of the wagon is pulled aside and Francesco Andreini's face appears. 'Bella, can you spare me a moment?'

'Of course, *caro*. Come in. We've just finished cobbling it all together, and are on the point of running through.'

Simone says, his face and voice distorting as he smothers a yawn, 'I could do with a piss, as it happens. I'll just go now, seeing as we're pausing.'

Sofia watches him push aside the back flap and vault, almost as nimbly as Beppe might have done, out of the rear of the wagon.

When he returns some moments later, there is an odd smile on his face, Sofia thinks, as though he is savouring the memory of a shared joke. She watches him, wondering if he has any intention of expounding on the cause of his amusement, but, after a swift glance in her direction, which seems to intensify his smile for a fraction of a second, his face straightens and he picks up the sheet of scribbled dialogue. Frowning down at it, lips moving silently and eyebrows lifting, he runs through the new lines, free hand gesticulating as he reads.

Once or twice he looks at her again and the strange, twitching half-smile returns.

Francesco Andreini edges between the others towards the back of the wagon. 'I'll leave you three to run through the new material. But you do agree, Bella, don't you, that we absolutely *have* to do the show there? We've been hoping for another invitation from them for months.' He pauses; then his face splits in a boyish smile. 'The Castello Estense . . .' he says, clenching a celebratory fist. 'To get one invitation seemed miraculous . . . a second is almost too good to be true. We've been asked back – the ultimate compliment. Who knows, it might become an annual event!'

Simone grins and claps. 'That's wonderful! When did this happen?'

'Just now. The duke sent a personal request. Written yesterday. Poor messenger must have been riding all night.'

Isabella Andreini holds Francesco's face between her hands and kisses him. 'Well done, you very clever man,' she says. 'It's wonderful. Tell Flaminio to come by when he has a moment, will you? We'll need to decide which show to give them this time.'

Francesco nods happily. Sofia can hear him whistling as he walks away.

'Now,' Isabella says, sitting back down and straightening her skirts. 'Let's run through what we've put together for this afternoon, shall we? We'll start with Colombina's speech. Can you remember—?'

'Every word.' Sofia pauses, breathing slowly for a moment, then looking up at Simone she says, *'Misfortune? There can be none greater than this! You might say that I am a creature of misfortune – in fact, if you sliced me in half, you'd find a core of misfortune running down through me from head to toe. And what greater adversity can there be than to be . . . falsely accused? Falsely accused, not of an infidelity – no, they are not saying I've been found in someone else's husband's bed! Not of a petty theft – no, they are not saying that I pilfered some bunch of ribbons, or a length of lace, or even snipped a lady's purse from her belt! No, I have been falsely accused . . . of . . .'*

Sofia sucks in a short breath and holds it for a second. Pointing a finger at Simone, she says, ' . . . *of* murder.'

'*Of murder?*' Simone's Arlecchino sounds astonished.

'*Of murder.*'

'*Who did you kill?*'

'*I said it was a* false *accusation.*'

Simone smacks himself in the forehead with the heel of his hand. '*Of course, a* false *accusation. So who did you kill – falsely?*'

Sofia sucks in a gasp of counterfeit irritation and glares at Simone. '*It won't be a false accusation in a moment, it'll be a real one, and it'll be* you *lying dead on the floor, you fool, not some lecherous nobleman in his castle.*'

Isabella Andreini brings her hands together a couple of times. Sofia glances at her; she is smiling widely. 'Perfect – you're good, you know. You have Colombina in a nutshell.'

Sofia swallows and, turning back to Simone, says, '*That horrible man is dead, even though I didn't kill him. But somebody did.*'

'*Who, though? Did you see anyone there?*'

Another sucked-in sigh of irritation, and a roll of the eyes. '*Of course I didn't see, you stupid, stupid man. I'd tell you who it was, wouldn't I, if I'd seen him? And* you *could go and kill him for me.*'

Simone's mouth drops open and he stands up suddenly. Turning to what would be the audience, he points at himself, jabbing himself in the chest and shrugging in disbelief, then he raises both hands, palm up, as though questioning Colombina's sanity.

Sofia grabs his arm. '*Listen, someone out there has the truth festering within them – like a tumour – I'm sure of that. Find them for me, will you? Find out who did this? I don't care how you do it – but find them.'*

And Simone – as Arlecchino – swells with pride, grinning at the thought of being thus chosen as a champion. He rubs his hands together gleefully, but then, his smile fading comically, he looks from right to left, as though ensuring he is not being overheard, and, leaning out towards the as yet non-existent audience, he begins to speak in a thrilling, carrying hiss-whisper.

37

The walk from the little tavern the next day, back to the Piazza di Porta Ravegnana, is no more than a matter of a moment or two. As they hurry towards where the Gelosi are now putting the finishing touches to the newly set stage, Sofia wastes no time in telling Niccolò more of the details of what she has agreed with the Andreinis. Ippo jumps up repeatedly, nosing at Sofia's skirts; she rubs his head distractedly, hardly aware that he is there, but as he utters an impatient bark, she looks down and sees Beppe's dog, happy to be with her, his mouth open in a wide, tongue-lolling grin, and a wash of sadness threatens to drown the excitement she has been feeling at the prospect of the impending performance. Her voice, when she speaks, sounds to her as though it is coming from the other side of a closed door. 'They've asked me to go with them when they move on, Niccolò.'

'What?' Niccolò stops and stares at her.

Sofia repeats herself.

'Go with them – the Gelosi? Oh, Sofia, that's wonderful. I can't believe it – you with the Gelosi! I couldn't be more pleased for you. You will go, won't you?'

She shrugs. 'I don't know.'

The prospect of days, weeks, *months* ahead without Beppe is filling her head, and for a moment she can hear nothing – just a thick silence – as she tries to examine her feelings. She heard what she heard. There is no getting away from the fact that she heard Beppe's own voice uttering the words: *I made a mistake. I hate to admit it but she's trouble. I should never have got close to her. I made a mistake. She's trouble. She's trouble.* It's not as if some other person had reported those words to her – that, she would never have believed. She thought he loved her. Until those last two days, that is, when he had begun to seem distracted and unlike himself.

But what if she is wrong?

A thin worm of doubt has begun to writhe in her belly.

She ran off so quickly – left without talking to Beppe, without asking him about what she heard; disappeared silently, unable to face the thought of confronting the unbearable. But what if she misheard – even though she knows she did not – what if she agrees to go with the Gelosi, all the way to France . . . and she is wrong? What if Beppe does still love her? What if, even as she thinks this through, he is as unhappy to be without her as she is to be without him? An image of him gazing up at the sky with misery etched over his dear, tilted face pushes into her mind and she holds her breath, squeezing her eyes tight shut for a second, trying to banish it. The thought that she might have brought this despair upon herself unnecessarily grips her scalp with ice-cold fingers.

' . . . and I think you'd – Sofia? What is it? Are you unwell?' Niccolò's voice interrupts her thoughts; taking her hand, he pulls her to a halt. 'You look as though you're in pain. What is it, child?'

They have arrived at the piazza; Simone da Bologna is up on the stage, as yet dressed in nothing more than untucked shirt and grubby breeches. He is smiling and has raised a hand, waggling his fingers in greeting. Sofia avoids having to give Niccolò an answer; shaking her head, and smiling at him, she merely says, 'Keep Ippo close, won't you?' and, after giving him a brief hug, she runs towards where Simone is holding an arm out to shepherd her away to the wagons.

Niccolò watches her go, then, glancing around the piazza, sees a stone seat over at the eastern side. Determining to sit until the show begins, he pulls a thin leather belt from around his waist and, threading the end through the buckle, makes a loop, which he puts over Ippo's head. Ippo submits affably to being thus tethered, and trots next to Niccolò as they cross over to the bench. Sitting first on his haunches, he then sinks to lie unmoving at Niccolò's feet, his nose between his two outstretched front paws. Only the continual twitching of his tufted eyebrows betrays the fact that he is not asleep.

Beppe spent last night in a doorway. In a wide street not far from the Piazza di Porta Ravegnana he found a deep, pilastered recess at the top of a flight of three steps, and there sat hunched, with his arms wrapped around his knees and his head resting against a wall. He is not sure, but thinks he might have slipped into sleep a couple of times. Standing now, rubbing his face and pushing his hands through hair that feels damp and knotted, he tries to ease the stiffness from his back, rolling each shoulder and shaking out each arm. His buttocks are chilled and numb; he rubs them now with the palms of both hands and, bouncing on the balls of his feet, he lifts first one knee, then the other, hugging each leg in turn close to his chest.

Despite his fatigue and the aches in his limbs, he cannot help smiling.

One way or another, he will see Sofia today.

He was astonished by what he learned yesterday. Thank God he happened upon that particular person! If the idea he suggested works as he hopes it will, Sofia will not be able to doubt his feelings for another moment. Thinking about her now, it is all he can do to stop himself running across the piazza and calling for her. But he must hold back until later – what was arranged yesterday will be the best way. He pictures the surprise on Sofia's face and his smile widens.

Niccolò is dozing, his chin dropped to his chest, his mouth a little open. He did not sleep well, having spent hours pacing the otherwise deserted upper room in the little tavern, anxious about Sofia and what might have been transpiring between her and the Gelosi, and here, on his bench in the warm October sun, his eyes have closed despite his best intentions. His hands are now lying limply in his lap, the thin leather strap threaded loosely between his fingers.

He does not stir for some time – not until Ippo scrabbles to his feet, barks, and races away. The leather belt tugs briefly at Niccolò's fingers, then slips free and Ippo is gone. Startled, Niccolò sits up straight and looks around him, disoriented. He catches a brief glimpse of Ippo's whip-thin tail disappearing between two long-coated men on the far side of the piazza and then the dog is lost from sight.

Getting to his feet, his heart racing, he sets off in pursuit – he cannot lose the dog. Sofia will be heartbroken. Why? Why has Ippo run like that? He has been so docile and obedient all the way from Faenza.

The piazza is more crowded than when he first closed his eyes at least an hour before. It was almost deserted when he first sat down, but now, over on the far side, where the dog vanished, quite a throng seems to have gathered – of apparently aimless men and boys, loitering and talking together. Niccolò realizes dimly, from the snatches of conversation that he gleans as he edges his breathless way through, that they have already begun staking out their places for the show later that afternoon. Word has clearly spread that the Gelosi are in town.

Reaching the spot where he saw Ippo disappear, he scans to right and left, but can see nothing. He begins to call the dog's name: it is a two-note, sing-song call to begin with, which hardens into a shout as no dog appears.

'Oh God, dog, where in heaven's name are you?' he mutters. 'I simply can't tell her I've lost you.' He shouts again. And again.

A narrow street leads away from the piazza a few yards to the left. It is the only way Ippo can have gone, Niccolò thinks now; he excuses himself as he sidles between a pair of corpulent elderly men whose faces register irritable disdain at the interruption, and then sets off down the little street, calling increasingly desperately as he goes. Several doors are open along the street; into each of these, Niccolò peers, shouting for Ippo. He has no response from three of these doorways, but an oath is snarled back from one and a lump of stale bread is thrown at him from another.

And then he turns a corner and sees him. Ippo is barking joyously, tail wagging, standing on his back legs, with his front paws up . . . against Beppe's legs. Beppe is bending over, and he is laughing and ruffling the dog's ears. Niccolò's mouth opens. Turning, Beppe sees him and the laugh widens into a broad, tilted smile. 'Niccolò!' he says, raising a hand.

'But ... but ...' Niccolò can manage nothing but a confused stammer.

Dropping back onto all fours, Ippo trots beside his master as Beppe strides over to hug Niccolò. 'Niccolò, I'm so glad to see you. How come you're here? Was Ippo with you?'

'She's here, Beppe. She's in one of the wagons with the Gelosi.'

'I know.'

'She said ... she said she overheard you saying—'

Beppe winces. 'Don't. Please don't. I think I know what she must have heard. But ... it was only a snatch of what I was saying – and it wasn't what she thought at all.'

'She told me what you said. She's heartbroken, Beppe.'

'I was only saying what I thought Angelo was trying to *make* me say – I was angry with him. What I *said* wasn't what I was *feeling*. Quite the opposite. I love her, Niccolò. So much. Losing her has been like losing a leg. I've been searching for her for days.'

'Oh, thank God for that.' Niccolò looks skyward for a second, crosses himself, then smiles back at Beppe. 'Come with me then. Let's go and find her.'

'No. Not yet.'

'What? Why not? She's just over there ...'

'I know.'

'Then why—?'

'If you see her, don't tell her I'm here. We have it worked out – I know what I'm doing.'

'*We?* Who—?'

And, squatting on his heels again, as he starts once more to fondle his dog, looking up at Niccolò and squinting against a shaft of sunlight, Beppe explains. Niccolò's mouth is an O of incredulity – an O which rapidly flattens and widens into a grin. 'Oh, that will be worth watching! I won't say a thing, Beppe, I promise. I doubt I will see her to talk to her before the performance, anyway.' He pauses. 'How are the rest of the Coraggiosi?'

'I don't know. I've not seen them for the best part of a week.'

'How are they managing without you?'

'I don't know that, either. I'm not too worried, though: I don't know if they are planning any performances, but if they are, Vico has stood in as Arlecchino before – that time when I broke my leg, do you remember?'

Niccolò nods.

'I've come away with their blessing. I just want to get Sofia back to them quickly.'

Niccolò hesitates, then says, 'Beppe, they've asked her if she'll go with them – the Gelosi. To France.'

'What?'

'Their Colombina is pregnant. They want Sofia to go with them until their girl is fit to perform again.' He pauses a second. 'She hasn't said no.'

Beppe stares at him for a moment and his face stiffens as he considers what Niccolò has said. 'Has she said yes?'

'No – not in so many words.'

'Good. Then let's go back to the piazza. You wait for the performance, Niccolò,' Beppe says. 'Take Ippo. I need to get ready for . . . well, for what I'm going to do later. Don't go far – and come and find us at the end of the show.'

'I wouldn't dream of doing anything else.'

Niccolò pats Beppe's shoulder again; then the two of them turn and walk back along the narrow street, back towards the Piazza di Porta Ravegnana. The dog's leash now held more tightly in his hand, Niccolò heads for the bench on which he had been sitting before, while Beppe, shouldering his leather bag, hesitates for a moment, then ducks into the shadows of the east-facing colonnade.

It is strange to watch this set of strangers preparing to perform, Sofia thinks as she watches the Gelosi going through all the same rigmaroles that she has witnessed with the Coraggiosi countless times. They have made up their faces, polished their masks, donned their costumes; Flaminio Scala, as Capitano Spavento, is now pacing with an endearingly familiar ponderous, bent-kneed stride around the back of the stage, his mouth below his mask screwed sideways in a leering grimace, running through his set speeches in a muttered undertone. Isabella and Francesco, both undeniably beautiful in their lavish costumes, are hand in hand, chins high, both exquisite faces expressionless as they breathe slowly and steady themselves for their opening scene. Five men to whom Sofia has not spoken are throwing a ball to each other: a white-faced Pedrolino, three indeterminate *ʒanni* characters and the hook-nosed, mustachioed Brighella in his white and green jacket and trousers. The speed with which the ball is passing from hand to hand is increasing by the minute. Not once do they let it drop.

She has whitened her face again – just as Beppe did for her before – though this time there is no pearl. With pinked cheeks and reddened lips, with coloured ribbons in her hair, in a dress borrowed from Prudenza – and pinned to fit – she is Colombina once more.

Simone da Bologna appears behind her; he takes her by the elbow. Seeing the diamond-patterned jacket and trousers, the black hat, the wooden bat stuck through his belt, her heart flips over yet again.

'Ready?' he says, smiling.

'As I'll ever be.'

'Want to run through it again?'

'Not the speech – just the run-up to it, if you wouldn't mind. I don't want to risk missing the moment.'

'You won't miss it. But let's walk it through again.' Simone stands back, glancing round to make sure he has enough space. 'We've written Colombina out of most of the *canovaccii*, so you have hardly any material to remember, apart from the new speech.'

Sofia nods, still privately astonished at the generosity of this group of strangers, who have been so quickly prepared to alter their entire afternoon's performance for her, with almost no notice, on little more than a whim.

'Then,' Simone says, 'after Arlecchino has asked you what's troubling you, you'll be so irritated with him that he has forgotten, yet again, that you'll stalk off right up to the leading edge of the stage and talk *to* him without looking *at* him. Look out over the audience – but not at them: as though they're not there. Arlecchino will listen for a moment as you begin to recount your misfortunes, then he'll pretend to lose interest and almost fall asleep on his feet. Like this . . .' Simone's jaw sags momentarily, his shoulders slump and his knees bend outwards. He looks the picture of vacant boredom.

'Yes.' Despite her tension, Sofia smiles at the sight of him.

'Then as you say that terrible word, "*murder*", he'll wake with a jump' – Simone straightens suddenly – 'looking horrified. It's only then that he'll start involving himself in that dialogue that we've been through several times now.'

'Yes, I'm quite happy with that part. But I just wanted to be quite sure that Colombina mustn't notice Arlecchino not listening to her.'

'No, she definitely mustn't — far funnier if she's passionately declaring her unfortunate state to the audience, and — so she thinks — to Arlecchino, while behind her in reality he's yawning and clearly bored by what she's saying, and edging as far away from her as possible to avoid the responsibility of having to take any notice of her.'

A thin, reedy trumpet sounds a jaunty fanfare.

'Here we go — a couple of minutes,' Simone says.

'Sofia, are you ready?' This from a huge-eyed Isabella, still hand in hand with her husband.

Sofia nods, hoping fervently that she is.

She sees Flaminio Scala, now staring up at the sky, shaking out his arms from fingertips to shoulders, sucking in a long breath and letting it out in a slow stream through a mouth puckered drawstring-tight. He and Simone will be opening this particular show, and Sofia watches as the two of them climb the little ladders up to the cramped space behind the backdrop. The reedy fanfare builds to a climax and ceases, leaving a long high note quivering across the piazza.

Then a plaintive tune begins, picked out on a lute from the side of the stage. Flaminio Scala pulls aside the backcloth, and he and Simone stride forwards.

Beppe has tucked himself in the shadows of an archway at the foot of the gigantic Torre degli Asinelli: the taller and straighter of the two central Bolognese towers. From here, he can see exactly who is doing what behind the backcloth, whilst remaining hidden.

He saw Sofia just now, deep in conversation with Simone da Bologna. The desire to run across the piazza and throw his arms around her almost overwhelmed him as he stood in the dark and watched the two of them talking with such animation, but, picturing her face in a few moments' time, he presses a fist against his mouth and stays where he is.

'*Speaking personally, I think I have been treated very shabbily,*' Sofia's Colombina says to Simone in his guise as Arlecchino. '*Very shabbily indeed.*'

The audience is a sea of faces, and every gaze is upon her.

'*You don't say! Ha! I could say the same thing about myself,*' Simone mutters, scowling. '*That word —* shabbily *— just about sums up how everyone treats poor Arlecchino, most of the time.*'

'*But I wasn't talking about you. I was talking about me — and the terrible things they have been saying about me.*'

Simone's shoulders droop, as he tries to look contrite. '*I'm sorry,*' he says in a voice of clearly deliberate sweetness, clasping his hands in front of his chest. '*You're right — in fact, it would be fair to say that you have been quite swamped by misfortune.*'

Sofia draws in a breath. This is her moment. '*Misfortune?*' she says, glaring at Arlecchino for a moment, then turning her back on him and staring out across the piazza. '*There can be none greater than this! You might say that I am a creature of misfortune — in fact, if you sliced me in half,*' she says, running a finger down her front from forehead to hip, '*you'd find a core of misfortune running down through me from head to toe. And what greater adversity can there be than to be . . . falsely accused?*' She clutches a clenched fist to her chest. The audience has sniggered quietly as she has been speaking – she presumes that, behind her back, Simone is amusing them by being 'bored'. Pointing an accusatory finger out at them, she says, '*Yes, I stand falsely accused! Not of an infidelity — no, they are not saying I've been found in someone else's husband's bed! Not of a petty theft — no, they are not saying that I pilfered some bunch of ribbons, or a length of lace, or even snipped a lady's purse from her belt. No, I have*' *been falsely accused . . . of . . .'* Sofia sucks in a short breath and holds it. Turning, and pointing her finger towards Arlecchino, who is now sitting slumped on an upturned barrel with his chin in his hand, drumming his fingers on his knee, she says, '. . . *of* murder.'

Arlecchino jumps up, hopping from foot to foot in consternation. '*Of murder?*' he says, and Sofia's eyes widen at the sound of his voice.

'*Yes, of murder.*'

'*Who did you kill?*' Even if the black mask and the woollen hat are hiding his features, the heavy, Bergamo accent is unmistakable. The hat is further back on his head than it was. And he is taller and thinner than Simone.

Sofia can hardly speak. In a voice that feels quite detached from the mouth that is uttering her words, she says, '*I said it was a* false *accusation.*'

Smacking himself in the forehead with the heel of his hand, Arlecchino then draws out his wooden bat and slaps it against the side of his leg with a ringing crack. '*Of course, that's what you said, isn't it? A* false *accusation.*' He points the bat at her. '*So who did you kill – falsely?*'

Sofia walks towards him, as if sleepwalking. She stands and stares at him for what seems an age; then, hearing as though from a far distance that unmistakable hum of concern from an audience aware of a clearly unplanned silence, she swallows, shakes her head and finds her line. '*It . . . it won't be a false accusation in a moment, it'll be a real one, and it'll be* you *lying dead on the floor, you fool, not some lecherous nobleman in the depths of his castle.*'

Arlecchino hangs his head like a scolded child and scuffs the trestle boards with the toe of his shoe.

'*That horrible man is dead, even though I didn't kill him. But somebody did.*'

'*Who though? Did you see anyone there?*'

Fighting to make herself speak, she says, '*Of course I didn't see, you stupid, stupid man. I'd tell you who it was, wouldn't I, if I'd seen him? And* you *could go and kill him for me.*'

Turning to the audience, Arlecchino shrugs high in open-mouthed disbelief, one finger pressed against his chest, the other hand out sideways, palm up, fingers splayed. '*Me?!*' he mouths, pulling a face, and the audience laughs.

Sofia grabs his arm, but, raising it quickly, he dislodges her grip and reaching for her hand, he links his fingers through hers. She gasps, draws a breath and manages to say, '*Listen, someone out there has the truth festering within them – like a tumour – I'm sure of it. Find them for me, will you? Find out who did this? I don't care how you do it – but find them.*'

Arlecchino cups her face in his hands – very, very gently – and kisses her full on the mouth. Sofia's heart stands still. The audience draws in a collective breath. Then he says, in a ringing voice, '*I'll do it. I'll find him and kill him – just for you!*'

The audience cheers.

With Colombina's hand firmly in his, Arlecchino walks down to the front of the stage. Gazing out at the audience, he says, '*Someone out there is wearing a piece of guilty knowledge tucked away inside his doublet. It's curled like a snake against the skin of his chest. That little snake wriggles and writhes from time to time – most often when it hears mention of . . . certain events. Important events for the person inside whose doublet it is nestling. It must be wriggling now, don't you think, signori and signore?*' Wooden *batocchio* tucked under his arm, Arlecchino raises his hands and wiggles his fingers. '*Inside somebody's shirt? When it's just been listening to a tale of such mis-adventure as our lovely Colombina has been telling you? Now – the trouble with snakes is . . . if you're not careful, they bite. It might not*

390

be just one person, either – that's the thing about guilt. It's infec-tious . . . ' Arlecchino snatches a look at Colombina; then, turning away, he puts a hand around the side of his mouth as though to keep his next loudly hissed utterance from her. ' *. . . like the pox.*' The audience laughs, but the laugh dies fast, as Arlecchino points out at them again, and says in a ringing voice, '*One person did this terrible thing. One person – and he might be standing right next to you now, this very minute – one person picked up a dirty great candlestick and whacked a man on the back of the head with it – and killed him.*' He stands silent for a moment, staring out at the audience. '*This city's buzzing with the news, is it not? Somebody made that choice and now a man is dead. That somebody's snake is probably particularly cold and slithery, and it most likely nips him quite often – just where it hurts most – when he's least expecting it. But he won't be alone: mark my words. There'll be others too, with their own little vipers – perhaps someone who saw and hasn't said. Someone who's been told and is too scared to speak out. Someone who's done the like before, themselves, and won't risk exposure. They'll all have their own wrigglers inside their shirts. You see if I'm not right.*'

Sofia cannot take her eyes from him. She stares and stares at him as he strides right to the front of the stage, pulls out his wooden bat, crouches down on his heels and points it at a man near the front of the crowd. '*What about you, signore? Got a wriggler? Or you, signora, tucked down inside that very lovely bodice . . .* ' Putting a hand down to the trestle floor, he leans out, craning his neck towards an amply bosomed woman to his left. '*A chilly little wriggler right down in there?*' He snorts, then licks his lips, sketching the outline of the woman's generous proportions with his hands. '*Ha! Can't imagine* that *one will want to come out very often.*' A snickering laugh trickles around the audience. '*Laugh if you will,*' Arlecchino says now, straightening, scowling and pointing the bat again, '*But if you're one of those people – the people who know, and won't say; the people who suspect but daren't admit – then expect your writhing little worm of guilt to grow and swell and become more and more of a nuisance to you. Because the only thing that gets rid of a guilt-wriggler is an admission. You think about it.*'

There is a clatter of footsteps on the stage behind them. Sofia turns, knowing full well that it will be Flaminio Scala, striding out as planned in his ridiculous long-nosed mask. Arlecchino grabs her hand. '*Quick!*' he says. '*We have to go! We don't want to be caught here by that pompous old windbag – we'll never get away!*' Turning back to the audience, he says, '*Don't forget what I said – it'll only get bigger and colder and wrigglier and end up by strangling you!*' Then, with Sofia's fingers laced through his, he runs across the stage and pushes his way through the gap in the backcloth.

Beppe cannot speak. Pushing his mask up and off his face so that it falls to the floor with a clatter, he puts his arms around Sofia and, without a word, he kisses her. His mouth is on hers, and her hands are in his hair, and her body is pressing against his, soft and pliant and eager. Stepping backwards, he feels the heavy folds of the backdrop shift behind him – another step in that direction and they will be on the stage. The ladder leading down from the trestles is a pace to the right.

'Go back down the steps.'

As Sofia reaches back with her foot to find the first rung of the ladder, Beppe lets go of her, vaults down off the trestles and then lifts his arms to her; she turns to him and he picks her off the ladder, starting to kiss her again even before her feet have reached the ground. They lean together against the ladder, arms around each other, so entirely engrossed in their embrace that they hear nothing of the stream of hissed comments that are now coming from Simone da Bologna.

'Quick! Stop it – let go of each other! You're on stage again in a minute! Sofia! Signor Bianchi, you'll have to wait until we—'

Neither Sofia nor Beppe are listening, though Beppe feels his shoulder being roughly shaken, and vaguely hears, as though from a distance, Simone da Bologna hiss-calling, 'Prudenza! Quick, come here.'

Beppe, his mouth on Sofia's, one hand at her back, the other in her hair, feels as though he could never have enough of her. He cannot hold her close enough. She is wriggling in against him, making soft little sounds of pleasure – not words, just inarticulate half-sighs – as she kisses him. Then other, bigger, male hands take hold of his upper arms and pull him back, away from Sofia. He jerks away, trying to free himself from whoever is holding him, but a laughing voice says, 'Don't worry – just get the jacket off him, will you? I'll take over – but I need my costume. And hurry! My cue is in a moment or two!'

The same hands reach around him from behind and Beppe feels unknown fingers beginning to unfasten the diamond-patterned jacket.

'Prudenza, get the dress off Sofia.'

Beppe hears a squeak from Sofia, and feels her grip on the back of his neck tightening as she is pulled backwards away from him. For a moment their bodies are held apart from each other, though they struggle to maintain their kiss and their mouths are still touching. Beppe feels the jacket being pulled off him, first one sleeve jerked down over an arm, then the second, and, glancing behind Sofia, he sees a dark-haired, plump woman, frantically unpinning and unlacing Colombina's dress and easing open the back of the bodice. She crouches behind Sofia for a moment and Beppe hears

393

her amused voice, saying, 'Quick, *cara*, step out of the skirts, will you?'

Sofia obliges, her arms now back around Beppe. She is dressed now only in shift and underskirt, he in nothing but the diamond-patterned leggings. He can feel her hands on the skin of his chest and back.

Simone's voice says, 'I'm not even going to try getting the leggings off him – I'll have to use my old ones. But where's my mask?'

'He dropped it up there, look.'

Another, unfamiliar voice. 'Here are the leggings, Simone.'

After a moment's frantic rustle of clothing, there is a muttered oath, then footsteps on the ladder, followed by a brief burst of applause and a couple of whistles from the crowd.

The play unfolds behind and above Beppe and Sofia, and they take in not one word of it: it is no more than a jumble of noise, interspersed with laughter and clapping. Seated as they are at the foot of the ladder, entwined in each other's arms, there are moments of interruption when unknown pairs of legs step over and around them, muttering apologies – once or twice Beppe thinks he hears a smothered snort of amusement – but not for a second does it occur to either of them to pause, to stop what they are doing, to search for a more suitable place to resume their redis-covery of each other.

'*Oh my word, but I am truly a fool,*' he says indistinctly, in between kisses. '*And you will never forgive me, will you?*' He wonders if Sofia will remember the lines.

'*No, now that you mention it, I'm not sure that I shall.*'

She mutters the response, her words almost indistinguishable as her mouth is on his, and he cannot help smiling.

'*Just one more chance?*' he says, pulling back for a second and holding her gaze. '*One more very small . . . extremely insignificant . . . little chance?*'

She stares at him, her expression taut and serious, and Beppe holds his breath. Then her face dissolves into a wide smile and her eyes are sparkling with tears. '*Very well. Just one.*' A pause. '*One last.*'

They carry on kissing as the final prolonged burst of applause from the crowd fills the air. They fail to stop even as the actors burst through the hanging and jostle down the ladder, stumbling over them, apologizing; one or two of them laugh and clap at the sight of the two oblivious lovers, while another offers a decidedly lewd suggestion as to what they should best do next and where.

38

'What did you say he called me?'

'An *underage* bardassa *with the morals of a tomcat*, I think it was,' Marco says, shaking his head, fiddling a shred of dry skin on his lip between his teeth. The tavern table in front of him is stained with ale and pitted with worm holes, and the tallow candle stub, stuck straight onto the wood, is giving out little more than a fitful, flickering, sheep-smelling glow.

Fabio da Correggio raises an eyebrow. Blowing out his cheeks and letting the air puff out of his mouth, he says, 'How bloody rude.' Then, grinning, he adds, 'Though I suppose he wasn't that far wrong, really, was he? Bastard.' The grin fades. 'God, though, I'd never have wanted that sort of an end for him. He was our cousin. Terrible. And they haven't caught whoever did it?'

Marco's heart flips over as he looks at his cousin: slight, smooth-cheeked, as fine-featured as many of the women of his acquaintance, as gaudily dressed as any of the performers at that last play. He decides to tell him the truth. 'No. They haven't. And you and I are getting off up to Verona fast, before they have time to think of accusing *me*.'

Fabio grins at him. 'You *didn't* do it, did you?'

'No I bloody didn't!' His voice comes out higher-pitched than he meant. There have been so many moments, since he sat in that room at Franceschina with Sebastiano's body, staring at the seeping stain on the pillow around his cousin's head, when he has anxiously wondered if he might have done. Done it and somehow forgotten. Though he knows he could never have lifted the candlestick and ... and brought it down onto the back of Sebastiano's head like that, every time he has heard people speculating about the possible identity of the killer over the past few days he has felt heat rising in his face, and has dreaded an unstoppable rush of colour proclaiming a guilt he knows he does not possess. Or *hopes* he does not possess. Because how many times had he in fact wished his cousin dead? On how many occasions, facing yet more of Sebastiano's snide comments and menace-heavy threats, did he wish he could just draw his dagger and put an end to it? Is that enough to make him guilty? It feels strangely as though it might be. God, he wishes now that he had never borrowed money from Sebastiano in the first place – in fact he is astonished that, given his own debts and insecurities, Sebastiano ever agreed to lend him a single *scudo*.

Perhaps blood ties do matter after all.

'What shall we be doing in Verona?' Fabio says into his thoughts, and Marco looks up at his other, younger cousin, whose mouth has now curled into a cat-like smirk of anticipatory excitement. He swallows uncomfortably. Sebastiano might repeatedly have risked too much for his laudanum and his desire for a beautiful woman, but he, Marco, knows that he is perhaps just as reckless in the pursuit of his own addiction. He is all too aware that

Fabio is nothing but trouble; he knows that Fabio cares nothing for anyone but himself; he is quite certain that as soon as the first hint of possible excitement somewhere else reaches Fabio's ears, the boy will be off, abandoning Marco without a qualm. But still he craves his young cousin's company – he longs for it – and he knows he will lap up every second of it he is offered, like a starving cat. He relishes the prospect of this trip to Verona with him, however terrible the reason for its undertaking: Fabio will be his alone for at least the next few days. Unless they meet someone who takes Fabio's fancy in a tavern or on a street corner, of course.

'In Verona?' he says. 'Oh, we'll find somewhere to live first – then I want to look up a moneylender friend of mine. What we do might depend on how generous he's feeling at the moment.'

Fabio laughs and Marco watches his small white teeth gleam in the candlelight.

39

The ugly donkey's taut hoof-beats ring out into the silence of the still evening and the iron-wrapped wheels of the little cart crunch over the loose stones of the track. A chilly mist has already risen as the October evening has begun to draw in, wreathing itself around trees and bushes, and hanging like a thick cobweb low over the ground. Spiralling wisps of the mist curl away from the cart as the donkey trots on down the ditch-bound track as though through watered milk.

Niccolò has his thickest woollen coat over his shoulders, while Sofia has bundled herself in two blankets: one around her shoulders, the other tucked over her knees. Ippo is sprawled across her lap. She is warmly wrapped but, even so, her fingers and toes are stiff with cold and she has been wriggling them repeatedly to try to prevent them from numbing.

Only Beppe seems unaffected by the sharp nip in the air. Dressed only in breeches and shirt and his old leather doublet – the one Sofia likes best – he has an arm around her shoulders and she can feel the heat from his body where he is pressed against her.

'There they are, look – over there,' he says, pointing. 'Can you see the smoke?'

'Where? Oh yes, I see. Is that really them? Can you be sure?'

'They said they'd stay put until I got back. That's where I left them.'

'How long, Niccolò?'

Niccolò pats her knee. 'A few minutes perhaps. No more. Just as well – I think poor Violetta has had quite enough of being on the road.'

'Oh, do let's hurry – I so want to see them all.'

'Shall we send Ippo on ahead when we get a bit nearer?' Beppe suggests.

The dog's ears prick at the sound of his name and he lifts his head.

Ruffling his ears, Sofia smiles. 'Oh yes – like a harbinger.'

Beppe raises an eyebrow and grins. 'A very scruffy and mud-covered harbinger.'

As the cart rounds a bend, the wagons are clearly visible, standing in a huddle near a stumpy group of trees, some paces back from the track. Sofia holds her breath at the sight of Agostino bending over the brazier, which is sending a column of grey smoke up into the still evening air. Cosima is holding his arm, pointing back towards the wagon, gesturing with her free hand, and Agostino is shaking his head. Cosima gives him a swift kiss and walks back to the cart.

Sofia grips Beppe's arm, suddenly nervous at the thought of meeting them all again; Beppe smiles at her in reassurance. He turns to the dog. 'Go on, then,' he says, holding Ippo's head in both his hands and pointing it in the direction of the wagons. 'Go on, boy. There's Ago! Ago! Seek! Go on – go find him!'

Scrabbling down from the cart, Ippo does not need to be told twice. He races off, ears flat against his head, back arching at each stride like a hound's, and Sofia feels her face stretching out into a smile as Agostino looks up in astonishment. Ippo jumps up, his joyous barks audible even at this distance. Sofia sees him turning in tight circles, chasing his tail with excitement; hears Ago shouting to Cosima, who all but falls out of the back of the wagon, she reappears with such haste; sees Vico's head peering out from the smallest wagon, his expression unreadable from this far away.

Agostino has seen them – he is waving wildly with both arms. He begins to run, his breath puffing in clouds before his face.

'Come on, let's go and meet him,' Beppe says. 'Nicco, can you follow on in the cart – do you mind?'

'Go on – hurry up! Get going!' is Niccolò's only reply.

Vaulting down from the cart, Beppe reaches back up and takes Sofia's hand. She jumps down, and, hand in hand, they too start to run. Their footsteps jar on the hard ground and Sofia stumbles, but Beppe's grip on her hand tightens, his arm lifts, and she rights herself without slowing.

As they near each other, Sofia can see the untidy smile on Agostino's face; he is out of breath now, and the smile has stretched out into a gasp for air, but his arms are wide and before she can speak, he has pulled both her and Beppe into a hug.

'Oh thank heavens – you've found her! Thank God! Genesius and Vitus were watching out for you after all! Oh, bless them – bless you! Cosima and I have been sending up our prayers nightly and' – Agostino looks upwards – 'heaven be praised, they have obviously intervened in the right places and . . . oh dear Lord . . . here you are and . . . who is that in the cart over there?'

'Niccolò.'

'Niccolò? Niccolò Zanetti? Oh *cielo*! How marvellous!'

Cosima has caught up and, gasping for breath, she too throws her arms around first Sofia, then Beppe. 'Oh, thank goodness he found you! Why? Why did you go like that? Where have you been? We've been so worried! Beppe, where was she? How did you—?'

Beppe is laughing. 'Enough! Enough! We'll tell you everything, but we're all badly in need of something to eat. It's been hours since—'

'Oh, my word, of course! Quick – I have a pot of my best soup on the brazier,' Cosima says, taking Sofia's hand and turning back towards the wagons.

Catching Sofia's eye, Beppe grins and raises an eyebrow. 'Soup. Still glad to be back?' he says, very quietly into her ear, and she laughs.

The little cart scrunches up beside them.

'Niccolò, bless you, how good to see you, my friend,' Agostino says, reaching up and taking one of Niccolò's hands in his. 'But I thought you were at your daughter's for the winter.'

'I was, Ago, I was. In fact I had absolutely no intention of moving from Anna's little place until the spring.' He smiles at Sofia. 'But then I was rudely uprooted from my hibernation by the arrival of your little Colombina. *No* regard for an old man's need for rest, she had – not a *moment's* thought given to—'

'Niccolò!' Sofia is suddenly anxious.

He laughs and blows her a kiss.

'Bring that donkey down here, Nicco,' Ago says, pointing towards where the Coraggiosi horses are tethered. 'She'll need hay and water.'

*

The brazier is blazing and the soup in its great iron pot is steaming – white wisps are tendrilling out from beneath the rim of the lid. The Coraggiosi have seated themselves around the fire on their usual odd assortment of boxes, barrels, cushions and blankets. Beppe and Sofia, in the midst of it all, are pressed close to each other and Beppe's arm is protectively around Sofia's shoulders. Ippo has curled himself at Beppe's feet, his nose tucked under his paws. Niccolò is in the only complete chair – a small painted wooden thing with a woven rush seat and no arms – while Lidia, Federico and Giovanni Battista, who is still tutting his teeth and shaking his head in bewilderment at the new arrivals, are side by side on a long wooden chest. Vico has picked up his guitar and is cross-legged on a folded blanket in front of Lidia's legs. Agostino has perched on an upturned half-barrel and Cosima is on her feet, wooden ladle in hand; removing the lid of the pot she begins spooning soup into bowls.

Just to the left of Giovanni Battista, Angelo is perched on an upturned wooden carton. He has said little since the newcomers were bustled in to sit near the brazier, and now is watching them intently, chewing the skin at the side of his thumbnail.

Sofia darts glances his way every now and again, unable to determine what she should be thinking about him. It is, after all, thanks to Angelo that she is not still incarcerated in that cramped and ill-smelling room in Bologna – or worse – but then Beppe's overheard and misunderstood outburst, which caused her to run off and spend so many days in abject misery, was also down to Angelo. Gratitude and resentment battle uncomfortably in her head.

Agostino's voice breaks into her thoughts. 'And then you overheard these Gelosi boys talking about Sofia's arrival ...' he is saying to Beppe, but then he stops, as though hearing his own words again in his head and turns instead to Sofia. 'Oh, Sofia, to think of it! The Gelosi! *You* have performed on the stage with the Gelosi. Our own Colombina, on stage with the Andreinis and Flaminio Scala. Oh my word, that is so entirely extraordinary!'

'Ago, they were lovely. They couldn't have been kinder. And they're doing what they can for us even now – as I told you. After what that man said, when he came and spoke to us after the performance, Isabella said she would petition on our behalf.'

'What man?' Agostino frowns in bemusement.

Beppe says, 'Did we not say? One of the Franceschina servants. Clearly no friend of his master's, though. Realized straight away what we were talking about, and told us da Correggio was sodden with opium and grappa much of the time and was asking for trouble. He said that he thought his master was selling the opium, too – not just taking the stuff himself.'

Agostino puts his head in his hands. 'Oh *cielo*! I knew it! It's all my fault!'

'What?'

'I chose to take us all to the home of an immoral reprobate. It's all my fault.'

'Don't be silly, Ago, how could you possibly have known?'

Everyone – Sofia perhaps most vocally – hurries to reassure Agostino, and Cosima changes the subject. 'Tell us more about this plan you hatched, Sofia.' She has perched herself on Agostino's lap. 'How did it work?'

Feeling everyone's eyes on her, Sofia says, 'Well, it seemed like the only chance I could possibly get of confronting whoever killed that man. I thought that if I could write it into a speech and try to . . . oh, I don't know . . . *flush them out*, make them feel guilty . . . I hoped that perhaps I'd be able to see it – *see* their reaction. I meant to describe the awfulness of it – the fact that someone actually did it. You know – that they picked up a great lump of metal like that, and actually hit it against a man's head.' She swallows. 'I thought it would shame whoever it was into reacting. I wanted to see someone gasping, looking shocked, reacting in some way that'd be obvious.' Stopping again, she puffs a resigned little laugh in her nose. 'It was stupid, really, wasn't it? I mean . . . to think that whoever it was would happen to have been there – watching me. On that very day.'

'I'm glad you did it,' Beppe says. 'If you hadn't, I wouldn't have found you, would I? Not so easily, anyway. And you nudged that servant into telling us what he knew.'

'I suppose so.'

Lidia smiles as Sofia lays her head on Beppe's shoulder.

Looking at her now, returning the smile, Sofia can see that there is a new fullness in Lidia's face, a soft pink in her cheeks, and, although it is hard to see from where she is sitting, it occurs to Sofia that Lidia's front-fastening bodice seems to be slightly looser-laced than before. Catching at her lower lip with her teeth, she wonders if these tiny changes signify what she thinks they might.

Vico has stopped playing his guitar. He is frowning at something to one side of her with his brow furrowed. Catching her eye, he holds her gaze for a second, then looks at Beppe. Some sort of understanding seems to pass between them, for Beppe nods briefly – though to what he is agreeing, Sofia has no idea at all.

'And tell us more about how you managed to get yourself onto that stage, Beppe,' Agostino continues, boomingly cheerful once more. 'Was it a total shock when you turned round and saw him, Sofia?'

'No – not when I *saw* him. The shock didn't come till I heard him speak.'

'How did you do it, Beppe? How did you come to be there?'

Beppe squeezes Sofia against him. 'I heard those boys up on the stage, like I told you, and I couldn't imagine who else they could have been talking about. I was on my way around to the back, to find which wagon Sofia and the others were in, when I saw him. Simone da Bologna. He was coming out of one of the carts. I recognized him from all those years ago, when I first saw the Gelosi back in Bergamo.'

'Then what?'

'I stopped him. "I'm looking for a girl called Sofia Genotti," I said.'

'What did he say?'

Beppe kisses the side of Sofia's head. 'He looked as though he was ready to punch my lights out, to be honest.' He demonstrates Simone's reactions as he describes them. 'His eyes narrowed . . . and his mouth pursed up tight . . . and he just said, "Who are you?" So I told him. Told him everything. Told him how long I'd been looking. Told him how desperate I was. Told him what I'd heard the little boys on the stage say – about the new material Sofia had suggested.'

'Was the idea of the substitution his or yours?' Vico asks.

'Mine. He was all for an immediate reunion. As soon as I said I'd been searching for Sofia for days, Simone suggested taking me back into the wagon right there and then, but I said no.'

'Why?' This from a furrowed-browed Cosima.

'I don't really know. I suppose . . . oh, you'll laugh . . . but . . .'

'What?'

Beppe shrugs. 'I'm a performer, aren't I? I can't help it. I just knew it would work on the stage, and it seemed right.'

Everyone laughs.

'Simone loved the plan. He said he would change the instructions he was giving Sofia, and that he'd tell her it would be funnier if she stared out front while pouring her heart out, and that Arlecchino would pretend to be bored behind her. He gave me the lines.'

Sofia is smiling now. 'Simone made me promise not to turn around.' She puts on Simone's voice. '*Far more amusing to the audience if you're totally unaware of him not listening behind you.*'

'But what she *didn't* know was that Simone gestured out at the audience to keep silent.' Beppe puts a finger to his lips now. 'Then he tiptoed off stage completely. He stripped off, I put on the costume – which didn't fit very well, I can tell you – and I crept back on in his place. No idea if the audience noticed the change of actor.'

Sofia says, 'When I turned around and he was sitting there, drumming his fingers on his knees and looking the very picture of boredom, I just presumed it was Simone. Why would I not? I thought that the audience's laughter had been because he had been fooling about behind my back.'

'And then . . . ?'

'And then he spoke. And I knew straight away. And it was as though I'd stopped knowing how to breathe.'

Beppe pulls her in tightly again and kisses her cheek. The softest murmur of appreciation passes around the various members of the Coraggiosi.

'But,' Agostino says proudly, 'but like a true and consummate actor, you carried on with the scene, and the audience were none the wiser that you were all but poleaxed.'

'She did indeed,' Beppe says. 'She was wonderful.'

'And you, Niccolò,' Agostino says now, and everyone turns to look at him. 'Without you, none of this would have come to pass, am I not right?'

Niccolò smiles. 'No, not me – it was my lovely daughter. It was Anna's idea that Sofia should go back.'

'But you came with her.'

'Of course. How could I have sat there and let her go back on her own?'

Agostino says, 'Do you know, if I did not have the very lovely Cosima upon my knee at this moment, I would stand and declare that you, Niccolò Zanetti, are now even more than an *honorary* member of the Coraggiosi. You are ... a ... oh *cielo*, I cannot think of a proud enough term. Help me out, someone!'

'Ha! The great and verbose Agostino Martinelli is lost for words! That has to say something about the immensity of his pronouncement, don't you reckon, Niccolò?' Federico says, grinning.

'I'd say Niccolò should be awarded the title of "*Fundamental* Member of the Coraggiosi",' Beppe says.

'Perfect, Beppe, perfect.' Agostino smiles widely. 'Cosima, my love, on your feet for a moment.'

Cosima stands.

Getting to his feet too, Agostino raises his glass. 'Signor Niccolò Zanetti: Fundamental Member of the Coraggiosi!'

Everyone takes a mouthful from their cup or glass and repeats Agostino's words. Niccolò's colour deepens dramatically.

Looking suddenly more serious, Agostino leans towards where Niccolò is sitting. 'Why don't you stay with us, Nicco? Travel with us? Don't go back to Faenza. You could set up stall wherever we stop and play and ... '

The rest of his sentence is lost in the babble of responses from everyone else, agreeing, exhorting Niccolò to consent, proclaiming the good sense of the suggestion. Niccolò raises both hands and the troupe falls silent.

'Agostino – all of you – I am truly honoured by your suggestion.'

'Will you come? Come with us? It's new territory – down here, down south – it'll take time to build up the audiences again, but. . .'

'We may be back in Emilia-Romagna, don't forget, Ago,' Vico says. 'Like Sofia said just now. The Andreinis are doing their best to have the banishment rescinded – that's what you said, isn't it?'

'Yes. They're performing at the Castello Estense any day now, and they are going to put it to the duke himself.'

'The duke himself? Oh dear God, that would be a gift from the heavens,' Agostino says, shaking his head. 'But wherever we are touring, Niccolò, we would like you to be with us. What do you say – will you come?'

Niccolò draws in a long breath, holds it . . . then nods. 'Very well. I will. I'll have to send word to Anna – but I'll do it. I'll come with you.'

Everyone claps.

Sofia looks around at the firelit faces of the members of the troupe. Their happy camaraderie – which she feared had been quite lost, immediately after her release from incarceration – is perhaps more vividly present here tonight than she has seen it before and everyone seems uncomplicatedly happy.

Everyone?

Glancing around again, this time more quickly, she sees that Angelo has slid away – yet again, as he has done on so many occasions, he has absented himself. She is about to point out his disappearance to Beppe, when Vico puts his guitar on the ground and leans over towards them.

'Beppe,' he mutters. 'Can we talk? Now?'

His smile has vanished and the seriousness of his expression, at odds with the joviality of the evening, suggests trouble; Sofia, looking from him to Beppe and back, is suddenly fearful. She sees Beppe nod. He starts to stand. She grips his hand. 'Can I come with you?'

Beppe looks back at Vico, eyebrows raised in question. Vico nods, jerking his head towards a deeper patch of shadow beneath a clump of beech trees. Arm around Lidia's shoulders, he sets off, with Beppe and Sofia close behind.

40

Sofia glances back over her shoulder. From here, in the deeper shadows of the trees, the still-burning brazier stands out brightly, and the near sides of the wagons are blocks of bright flickering colour in the otherwise dark blue night. Thick clouds are obscuring the moon and there is a velvety quality to the darkness. She can see little of her companions out here, other than faint silvery highlights along the edges of their faces and limbs and the odd gleam in an eye. Those few leaves still remaining on the beech branches have crisped and curled, and they are rustling softly overhead now, as though, Sofia thinks, they are whispering between them, curious about what might be transpiring below.

'Did you see his face just now?' Vico says.

'What – Angelo's?'

'Who else? Listen.' Vico hesitates before he speaks. 'As Sofia described her plan, I was watching him. He was following every word, even if he wasn't looking at her – and that in itself says something, doesn't it? Everyone else's eyes were on you, Sofia, except his – he was staring over at the horses.'

Sofia does not know what to say.

Vico continues. 'He might not have been *looking* at you, but he was definitely *listening*: his expression kept changing as you were speaking – and when you said whatever it was you said about the candlestick and what happened to that man, he winced. He really winced, and swallowed uncomfortably. He coloured up, and something odd shifted in his eyes – I can't describe it, but I could see him clearly and I know I'm not mistaken.'

Beppe chews at his lip for a second before saying: 'Are you accusing him, then?'

A long pause.

'Yes.'

'Of the murder?'

'Yes.'

'There's no proof.'

'No. I know.'

'He might just have been upset by the description.'

'I know.'

'What makes you so sure?'

'Several things. It's starting to knit together. That little brown bottle I found in his bag, and his reaction when I asked about it. What you've just said about that piece of scum, Sebastiano da Correggio, and his fondness for opium, and his selling the stuff. It fits, doesn't it?'

Beppe frowns. 'I suppose so. But . . . Angelo was the one who went out of his way to get Sofia released. Why would he have done that if he was guilty of the murder? Wouldn't it have been safer for him to leave her locked up for it if he'd done it?'

'You heard what he said, when we talked about that before,' Vico says, shaking his head. 'He said he knew she wasn't guilty. Said that he didn't like to think of someone innocent being punished.' He pauses. 'That fits, doesn't it? Guilt getting the better of him?'

Beppe sucks in a shocked breath. 'Oh my God,' he says in a slow whisper.

'What?' Sofia is staring up at him, wide-eyed. 'What is it?'

Beppe shakes his head. 'No, it can't be – not after all this time.'

'Beppe?'

'I think you may be right,' Beppe says, pushing the fingers of one hand up into his hair, making it stand on end. 'I think guilt *may* have got the better of him.'

'What do you mean? What are you saying?'

Beppe draws in a long, shivering breath. 'I don't want to go into details now . . . but I do think you may be right.'

Everyone is staring at him. Sofia takes one of his hands in both her own.

Gripping her fingers, running his tongue along his lip, Beppe says, slowly, 'Do you know – I think Fosca might get it out of him.'

Vico whistles.

Lidia draws in a breath.

Not understanding, Sofia looks from Beppe to Vico. 'Who's Fosca?' she says.

After a pause, Beppe says, 'Someone extraordinary, who has a way of goading the guilty into revealing their inner thoughts.'

'I don't understand.'

Beppe explains and Sofia listens, frowning with concentration. 'So you intend to surprise him with it?' she says. 'Angelo? Actually in a performance? Unrehearsed?'

'Best way, I'd say.'

'When?' Lidia says, sounding concerned. 'Beppe, we can't afford to jeopardize any—'

Vico interrupts her. 'Agostino's fixed up a show at a big house near Borgo San Lorenzo next week. Some rich merchant with more money than he knows what to do with. God knows who. I think Fosca might be able to make an appearance there.'

'Which *scenario*?' Beppe asks.

'Ago's basing it on Flaminio Scala's *The Just Punishment* – which seems highly appropriate, don't you think?'

Sofia hears Beppe snort a soft laugh in his nose.

'But,' Vico continues, 'he's writing a few new elements even as we speak, so the final plot will be something new – different from the original. Just right for introducing our friend Fosca to the proceedings at the last minute, I would say.'

'I agree,' Beppe says. 'Just right.'

'Don't say anything to Ago or Cosima, or the others – any of you. I'll let him know what he needs to know – but at the last minute.' Vico sounds almost angry, Sofia thinks. Reaching out, she slips her fingers into Beppe's palm and he squeezes her hand.

'Not a word.' Beppe puts an arm around Sofia's shoulders. 'Let's get back.' With his mouth close to Sofia's ear, he says, 'Nicco offered to sleep in the yellow wagon with Giovanni Battista and Federico tonight. Said we could have his cart.'

Sofia turns her face quickly towards Beppe's and kisses his mouth.

'This, my friends, is the beginning of the conquest of our new territories!' Agostino explains over welcome bowls of bread, ricotta and honey the next morning. 'In the face of rank injustice, bigoted authoritarianism and unreasoned accusation, we have bade farewell to the familiar landscape of Emilia-Romagna, we have crossed the mountains in our bid to flee from those who no longer care for our expertise, and we stand now, trembling in anticipation, up to our ankles in the shallows of the unknown, like Amerigo Vespucci on the shores of the New World.'

Several people, their hands too busy with their breakfast to applaud and their mouths too full to cheer, tink their spoons against the sides of their bowls in appreciation of Agostino's enthusiasm. Untidily swallowing a mouthful of his ricotta, Vico whistles.

Niccolò catches Sofia's eye and winks.

'We begin to rehearse *The Just Punishment* in earnest this morning,' Agostino continues, in a rather more prosaic voice. 'Now that Beppe and Sofia are back with us—'

More tinking of spoons.

'—we must put all our efforts into perfecting *The Just Punishment*. We've performed it before and we did it well, and we'll do it justice now. I've written a couple of new speeches – Federico: one for you, and Cosima and Angelo: a dialogue for the pair of you – but otherwise, it's pretty much as it was.' Agostino turns to Sofia and draws in a long breath. 'It feels quite momentous, beginning work on a Flaminio Scala play, when you've performed on stage in his presence. Actually on stage with him.'

'Beppe did too,' Sofia says. 'When he substituted for Simone.'

Beppe laughs. 'Ha! If you remember, as soon as I heard Scala's footsteps coming up on to the stage, I called him a pompous windbag and said we ought to get away as fast as possible, and we scarpered, didn't we?'

Agostino still looks awed. 'But, nonetheless, you shared a stage. If only for a fraction of a second.'

'If you like.'

Shaking his head as though in wonder, Agostino tuts his tongue against his teeth, his eyes momentarily unfocused. Then, puffing out a breath and standing up, he points his spoon at the troupe and says, 'Right! That's enough of that! On your feet, all of you! We have a great deal to do!'

'And the four of us have still more, which will have to wait until after the rehearsal,' Beppe mutters to Sofia, Vico and Lidia. 'Fosca needs to be properly woken up and told what he has to achieve.' Turning to Sofia, he adds, 'He's apt to misbehave, if you don't treat him with enough respect.'

'Isn't his misbehaviour just what we're after?' Vico says quietly. 'Let's take ourselves off after the rehearsal. We need to plan this carefully.'

'We do indeed. I have it pretty clear in my mind what we need to do.'

'Where shall we go?' Sofia asks, turning from Beppe to Vico and back.

'Good question. It's too cold now to sit out.'

'I could ask Nicco for the little cart.'

Beppe nods. 'Perfect. Tell him . . .' He considers.

'Tell him the truth?' Sofia suggests.

Beppe, Vico and Lidia all stare at her for a second, then Beppe says, 'Yes. Tell him the truth.'

A mile or so away down the road, Beppe steers Nicco's cart off the track and onto a flat piece of waste ground. 'Here will do as well as anywhere,' he says, pulling Violetta to a stop under a tree, knotting the reins and draping the resultant loop over a peg on the side of the cart. Picking a net full of hay from under the seat, he hangs it on a low branch and Violetta begins at once to tear the contents from it, shaking her head when wisps catch on the mesh as she pulls.

Sofia jumps down from where she has been sitting beside him

up front, while Vico and Lidia climb out of the covered space at the back.

'So, Niccolò wasn't surprised when you told him what we think?' Vico asks.

Beppe shakes his head. 'No. He just nodded – sort of screwing up his mouth as though sad that he'd had the same thoughts himself.'

'And he thinks it's a good idea to introduce Fosca into the proceedings?'

'His exact words? He said it was *a stroke of genius* . . .'

'Good, so let's—' Vico begins to speak, but Beppe interrupts. 'I think you'll want to know what else he said.' He pauses.

Vico and Lidia are frowning curiously, but Sofia, having been told this already, holds her breath, feeling her heartbeat high in her chest.

'I told him what you'd said about the contents of that little brown bottle, and the way Angelo had snatched it from you that time – and he looked badly shocked. He says he thinks . . .'

'What?'

' . . . that it's something called laudanum.'

Vico whistles, but Lidia says, 'What's laudanum?'

'Opium,' Beppe says, and Lidia gasps. Beppe nods. 'Yes, exactly. But – so Nicco told me – it's opium in a new form, which some man in Switzerland invented a few years ago, to use to treat pain more efficiently. Made from opium, crushed pearls, musk, amber and saffron, he said, and a number of other things I can't remember, dissolved in alcohol. Nicco says that he's heard it works really well, though he's only ever come across it once before . . . but because it's so strong, he says, people have started taking it for the wrong reasons. I think this must be what Sebastiano da Correggio has been selling.'

'Crushed pearls . . .' Sofia says quietly to herself.

He says, 'It was the smell that proved it to Nicco, I think. When I told him what you'd said the contents of that bottle smelled like, Vico, his mouth opened and he said that, given how Angelo had reacted, he was fairly certain that's what it was in there. Nicco says once someone has started using it, this laudanum, they'll do . . . almost anything . . . to keep up the supply.'

'Almost anything?' Lidia says softly.

'Exactly.'

'So – should Fosca know about it? About the laudanum?' Vico says.

Beppe nods. 'Oh yes, definitely. And, now you come to mention him, I think now is probably as good a time as any for Sofia to meet our friend Signor Fosca, now we're away from the others.'

Vico and Lidia murmur their agreement.

Looking around, wondering where this new person is supposed to be coming from, Sofia sees Beppe reaching back up into the cart. He grabs his leather bag. Turning his back on the others, he opens the drawstrings and pulls from it firstly a black object that appears to be a hat, then something else she cannot properly see. She sees him duck his head; then, straightening, he pulls on the hat: another black woollen hat, but taller and stiffer than Arlecchino's – quite a different shape.

He turns to look at them then and Sofia gasps aloud, putting her hands over her mouth.

Almost the whole of Beppe's face has been covered by what looks like a decaying skull. Bone-white and cracked, the face has two expressionless black eyeholes and small elongated pits for nostrils. Only his mouth is showing and now he speaks, in a voice Sofia has never heard him use. The Bergamo lilt that she loves has gone; this accent is cold and hard, an aristocratic Venetian, and there is a rasp to it that seems to suck the very life out of the air around them. The hairs rise up on the back of her neck and along her forearms.

'Signorina,' the creature says. Sofia finds she cannot think of it as Beppe.

She does not answer.

'I think we have come close to meeting, more than once.'

Sofia stares, still silent.

Fosca comes up to stand close behind her. She does not turn around. He leans out to one side of her and whispers into her ear. 'On those days when you feared for your life, signorina, are you aware that I was just around the corner, waiting for you?' He pauses, then, laying a hand on each of her shoulders, he says, 'I so hoped you'd come.'

Not daring to move, Sofia remains facing forwards. She glances at Lidia and Vico; Vico raises an eyebrow, but other than this, neither of them moves or speaks.

'I was badly disappointed,' Fosca says. 'We must make a more binding arrangement to meet next time. And that next time must be soon.' He runs a finger down one of her cheeks.

Sofia's heart is racing now. This is Beppe – her sweet, funny, familiar Beppe. But here, in this mask, using this voice, he is frightening her. She swallows uncomfortably.

Then Beppe strides around to stand in front of her. Puffing out a breath, he pushes the mask up onto the top of his head and the hat falls to the ground behind him. 'There you are,' he says in his normal voice, crouching to pick it up. 'That's Fosca.'

Sofia does not know what to say.

'He's not the most comfortable of companions, really, is he?'

'What is ...? When did ...? Did you *invent* him?' Sofia is struggling to find her words, so unnerved has she been by what has just occurred.

'No. He's part of the tradition. Doesn't often make an appearance, though. He hasn't turned up in a Coraggiosi play for years. The mask was made for me by a man in Napoli, years ago. I've only used it a couple of times.'

Still unsure how to react, Sofia finds herself staring up at the mask, now perched jauntily on the top of Beppe's untidy head. He sees her gaze and, reaching up and pulling it off, hands it to her. She takes it gingerly, holding it at arm's length, as though she expects it to speak to her again from within her grasp. It seems to have been formed, like the other masks, from thick leather, moulded and shaped to sit comfortably on an actor's face. Two real teeth have been inserted into the leather to sit above the wearer's upper lip.

'Isn't Ago going to be angry if we just throw this new material into a finished performance, in front of a paying patron?' Lidia asks now, and Sofia looks up from her contemplation of the death mask.

Beppe hesitates. 'Yes, I suppose he might be.' Lidia opens her mouth to reply, but Beppe interrupts. 'Would you rather we didn't do it?'

Vico answers for her. 'Of course we're going to do it. If Angelo killed that man, we need to know, don't we?'

'But what if he didn't?' Sofia asks.

They all turn and stare at her. Beppe nods. 'Mmm. There's always the chance that we're wrong.' Frowning, he pauses for a moment, then says, 'Fosca just needs to phrase things carefully, so it's not a direct accusation.'

Lidia seems determined to consider every possible problem. 'What about the others, though? Whether Angelo is guilty or not, how are we going to prevent the whole show breaking down?'

'Oh, don't worry about that – we're all capable improvisers, aren't we? Look at Sofia – the least experienced of all of us, and she managed to keep going on that stage when I turned up and left her almost speechless. Unexpected things have happened in performances before, haven't they? Remember that pig in Ravenna?'

The stage is set. The banqueting room at the merchant's large villa in Borgo San Lorenzo is wide and long, low-ceilinged, with deep, brightly painted parallel beams like the vividly coloured ribs of some giant creature. The walls are lined in bright tapestries, rushes cover the wooden floor, and dozens of dribbling candles are filling the room with a shifting yellow light. The three dozen or so members of the audience – seated nobles, and servants standing in groups at the sides of the room – are eagerly awaiting the start of the performance and an anticipatory hum of murmured conversation is filling the air. Sofia, who has peeped out at them from behind the backdrop, is anxious, reminded all too forcefully of the scene at Franceschina moments before the start of that ill-fated show. Their host here, though, is a very different prospect to Sebastiano da Correggio: heavy-bellied, grey-haired, red-faced and widely smiling, the wealthy merchant is sitting in the front seats with his equally plump wife and their several children, beaming out at his guests, gesticulating and pointing out features of the stage with a thick forefinger, clearly delighted at the prospect of the evening's entertainment.

'Oh God, Beppe, I hope we are doing the right thing,' she mutters as Beppe, standing beside her, runs his finger down the pinned *canovaccii*.

He does not reply directly, just says, 'Look, there – remember this. It'll be just after *that* moment there . . . ' He points to one of the scraps of paper. ' . . . just after Vico has crept away from

Cosima and Angelo, and just before you and I are due back on for this scene here, look.'

Sofia nods. Her chalked and pearled face is itching again, but she resists the temptation to scratch.

'It'll just be you on the stage with Cosima and Angelo, then Cosima will go off *there*, see, to find Vico, and I'll be there, ready in Fosca's mask and hat and a long black coat. Vico won't need to be on stage until *then*' – a finger on the relevant scrap – 'and he'll be waiting behind the backcloth to come on and react to Fosca's announcement.'

Agostino appears, costumed, his face now thickly white-painted. 'All ready?' he says cheerfully.

Sofia swallows awkwardly as she assures him that she is looking forward to the start of the performance.

'Not too anxious – after last time?'

'Just a little.'

'Good, good. *Just a little* is just what we want – a performance is never as good without that flutter of fear in the belly beforehand, I always say, don't I, Beppe?'

'You do – and you're quite right.'

Appearing from the room behind, Federico nods to Agostino. 'Shall I blow the trumpet? Are we all ready?'

'Yes, I think so, don't you?'

Federico smiles, then slips out between the two halves of the backdrop. Sofia hears the reedy notes of his trumpet, heralding the beginning of the play. As they have done each time, her insides begin to squirm.

Beppe squeezes her hand. 'All will be well,' he says, bending and planting a swift kiss on the top of her head.

Cosima and Lidia are there, ready to go on with Sofia. Cosima is as beautiful as ever in one of her most sumptuous dresses, mended and rebeaded by Sofia last night; Lidia looks pink-cheeked and pretty, and Sofia wonders again – if only momentarily – about the reason for the slight thickening of her friend's waist.

Over to one side stands Angelo. A muscle is twitching in his jaw, and he is chewing at his lower lip, but otherwise he is still and silent, his arms hanging by his sides. Sofia looks at his hands, wondering. Are those hands guilty of what she and the others believe them to be? Angelo glances up and meets her gaze; she looks away quickly, glad that the flush of colour she can feel rising will be hidden by the chalk and the pearl.

The fanfare dies away.

'Come on, off we go,' Cosima whispers. Pushing aside the hanging, she walks out onto the stage, already in conversation with Lidia. Sofia trots behind, a small basket in one hand.

'*I cannot deny that you are still beautiful,*' Angelo says to Cosima.

'*And I cannot deny that your charm would – still – bewitch an angel.*'

'*But it has to be said . . .*'

'*That I curse the very day . . .*' Cosima points an accusatory finger, her face set as though she has a mind to spit at him.

'*The very day?*'

'*That I set eyes upon you.*'

'*What use is beauty . . .*' Angelo sneers the words.

'*If it is tainted with lies?*'

'*Stained with falsehood?*'

'*Defaced by deceit!*'

'*You have proved yourself false,*' Angelo says dismissively, and Cosima rounds on him.

'*I will not stay a moment longer—*'

'*If you won't stay, then go!*'

'*Do not expect to see me again . . .*' Cosima says in a voice of deadly quiet. Chin tilted high, she spins on one slipper-shod foot and, flipping aside the backdrop, disappears from the stage. Sofia can hear the audience shifting in their seats and murmuring to each other.

Angelo turns to her. '*And what are you staring at, signorina?*' he says. Knowing what is about to happen, Sofia draws out the pause before she speaks.

'*I'm staring at a man who has little idea what consequences his actions are about to pull down upon his head,*' she says, and Angelo's frown of incomprehension is genuine. This is a line he has not once heard in rehearsal. '*Deceit and falsehood are sinister companions,*' Sofia says now. '*Once they have been invited to spend time with a man, that man will often find that they are reluctant to part company with him – and they frequently invite other, even less welcome, friends to join them. It can end up as quite a crowd.*'

The hangings move behind her as she speaks, and a figure in a long black coat and hat slips out, keeping his back to the audience. He sidles along towards where Sofia and Angelo are facing each other, then turns around slowly so that he stands a little behind and to one side of Sofia, facing Angelo. Sofia hears a gasp ripple through the audience and knows, even though she cannot fully see, that Fosca's masked face has shocked them.

Death is a constant near neighbour to all of us, after all, she thinks. He is feared and disliked – dreaded – and his unexpected appearance in such a guise on a stage is unsettling. Even she is unnerved by Beppe as Fosca, and she was expecting his appearance.

Angelo's mouth has dropped open and his eyes are wide.

'*You seem surprised to see me, signore,*' Fosca says, his voice a hard, aristocratic drawl to match Angelo's own.

Angelo does not reply.

'*Though by rights you should have been expecting me, should you not?*'

The uncomprehending frown deepens between Angelo's brows.

'*You've been playing me at my own game, haven't you? Doing it for years, so I've been told.*'

'I don't know what you mean.'

'I'm *the one who decides when someone is at the end of his allotted span, am I not? I'm the one – the only one – who has been given the liberty of creeping up behind a man unannounced . . .* ' Fosca moves stealthily around to stand behind Angelo, bent-kneed, each foot placed slowly and silently. He lowers his voice to a piercing hiss. '*. . . yes, unannounced. It is I who have the right to whisper to him that his time has come, and to tell him that he should accompany me.*' He shakes his head and, taking a handful of Angelo's hair, pulls his head a little backwards. 'I *should be doing that. Not you.*'

Angelo's mouth opens slightly wider as his head tilts back.

'*It's far easier to end a life by omission than by action, do you not think?*' Fosca says in a voice of silk. '*I do it often. I frequently, for example, stand by and watch as a man gasps his last, when I know that a simple draught might have saved him. And on a number of occasions I have watched as a man has been put to death, when a mere word in the right ear could have prevented it. Has such a thing ever happened to you?*'

Fosca's face is close to Angelo's now; he is holding Angelo's head in against his in a parody of a lover's embrace, his mouth next to Angelo's cheek, his fingers in Angelo's hair. Sofia can see from where she is standing that Angelo is trembling.

Pointing out across the audience now, his arm stretching out over Angelo's shoulder, Fosca says, '*Imagine the scene . . . a man . . . let's call him a cook . . . is accused of a murder he did not commit. He is dragged to the gibbet, protesting his innocence, sobbing out his terror at the thought of ... of meeting* me ... ' Fosca smiles out at the audience, who are motionless and silent. '*What would you do, signore? You know he's innocent. You have the power to stop what is happening. But you ... say nothing, fancying yourself, perhaps, as Fosca's apprentice? Was that what it was? Is that what happened that day? You fancied yourself my apprentice?*'

The audience murmurs at this.

'I don't know what you—'

'*Oh, I think you do.*' Fosca pauses.

The audience waits in breath-held silence.

Then, releasing his hold, Fosca strides back towards Sofia, who, as Colombina, shrinks away from him, her hands clasped in front of her mouth, her eyes wide with fear – a fear that is not altogether counterfeit. Fosca eyes her for a moment with the blank, dead eye-sockets, then appears to dismiss her.

Angelo's gaze is fixed upon the grotesque death mask.

Staring at Angelo now, Fosca moves backwards down to the front of the stage. There is a shifting in the audience as he comes closer – a drawing back – then a gasp as he spins round and stares from one individual to another. Crouching on his heels, he leans precariously out towards those people closest to the stage; then, swinging down from the trestles, he steps forwards towards the front row.

'*Oh yes, nearly time for this one to come with me,*' he says, grinning and ruffling the hair of a big man with sparse, greying hair seated near the host's family. '*Won't be long now, chick.*'

The man stiffens, saying nothing. His friends laugh nervously, but his own face remains stolidly unsmiling.

'*And you, signore, I'll be back for you before long,*' Fosca croons to another greying man in a finely embroidered doublet, running a hand around the curve of his jaw, then patting his cheek. '*Once I've dealt with our friend back there. Him first, I think, given the liberties he's been taking.*'

He vaults back onto the stage in one swift movement, and the audience gasps again. Pushing a hand into a deep pocket, he pulls out a small brown glass bottle. '*See this?*' he says, holding it high to show it to the audience. '*See this? Oblivion in a bottle, this is. A liquid counterfeit of the pleasures of my company. And he*' – he points back towards Angelo – '*has come to rely on it. A little too much.*'

Angelo's mouth has opened in outrage, though he says nothing.

Fosca continues: '*Be assured, signori and signore, that desire for that oblivion grows by what it feeds on.*' He throws the little bottle high and catches it neatly one-handed. '*It grows to be irresistible in the end. Quite irresistible.*' Striding back to Angelo, he moves around behind him again, and speaks into his ear. '*And the things one will do when desire has become . . . irresistible . . . can be very terrible, can they not, signore?*'

Again, Angelo says, 'I don't know what you mean.'

Fosca crosses to where Sofia is still standing, hands clasped, eyes wide. He moves to stand directly behind her. '*Imagine, signore, that this little girl here was standing in between me and the realization of my desires. How might I dispose of her as an obstacle, do you think?*' He places a hand on each of Sofia's shoulders. Running them down her arms, he grips hard around the crooks of her elbows and lifts. Sofia's feet leave the ground. She squeals. '*Pick her up and dump her elsewhere?*' He puts her down. '*I think not.*'

'What the hell is this—' Angelo begins, but Fosca ignores him.

Pulling a long length of fine dark-coloured lawn out from under his coat, he wraps it tightly around Sofia's body. '*Cocoon her in silk like a spider's supper and send her spinning off into nowhere?*' He flaps at one end of the lawn, and Sofia staggers a little, turning around and around as it unwinds. '*No, I don't think so.*'

Then, bending into the shadows at the edge of the stage, where the backcloth touches the trestle boards, Fosca picks up a candlestick. Holding it high above Sofia's head, he says, '*Or how about this?*' He swings it around and feints a downward lunge with it and several people in the audience shout out their shock. Sofia screws up her eyes and hunches her shoulders in anticipation, but Fosca pulls up short before the candlestick strikes her skull. He spins it and holds it up on the tips of the fingers of one hand. '*That would work, would it not?*' he says. '*A quick and easy way to rid oneself of a problem one had come to despise . . . ?*'

Angelo's face has drained of all colour. 'I'm not staying here to listen to this,' he says, turning to leave the stage.

Fosca shakes his head. '*Go if you will, signore. But I'll find you when I want you, don't worry. I always do.*'

Angelo pushes his way untidily through the gap in the hangings and disappears to a spatter of applause from the audience. Even as he leaves, Vico appears, apparently unconcerned, whistling and walking jauntily with his hands pushed deep into his pockets. Seeing Fosca, he starts wildly, leaping backwards with a strangled yelp of shock, and rolling onto his backside. The audience laughs nervously.

'*Oh my dear heavens!*' he says.

Fosca chuckles. '*Don't worry, little man,*' he says. '*I'm not expecting your company any time soon.*' He turns to Sofia. '*Or yours, chick.*' Bowing low, he adds, '*We'll see each other again one day – but not for a while.*' He blows her a kiss. '*In the meantime, I have a nobleman to find. If you will both excuse me . . .*' Picking up the candlestick, which appears surprisingly light, he balances it on the tip of a forefinger for a second, then tucks it under one arm, bowing equally low out towards the audience. They cheer loudly as he leaves, clearly relieved at his departure.

The flush of bewildered anger on Agostino's face is visible even under the thick white paint; an ugly, pinkish stain has spread across both cheeks. As Beppe appears behind the backdrop and starts stripping off Fosca's mask, hat and coat, and reaching for Arlecchino's diamond-patterned jacket, he rounds on him.

'What the hell are you doing, Beppe? What in God's name is going on out there?'

'We couldn't tell you beforehand, Ago—'

Agostino jabs his fingers into his hair, clutching at a clump near the top of his scalp. 'Why? Why not? What on earth—?'

Beppe drops his voice and leans in close to Agostino. 'He did it, Ago. We're sure he killed da Correggio. We wanted Fosca to frighten him into admitting it.'

'What? How do—? What in heaven's name makes you th—? But—' Agostino can do no more than splutter. He glances at the scenario board. 'Oh, for God's sake, I'm due on in a moment. There are ...' He checks the board more carefully. '... four *canovaccii* to go. The moment we've finished, Beppe, I want a proper explanation.' He points an accusatory forefinger at him. 'The very moment. And where the hell is Angelo? He's due on in a second.'

Angelo elbows past Beppe, without looking at him. 'I know when I'm due on, thank you, Agostino,' he says, and his voice cracks as he speaks. 'And I'll be on stage exactly when I'm needed, no thanks to that fucking Bergamese peasant there.' Glaring at Beppe, he hesitates for a moment, breathing slowly though an open mouth, then he climbs the ladder up to the space behind the back-cloth.

41

The large and florid merchant embraces Agostino, then Cosima, then Sofia and Lidia in turn. He bows low to the other members of the troupe, his smile so wide it distorts his voice when he finally manages to speak. 'Oh my dears, that was a triumph! A triumph! I'm so very proud that we are the first household in the area to have succeeded in engaging such a . . .' He struggles to find the apposite word. '. . . such an *extraordinary* group of performers so soon after their arrival in the province. You will go on to great things in Toscana, I'm quite certain. Great things. And you performed here first!'

Agostino's smile of gratitude is equally wide and clearly heart-felt, though Sofia can see anxiety tautening his features. 'You are too generous, signore,' he says, bowing to the nobleman.

'Indeed I am not. Merely honest.' The merchant clears his throat. 'Now, you shall have a couple of rooms here in the villa in which to stay tonight, if you want them, and as much as you wish to eat and drink.'

Agostino opens his mouth to speak, but the merchant, frowning a little now, continues, this time with a note of apology in his voice. 'I do most earnestly beg your forgiveness, though ... I shall be unable to join you for your meal this evening. I had so very much hoped to do so, but I'm afraid another – far less enjoyable – commitment has arisen and is rudely demanding my presence.'

Agostino assures him that his absence, though of course regrettable, will not diminish their pleasure in the extremely generous hospitality he has offered them, and, amidst numerous bows, and smiles and handshakes and repeated paeans of praise, the merchant takes his leave, leaving the Coraggiosi in the care of three of his servants, who immediately show the troupe through to a large room at one end of which a vast fire is merrily blazing.

'Signori and signore, we shall return shortly with food,' the thinnest of the servants assures the Coraggiosi, backing out of the room with his two companions. 'Please make yourselves comfortable whilst you wait.'

As the door shuts behind the servants, Agostino turns to the troupe, and, with a frisson of anxiety, Sofia sees that the smile has quite faded from his face.

'We have much to discuss, I think,' he says. His voice is quiet, but it carries across the big room with ease.

Beppe puts an arm around Sofia's shoulders; she bends her arm up and links her fingers through his.

'Beppe,' Agostino says. 'Perhaps you would like to explain the changes you made to this evening's performance. And – *NO!*' His voice is suddenly thunderous. 'Angelo, you will *not* leave the room! You will stay and listen – and speak when it is time for you to do so. I think you may have much to say – and there may well be much from you that we shall want to hear.'

Looking around, Sofia sees that Angelo has frozen with one hand on the handle of the door through which the servants have just left. He releases his grip and slouches over to sit on a nearby cross-framed chair, arms folded tightly across his chest.

'Beppe, explain!'

Vico clears his throat and interrupts. 'Ago, it wasn't just Beppe. He had the idea of using Fosca only because of my suspicions. I began this.'

'Very well. But I'm waiting to hear anything – from *either* of you – that can *begin* to explain why you chose to jeopardize the success of such an important performance. You *knew* how vital this show was to our establishing a presence down here! You *knew* that word would spread quickly from here and that other potential patrons would undoubtedly hear from our host tonight about the quality of the play he commissioned.' Agostino wipes the back of his hand across his mouth. 'And yet you chose to ... to ... undermine one of the most important performers by hurling unrehearsed material at him in front of an audience. How *could* you? If it hadn't been for Angelo's level head, the show might have collapsed entirely!'

Beppe glances across at Vico. 'We had good reasons, Ago.'

'Explain them.'

And between the two of them, Beppe and Vico attempt to do just that.

As the story unfolds, Sofia, whose gaze is flicking from Beppe and Vico to Angelo and back, sees the latter losing colour and stiffening. His exquisitely proportioned face has rapidly become drawn and white, and a muscle is twitching in his jaw, deepening the hollow there. Every few seconds, he runs his tongue over his lips.

Agostino and the others listen to Beppe and Vico without a word: Agostino is stony-faced; Cosima tight-lipped and miserable; Federico is shaking his head and Giovanni Battista frowning with

432

bemusement. Niccolò is warily shifting his gaze from Agostino to Angelo and back, his expression set and taut.

'And', Beppe says, finishing his story, 'I suppose it was following on from Sofia's idea in Bologna – of creating a scene to flush the guilty party out by confronting them with their crimes – that I thought of Fosca.' He swallows uncomfortably. 'Fosca does that better than anyone. We knew we had no certain evidence, so we wanted to do something that would at least bring things out into the open, if not actually provide any proof.'

A long and very uncomfortable pause stretches out.

Agostino then opens his mouth to speak, but before he can utter a word, there is a knock at the door of the big chamber and the three servants come back in, smiling broadly and bearing trays laden with food.

Thanks are given, the servants' requests for the food to be served are politely refused, respectful bows are made and the servants leave the room once more.

Staring at the closed door for several seconds, Agostino hesitates, then turns to Angelo. 'Well?' he says. 'What do you have to say to all this?'

Angelo snorts. 'I don't have to answer to *them*.'

'Perhaps not,' Agostino says coldly, 'but, given my position as the head of the Coraggiosi, you *do* have to answer to *me*.' He glances across at Beppe, who is now hand in hand with Sofia on a low seat near the fire. 'What do you say to these charges, Angelo?'

'They're ridiculous.'

'Is there any basis of fact in anything these two have said? Anything at all?'

Angelo's pallor flushes dark. He says nothing.

'This opium?' Agostino says. 'What about that?'

'I'd rather not say.'

Agostino glares at him. 'Well, *I* would rather that you *did* say.'

'Well, then, yes. I have taken it – at least I've taken laudanum – in the past.' Angelo sounds defensive and irritable.

'The recent past?'

A sulky shrug is the only answer Agostino receives.

'And from where have you obtained it? From one particular source? Or a variety?'

There is something inexorable and irresistible about Agostino's voice and his unwavering stare. Watching, breath held and with heartbeat racing, Sofia sees Angelo's tightly set mouth twitch, sees the tip of a red tongue dart out to wet his lower lip and knows that he is about to reveal the truth.

'One in particular,' he says.

'Who was that?'

There is another long and painful pause. 'Sebastiano da Correggio.'

A soft intake of breath can be heard from everyone in the room.

Agostino waits a second or two, then says in a slow and expressionless voice, 'Angelo, did you have anything to do with that man's death?'

Turning his head away, Angelo stares hard at the floor. His arms are tightly folded in front of his chest and his shoulders have hunched as though to avoid a physical blow. He shrugs again.

'Tell us what happened.' Agostino's voice is now little more than a whisper, and his expression is terrible. Watching him now, Sofia thinks that it will certainly be something like this facing the recording angel; Angelo surely cannot refuse this steely demand for the truth.

He draws in a long breath, holds it for several seconds, then releases it in a puff. In a fast, clipped monotone he begins to speak. 'Sebastiano had a friend in Switzerland – a man who worked with an old apothecary called von Hohenheim. A few years ago this friend told him that von Hohenheim had invented a way of preserving opium in alcohol. It kills pain better than any other substance yet found.'

Everyone turns to look at Niccolò, who nods his agreement with this.

Angelo flicks a glance at Niccolò, then stares resolutely back at the rush-strewn floor. 'But it doesn't just kill pain.' Glancing up at Agostino, his eyes are burning. 'It makes you feel . . . oh God, it makes you feel . . . *released* . . . when you take it. Ecstatic. It's almost impossible to find in Italy – it's still practically unknown here – but Sebastiano knew this friend of von Hohenheim and he was able to receive regular deliveries.'

No one speaks or moves. All eyes are now on Angelo.

He shrugs and says, 'It was easy to start with, but, after a couple of times when I was late paying him, Sebastiano started to be difficult about dealing with me. Unpleasant, to be honest. I should have walked away from him – but . . . when you need the stuff as badly as . . . I . . . I mean . . . I didn't know how to stop.'

Beppe's grip on Sofia's hand tightens. Glancing up at him, she sees that his expression is easily as stony and angry as Agostino's.

'Just before we went to Franceschina,' Angelo continues, 'I saw da Correggio in Bologna, and he refused to allow me to take a promised delivery . . . without paying in full. I'd already told him I'd get all the money to him after the performance, once I'd been paid myself, but . . . but he took great delight in refusing, and packing me off out of his house like a scolded child. He said he'd give me what I wanted only when I'd handed over the money.'

Angelo pushes his fingers through his hair.

'Go on,' Agostino says.

Glancing at him, then dropping his gaze to the floor again,

Angelo says, 'He let me have one tiny bottle, part-full, to last me until I saw him again, but I tripped on the way back to the wagons and broke it and lost the contents, so when we arrived at Franceschina, I was pretty near desperate. I spoke to da Correggio and asked him for the bottles he'd promised me, but he was adamant. Said he didn't want to deal with me any more. He taunted me – he'd had a big delivery from Switzerland the day before, he told me, but he'd decided to keep it, and to sell it on to more . . . more . . . reliable payers. I couldn't bear the thought of doing without, though, so I . . . I suggested an alternative way of paying him. Something I thought would catch his attention. And it did.'

A log crumbles in the big fireplace, sending a shower of sputtering red out onto the rush-strewn hearth. Federico reaches out a foot and presses his heel down upon the tiny glowing specks.

Angelo glances at Sofia, but looks away quickly. 'I had seen him watching . . . watching Sofia earlier in the day. I'd seen how he was looking at her. It gave me an idea.' Angelo's voice is now almost inaudible and he is massaging one hand with the fingers of the other, pushing the ball of his thumb fiercely into the opposite palm. 'I suggested to him that I could . . . steer Sofia his way after the show. I think that was how I phrased it to him.'

Sofia's mouth drops open. Her skin is prickling and her lips feel cold. She seems to have forgotten how to blink, and her eyes quickly begin to sting as she stares at Angelo. Beppe mutters something she cannot hear. His hold on her hand is now so tight it is almost painful. She wriggles her fingers and he starts, glances at her, then lifts her hand to his mouth and kisses her knuckles.

Swallowing twice, Angelo pulls in a couple of long breaths before continuing. Other than his voice, the room is in total silence. 'Sebastiano seemed excited by the idea. He agreed that . . .

in return for an hour of Sofia's time, I could have a bottle.' He turns to Beppe. 'Obviously, I needed to get you out of the way, so I went out to the wagons . . . and . . . '

Beppe shakes his head slowly, and Sofia can hear him whispering, almost inaudibly, 'No – no, you can't have done . . . '

'I cut the dog. Cut its leg.'

Everyone in the room draws in a shocked breath. Cosima says, 'No!'

Beppe begins to rise to his feet, but Sofia grabs his wrist and he sits back down without a word.

'Once I'd done it, I let the dog out of the wagon and shooed it over towards the kitchen entrance of the castle. There were people there. I saw someone take hold of it and carry it indoors, then I went back to the banqueting hall and told you the animal had been injured.'

Memories of that evening, sharp as if they had happened an hour since, flood into Sofia's mind and her pulse races.

'Moments later,' Angelo says now, 'I saw da Correggio get up with Sofia's hand in his. I knew what was going to happen. I could have stopped it but I needed a dose so badly by then that I knew I wouldn't do anything that might jeopardize the deal.'

He stops, and breathes deeply for a few seconds.

'He and Sofia left the room, and before long the rest of us were all talking about going off up to the chambers we had been given, and sleeping. My mind was filled with pictures of what must be happening between Sofia and Sebastiano. Beppe came back in with the dog in his arms and asked where Sofia was. I didn't say – and nobody else knew. He left the room again straight away.'

Remembering her struggles with Correggio in his darkened study, Sofia shivers, feeling nauseous.

'Then, a few moments later, just as we were leaving the

banqueting room, Beppe came racing in saying that Sebastiano had gone for Sofia and that he – Beppe – had hit him and all but knocked him out. I panicked, terrified that I was not going to get the laudanum I had been promised. Sebastiano had not had his time with Sofia – and on top of this, he had been attacked by one of the troupe. I couldn't imagine he would agree to give it to me.' He winces. 'I suppose I shouldn't have gone anywhere near him, but – oh God! – I wanted that dose so badly by then, it was as though there was someone just behind me, goading me into doing it. Beppe was trying to get everyone out and I should have just gone too. But I didn't.'

He draws in a long breath and sighs it out again slowly.

'I ran off towards where Beppe said it had happened, and found the study with little difficulty. Sebastiano was there, just like Beppe had said, still sprawled on the floor, swearing foully and clutching his face. His nose was bleeding. I confronted him. "I've kept to my side of the bargain," I said. "It's not my fault things went wrong. You owe me what you promised. I'll help you upstairs, if that's where it is." He laughed at me. Sitting there in the dust on the floor, he laughed at me and said I was ... I was ... said I was pathetic. Said I couldn't even manage a simple pimping job without cocking it up, and that he wouldn't ever deal with me again.'

There are tears in Angelo's eyes now and his voice is shaking.

'He stood up, steadying himself against the bedpost, still laughing, then bent to pick up his doublet, which was on the floor. And ... I hit him. I did it without thinking. I was so angry with him, and so desperate. I picked up an iron candlestick from the table and swung it around and hit him with it. It caught him on the back of the head and he went down. There was a row of bottles on the table – I pulled a cork and sniffed to make sure it was what

I wanted, then grabbed what I could fit into my pockets . . . and ran.'

No one speaks for several minutes. The only sounds in the room are those from the softly crackling fire.

Angelo turns enormous eyes to Agostino. 'You wanted the truth, and you have had it. So: when will you be informing the authorities?'

Agostino's mouth opens, but no sound comes out. Sofia looks from him to Angelo; Angelo is staring at him, silently demanding an answer he cannot possibly want to hear.

No one speaks or moves.

Another log shifts and falls; this time a little knot of wood bounces out onto the hearth. Once again, it is Federico who reaches forward. Picking up the still burning fragment between finger and thumb, he flicks it back into the blaze.

Beppe draws in a breath. 'We could hold a *congedo*,' he says into the stifling silence.

Agostino's head snaps around. 'What? What did you say?'

'A *congedo*.' He pauses. 'It's a possible alternative course of action, if you don't like the idea of handing a fellow actor over to the *podestà*. Which, even now, I don't think *I* like very much at all.'

'A *congedo*? But . . . but we've never had to do such a thing. I've never heard of one being done in my lifetime, and—'

'Perhaps no one has deserved it in your lifetime.'

Agostino looks stricken. Cosima reaches across and takes his hand, and at her touch he seems to rally. He holds Beppe's gaze for several seconds, then nods. 'Yes, Beppe, you're right. Though I'm not sure I know . . .'

'I've heard it described.' Niccolò clears his throat. 'I know what should happen.' He looks grave. 'There can be no going back once it has begun, though, so you must be very certain you want it to go ahead.'

Agostino breathes deeply three, four, five times, then nods. Turning to each troupe member in turn as he speaks, he says, 'I think Beppe's right. I cannot contemplate deliberately handing a fellow performer over to the authorities – whatever he has done.'

Remembering her terrible, fear-soaked hours in the locked room in Bologna, Sofia glances over to Angelo, imagining the thoughts that must be fighting themselves in his mind. His expression, however, is unreadable. In the flickering candlelight, she thinks, he looks like an exquisite statue.

'Do you all agree with Beppe's suggestion, that a *congedo* is an alternative?'

There is a murmur of agreement from everyone in the room. Sofia, however, says quietly to Beppe, 'What is this? What does it mean?'

'It's for the best. Watch, and you'll see.'

Agostino coughs, and seems to be on the point of speaking again, when Cosima stands and says, 'Before we begin anything, perhaps we should eat. Our hosts have been kind enough to provide for us, and we are letting their good food go cold. They will think us ungrateful if we leave what they have provided.'

Everyone nods, without speaking. In silence, Cosima puts sliced meat, braised vegetables and torn quarters of bread onto plates and hands them out, one by one. The food, which had been hot on delivery, has cooled somewhat and congealed, but everyone in the room eats without comment. Only Angelo shakes his head as a plate is handed to him, and sits, wordlessly fiddling with the ring on his little finger, turning it around and around, pulling it up to the swell of the joint and pushing it back down again.

'Very well,' Agostino says a little while later, after the empty plates have been neatly stacked on one of the trays, and the cups that had contained ale have been put to one side. 'It's time. Niccolò, can you advise as to how we should best begin?'

'It's like the *scelta* ceremony in reverse,' Niccolò says quietly, 'only now the person accused must speak for himself. No one can speak on his behalf.'

The expression on Niccolò's face is so grave and his eyes so dark and hollowed that Sofia fancies for a moment that it is Fosca who stands before her ready to do ... whatever is about to be done. She watches as Niccolò leans in close to Agostino and mutters an inaudible explanation of how the ceremony should proceed and, as Agostino nods, images from her own *scelta* ceremony flood into her mind; she puts the corner of her thumb into her mouth and bites at a shred of skin; it tears as she pulls at it, and a small bead of blood swells.

'I don't think music really appropriate to the occasion. But we need something. Vico, will you find something to use as a drum?' Agostino says.

Nodding, Vico crosses behind Federico and Giovanni Battista and picks up the small barrel which had contained their ale. He returns to sit beside Lidia and up-ends the barrel over his knees. 'Pass the ladle over, will you?' he mutters, and Cosima takes the wooden ladle from the vegetable bowl and hands it to him. He begins a slow and insistent beat with the handle of the ladle and with his fingertips, a soft pulse that rings out into the quiet of the big chamber. Sofia feels her own heartbeat quicken at the sound.

'Angelo,' Agostino says now. 'Come and stand here by the fire.'

Without a word, Angelo moves to stand before Agostino and Cosima.

'Angelo da Bagnacavallo, you have here been accused of a heinous and dreadful crime by two members of the troupe, and you have confirmed that accusation with your own words.'

'I have.'

'Do you stand by that confirmation, or do you wish to retract it?'

Angelo shakes his head. 'I have no choice but to stand by it.'

Looking close to tears, Agostino says, 'Are you ready . . . to take the consequences of having embarked upon a course of action incompatible with the life of a member of the Coraggiosi?'

'I suppose I have to be. Yes. I am.'

The soft drumbeat quickens a pace.

'I need to hear a declaration from you that you will set forth from here tonight with no malice, with no intent to bring disrepute upon the troupe, with no wish to cause harm to any member at any time in the future. Remember you are bound by the Tenure of the Road, as are we all.'

'I so declare.'

Niccolò mutters something in Agostino's ear, and he nods. 'For should word reach us of any such defamation or harmful intent,' he says, 'the Tenure of the Road – shared by every member of every troupe upon the road – would be dissolved between us and we would feel obliged to alert the authorities immediately, laying before them all the facts as you have made clear this evening.'

Angelo swallows visibly. After a deep breath, he says, 'I shall cause no harm to be brought upon the troupe.'

Vico's drumbeat speeds up still further.

'Then, Angelo da Bagnacavallo, despite the damage you have done to us and to others, I ask Genesius and Vitus to travel with you and to keep you safe, as a Brother of the Road.' Agostino closes his eyes and clasps his hands. 'Genesius and Vitus, keep our brother here safe from harm . . . but keep him too away from us. We do not wish to see him amongst us again.'

Niccolò whispers in Agostino's ear again, and, opening his eyes once more, he nods, his face taut and miserable. 'Angelo da Bagnacavallo,' he says in a ringing voice, 'take this handful of dust.' And, reaching over to the outer edges of the hearth, he bends down and scrapes up a fistful of ash.

Angelo frowns slightly, as though unsure how to proceed, but he holds a hand, palm up, beneath the fist as Agostino allows the ash to trickle out, then he closes his fingers loosely over the little pile in his palm.

'Mingle with that a pinch of the dust of the Coraggiosi.' Agostino now has in his hand the small corked pot which Sofia last saw on the day of her *scelta* ceremony. He pulls the cork, puts finger and thumb into the neck of the pot and brings out a small pinch of dirt. Opening his fingers, Angelo allows Agostino to drop the dirt onto the pile in his palm.

'Take with you now this fragment of the dust of the Tenure of the Road,' Agostino says, and Sofia thinks his voice is now perilously near cracking. 'It is time for you to go. You may be a road-dweller for the rest of your days or you may choose to renounce it and live within walls, but as from this moment, wherever you are, you are ... you are no longer a member of the Coraggiosi.'

Angelo stares around at them all without speaking for several long seconds. Then he speaks, and his words fall like hard pebbles into the silence. 'May I say something before I leave?'

Agostino darts a glance towards Niccolò, then nods.

Angelo, staring now at Beppe with deadened eyes, says in an expressionless voice, 'I should have prevented your father's death, Bianchi. I could have done it, but I chose not to. Papa discovered my friendship with you a few days after your father was arrested – one of his servants had told him – and he forbade me to see you again, or to have any contact with you. *It was an acquaintance that reflected particularly poorly upon the family's social standing*, he said. He was angry – he shouted at me for hours. I was very much afraid of him. I had disappointed him in almost everything I'd done up until that point, and I knew that I was going to disappoint him most of all in the request I was saving up to make: the fact that I wanted to be an actor and I needed money from him to do so. Even at thirteen I knew it was all I wanted – an ambition first born out of our wild games together, I suppose. Papa, however, saw actors as little better than criminals. I knew that if I asked him to speak out for your father, it would reflect badly upon me and threaten my ambitions. So I stayed silent. I stayed silent and your father died a most terrible death, when he might have walked free.'

Beppe's mouth is slightly open and he is breathing fast. Sofia's gaze flicks from him to Angelo and back, her eyes wide, her lips dry and cold.

Angelo turns to Agostino. 'I stayed silent at Franceschina, too, and Sofia nearly paid the price for that, as Beppe's father had done before . . . because of me. So I spoke up for her in Bologna to try to . . . to try to smother the accusing voices in my head: the ever-present voices. Voices . . . that even the laudanum never fully manages to silence.'

And, crossing the room in a few long strides, he throws his handful of ash into the fire and wipes his hands, first one against the other, then both against the sides of his breeches. Snatching up one of the bags from the pile near the door, he stares at each member of the troupe in turn, then leaves the room without a word. The door bangs behind him and the echo of the noise hangs in the air like the rising curl of smoke after a cannon-shot. His footsteps ring out for a moment on the steps outside and then fade.

No one utters a sound or moves a muscle.

The silence is almost suffocating.

Then Lidia begins to sing: a soft lament, which raises the hairs on Sofia's arms and neck. Vico picks up the ale barrel and taps out an accompaniment on its base with his fingers, humming a wordless harmony beneath Lidia's haunting tune.

Sofia clasps her hands and presses them against her mouth. Tears sting in the corners of her eyes. Despite everything – despite the betrayal and the anger and the pain Angelo has caused – she knows he has walked away from them wrapped in a stinking fog of self-loathing and loneliness and her heart clenches tight at the thought of it. She wipes her eyes with the back of her index finger.

Beppe puts an arm around her shoulders and she leans in against him.

42

Fabio da Correggio laughs, and at the sight of his cousin's gleeful, upturned mouth and the gleam of wetness along the line of the boy's lower lip, Marco's insides lurch painfully. Seated at his table under the window in the small Verona apartment, he forces himself to look back at the letter in front of him.

He will not beg.

'And anyway, I won't be long, Marco,' Fabio says. 'Like I said: he only has to deliver the finished painting. He says he just wants a companion for the journey. We won't be more than a few weeks. I can't turn down an adventure like this – God, I've wanted to go to Venezia for years! You'll be happy here until I get back, won't you?'

Marco hears the dismissal in Fabio's voice and knows that the moment has come, the moment he has known all along would be inevitable. His hedonistic, self-centred, amoral tomcat of a cousin has tired of him. Their weeks in Verona have been wild and exhausting and – to Marco at least – exquisite, but, as he has known all along would happen, Fabio has finally lost interest. The young artist with whom he has been spending increasingly more of his time over the past few days has proved too much of an attraction to resist. Feigning a continuing concern with his letter, Marco smooths out the paper and frowns at the words scrawled illegibly upon it as though they have some significance for him.

'Of course,' he lies, glancing up and flashing a brief and wintry smile. 'I'll be here – I have plenty to do until your return.'

Fabio puffs a short breath. 'Good. I've said I'll meet Enrico later this evening. I might stay at his rooms, in fact, as we're setting off at first light tomorrow. So, I might not see you again until I return from Venezia.'

Fully aware that Fabio might not choose to return at all, and that this might perhaps be the last time he ever lays eyes on the boy, Marco struggles with himself as a howling cry of despair balloons in his throat. Swallowing it down with an effort that leaves him light-headed, he gets to his feet. 'Travel safely, Fabio,' he says, forcing a smile. 'I shall lay in some wine for your return.'

'Excellent – oh, and steer clear of those boys we met last week, won't you?' Fabio says cheerfully. 'They seemed most entertaining, but I got the feeling they might only be after your *scudi*.'

Standing in the little chapel, gazing down at Maddalena's body with its smoothly domed belly, the swell almost hidden now beneath her finest silk and lawn, Paolo di Maccio finds that he cannot summon up any emotion at all. No anger; no desire for revenge; no sadness; no relief; no regret. Just a blankness. An absence of feelings. An empty space.

Maddalena's panicked wail – the noise that woke him two nights ago and which has resonated in his head ever since – and the racking seizures that followed within minutes of her gasped-out pleas for help have left him shaken, he cannot deny that. But surprised –

no, he was not surprised. Maddalena was carrying da Correggio's child, and it was abundantly clear from his mocking taunts that evening at Franceschina that da Correggio had thoroughly enjoyed imparting the news. The reasons for her liaison with him were clear: the little brown bottle beneath Maddalena's pillow and the upturned glass on her table both told their own story; the rumours had indeed been true. All in all, he thinks to himself now, as he runs a finger gently along the back of one of Maddalena's thin, chilled hands, it has all probably worked itself out for the best.

Gripping his dead wife's fingers in his for the briefest moment, he turns and leaves the little chapel.

43

'A letter came for you earlier, Sofia,' Vico says, flapping it out towards her as she returns from the market two mornings after Angelo's departure. She takes it from him and he strides away. Still unable to read more than a few words, she hands it straight to Beppe. 'Read it for me, please,' she says. 'Who is it from?'

Beppe cracks open the little blobbed seal and unfolds the letter. 'What do you know?' he says, grinning at Sofia. 'It's from Signora Andreini. You have a message from the Gelosi them-selves, no less.'

'From Isabella? Oh, Beppe, read it for me – what does she say?'

Beppe clears his throat and reads.

' *Sofia, cara,*

   '*As I said I would, I have spoken with His Grace the Duke of Ferrara on your behalf – on behalf of the whole of the Coraggiosi troupe, in fact. Oh, my dear, you will be so happy – the duke is simply outraged at the injustice of* the treatment you have received at the hands of his representatives in Bologna! While we were dining with him in the great hall at the Castello Estense after the Gelosi performance yesterday (you must believe me, <u>cara</u>, the duke's palace is a truly frightening building — more like being in a prison than a castle, if you want an honest opinion ...), I took the opportunity to put to him just how dreadfully you had all been treated. I made sure to paint a truly distressing picture of everything that had happened — and in the event Signor d'Este was deeply shocked, as indeed was the duchess.

'I shall not tell you everything here, but suffice it to say, my dear, that Signor d'Este has for some time been concerned at the heavy-handed justice (or lack of it) in some of the cities in the Duchy of Ferrara, and Signor da Budrio is one of those on whom he has been keeping a very careful eye. This was, I understand, one injustice too many. He is even now instructing the said signore to rescind the banishment order forthwith and — are you sitting down, my dear? — perhaps just to underline how very much he disapproves of what has taken place, he intends to commission a performance from the Coraggiosi in the days leading up to Christmas! A greater honour I simply cannot imagine! I'm <u>so</u> happy to have been instrumental in obtaining it for you.

'We in the Gelosi will all be heading off to France to perform at the French court next week and will be in France a year or more, otherwise I would insist on our spending some time together when you come to Ferrara. I am so very sad that you will not be joining us after all — but of course I understand. Perhaps particularly as

actresses, we know all too well that the course of true love
must triumph over all else, do you not think, <u>cara</u>? (And
having met your charming Arlecchino, even briefly, I can
<u>quite</u> see why you are staying put in Italy …)'

Here Beppe coughs and waves a hand in front of his face, feigning embarrassment, and Sofia laughs. Leaning forwards, she kisses his mouth. 'Get on with it, will you?'

Straightening his face, he continues.

'You will no doubt be receiving your invitation directly
from the duke — but in case it is delayed for any reason,
know that he is expecting you all at the <u>castello</u> for a
performance a couple of days before Christmas. Put
something <u>wonderful</u> together for him! I have told him
how impressed I was, particularly with you, my dear.

  'Francesco and I send you all our fondest wishes, and
Flaminio says I am to tell you that he is writing
Colombina's lines for his new scenario with you in mind —
whether you are to play the role or not. You made a <u>great</u>
impression on him, <u>cara</u>.

  'Your friend,
  'Isabella'

There is a moment's silence, then Beppe whistles. 'We must tell Ago and Cosima straight away – this is better news than we could possibly have hoped for.'

'Is it true – does she mean it?'

'I can't imagine she would make up such a thing.'

'I'm not sure I understand, though,' Sofia says, puzzled. 'Why on earth should someone as powerful as the Duke of Ferrara care at all about what has happened to someone like me? Someone he has never heard of?'

Beppe looks back at the letter. 'Do you know what I think?' he says, folding it back up and tapping his mouth with the folded edge. 'I think it might just be that Signor d'Este was more struck by the teller of the tale than by the tale itself.'

'What do you mean?'

He points the letter at her. 'Well ... she's beautiful, isn't she, Isabella Andreini?'

Sofia nods.

'And very ... excitable ... and passionate. I think the duke might just have been swept away by her story and ... well ... decided to do whatever he thought might please her the most.'

'Do you think so?'

'Mmm. Not that it matters, though. All that matters is the commission. Come on, let's go and tell Agostino.'

44

The Castello Estense, Ferrara, December

It has been an unusually cold December. Everyone in Ferrara is talking about how long it is since there has been such a freeze in the city and, since this morning's particularly hard frost, the Ferrarese have only been venturing out when they absolutely have to, bundled in as many layers of clothing as they can gather together. Snow began to fall a couple of days ago, and now most of the city's roofs are smoothly white. Many of the narrower streets have already been trodden into dirty grey ruts, but the piazza outside the front of the Castello Estense has been deliberately roped off and still lies pristine white, its surface broken only by the tiny three-toed prints of birds and one single child-sized boot-print, daringly placed inside the cordon, right at the far western edge.

Within the castle walls, in the great central *cortile*, the snow — undisturbed here by wind and scuffed by no more than the occasional passage of feet — lies thicker than elsewhere: each bare twig of the dozen or so potted cherry trees is plumply white, every sill of every window seems pillowed with snow and tiny scuffs of the stuff are clinging to each minute irregularity in the bricks of the massive castle walls, giving them an unusually soft, speckled appearance.

It is five days before Christmas. The afternoon light has not yet begun to fade, but the many lanterns and torches burning within the castle are already shining out into the shadowed *cortile*, and their yellow light is casting vivid blue-purple shadows across the snow into the darker corners.

Inside, at the far end of the long North Hall, below where a pretty wooden gallery stretches across the width of the wall, a stage is being set. Above the gallery is a fresco – a huge, vividly painted, beautiful depiction of a mythological scene – and all along the gallery's balustrade, candles in little glass pots have been placed ready to be lit when the light finally fades.

The trestles are in place, the backcloths have been thrown up and over their tightly stretched ropes and three people are crouched on the ground in front of the trestles, busily hooking up the drapery which conceals the below-stage area from the audience's view. Sofia, Beppe and Niccolò are making their way along the row of hooks, Sofia at one end of the stage, Niccolò at the other, working in towards where Beppe is busy in the centre.

'What's left to do?' Niccolò asks, sitting back on his heels.

'Not much.' Beppe pushes a hand through his hair. 'Vico's dealing with the props and Agostino will put the scenario board with the *canovaccii* up in a moment. We're almost ready.'

'Can you believe this?' Sofia says, staring around the enormous room, where a dozen or so servants are busily setting out chairs and benches, refilling rushlight holders with oil and setting branched candlesticks out on the many windowsills. 'Look at it all – look at *us*! Can you believe it? The Coraggiosi, performing at the Castello Estense?'

Beppe grins at her. 'I told you right at the start that you'd bring us luck, didn't I?'

'Did you?'

Frowning, Beppe considers. 'I think I did. Well, if I didn't say it, I thought it.'

Sofia is smiling at this when a tall, thin, elderly castle servant, dressed in black, with a shock of thinning white hair and a worried expression on his rather furrowed face, approaches the stage, looking, Sofia thinks, like a rather nervous and aged heron. Clearing his throat, he pecks a bow towards the actors.

Beppe stands and nods a bow in return. 'Signore?'

'Ahem,' the man says. 'I need to ascertain that everything is set and ready to begin at the time we specified.'

'Indeed it is, signore. Only the last few bits and pieces to place in position, and then all we have to do is to put on our costumes and masks.'

'Beppe! Beppe!'

Everyone starts as Agostino hurries out onto the stage and, crouching at the front edge, bends down towards Beppe. 'Beppe, *caro*, we have a problem!'

'What? What's the matter?'

'Signore,' says the white-haired servant. 'If there is a problem, may I be of any assistance?'

'Oh, thank you, thank you, Signor . . . Signor . . . ?'

'Guarniero, signore – Franco Guarniero.'

'Signor Guarniero,' Agostino repeats politely. 'Thank you, you are most kind, signore. We have . . . er . . . a slight issue with a costume, and are in urgent need of some strips of buckram with which to repair it. Do you know of anywhere in the vicinity we might be able to find some?'

Guarniero frowns for a second, then says, 'Yes indeed. I will send one of the servants straight away. There is a row of little covered shops along the far side wall of the cathedral. One of them I know sells silks and linens and threads – and I hope very much that they will have the buckram you require.'

'That's marvellous! I think though that we should perhaps make the trip ourselves, signore, to be sure the stuff is exactly what we need. Is the place hard to find?' Agostino says.

'Not in the least. If you are quite certain you wish to go yourselves . . .'

Agostino assures him that this is the case.

' . . . then I shall take you to the door in person, and point you in the right direction. It is very close, and you simply cannot miss it.'

Agostino beams at him, then turns to Beppe. 'Beppe, *caro*, will you go, and take Sofia with you?'

'Of course. What's the problem – what do we need the buckram for?'

'So silly – Giovanni Battista's belly padding is about to fall to pieces. It was just holding together, but pulling it out of the box just now, I fear its hours are numbered. It would be too dreadful if it collapsed during the performance. We're just going to need a few yards of those stiffened buckram strips to give it a bit of solidity. Sofia, if we find some, will you be able to mend the thing for us in time?'

Together, Beppe and Sofia reassure Agostino that both the trip and the mend can easily be accomplished and he hands them a little drawstring purse filled with clinking coins. They follow the still-anxious-looking Guarniero down through the *castello* to one of the four main entrances, from where he explains the route, leaning out into the snow, pointing towards the cathedral and jabbing a finger around to the left as he details the directions.

*

It is a matter of a moment's walk from the Castello Estense to the great cathedral, whose façade today is shrouded in white. Walking quickly, hand in hand, with snow crunching underfoot at each step, Beppe and Sofia round the front of the cathedral and turn left, where, along the long side wall there is, as Signor Guarniero described, a row of tiny shops, nestling under the sheltering bulk of the massive church.

The first shop proves to be a purveyor of leather goods: belts and shoes, jerkins and boots, scabbards, purses and bags. The second sells glass. The third is empty; the door is ajar and the interior of the little room, when Beppe and Sofia tentatively push it open and peer inside, is dank and musty-smelling. A dirty flurry of snow has swept in from outside and scattered across the first few feet of floor. The fourth shop, however, is lantern-lit and glows in jewelled colours.

Sofia's mouth opens in astonishment as they push open the door and step inside.

The room is tiny – perhaps no more than twelve feet square – but despite its size, dozens of bolts of silks and velvets, lawns and damasks and cypress-gauzes of all colours have been stacked one on top of the other on deep shelves along the narrow back wall. Tawny oranges, vivid blues, wine reds and coral pinks; pristine white lawn and black fustian; a watered damask the colour of a storm cloud. Several yards of a ruby-coloured silk have been pulled from the bolt and lie untidily bundled on a table top, where an elderly man – bent of back and bald of head – is running it appraisingly through his fingers. He looks up as Beppe and Sofia enter the shop.

'Signore? Signora?'

Beppe clears his throat. 'Signore, we're looking for some stiffened buckram strips – might you possibly . . . ?'

The old man smiles widely. 'Buckram? Indeed, I have just the thing.' Turning to a tiny door in the far corner of the room, he leans through it and calls. 'Dario?' He pauses, then calls again. 'Dario! We need some buckram. There's a reel in the painted chest. Bring it, will you?'

A moment passes, and Sofia hears quick, light footsteps on what sounds like a set of wooden steps out behind the shop's front room; then the tiny door opens and a scrawny young man with untidy fairish hair ducks under the lintel, a narrow roll of cream-coloured stiff fabric in his arms. Much to her surprise, Sofia finds there is something familiar about the new arrival, and she stares at him, wondering where on earth she has seen him before.

He does not notice her straight away, but, muttering something to the elderly proprietor, pushes the pile of red silk to one end of the table to make room for the roll of buckram. Then, glancing across at the newcomers as he turns to leave the shop once more, he stops and his mouth opens a little. His gaze is fixed upon Sofia.

Beppe looks from her to the boy and back, puzzled.

The boy is frowning, clearly trying to place Sofia in his mind, but even as he stares at her, with a jolt of recognition Sofia realizes who he is. She bites her lip. 'Beppe, have you the purse?' she says quietly, her gaze on the boy's face. Without questioning, Beppe pushes a hand into his breeches pocket and pulls out the little draw-string pouch.

Taking it from him, Sofia opens it, rummages and picks out a couple of coins. She holds them out. 'I think I owe you some money, signore,' she says. 'Ten *baiocchi*, wasn't it?'

The boy's face cracks into a wide grin, snapping his fingers in realization. Pointing at her, he says, 'Yes, signorina, that was it. Exactly! Ten *baiocchi*.'

'Dario?' The old proprietor looks puzzled. 'What is this? Do you know the lady?'

Sofia says, 'Your boy was very kind to me some time ago, signore. Back in Bologna. He gave me a pair of crimson ribbons. I had no money but he saw that I loved them and longed to have them and he gave them to me. I promised then that I'd pay him back when I saw him again.' She shrugs. 'I'm just keeping my promise.'

'In Bologna? Dario, when was this?'

Dario pulls his gaze from Sofia's face and turns to the old man. 'Few months ago, Tommaso, just before I came to Ferrara.'

'You were so kind, signore.'

Dario shrugs, his grin wide and happy.

'I still have the ribbons. I wear them each time I perform. In my hair. I'm an actress now.'

'An actress?'

'Yes.' Sofia reaches for Beppe's hand. 'With a troupe: the Coraggiosi.'

Dario frowns. 'The Coraggiosi? Isn't that ... Tommaso, isn't that the name of the troupe Bigo Ghisilieri was talking about?' Not waiting for an answer, he turns to Sofia. 'Isn't it your people the duke has invited to play at the *castello*?'

Sofia nods. 'Today. In about two hours, in fact.'

Dario's eyebrows lift, and his mouth puckers into a silent whistle of admiration. 'Your troupe is quite something, so my friend Bigo says.'

Beppe puts an arm around Sofia's shoulders. 'We do our best,' he says, smiling.

'Do you work here all the time now?' Sofia asks.

Dario nods. He grins at the old man. 'Better than lugging that great pack around all over Emilia-Romagna, eh, Tommaso?'

'He's a good boy,' the old man says a little ponderously. 'A capable boy.' There is a pause, then he pats the roll of buckram and adds, 'Now . . . how much of this do you need?' and Sofia, Beppe and Dario all start slightly, jolted out of an odd stillness that seemed to have quite overtaken them.

Beppe says, 'Oh yes. Five yards. Five yards, if you have them, please.'

The buckram is unrolled and measured, cut and wrapped and paid for, thanks are offered, smiles are exchanged, promises to look in next time they are in the city are made and hands are shaken. Beppe and Sofia hurry back to the *castello*, pausing only for Beppe to duck down, form a handful of snowballs between cupped and reddening palms and begin juggling with them.

In the ante-room behind the stage, with a little over an hour to go before the performance is due to begin, everything is ready. Every item is in exactly the right place: costumes are hanging on hooks; every sponge, every box of charcoal sticks, every pot of chalk has been laid out on tables ready for use. (The precious crushed pearl has been tucked away in Beppe's breeches pocket.) Ranks of candles and lamps stand ready to be lit when the light finally fails, and the actors have run through the whole show once already. Agostino is happy and he has told the troupe to rest for a while before the performance. Lidia, who is indeed with child – Sofia's instincts have been proved right, much to her delight – has said she wishes to lie down, and has been given a small palliasse by the castle servants. Tucked under a blanket, she has her eyes closed. Vico, whittling at a small piece of wood with a knife, is sitting cross-legged beside her. Agostino and Cosima have ensconced themselves on a window seat near the fireplace; Cosima has always hated the cold, and today she has a thick woollen wrap around her shoulders and a scowl is crumpling her beautiful features. Federico and Giovanni Battista are engaged in a game of cards with one of Signor d'Este's young assistants and Benedetto Morello, the Coraggiosi's new *inamorato*. Slight, with fair hair, grey eyes and a neat, straight nose, Signor Morello does not have anything like the perfect looks of his complex predecessor, though he is, Sofia has thought privately, handsome enough. But his witty and affectionate personality has quickly endeared him to every member of the troupe, and, to everyone's delight, he has struck up a particular friendship with the elderly Giovanni Battista, who seems happier now than anyone can remember his being for years.

Niccolò, with Beppe's dog curled at his feet, has seated himself on the opposite side of the fireplace to Agostino and Cosima. The wood has been heaped high and the flames are fierce and loud. Heat is pushing out into the room as he stares; his eyes begin to sting, but he does not draw back. Gazing into the flames, he half listens to Agostino and Cosima's muttered conversation, and to the staccato bursts of speech from the card-players, but joins in none of it.

He thinks of Anna and her husband, back in the little house in Faenza; this will be the first Christmas he has spent without his daughter. He is happy to be here with the troupe – more than happy – but he will certainly miss seeing Anna. Sofia reminds him so much of Anna. Perhaps he can take her up to Faenza later in the New Year – and Beppe too. If Agostino can spare them.

'I'm sure Anna would like to see them,' he murmurs aloud.

'What was that, Niccolò? What did you say?' It is Sofia's voice; she is leaning over his shoulder, her hands on each of his upper arms, and he sees that there is snow in her hair; her face is glowing outdoors-pink and her eyes are shining. 'Did you say something? Ooh, you're so warm!'

She kisses his cheek, and her mouth is chilled. Smiling at her, he lifts a hand to his face.

'What's the matter, Nicco?' Sofia says. 'You look very pale.' She has crouched down next to where he is sitting, and has taken his hand in both of her own. 'Are you sure you're well?'

Niccolò nods, but Sofia is staring up at him intently now, her eyes flicking from one of his to the other, back and forth. 'Nicco, what is it?'

'Nothing, child, nothing.' He pauses, shaking his head, then says, 'Just thinking about my Anna, and how I shall miss her this Christmas.'

'Oh, Nicco . . .'

Niccolò puts his suggestion to her.

'To the house in Faenza? Oh yes, I should love that,' Sofia says. 'And Beppe would too, I'm sure. Let's ask Ago after the show.'

The grand North Hall at the Castello Estense is humming with conversation. There must be at least two hundred candles alight. In every one of the long window recesses at least a dozen are burning brightly, and every flame is reflected in the glass behind; several dozen torches are burning in brackets at intervals along each of the two longest walls. No flowers are growing at this time of year, of course, but around the edges of the room many garlands of little branches of beech and ash and holly, plucked from goodness knows where (this is, after all, a truly city-bound castle), festoon the sills and the tops of the doors, and every branch has been lavishly adorned with ribbons and laces, scraps of golden paper and dozens and dozens of bunches of red berries. The golden paper is gleaming in the candlelight. Two huge gold-paste angels stand, trumpets in hand, on either side of the great double doors.

The trestle stage at the other end of the room is complete now. The backdrop depicts a deserted street, and a little raised platform, draped in swagged cloth, stands to one side: a mountebank's stall. Leaning against the stall is a lute.

Standing on the little space behind the backcloths, Sofia peeps through the narrow chink between the two canvases and peers out at the audience that awaits them. Seated in the two largest and finest seats at the front are the duke – middle-aged, bearded, stern-looking, dressed entirely in black – and his latest duchess, the third in line, the little Spaniard who cannot, Sofia is sure, be much more than seventeen or eighteen. Wide-eyed and fresh-skinned, she looks more like Signor d'Este's daughter than his wife, though it is well known that the Duke of Ferrara has no children.

Beside and behind the duke and duchess are some three or four dozen dignitaries, all finely dressed in rich, vivid silks and damasks. Many gems and precious metals are glinting on necks and ears and fingers in the candlelight. It is, Sofia thinks, by far the most prestigious and glittering audience she has seen, and a moment's unease settles on her at the sight of them, making her pulse race and her stomach churn.

Beppe comes to stand just behind her.

Turning, Sofia tilts her face up to his and he makes as though to kiss her, though stopping short a fraction of an inch from her carefully painted mouth. 'Ready?' he says quietly.

Sofia sucks in a long breath and lets it out slowly through pursed lips, nodding as she does so. 'I think so. It's a bit more frightening when the audience is so . . . so . . .'

'Well dressed?' Beppe suggests. 'That's the only difference between them and any other audience, I reckon. They'll laugh and cry in all the same places as any other audience, if we do our job well, won't they?'

The others are beginning to gather at the foot of the little ladder: Cosima and Benedetto Morello, both beautiful and elegant and serene; Federico in his long-nosed and highly shining mask and Giovanni Battista with the newly mended fat belly which Sofia has carefully cobbled together with Dario's buckram strips. The two older men are standing close to white-faced Agostino, who is muttering his lines to himself with silent animation. Lidia, padded up to look more stoutly matronly, nonetheless still looks sweet-faced and pretty; Vico, scratching up under his mask with a finger, bends towards her and whispers something in her ear. Shaking her head, she looks down at her belly, rubbing a hand gently over the as yet hardly visible swelling there.

Sofia gazes at them all, and feels her mouth stretch out into a smile. The chalk and pearl 'skin' tweaks as she does so and, as always, she has to fight not to reach up and scratch.

'Happy?' Beppe whispers.

Sofia looks up at him. 'Oh yes.'

'Right,' Vico says, scrambling up the ladder and edging past Beppe and Sofia. 'Off we go. Twenty bars from me on the lute, then you're on.' He flashes a quick grin at Sofia, then slips out between the two hangings, and, at the sight of him in his grubby flour-sack costume, the audience begins to applaud. The sound crackles around the room like flame and the players straighten, readying themselves for the start of the show.

Sofia looks fondly at them all again, then sideways at Beppe. '*As much as actors love applause*,' she says quietly.

'What? What's that?'

'Nothing. Just remembering that day in the little clearing near Malalbergo.'

Beppe tilts his head enquiringly.

'The day you started teaching me to act.' She pauses. 'That pile of declarations – remember? *Just how much do you love me? As much as actors love applause.*'

'Oh yes – what was the other one . . . *as much as a blade loves a whetstone?* God, it seems so long ago.' Lifting her hand to his mouth, he kisses her knuckles. 'Before you ask, I think if you asked me the same question today, my answer would be . . . *as much as . . . ooh, as much as Arlecchino loves to cause trouble.*'

'That much?' Sofia is smiling. 'Surely not.'

Head on one side, Beppe considers. He grins and shrugs. Running a thumb along her cheekbone, he says, 'Well, now you ask, probably a little more than that, but it'll do for now.'

Vico's music builds to a crescendo and stops. In the second's hiatus of silence that follows, Beppe holds aside the backdrop and he and Sofia step onto the stage.

Reading Group Questions

1. How much do you think Sofia is affected by what happened to her mother years ago?

2. It's often said that clowns turn to comedy in the first place because of a need to overcome sadness in in their past. How true do you think this is for Beppe?

3. What role does Niccolò Zanetti play in the story?

4. Do you feel at all sorry for Angelo? How much do you blame him for Sofia's ordeal?

5. How well does the novel portray the practicalities of life in a travelling troupe of actors?

6. The novel deals with the aftermath of several false accusations – which of those accusations do you think has the greatest bearing on the course of the story?

7. Will the Corraggiosi go on to become as proficient and well-known as the Gelosi, do you think?

8. How well does the novel explain the traditions of *Commedia dell'Arte*? Can you see its legacy in any of the comedians and actors you know today?

9. If you had to describe first Sofia, and then Beppe, in three words, what would they be?

10. If you could pick out just one of the minor characters in the book who made an impression on you, who would it be, and why?